THE WORLDS BEHIND HER EYELIDS

ALEXA LEE

INESCAPABLE ESCAPISM

VOLUME 1

CONTENTS

CHAPTER ONE

"Your father is such a moron."

The words should have been jarring but they meant nothing to me anymore. Logically, I knew that they should have been hard to hear, but my mom had said them so many times that they'd lost all impact.

She sat on the end of my bed and threw her long blonde hair back from her face. My bedroom door was open, he could have easily heard, but I knew she didn't care. It was probably a conscious decision. She wanted him to hear.

"He just never listens to anything I say," she continued angrily, not seeming to care that I wasn't listening either.

I'd learnt a lot from her tirades over the years. When I was younger, I'd tried to listen more actively, to suggest things that might help, but I'd learnt that it was pointless. She didn't want solutions or for things to get better, she just wanted to complain about him.

They'd been together for twenty years, married after two years, had me just under two years after that, and from what I could gather, they'd never had a good relationship. Sometimes, she'd tell stories of when they first got together, how incompetent and clueless he'd been. She'd apparently been chased by so many men, all of whom were better than my dad, but she'd settled for him.

I didn't believe her stories though. She liked to exaggerate things. She always wanted her life to sound grander and more interesting than it really was. I got that, to a certain extent. I didn't really like my life either.

It was fine. I couldn't really complain. I went to a good school, didn't do too badly, was an only kid, had a pretty nice room to myself, and a couple of friends. It was fine, unless I thought about it too hard, and then it got a little less fine. I barely slept and was constantly kept awake by the stink of cigarette smoke and the almost deafening sound of the television that came from downstairs.

They always had it like that. That way they didn't need to talk to each other. They spent every evening watching countless shows and movies, basically ignoring the other person. It was for the best. Whenever they talked, they just argued and then my mom would come up to complain about him.

She didn't care what time it was or if I was pretending to sleep. She'd slam the door open and drop down on the end of my bed, where she was now, sometimes trailing cigarette ash with her.

I'd once made the mistake of asking her not to smoke in my room because it made me cough and her reaction had been… well. Exactly as expected. She'd accused me of trying to kick her out of her own house. It wasn't worth the fight.

There was a lull in her conversation as she paused to draw a breath.

"Mmm," I said noncommittally, knowing that it was all I needed to say to keep her happy.

I sucked in a deep breath, being careful not to let it out too heavily in case she mistook it for a sigh again. That had almost been worse than when I had asked her not to smoke; she'd accused me of being bored of her. Which I was, but then she'd started ranting about how she'd given up her life to raise me, and if it weren't for me and my father, she'd be running a very successful business by now or modelling or doing some other fantastical thing.

I leaned my head back against my headboard and stared longing at the wall of books. My dad never hesitated to buy me a book. I didn't like asking them for anything but he always went out of his way to get me some. I don't know if it was guilt or if he recognised my need to escape.

I yearned to be reading one of those books as Mom continued, her face turning redder and her voice getting louder, but instead, I was stuck staring around my room. Dark blue carpets with a couple of burn holes near the end of my bed where mom sat lined the floor, complemented by the light cream walls. A huge window lay at the end of the room overlooking our garden. I'd run out there sometimes when my parents were fighting, slip through the fence at the back, and venture into the wilderness beyond.

A field stretched out behind the house but beyond that was a luscious forest. Moss lined the ground and a thick canopy protected me from the light above. It felt almost like slipping into another world. One where it was quiet and I was safe.

"You know?" my mom demanded, looking at me expectantly.

"Yeah," I agreed flatly, not bothering or needing to inject any feeling into my voice.

It didn't matter, she wasn't listening.

"Exactly! And yet, he never learns!" she continued, but I'd already stopped listening.

My eyes fell on my desk, which was piled high with half-complete homework. I really needed to get it done tonight. I'd fallen behind weeks ago and just didn't have the motivation to do anything about it. I needed to get my parents to sign my planner, acknowledging that they were aware that I wasn't doing my homework and that they would help me with it, but I couldn't do that now. Mom would be too furious. I'd wait for the morning when her hangover had set in. She wouldn't be bothered to read the note and just sign it.

I briefly debated telling her I had homework to do and asking her to leave so that I could work on it but there was no point. She wouldn't care.

I stared back at her enraged face, watching detachedly as she waved her hands around, coming close to hitting the high wooden end of my bed but not seeming to notice. My eyes swam out of focus as I searched desperately for a distraction, something to stop me from being trapped in my room with her.

My eyes landed on my books again, tracing the blue spine of my favourite book, as an idea slowly came to me. If I couldn't read to escape, maybe I could do it mentally. Just use my imagination to get away from the situation.

I breathed slowly and held it, a spark of excitement lighting in my chest. I wanted to go somewhere completely the opposite of where I was now. Somewhere where I felt free and the world was silent.

I let the breath out slowly, letting my eyes unfocus completely.

The colours blurred, swarming together until they changed into something completely different. A vivid green overwhelmed my vision and I blinked, trying to bring it back into focus.

A wild, overgrown field surrounded me, dappled with flowers. The beautiful, bright blue sky lay above me, unmarked by clouds. A gentle breeze caressed my skin and blew my light blonde hair back. Despite knowing I was sitting on my bed, I could almost feel the soft carpet of grass beneath my feet.

It smelt so fresh.

A giggle slipped out of my mouth, but it was lost in the natural symphony of the world. Trees rustled loudly in the wind and a hare raced from the underbrush towards me. I froze, worried that my movement might startle the animal, but it seemed unbothered. It stopped right beside me, its giant ears twitching as it stared.

Slowly, so as not to scare it, I leant down and reached my hand out. I half expected it to run away or bite me, like I'd been told they would. Wild animals were unpredictable, dangerous. They'd attack if they go the chance. But the hare didn't. It just waited patiently as I gently stroked its soft fur, its eyes shutting in pleasure.

I stood again, watching as the hare hopped off again and disappeared down the slight hill, then wiped my hands on my dress skirt. I started to walk before stopping again and staring down at the dress I was wearing. It wasn't what I was wearing in real life but I still recognised it. I'd seen someone wearing it online or on television, I wasn't sure. It was an off the shoulder dress in light blue with a gently flared skirt. The small embroidered daisies perfectly matched the wild daisies around me.

I ran my hands over the soft tulle skirt, staring in wonder. From the moment I'd seen it, I wanted it but I knew there was no point in asking my mom for it. She would buy me the basics, enough so that I looked well cared for, but nothing special. I could have asked my dad. He generally bought me stuff if I asked but it wasn't worth it.

Mom always kicked off if I went to him for anything instead of her. She accused me of trying to drive a wedge between them or said that the only reason I went to him was because I was lying about what I wanted to do with the money or the clothes.

"Are you even listening?" Mom demanded, her voice cutting through my dreams.

"Of course," I replied, my fantasy world taking on a blurry dreamlike quality as I forced myself to focus on my mom.

She scoffed and rolled her eyes, barely pausing before launching back into her rant.

I tried to listen, but the wonderful world I'd created in my mind called out to me and I slipped back into it, my heart growing a little lighter.

"Grace! It's almost dinner time!" a voice called to me across the field.

Confusion made me stumble to a halt. It sounded like my mom but something was different. I stared towards the house in the distance; I hadn't paid any attention to it just moments before.

In fact, I hadn't even noticed it was there.

It looked like my house but the red bricks were brighter instead of dulled by age. I could see into the back garden from where I stood on the gently sloping hill. The first thought that I was struck by was that it had everything I'd wanted as a kid. That same trampoline that most of the neighbours had, a treehouse, and a swing set. Even a climbing frame, similar to the one at my friend's house.

I walked towards the stile built into the fence. It didn't exist in real life. I just had to climb the fence or squeeze through the bit I had pried away from the post years ago, but I appreciated it in my fantasy. It made it easier to get into my garden.

That made me hesitate. The grass was wrong. Normally, Mom made my dad mow it every Saturday morning, just in case someone was walking through the field and noticed that it was unkempt. Not that anyone ever used the field apart from a couple of farmers, sheep and me.

The big glass windows were wide open, the red curtains fluttering softly in the wind and sending the aroma of freshly baked cookies towards me. Even in real life, my mouth started to water. They smelt so good.

I'd just stepped into the house when a voice shouted at me again.

"Don't forget to wipe your feet before you step on the carpet!" that almost-my-mom's voice called.

I hastened to wipe my feet, worried about making her angry despite knowing that I was in a fantasy and that she wouldn't get mad unless I wanted her to before stepping further into my lounge.

It was cleaner than usual. The blanket on the pull-out sofa in front of the television, which I normally left in a heap wherever I discarded it, was neatly folded. The room was much lighter and airier than ever, even though it basically looked the same, and the smell of freshly baked cookies had permeated the room, wafting in gently from the kitchen.

Despite knowing that it was a dream, I still felt a flutter of the usual anxiety as I left my lounge and headed towards my mom's voice.

"Hello, darling," the woman standing in the kitchen said in a happy tone.

I froze, staring at the person before me.

It was clear that she was my mother but at the same time, she looked completely different.

Her normally long blonde hair was cut just below her shoulders and bounced in happy waves. It was lighter than normal. Mom always dyed it a little darker, claiming that no one would take her seriously if it were too light. I always hated when she said that because every time she'd sneer at me, as if silently telling me that my almost white-blonde hair was a problem.

The woman before me smiled even wider and turned to grab a plate of cookies off the side.

"Do you want one? They've not set up yet but they should still be tasty even if they're a little soft."

I reached out numbly and took one, still unable to tear my eyes away from her. I knew that she was just a figment of my imagination, but it still filled me with a sad longing as I looked at her.

Her face was much paler than my real mom's, less sun-damaged, but the main thing that hurt was the expression on her face. There was no anger, no hatred. She just seemed happy to see me.

Unexpected tears started to well in my eyes.

"Is it too hot?" she asked, glancing at the forgotten cookie in my hand.

"No," I said finally, forcing myself to take a bite and blinking quickly.

Disappointment rushed through me. I couldn't taste anything. I shouldn't have expected to be able to, it was a fantasy, nothing more. I wasn't actually in that beautiful world, I was stuck sitting on my bed and watching my mom get slowly more flushed as she ranted about my dad and how she never should have married him.

"So?" my fake mom asked, watching me chew in eager anticipation.

I swallowed and smiled, wanting to make her happy.

"It's delicious."

Her face lit up.

"Oh, good! Do you want another?"

I shook my head, wishing that I could taste them for real.

"I'm okay. Don't want to fill up before dinner," I said, glancing at the clock on the wall above the table.

"Are you sure? You're a growing girl, you need to be eating more!" she insisted.

A smile came over my face.

"I'm sure, I'm not hungry at the moment anyway."

"Hmm... okay, make sure you have a big dinner at least. I'm making your favourite, lasagne!"

I swallowed down a bitter lump of sadness and blinked myself back into my bedroom. My mom hadn't made my favourite dish in years. Most of the time, the cooking fell to me to do because my dad got home too late from work and my mom was always just 'busy'. I didn't mind it too much, I quite liked cooking, but after school sometimes I just settled for eating plain pasta or some toast because I was too tired to make anything else.

"Honestly, he just doesn't get it!" my real mom exclaimed before standing with a heavy sigh and strid-ing out of the room.

I slumped back against my headboard, letting out a soft breath, my mind straying back to the fantasy I'd created before.

It hadn't felt just like I was using my imagination, it had felt more real. It had never felt like that before. I'd been able to feel the wind against my skin, smell the delicious aroma of the cookies and feel the floor beneath my feet.

It was wonderful and it immediately made me hungry

for more. If I could make a better world where I could be happy and have everything I wanted, could I do better? What if I could do something a bit more... fun?

My eyes landed on my bookshelf again, finding a small book with a navy blue cover. My lips slowly rose into a smile as a slight dizziness washed over me and I let my eyes drift shut.

The boat rocked under me and the hard plastic seat I was perched on felt cold even through the wetsuit that I was wearing. The sharp, salty tang of the sea burnt my nostrils as I slowly blinked my eyes open and glanced around at my surroundings.

The light was almost blinding but my eyes quickly adjusted and once they had, my mouth almost dropped open. The sun reflected harshly off the water surrounding our boat as we sped towards the dark coloured, jutting stone cliffs.

The balmy breeze and the way the warmth settled against my cheeks, despite how fast we were moving, made me certain that we weren't in England anymore.

"Okay, kid," an older man I didn't recognise started loudly over the roar of the speedboat's engine, "once we get closer to the drop point, I'll bring us to a stop and then you can dive down and look for our target."

A small trill of excitement burst in me as I looked down at the iPad on my lap which showed a grainy image of a scan of the seabed. Raised shapes stood out clearly but I had no clue what they could be.

That wasn't in the book.

"Then what?" I asked uncertainly.

He looked at me like I'd said something very dumb.

"Then, you use the winch to bring it back up. Honestly, kid, we've done this a bunch of times. Are you really not used to it by now?"

His tone was concerned and his tanned face was wrinkled with worry.

"Sorry," I said quickly. "I just want to make sure I've got everything right before I go. Wouldn't want to make another mistake like last time."

My lie came out surprisingly easily and the old man laughed.

"Damn right, kid. If you break one more priceless artefact, I'm going to drop you back in that bar where I found you," he chuckled but his tone made it clear he was joking.

"Okay, so I dive down, find the thing and then attach the winch? Easy," I said with feigned confidence.

"Good. Get your gear on, we can't spend too long here otherwise those damn pirates are going to find us again," he grumbled darkly.

I had been starting to stand to walk towards the scuba gear at the back of the boat but my feet stilled.

"Pirates?" I said.

That definitely hadn't been in the book. But, then again, the guy in front of me was nothing like the crotchety old mentor from the book I'd read. And, in the book, they hadn't met in a bar.

I wasn't even old enough to go to a bar, I was fifteen.

Excitement built within me as I realised that I'd made these details up subconsciously, no doubt to make it more fun than the book had been. What's the point of living out a story if you already know how it ends?

"Pirates, mercenaries, same thing. Either way, they're trying to get to this before us and if they do, we'll never be able to make any money from it. Or did you forget what happened last time when those assholes almost blew you to smithereens?" he asked, his eyes narrowed behind his sunglasses.

I swallowed.

Despite knowing it was a dream, it was a little scary. I knew that I couldn't be hurt but still, I didn't want it to go badly. It might have just been my perfectionist streak, but I didn't want to let the man down. Plus, I wanted to see what the treasure sitting at the bottom of the ocean was.

"Hurry up, kid! I just said we don't have time to waste and you're faffing! Get that tank on now!" he called, breaking me from my worries.

I continued towards the back of the boat, my brain spinning with information. It was too different from the story. I wouldn't be able to do it just based on my knowledge of how they'd found the treasure in the book, I needed to go back. Maybe to the bar where this guy said we'd first met.

I blinked my eyes open, a shiver coming over me. It had started to get dark out. I could see through my window that the sun was dropping lower in the sky, setting it alight with vivid orange hues.

My stomach growled with hunger and my legs cramped as I stretched them out, unaware of how long I'd been sitting huddled up on my bed. It had only felt like a few minutes but I was sure that it had still been fully light outside when my mom left the room.

My daydreams would have to wait. Despite how little I wanted to leave my room, I needed to have some food and get ready for bed.

But still, the fantasy hovered at the back of my mind, begging me to slip back into it.

CHAPTER TWO

Full but not yet satisfied, I reclined back on my bed and pulled the duvet even higher. Dinner had been sad, even by my standards. I'd settled for noodles fried quickly with a dash of soy sauce. I wanted to be in and out of the kitchen before my mom got the chance to come down so I settled for the quickest thing I could make.

I'd wolfed it down as quickly as possible too, not daring to eat in my room with how furious she still was. She'd locked herself in their bedroom, probably banishing my dad to the guest room for the night again, but I'd still heard her stomping around up there. Every so often, just when I'd managed to get my anxiety back under control, she'd throw something or slam a door and my heart would start racing again.

A soft knock came from the door before it opened, spilling a harsh light into my darkened room.

"Night, darling," my dad said softly as he poked his

head around the door. "I'm sorry about that earlier."

I pushed myself up slightly and shook my head.

"It's fine, dad. It wasn't your fault," I said.

He smiled wryly at me.

"I'm sure your mother would probably disagree with that," he joked but it fell flat. "Did you manage to get all your homework done?"

"Yep," I said quickly, not wanting to tell him the truth because I knew he'd just worry.

He smiled softly. This time it was much more genuine than the one before.

"Good girl, I'm proud of you. Sleep well."

"Thanks, you too," I said, feeling my heart deflate slightly with shame.

He closed the door. Again, my eyes fell on the stack of books on my desk.

I hadn't had a chance to do any of my homework for the next day and I knew he'd blame himself if I told him the truth. Part of me wanted to get out of bed and do some now, at least my French homework as I had that first thing, but I knew it wasn't worth it.

If Mom managed to convince herself that I was up to no good or sneaking out, she'd come and check on me at some point. If she caught me up and doing my homework, I probably wouldn't get any sleep. I'd have to put up with comments from her about how I am lazy or stupid and will probably never amount to anything. I didn't want to deal with that. I could just do them in the morning or during form time.

Plus, my brain kept floating back to the imaginary world I'd created earlier. I wanted the chance to explore it properly. It had been so hard to keep myself from slipping into it whilst cooking and getting ready for bed, but now there was nothing stopping me.

I blew out a soft breath, letting that gentle wave of vertigo wash over me, and let my eyes shut. I opened them again cautiously.

Loud music immediately assaulted my ears and I had to resist the urge to cover them with my hands. If I did that, I'd give away my position.

I was perched on a fairly low wall overlooking a pub garden. The people in it weren't paying me any attention and I was basically shrouded in darkness because all of the lights were pointed at the small, hastily thrown together stage where a band was playing music. Well, I'm not sure that music was the right term. It was more just a solid wall of noise that threatened to overwhelm me.

I wasn't quite sure why I was sneaking in but it didn't matter, I knew I needed to get inside. Not inside the beer garden, but into the pub itself. There was someone in there, I wasn't quite sure who, but I knew that if I saw them, I'd recognise them immediately.

I smoothed my palms down my front, hoping to wipe away some of the sweat that was building there, but what I felt made me freeze and glance down.

Again, I was wearing clothes I'd never worn before

and definitely didn't own. The black skinny jeans hugged my legs tightly and the semi low-cut top I'd apparently thrown on under my leather jacket was far more daring than anything I'd wear in real life.

I didn't even own a leather jacket! Mom had told me that they were a symbol of rebellion and stupidity and said if I ever came home wearing one, she'd throw it in a fire immediately. Which, of course, made me want one even more.

With another glance at the people standing below me, I realised that I looked pretty similar to them. They were mostly wearing dark clothes and there were more leather jackets down there than I'd ever seen before.

I snorted a quiet laugh. It was basically my mom's nightmare. My mouth twitched up in a smile as I imagined her amongst the revellers down there. They all looked drunk and, despite the fact she often polished off a bottle of wine or more in one night (amongst other things), she had a hatred for people who drank often. It was hilariously ironic to me but I'd never point it out to her.

Bringing my mind to the present, I leant back against the cool bricks and looked down at the wall I was on. It wasn't too high, probably only a little taller than my own height. I wasn't sure if it was to keep people out of the garden or just to stop others from seeing in.

Glancing along the wall, I realised there was an easy way into the garden; giant bins lined the outside of it.

From there, anyone on the street outside would have been able to climb up, hop the fence and get into the garden.

Actually, I realised as I looked around the garden and the street beyond, it looked a lot like the pub in the village next to mine.

It was infamous for serving people who were under-age and apparently, it was pretty easy to get into. But that wasn't why I was there. I was there to find someone and I couldn't do that if I spent all night perched on the wall, just waiting to be caught.

The band finished their song to tremulous cheers again and I seized the opportunity to carefully jump down, the drop jarring my legs for just a moment and making me stumble forwards into a guy who had just come out of the pub.

Luckily, he'd been watching the band but he looked around at me as I collided with him.

"Watch where you're—" He stopped suddenly, his eyes scanning me up and down, lingering for slightly too long on my flushed chest. "Sorry about that, you startled me. You ought to be careful, if you run into the wrong guy like that, you never know what could happen."

I resisted a shudder at his flirtatious growl, feeling the urge to cover myself up and run away from him in disgust, but I forced myself to smile playfully.

"Sorry about that," I said coolly. "And, thanks for catching me."

I shot him a smile and started to move past him.

"Hey now," he said, catching my arm in his. "You're welcome. Why don't you buy me a drink to say thank you?"

His eyes lingered on my chest for just a moment too long and I pried my arm out of his claw-like grip.

"Ah, another night. I'm actually on my way out," I said with a calm smile, turning away from him and moving towards the door.

Luckily, the band drowned out his reply which, based on his expression, I was sure would have been insulting.

The door closed behind me, muffling the din of the band, and I moved along the dark corridor, my hand trailing gently on the slightly sticky painted wall.

Once upon a time, it would have been a very pretty bar, but the natural wood panelling on the walls had been painted a tar-like black that was somehow tacky.

Instinctively, I held my breath as I passed the toilets and slipped into the main room of the bar.

It was quieter than outside but not by much. People huddled around tables, drinking watered-down alcohol and laughing loudly. Bits of conversations reached out towards me but I didn't care. They weren't who I was looking for, I was looking for the man who was sitting at the bar, silently nursing a whiskey.

I couldn't go right over to him. I knew that he listened to me and accepted my proposal because he was the same man from the boat but still, I knew I'd need to convince him.

I made my way through the crowded room, dodging wandering hands and drunk guys like I had a lot of experience and leant on the bar, waiting for the bartender to notice me.

He came to the woman beside me first, which was lucky because I hadn't worked out what to order yet. I wasn't a particularly big drinker. Sure, I'd drank before, what fifteen-year-old hadn't, but I didn't drink much. I mostly just drank whatever was around, normally vodka because people always had that at parties.

I didn't go to many though. Parties made me uncomfortable and my mom rarely let me go anyway. I think she was convinced that, if she let me go to a party, I'd end up a drunk and then she'd never get rid of me. She'd actually told me that a few times.

More than a few.

"Spiced rum and diet coke," the woman beside me said in a raspy voice.

"Got it," the bartender said with a smile before turning to me. "You two together?"

"Nah," I said, trying to sound as calm and collected as she had.

His eyes scanned my face for a second as he poured her drink and I could tell that he was debating asking me for my ID, which I didn't think I had, before he placed her drink on the counter and shrugged.

"What do you want?" he said as he took her money and gave her the change.

"Same as her actually," I said with a smile.

"Good call! It's the best, isn't it?" the woman cried with a smile as she sipped the drink.

"Yeah, I love it!"

That was a lie, I'd never had rum before.

"Are you here by yourself?" she asked with an easy smile as the bartender poured my drink. "Do you want to come hang out with my friends?"

I glanced over her shoulder at the group she'd gestured towards. They were all women, seeming to be in their early twenties like her, and they were giggling freely.

A pit of longing opened in my stomach. Part of me did want to go hang out with her and her friends and completely forget about the reason I'd even gone to the bar in the first place. They seemed so nice and I'd always longed for a group of friends that I felt comfortable with. Not that I didn't have friends or like them, but the idea of a big group of friends always filled me with longing.

But I couldn't just blow off the reason I was in the pub.

"Sorry," I said with a genuine and regretful smile, "I'm meeting someone."

I jerked my head towards where the guy was sitting causing the girl and the bartender to look over at him.

"Okay, I see it. He's kind of cute in a rugged, old way. Is he rich?" the girl asked, sipping her drink whilst still watching him.

The bartender placed my drink in front of me, waiting for my answer too.

I had no idea what to say so I forced myself to laugh as I slipped a crumpled note from my pocket.

"I hope so," I said, shooting her a wink before picking up my drink and slipping through the crowd towards him, not bothering to wait for my change.

Taking a sip from the thin black straw, I found myself grateful that I couldn't taste the undoubtedly acrid drink, if my experience with alcohol taught me anything. The smell alone was enough to warn me off it. It was strangely warm and comforting but there was a definite note of paint stripper underneath.

"Is this seat taken?" I asked as I approached the man.

"I wish it was," he muttered, not taking his eyes off the phone clutched in his hand.

I hopped onto it, turning back towards the crowd and subtly glancing at the screen as I did so.

It was clear that he was looking at a map on it but I wasn't sure what it was a map of. There was a big rectangular building in the middle and a lot of empty space around it.

"I'm Grace," I said over the noise.

His eyes flicked up to my face for a second before he looked away again but I forced myself to keep my eyes on the crowd. I wasn't quite sure what I was looking for but it was definitely something.

"Who are you?" I asked finally when it became clear that he wasn't going to answer me.

"Uninterested," he said shortly. "And about twenty years too old."

I snorted.

"That wasn't my question."

"Does it matter?" he asked, looking away from the map in exasperation.

"Does anything?" I almost winced as the words came out of my mouth.

I'd meant it to sound snappy and cool but I just sounded like an idiot.

"No. Life is mostly void of meaning but there are still a few good things in it," he said, taking a sip of his drink.

"Like what?"

He took a deep breath, clearly annoyed by my continued questioning.

"Good whiskey, not this swill, obviously, cigars, women and silence."

I wasn't sure how to respond to that, but I couldn't stop the laugh that slipped out of my mouth.

"So, where are you from? It's clear that accent isn't from around here," I said after a moment.

He sighed heavily and locked his phone before turning towards me.

"God, you're a persistent little thing, aren't you?" he asked.

I cocked an eyebrow and took another sip as I

waited for his response.

"Kentucky, originally. Spent some time in the Caribbean, Greece, even lived in Ireland for a spell. You're from 'round these parts," he said simply.

It wasn't a question but I felt the need to answer it anyway.

"Eh, kind of. Started off in London but didn't last there long, went to Northampton after that then got sent further up north for a bit. Nottingham/Lincoln area," I said, the words spilling out effortlessly. "And now I'm here."

I wasn't sure where that lie came from but it must have sparked some interest in him because he looked away from the mirror behind the bar and examined me shrewdly.

"You're pretty young to have lived in all those places. How old are you?" he asked, his head cocking to one side.

"Young enough to not want to answer too loudly in here," I said.

He laughed loudly and unexpectedly.

"So, definitely underage? What are you doing here then?"

He hadn't asked it in a rude way but still, I hesitated before answering him.

I couldn't tell him the truth. Even though it was just a fantasy, I wanted to play it cool.

"Looking for a way to pass the time."

The crease in between his eyebrows deepened.

"Is that so? Well, unfortunately for you, kid, you're about twenty years too young for my liking," he said with barely a look in my direction.

I suppressed the urge to roll my eyes at him.

"Yes, because that's the only way someone can pass the time," I said flatly, hoping that he'd understand my sarcasm.

His lips twitched under his bushy moustache.

"Alright, what were you thinking then?" he asked, still looking at me instead of at the bar.

I looked away from him, taking a deep breath to steady myself so that I could answer him but instead, something caught my eye.

People were watching us. And not just in a slightly creepy yet innocent people-watching way. They were watching us. Intently. I swallowed and tried to look casual as I glanced around the crowded pub.

Six.

Six people were watching us. They were pretty obvious to spot, they weren't even trying to blend in. They hadn't gotten drinks and they weren't wearing the typical 'pub' attire either. From what I could see, they were dressed all in black with strange utility vests, and their eyes were fixed on us.

"Umm," I started.

The old guy must have realised something was wrong, because his head whipped around to the mirror and I saw him scanning the pub.

"Did you bring them in here?" he demanded quietly.

"No!"

"Did they follow you?"

"I don't think so," I cried as softly as possible, not wanting the people who were watching to catch on to my panic.

Even though I knew it was fake, my heart was pounding in my chest.

"How did you get here?" he asked, pretending to take a sip of his drink whilst he scanned the mirror again.

"I snuck in! Climbed the back wall. Do you think they followed me?"

He nodded, his expression grim.

"They could have, but I'm not sure." He took another sip. "Okay, kid, go hide in the bathroom, I'll lure these assholes out of here and then, in a couple of hours or so, you can go back home safely."

My eyebrows drew together at that horrible plan.

It wouldn't work and I needed to find a way to go with him, if I didn't then it would have all been for nothing.

"Well, as great as that plan sounds, it's pretty terrible. Do you really think that none of those people have seen my face or that they won't follow me into the bathroom?" I said, raising one eyebrow at him.

"Crap," he muttered under his breath. "Alright, fine. New plan, I'm going to go out the front and lure them into the alley beside the pub. You wait a minute until most of them leave and then go out the back. Hop the wall and hide until I've taken them all down, then I'll find you and we'll try and work out a way to get you home safely."

I opened my mouth to ask what to do if there were more people waiting out there, but he'd already drained his drink and pushed away from the bar.

My heart started pounding as my eyes followed him. He weaved his way through the bar, not even bothering to try and hide, and disappeared through the door. Automatically, I glanced at the people who'd been watching us. Most of them had left but one stayed behind.

His eyes were fixed on me and when my gaze met theirs, his lips slowly broke into a cruel smile that made my heart stutter.

CHAPTER THREE

My heart started pounding in my chest as the guy's smile grew even wider. His dark green eyes never left my face as he slowly pushed away from the table and started to weave sinuously through the crowd towards me. There was no point in waiting, I needed to leave now.

I put my drink down on the counter and slipped off the stool I'd been perched on. I needed to get out before he could reach me. I ducked behind a group of people who were talking loudly, squeezing up against the wall so that I could pass without them noticing.

I managed to make it into the corridor without attracting too much attention but I had to force myself not to break into a run. If I didn't hurry up, not only would that old guy not wait for me, but the guy following me would catch up and I didn't know what would happen then. But, running felt too obvious. People would stare.

Just as I reached the door to the garden, I heard the other door open behind me but I couldn't risk looking back. I pushed the surprisingly heavy door, barely noticing the biting wind as I burst into the garden.

The band was still playing a punishingly loud song and the garden was dark except for the stage but that was better. It meant that I could slip into the crowd unnoticed as I surveyed the wall, trying to work out how to climb it.

I needed a way to get over it but I was too short to just pull myself up and there were no bins on this side for me to climb onto.

Wait, no. There was one. A small open-topped trash can overflowing with clear plastic cups lay near the back corner. If I could climb onto there, I could probably pull myself up onto the wall.

I'd need to be careful though, I really didn't want to fall into that bin.

My heart echoed in my ears as I edged closer, trying not to be obvious about it in case the guy who was following me saw and tried to cut me off. People surrounded me on all sides, most of them taller than me and swaying to the music. Normally, it would have been overwhelming but for once, I appreciated being short. It meant that I was essentially hidden.

I reached the edge of the crowd, the acrid stench of cigarette smoke filling my nose, and stared at the bin. If I moved quickly and perched just on the edges, I'd be able to get up onto the wall before I was seen. I just needed to get there quickly.

Taking a deep breath, I dashed towards the bin and threw myself onto it. Scrabbling to avoid slipping into the rubbish, I barely managed to climb up before a shout from the crowd grabbed my attention. I couldn't stop myself. I glanced behind me, seeing the guy force his way through the people, his eyes still fixed on me.

Panic raced through me and I managed to throw my arms over the wall, stretching one leg up onto it before gloved fingers found my other ankle. My eyes widened in fear and I kicked my leg, furiously trying to escape his grasp, but he was too strong. He was trying to drag me back.

I peered over the wall, hoping that somehow the old guy would be there to help me, but I could see him disappearing around the corner at the end of the alley next to the wall.

The people in black were following him.

I didn't have a chance to worry about him though because a shout came from behind me.

"Hey! What's going on there?"

Hope fluttered in my chest as the commotion behind me grew.

"Help! He won't let go!" I cried, making my voice as shrill and panicked as possible.

It wasn't hard.

"What the hell, man?" someone shouted and I risked

another look backwards.

A few people were huddled around the guy, grabbing at him and trying to pull him off me. I grasped the wall even tighter, my slippery hands making it difficult, and kicked out.

My leg finally came free and I hauled myself up onto the wall but the momentum sent me tumbling off the other side, landing heavily on the plastic bins before crashing to the floor.

The air was knocked out of me but luckily, pain couldn't reach me in the fantasy. I rolled to my feet, sucking in air and looked up.

"Crap," slipped out of my mouth.

The people who had been chasing after the old guy must have heard me because they'd turned and were slowly advancing towards me, having abandoned their chase in favour of me.

I turned, my hands shaking with nervousness, and started sprinting towards the road that was somewhere behind me. Their footsteps pounded against the tarmac behind me, spurring me on.

I emerged from the alley and raced along the street, glancing at the houses that I passed. I could have easily banged on the doors and hoped that someone came out and helped but I knew it was pointless. I needed to find a way to find the old guy but I didn't know where he'd gone. He'd said that he would find me but I wasn't sure how he planned on doing that.

Annoyance at myself washed through me despite my panic. I'd screwed it up and I was half tempted to try again. I controlled the fantasy. I could go back and start over, spot the bad guys before it got that far and insist that we escape together.

I reached the end of the street and ran out into the road without looking, my heart almost stopping when a screech of tires erupted behind me. I leapt to the side, hoping that it wouldn't hit me or, if it did, that I wouldn't feel it, and spun around.

An old-looking cream car had come to a stop not far from where I'd been standing just moments before and behind the wheel, the old man's face was pale.

Relief washed through me.

"What are you standing around for, kid?" the man demanded. "Get in!"

I didn't even hesitate.

I threw myself over the bonnet of the car and ripped the door open, diving inside. I slipped on the leather seat as the wheels spun into motion and we sped along the street.

"Get that seatbelt on, kid. I've almost killed you once today, I ain't doing it again," he growled, glancing in his mirrors to watch the people standing in the road behind us.

I reached blindly for the belt, not wanting to take my eyes off the people behind me, but we turned a corner before long and they were lost from sight. I was finally able to breathe properly as we sped past the church, the road still empty behind us.

"Who the hell were those people and why were they chasing us?" I asked, my voice wavering with anxiety.

It was just a fantasy, I tried to remind myself but it was difficult. It felt real. I could feel the cold leather seat under me and my body swayed in time with the car's movements. Even when that guy had grabbed me earlier, it had felt real. I had felt his leather glove wrap so tightly around my bare ankle that, even now, it still throbbed slightly.

"Assholes," the guy growled. "They've been following me since I crossed the channel. I've switched cars three times and yet they still keep finding me. I thought I'd be safe in this backwater town but they even managed to find me here."

My head swam from the information, but I forced myself to repeat the question.

"Who are they and what did they want?"

He took his eyes away from the road for a second to glance at me before he cleared his throat.

"That's a complicated question with an even more complicated answer," he answered finally.

"We got time," I said as my hands tightened on the edges of the seat.

"No, we don't. I need to find a safe place to stash you. Do you live near here?" he asked, his eyes flicking to the mirrors often.

"Kinda," the answer slipped out of my mouth. "Got a foster home nearby."

His eyes narrowed and he glanced at me again.

"You like it there?" he asked carefully.

I scrunched up my nose, a little unsure how to answer.

"Not really," I said finally, thinking of my real home. "I mean, it's not too bad. Lot of arguments though."

The guy was silent as we slipped through the streets.

"Do they treat you right? Look after you properly? Make sure you got food and all?" he asked after a while.

I swallowed as a wave of unexpected sorrow washed over me but I couldn't shake the lump in my throat so I just shook my head.

Tears threatened my eyes as I stared at the darkened dashboard. I could feel his eyes on me but I couldn't look up. I couldn't do anything as hopelessness washed over me.

The answer was no. My parents didn't treat me right. They didn't look after me properly or make sure I had food.

My dad tried but he worked too much. He was barely home. But Mom… She didn't even try.

"Alright, kid. I'm not going to force you to go back if you don't want to. I know what it's like to grow up in a place where you're not wanted," he said so gently that it made a tear slip from my eyes.

"I have nowhere else to go," I admitted quietly.

I didn't. What was I meant to do? Run away and hope that someone takes me in? Maybe some of my family would but not if it meant risking my mom's wrath. Plus, they believed that any issues should be settled within our family so they wouldn't get involved with what was going on with her, no matter how miserable I was.

I sniffed and stared out the window at the shadowy world slipping by. I could tell that the guy was struggling with something, but I was too trapped within my own sorrow to say anything.

My stomach ached with sadness, leaving me hollow.

"What if you did?" he asked finally.

I shook my head.

"It doesn't matter, I don't."

"But what if you did?" he pressed.

"Where?" I asked flatly.

He glanced up at the mirror again.

"Couple of options. I know a nice family that would take you in, friends pretty high up in social services that could help gloss over the foster placement too. Or…"

He trailed off and I waited for him to continue.

The ache in my stomach subsided for a moment as he thought for a minute.

"You were pretty good back there. You spotted them in the bar before I did, managed to get away from them too. Do you fight?"

I shrugged, not sure why he asked.

"I did karate when I was younger."

That was true. My mom liked to tell people very loudly that she was making sure I could look after myself if needed.

"You ever been in a real fight? It's pretty different to karate but that can give you a good basis."

"Couple of times, nothing big though."

That one was a lie but in my fantasy, anything could be the truth.

"You're a pretty fast runner, I saw that much. Can you swim?"

"Yeah," I said.

I wasn't sure where he was going but excitement was building within me.

"What about climbing? You ever done rock climbing?"

I shook my head.

When I was in primary school, I'd gone to a rock climbing party but I felt like that didn't count.

"No? That's fine, you can pick that up quickly enough. What about heights? Scared of them?"

I considered it.

In real life, they made me a little uneasy. I wasn't the most graceful person in the world and I was always a little worried that at some point, I'd slip and fall if I went too close to the edge. But, he didn't need to know that.

"Don't think so. Why?"

"Are you smart? Do you do well at school?" he asked,

ignoring my question.

My face scrunched up at that.

I wasn't dumb but school wasn't for me. I did well when I tried or cared about what we were learning about but the rest of the time, I didn't have it in me to try.

"Kind of, but I don't really like school," I said awkwardly.

"Why not?"

I considered my answer carefully, feeling like my answer was important.

"It's boring, I know I'll never use half the stuff we learn there and even the teachers know that."

He snorted.

"You sure about that? I mean, I used to feel the same way but being out in the world changed things. I mean, travelling is pretty tough with no knowledge of geography. And, how are you meant to know where to anchor ropes for climbing if you don't know about the rock types?" he asked gently.

"Umm..." I started but he wasn't finished talking.

"And with no knowledge of chemistry, how are you meant to know how to mix explosive substances? Do you know how often that comes in handy out there?"

I shook my head but didn't speak.

"Exactly! And if you've never studied biology, how would you deal with a bullet wound or an infection? Do you know what to look out for? How would you deal with a snake bite? Damn, if you don't pay attention in school, you're screwed out there," he sighed and shook his head.

I was aware that I was gaping at him and finally managed to make my mouth form words.

"I don't think we've ever learnt anything like that in school," I said finally.

He snorted again.

"Then, your school has failed you," he said with a heavy sigh. "Maybe it wouldn't be the end of the world if you were to drop out..."

"Why would I drop out?" I asked quickly.

I was unsure whether to be scared or excited by where the conversation was going. It was mostly excitement though. I knew I was still back in my bed, in the early hours of the morning. I couldn't be hurt.

He sighed heavily.

"I have an offer," he said, his tone almost regretful. "You were useful back there and I think you'll continue to be useful. You can come with me. We'll travel and you'll essentially be homeschooled. You'll still have to have lessons and learn but I guarantee that it'll be a lot more interesting than you sitting in a classroom bored out of your wits. I'm not a teacher but I'll try to make sure you learn and stay safe."

My tongue darted out to wet my lips. It was a terrible idea and I knew it. If it were in real life, I would never have agreed to it. I wouldn't have gotten in the car with that strange man who still hadn't told me his name but...

it wasn't real life. There was no real risk to me.

Still, I wanted to know.

"Why?" I asked. "Why would you do this for me?"

There was a pause and I examined what I could see of his face, searching for answers.

"Hell, I don't even know why I'm doing this but I've been in your shoes before and you deserve better than what you have. Every kid deserves to be happy and treated properly. I'll do my best to make sure that you're protected and have more chances than you would have here," he said softly.

I reminded him of himself, I realised slowly.

Guilt washed over me. I was manipulating him. I'd made him believe that I was in foster care and treated badly. Maybe I was treated badly but at least I had a dad who cared about me.

"It's completely your choice, kid. I can drop you back with your foster family, take you anywhere you want, find you a better foster family or you can come with me," he said softly.

"Where would we go?" I asked quietly.

"I mean, firstly we'll probably have to swing by a buddy of mine who works in child services and child protection so that I don't get done for kidnapping, then... Scotland. And, don't worry, when we're staying in hotels, you'll get your own room. I meant what I said before, I ain't looking for anything from you. I'm easily old enough to be your dad."

My head snapped up and I nodded at the uncomfortable edge to his voice but I chose not to address it any more.

"Why Scotland?" I asked.

I'd been there. My mom took me there to visit family every summer.

"I'm looking for something. Or, at least, information on something," he answered cagily.

"What is it?"

Interest prickled in my stomach, chasing out all traces of guilt.

He sighed heavily.

"Well, this might influence your decision and probably not in a good way but… treasure."

My mouth dropped open again even though I had been expecting it.

"Treasure?" I asked, needing to make sure I'd heard him correctly.

"I know it sounds crazy but it ain't. That's what I do, I'm a treasure hunter for private clients generally," he explained.

"You're a treasure hunter?"

"Yep. Have been since I was pretty young myself. Stumbled onto it by accident and here I am some thirty years later."

Interest and confusion washed over me.

"How do you stumble onto treasure hunting?" I asked.

He snorted a laugh.

"I ran away. Things were a little different when I was a kid so it was pretty easy to get far enough away from the assholes who'd been looking for me. I heard some people talking in a pub one night, talking about one of their new recruits who didn't know shit and that they were pretty sure no one even screened them because they just showed up at camp one day and honestly, that sounded interesting so I followed them back to where they were staying and, the next morning, did the exact same thing."

A wistful smile came over his face and he chuckled.

"What happened? Did they question you or just go along with it?" I asked, fascinated and desperate to know more.

"Oh yeah. I'm not sure if it was their recruitment style or if they were just used to picking up strays but they didn't even question it. Within the day, I had a new identity, new passport, hell, I even had a new wardrobe. They took care of everything and we flew out that evening. I got a crash course in how to find things no one wants you to find and by the end of my time with them, I was pretty good."

"Why did you leave?"

I regretted the question as soon as it came out. His face tightened noticeably and his hands clenched around the steering wheel.

"Let's just say we had some conflicting morals," he said finally.

I nodded, wanting to know more but I figured I'd find out at some point.

A yawn fought its way out of my mouth and I clenched my hand, digging my nails into my palms in an attempt to stay awake.

"So, kid. What's your answer?"

"I want to be a treasure hunter," I said immediately.

I did. In real life and in the fantasy. He made it sound so fascinating.

I knew it would be dangerous to run off with a guy so much older than me and I never would have done it in real life but, in my fantasy, I was safe. He wouldn't touch me. Plus, he had sounded genuine when he'd said he wouldn't.

I had nothing to lose.

"Okay, kid. But it won't be like the video games. It's a lot of work and you have to train. Mentally and physically. We'll swing by a friend's office in the morning and get it all squared up and get you registered for homeschooling. I meant what I said; I'm not a good teacher but I'll try my best. I'm going to need you to meet me halfway though," he said, shooting me a look out of the corner of his eye.

I nodded eagerly.

"Okay. Do you need anything from your foster house? We can go back," he offered.

I shook my head.

"Okay, we'll switch out the car and then head to

London," he said. "Find Betty and go from there."

"Who's Betty?" I asked.

Sleep was pulling at my mind and sapping the colour from my fantasy.

"She's an old friend," he said with a slight smile. "Wait, did you tell me your name before? I don't remember it."

"Grace," I said softly.

"Well, it's lovely to meet you, Grace. I'm Mitch."

CHAPTER FOUR

"Okay, turn to page forty-seven. We'll be picking up from where we stopped last time," my English teacher, Mrs Govern, said in her usual nasal tone.

I watched her blankly, my interest in the book being sapped out of me the longer I sat in the classroom. She was wearing her usual thin scarf, striped jumper, and long skirt. Her short hair stuck out at every angle, as always, giving her a vaguely electrocuted look.

"I'm going to need some characters. Who would like to read today?" she asked, looking around the room with an overtly enthusiastic grin that bordered on manic.

I stared down at my open book intently.

I did not want to be chosen. Don't get me wrong, I enjoyed reading, of course I did, but there were few things I disliked more than reading in front of the class. I always tripped over my words and hated every moment. Every time, I could feel Sophia's eyes burning into my red face, and I knew that she was smirking, waiting for me to struggle so that she could laugh. She always did. She was the ringleader who made the others laugh too.

I think it was at least slightly out of fear. If people laughed along and pretended to like her, she wouldn't turn on them too.

"Emily, I'd like you to play Viola," Mrs Govern started.

"Yes!" Emily hissed under her breath but loud enough for everyone to hear.

Mrs Govern just smiled at her indulgently before looking around for another person to choose.

"Alex, you can read the Duke and we'll choose the others as and when they come up. Okay, Emily, start at the top of the page."

Relief washed through me, only slightly tinged with annoyance, as Emily cleared her throat and started reading in an overdramatic and loud voice. Her voice felt like it echoed around the room, easily reaching everyone in the classroom.

She didn't need to be talking so loudly, there were only about thirty of us so it wasn't a particularly large room. We were seated in rows and, as usual, she was right at the front. Even so, she felt the need to almost shout.

I scanned the pages, blocking out Emily's voice as

much as I could. I didn't hate the book, it was fine, I just didn't like how we were reading it in school. Mrs Govern always made us read through as a class and told us off if we had the audacity to read ahead.

Apparently, that would ruin our enjoyment which always made me smirk a little. As if hearing Emily try to put on a masculine voice and read Cesario's lines added anything to the reading experience. I'd already finished the book. I'd managed to do it over the first couple of classes. Now, I had weeks stretching ahead of me where I'd just be expected to sit silently and read painfully slowly through the book with others acting out the lines.

It happened every time we started a new book in class. I'd enjoy it for the first lesson, finish it in the next few and then slowly start to hate it as I was trapped slowly reading through it and being asked every couple of lines to examine it deeper and try to consider the inspirations behind everything or why something was written in a certain way.

There was always some deep and convoluted reason that Mrs Govern came up with and it was always more than 'because they wanted to'. I doubted she ever got it actually right. I knew that she studied English at university, she'd bragged about that enough times, but still, it seemed unlikely. Some of her theories were so farfetched.

Why couldn't a line be written in a certain way just because the author wanted it to be read that way? Or was every single word carefully thought out and consid-ered? No, that seemed ridiculous. Surely, that would take too long.

My eyes widened slightly and a smile came to my face as I realised something. Without conscious thought, I slipped back into my daydream with a wave of dizziness.

"Kid," Mitch's soft voice said. "Kid! Wake up, we're here."

I cracked my eyes open, blinking rapidly against the dazzling brightness.

"Where are we?" I asked before fear shot through me and I opened my eyes in real life.

I don't think I'd even had them closed but I stared around the classroom carefully, fearful that I'd spoken out loud and was about to be mocked. But no one was looking at me. Everyone was either staring into space or staring blankly at their books.

Relief, so strong it made me lightheaded, washed through me and I blinked back into the other world.

The sun blazed down, reflecting off the other cars around us and threatening to blind me. There weren't even any clouds to protect my eyes, just an endless bright blue sky.

"Car park in London. The only open-top one I could find near here," he said gruffly.

I stared around the cars surrounding me, shining brightly in the morning sun.

"Why?" I asked.

"If things get bad, I can call a buddy with a helicopter to come get us. It's not exactly legal but we can find a way around it."

My head spun and I was at a loss for what to say.

I wanted to ask a million questions, like why would things get bad and were those people still following us. Also, who was his buddy and why did he never refer to any of them by name? Or even how would they find a way around the law, surely that was pretty set in stone?

But then my eyes fell on the dashboard of the car we were in. It was different to the night before. That one hadn't had the silver accent that this one had.

"Is this a different car?" I asked before I could stop myself.

"Yeah, do you not remember switching it last night?" he asked, shooting me a look.

"No, not at all," I answered honestly.

He snorted.

"I'm not surprised. I doubt your eyes even opened once. Had to check you were still breathing a couple of times."

I felt myself laugh softly.

"What now?" I asked.

"Now, we get breakfast. You hungry?"

It didn't matter, I couldn't taste anything in my fantasies.

"Sure," I lied.

"Great. There's a cafe on the ground floor of this

multi-storey. Will you go down and pick me up an espresso, the largest one they do, and some kind of breakfast sandwich and get something for you too?" he asked with a cheeky grin.

"Hey! Why can't you do it?" I complained but it was hard to keep the smile off my face.

I didn't really mind though.

"More people are looking for me, I gotta lay low, but they probably won't be looking for you. One sec, I'll grab a couple phones out the back."

He disappeared out the door before I could say anything else and my eyes scanned the car park as he made his way around to the back of the car and rooted around in the boot.

He returned before long, holding out an iPhone to me.

"You know how to pay using this?" he asked.

I nodded. I'd used Apple Pay before.

"Great. The password is four zeros, you got it?" he said, his expression intense.

I nodded again.

"Now, don't think about running away and using my card. There's a limit to how much can be spent on there and it's a burner account. Get down there and come up quickly. If you think it's going to take more than ten minutes, text me. Otherwise, I'll assume you're working with the others and I'll leave you here then wipe that phone, got it?"

"Yep," I said, my mouth dry.

"Great. My number is saved under the name 'one'. If something feels wrong or you get held up, text me just the letter 'Q' and I'll come help, okay?"

I nodded again, fear washing through me.

I hoped nothing happened. I was in class still and I could vaguely hear the droning voices of Emily and Alex so I didn't want anything too exciting or cool to happen. I knew that I needed to stay at least a little bit aware of what was happening in the real world, which would be hard if a fight or something happened in the fantasy.

My face started to flush with embarrassment as I imagined what would happen if the bell rang and we were dismissed but I was too distracted by being chased again or something.

"Well, what are you waiting for? We only have twenty minutes before Betty's office opens, go!"

I threw the door open and rushed out, painfully aware of the time limit he'd set for me. As I rushed across the car park, trying hard not to look suspicious whilst also moving quickly and checking that I wasn't being followed, I checked the time. It was a little after seven in the morning, her office must open at seven-thirty.

I'd need to be quick.

I yanked the heavy door open to the staircase and raced down the steps, the phone slippery in my sweaty hand. My footsteps echoed loudly in the staircase and my heart raced with a combination of anxiety and exertion.

After what felt like far too long, I burst out into the bright sunlight, blinking and squinting so that I could just about see.

My gaze quickly fell on the cafe that Mitch had mentioned and I joined the busy foot traffic towards it. It was attached to the multi-storey but I couldn't see any way to get into it from the inside of the car park so I settled for entering from the street.

The glass front allowed me to quickly survey the people sitting inside as I approached but it did little to reduce my anxiety. I didn't recognise anyone sitting at any of the wooden tables but that didn't make me feel better.

The soft and welcoming aroma of coffee washed over me as I pulled the door open, making my mouth water. I continued to watch everyone as carefully as I could as I walked towards the refrigerated units before my eyes fell on the rows of sandwiches and rolls.

I quickly found the heated display of warm food where the breakfast sandwiches were but from there, I was stumped.

There were too many options.

I turned the phone in my hand as I examined them carefully and debated texting Mitch.

Sausage, bacon, both or vegetarian? I pondered as I unlocked the phone and pulled up the messaging app before stopping myself.

I couldn't go running to him with every single little

question I had. That would get so annoying so quickly. I needed to show him that I could be decisive.

Before I could change my mind, I reached out and grabbed the breakfast sandwich with bacon, sausage and egg but then I froze.

What if he doesn't like eggs? I thought, worry shooting through me.

Some people didn't. Hell, I didn't and I didn't want to get him a sandwich he didn't like.

The phone buzzed in my hand, startling me, and I stared down at the words that had appeared.

I'm hungry, get two.

I quickly typed '*okay*' and sent it back to him before grabbing a sausage sandwich as well and one of the vegetarian sandwiches. That way, all bases were covered. I'd offer him all of them and then, if he didn't want it, I'd eat the vegetarian one.

Almost content with my decision and the breakfast sandwiches just about clenched in my hands, I scanned the cafe again and joined the queue. My heart raced as I watched the time slowly tick down and the queue crawled forwards at a painfully slow rate.

It took far too long before I reached the counter and clumsily dropped the sandwiches onto it.

"One breakfast sandwich, one vegetarian breakfast sandwich and a sausage sandwich. Can I get anything else for you?" the blue-haired woman behind the counter asked in a falsely bright tone.

"Um, an Espresso, please. The largest you do," I added hastily.

"Sure," she said, typing on the screen. "Anything else?"

I stared up at the menu above her.

I didn't drink coffee in the real world, it was too bitter, but I liked the smell. I could have one in my fantasy world, there was nothing stopping me.

"Can I get a latte, please?" I said, ordering my dad's go-to. "With caramel syrup?"

"Sure, anything else?"

"That's it, thanks."

"Great," she said flatly. "How are you paying?"

A trill of anxiety burst through me as I lifted the phone. What if it didn't work? I'd look like such an idiot.

"Do you accept this?" I asked with what I hoped was a lighthearted smile.

"Sure, just tap it on there when you're ready."

The woman gestured towards the card reader and I double tapped the button on the phone to activate the payment system, quickly typing in the code when prompted to do so.

I could hear my heart pounding in my ears as I waited for it to be accepted, almost pulling the phone away to check that it was working and I was using the right card before the phone buzzed slightly, sending a wave of relief through me.

"Great, that's all gone through. If you wait down there by that counter, someone will put your drinks there once they've been made. Do you want a bag for those by the way?"

"Oh, yes, please," I said, sending her a relieved smile.

She returned it halfheartedly as she bagged my sandwiches and pushed it towards me.

I took the bag and walked towards the counter she'd pointed at, watching the others in the cafe. No one was wearing the telltale all-black uniform as those who had followed us the night before, but that didn't mean I was safe. They could be dressed in normal clothes.

There was someone sitting at one of the tables who was watching me. He was dressed in a crisp dark suit and his blonde hair was pushed back away from his face. It looked like he'd just swept it back but I knew it probably took him ages to get it to just the right level of dishevelled.

His lips broke into a wide, smarmy smile as he noticed my eyes on him and he slowly pushed away from his table. My heart started to speed up as he made his way over to me, blatantly checking me out.

"Hey," he said in a surprisingly deep tone, sending me another smile that showed his bright white teeth.

"Hi," I said with a tight smile before looking away.

"Come here often?" he asked, ignoring my obvious disinterest.

"Nope, first time."

"Ah, a virgin? Well, I'm glad I could share this experience with you."

He smiled again, clearly thinking that he was being clever but my stomach turned.

I glanced at the people who were making my coffee, smiling as one to-go cup was put on the counter.

"Caramel latte?" they asked.

"Thanks," I said quickly, glancing at the other baristas and trying to work out who was making the espresso.

I really needed them to hurry up so I could get away from the creep who was still eyeing me up.

"So, are you sticking around for a while or have you got plans?" he tried again.

"I have plans."

"Anything interesting?"

My mind raced as I tried to think of something to say that would get rid of him. In real life, I would have just had a conversation with him and then left as soon as possible but... I didn't need to here. I could mess with him with no worries of repercussions.

"Meeting my lawyer actually," I said in a brighter tone and was rewarded with a look of concern that briefly flitted over his face.

"Oh?" he asked, sounding a little uncertain for the first time.

"Yeah, it's nothing major, just a light assault case. She reckons she should be able to get the charges dropped pretty easily," I said with a grin, holding up my fingers which I'd crossed for luck.

"Espresso?" one of the baristas asked, holding up a cup.

"Oh, that's mine too! Thanks!" I said, juggling the things I was holding around so that the bag was looped on my wrists and the phone was clutched between my fingers around the cup. "Well, actually, it's my lawyer's. You know what they're like, it never hurts to bribe them a little. It was nice talking to you."

I breezed away from him without looking back and shouldered the door open before I let myself glance behind me to make sure he hadn't followed.

He hadn't. He'd slowly lowered himself back into his seat, a slightly bewildered look on his face.

I let myself smile, enjoying the fact that I'd actually managed to get him to leave me alone, and crossed the street towards the urine scented staircase. I raced up the stairs as quickly as I could with the two hot cups of coffee threatening to overflow at any moment, despite their lids.

Pushing the door open at the top of the stairs, I realised that I had no idea how long had passed since I left Mitch. Fear blossomed in my stomach again as I scanned the cars quickly, looking for the silver car he'd been in. Breathing out a sigh, I spotted it and raced towards it.

Mitch looked almost relieved to see me but he quickly hid it behind grouchiness.

"You took your time, didn't you?" he grumbled once I'd managed to get back into the car.

"I ran all the way there and back!" I insisted, holding out the coffee to him.

"Did you now? Well, maybe you aren't as fast as I thought. We'll work on that. What sandwiches did you get?"

I ignored the dig and put my coffee into the cupholder before pulling the bag off my wrist.

"Take whichever ones you want," I said, holding the bag out to him.

He peered into the bag suspiciously, examining the content.

"Did you get the veggie one for me or you?" he asked.

"You can have it if you want."

He narrowed his eyes at me.

"I'm good with these two," he said after a pause, pulling out the other two sandwiches and handing the bag back to me.

"Good," I replied with a smile as I pushed the bag onto the floor and grabbed my sandwich.

"So," he said after taking a few bites of the first sandwich. "You're a vegetarian."

It wasn't a question and it didn't need an answer but still, I gave one.

"Yeah."

"How long's that been going on?"

His tone wasn't judgemental, just curious.

"A few years," I replied.

"Bet the foster homes hate that," he said with a good-hearted smile. "I'm not going to stop eating meat around you."

"I wouldn't expect you to," I said with a shrug, taking another bite of the sandwich.

I still couldn't taste anything but I could smell it and it smelt good. It almost made me want to hunt down the cafe in real life. It wouldn't be hard, there were hundreds of them across the country.

"But I will make sure there's always food you can eat wherever we go."

That sent warmth through me. Even though I knew he was a figment of my imagination, it made me happy that someone thought of that for me. Maybe I just wanted to be cared for like that and I knew I wouldn't get it from my mom.

A jarring bell broke through my consciousness and I looked around the car in fear before realising it was happening in real life. I blinked back into reality and let my eyes focus on Mrs Govern at the front of the classroom. My hand moved mechanically as I wrote down the homework assignment, barely even paying attention to it as my brain begged to slip back into the fantasy.

CHAPTER FIVE

The entire day dragged.

We'd had maths right after English class and even that had been boring for once. Normally, I enjoyed it, but I couldn't stop my mind from wandering.

I wanted to step back into that fantasy world where I was about to be adopted or fostered by Mitch and then become a treasure hunter. I didn't really know what I'd be doing as a treasure hunter, but that small glimpse where I was on the boat and about to scuba dive, had filled me with excitement. And a bit of fear, but it was a fantasy. I wouldn't be hurt so it didn't matter.

I'd basically run home as soon as class was finished for the day, calling a quick goodbye to my friend before rushing out the door and towards the quiet path home. The shadowy canopy protected me from the punishingly hot summer sun and the world took on a hushed quality as I slowly made my way along the old railway walk.

Years ago, way before I was even born, there had

been a railway that cut through my town, but it was abandoned now. Most of the tracks had been pulled up and the materials used for something better. They'd pathed the majority of the walk but it was bumpy and uneven. Pitted slabs of concrete fought with the strong tree roots, but mostly the trees won.

The path always smelled a little… off. Even in winter, the scent of rust and rot lingered in the air. It came from the weak, stagnant, and alarmingly orange water that lined one side of the path. The other side was mostly a mud and tree-covered bank.

If I paused for even a moment, the trees came alive. I could hear tiny animals scampering around, birds flapping and crying above me, and something splashing in the water.

Despite all of that, I always felt somewhat calm as I walked. I knew that I shouldn't linger, someone could easily follow me down the path and I was too far away from the school or any houses for anyone to hear me if I shouted, but I couldn't help myself.

It was my brief respite before I got home.

But on that day, I rushed. I skipped over the bumpy pavement, ran across the road beyond and hopped the fence into the field on the other side. It wasn't the safest or the smartest route but it was the quietest so it was my favourite.

The sheep weren't in the field on that day. They sometimes were at that time, but it varied. I was a little glad that they weren't; it meant that I could get home quicker. Edging around piles of sheep poo and holding my breath when needed, I managed to make it across the field and slip out the gate without any difficulty.

As I traversed the dry field beyond, my heart sank. I was almost home, which was good because it meant that I could go back to that treasure hunting fantasy, but also I'd need to deal with my mom. I wasn't sure what kind of mood she'd be in. I hadn't received any texts from her during the day but that didn't mean anything. It was just as likely that I'd walk through the door to find her glaring furiously and ready to fight or passed out on the sofa already.

I wasn't sure which I preferred.

At least if she were asleep, I'd be able to sneak past her and get upstairs. Then, I might be safe from having to deal with her for the evening. I'd be able to get my homework done before slipping back into the fantasy world.

Or maybe, I wouldn't wait. I didn't have to. I could do my homework during registration in the morning.

Plus, it was the run up to the school holidays; we only had a few days left. As much as the teachers tried to pretend, no one really cared what we did anymore. I'd finished my exams for the year. Now, they were just having us 'get an early start on next year' but it was half-hearted at best.

Some teachers didn't care at all and didn't even

bother trying to set us work, like my wonderful chemistry teacher Mr Gais, but others did. Mrs Govern obviously didn't mind setting us work even though we'd just finished our exams. Neither did Madame Noel.

Even so, I doubted any of the teachers would mind that much if I didn't hand in the homework, so if I didn't have time to do it during registration, it didn't matter that much.

I climbed over the fence at the back of my garden and stumbled as I landed heavily on the other side. Despite climbing over the fence most school days, it still caught me out at times. Normally, it was whenever I was distracted but at least this time I managed to catch myself before I fell on my face.

I crossed the garden, edging around the patches of weeds that my dad would have to sort out at the weekend, and pulled on the handle on the back door. It was locked.

I breathed out a sigh of annoyance and walked around the side gate towards the front door. If it was locked, it meant that Mom had gone out at some point today. That was good, kind of. It meant there'd probably be food in the fridge, but also it meant that she was less likely to be passed out on the sofa already.

I pulled my keys out, carefully inserting them into the lock and turning as quietly as possible before pushing the door open. I padded in before pausing and listening carefully.

The house was almost silent, which could mean anything. Only the quiet buzz of the television could be heard. I slipped my shoes off and moved towards the noise, my body tensing in preparation for what could be waiting in the lounge. Just before I reached the edge of the door, I realised I could hear another sound. Soft, snuffly breathing.

She was asleep.

My shoulders drooped with relief and I peeked around the door frame, spotting my mom lying on the sofa with a blanket haphazardly draped over her. A half-empty glass of white wine lay on the table before her and some boring show was playing on the TV.

A smile came over my face as I turned and padded towards the kitchen. I'd be able to grab some food and then go upstairs without being disturbed. I could spend the rest of the day fantasising and finding out what happened next! I couldn't wait.

I grabbed a bag of crisps and a cereal bar from the cupboard and quietly edged up the stairs, avoiding the fifth step which always creaked loudly, before racing into my bedroom and shutting the door behind me. I dropped my bag down by my desk and threw the food onto it.

I needed to look like I was doing work. If I was just sitting in my bed blankly and staring into space when my mom woke up and came to check that I'd come home, she would definitely accuse me of being high or something ridiculous.

I ripped my bag open, my mind reaching out towards the fantasy, and pulled out my French books.

They would do; I did have French homework after all.

A smile came over my face as I dropped into my chair and opened the books.

"Don't worry, Betty will be able to sort everything out," Mitch said with a soft smile. "She'll get it all squared away so that I'm fostering you and your other foster parents know what's going on."

I glanced around quickly, blinking quickly to try and get rid of the lingering sense of dizziness.

Mitch glanced back at me before stopping in the middle of the busy street and pulling me into a doorway.

"Kid, don't worry. Everything is going to be alright. Betty's good at what she does. You can trust her," he said, thinking that my lack of response was due to anxiety.

I nodded, taking a deep breath of lightly urine-scented air.

"Plus, we have to be quick. We're heading up to Edinburgh after this and it is quite the drive," he said with a smile.

"How long is it?" I asked, finally able to speak.

He hesitated.

"How do you feel about long journeys?" he asked cagily.

"Fine…" I replied hesitantly.

I actually really enjoyed them. They felt a little bit like the fantasies, like they were separate worlds of endless motion and music.

My mom and I always took a long drive up to Scotland during the summer to go stay at my grandparent's house for a few weeks. It was one of the few times we got on well. Her anger was always directed at her mom until they inevitably left for their other house.

They always vaguely hinted that they'd stay with us for the whole time, but after a few days, they got bored of our company and would leave. I didn't mind that too much. It was always good to see them but I wasn't particularly close with them and the atmosphere was generally much nicer once they left.

"'Bout six hours but it'll probably be more due to all the detours and pit stops we're going to have to make," Mitch said finally.

"Why are we going to have to make so many?" I asked as he peeked out onto the street before gesturing for me to start walking again.

"We can't go right there, people might still be following us," he said, surreptitiously eyeing the others walking around us. "We're going to take a small detour to a garage outside Sheffield where a buddy of mine has a car for us which should add some extra time too. Plus, I like snacks. Here, it should be this one."

I glanced up at the glossy red door we'd stopped in

front of, fear suddenly bubbling within me.

I wasn't sure what awaited me on the other side and that made me anxious, which I knew was silly.

"I've not been to this office yet, but Betty should be on… floor six," he said as he scanned the labels next to the buzzers on the left of the door. "There we go! Child Protection, that's her!"

My eyebrows drew together as Mitch pressed the buzzer.

It didn't say anything more than just 'Child Protection', but all the other labels had actual business names. Confusion buzzed in my head, but I couldn't work out if it was just my brain being lazy or if the label was purposefully vague.

"Hello," a voice said over the speaker in a clipped, professional tone.

"Hi there, can you please tell Betty that Mitch is here to see her?" Mitch replied in a light tone.

There was a pause and I glanced worriedly back at Mitch.

"Don't worry," he said with a smile. "She'll see us."

I opened my mouth to ask him why he was so certain but, before I could speak, the door made a loud thunk.

"Come on up, please," the woman said.

"See?" Mitch asked before grasping the metal door handle and pushing.

I wasn't sure what I expected to see on the other side but I was surprised by the wide, open corridor.

The black and white chequered marble floor was

shiny and perfectly polished, causing our footsteps to echo loudly until the corridor opened out into a circular space lined with chairs. To the right, a man in a carefully tailored suit waited behind a dark wooden counter, with a pleasant smile.

"Hello," he said as we approached. "If you could please sign in here, I'll take you up to the sixth floor."

Mitch smiled at him politely and picked up the pen, leaning over the thick, leather-bound book. I leant around him to peek at what he was writing, noting with a smirk that he definitely hadn't signed his real name.

"Does the kid need to sign in too?" Mitch asked as he straightened again. "It would be better if she didn't, you know, in case anyone comes looking for her."

"Don't worry," the man said with a smile, showing his straight white teeth and giving the vague impression of a shark. "We never ask any minors to sign in when they're visiting Child Protection."

I tried to smile back at him but it died on my lips.

"Great. You don't need to show us up," Mitch said, already turning and striding towards the golden elevator doors.

I hurried after him, expecting the man to follow us but he stayed at his desk, his attention already turned back to the computer screen in front of him.

"Hate that guy," Mitch muttered as he stabbed at the button. "Smarmy git."

"You know him?" I asked quietly.

He hadn't done anything that smarmy as far as I was aware. I mean, he was a little… condescending, but basically fine.

"Do I just. That asshole has been working with Child Protection for almost as long as Betty has. I don't know what it is about him, but I hate him."

I smirked and stepped into the lift.

"I get it," I said, eyeing him as the doors closed. "I think it's his smile."

"Damn right. That boy looks like he could use a good punch in the face."

I snorted at how accurate that description was before the elevator dinged lightly and the doors opened.

Anxiety started to churn within me again. What if Betty was mean or wanted to send me back home? Mitch had said that she was nice and that she'd get it but what if he was wrong?

The corridor on the other side of the doors was bright and cheerful, which immediately set me more at ease. The red carpet was plush but worn and the walls were covered in framed children's drawings. Some were really bad, little more than scribbles, but they'd been framed nonetheless. The wide windows were open, letting in the bright morning sun, and a woman sat behind a desk facing us.

She looked up as we exited the lift, a joyous smile crossing her face.

"Mitch McHoughen. What a sight for sore eyes you

are," she called, leaning back and shaking her head, causing her curly blonde hair to bounce around her shoulders before pushing away from her chair. "How long has it been? And there I was thinking you'd be dead in a ditch somewhere!"

They both laughed as they embraced warmly.

"More like you hoped!" he chuckled fondly. "Did Bets get my message? She knows I'm coming, right?"

"You mean your frantic message at three in the morning? Something along the lines of 'I kidnapped a kid, but it ain't that big a deal. I am gunna need your help though'? Yeah, judging by the state she was in this morning, she got that message," the woman said, her voice brimming with laughter as she stepped away from Mitch and turned to me. "And this must be your little abductee! I'm Kelly, what's your name, ducky?"

"Grace," I said before feeling the need to quickly add, "and it wasn't so much of an abduction. I did go with him willingly."

Kelly chuckled and readjusted her bright blue blazer which had ridden up slightly when she'd hugged Mitch.

"Well, that is good to know at least. Alright, you can find her office, right, Mitch? Go on in, she's been waiting for you," she said, gesturing down the corridor.

I stepped forwards but Mitch hesitated.

"How's she doing today? Is this a 'one cup of coffee' kinda morning or..." He trailed off, waiting for Kelly to jump in.

"Oh no, sweetie, she had two cups before she even got in this morning. And she's waiting for another cup to be delivered."

Mitch winced.

"Well, time to rip that band-aid right off, I guess?" he said, shrugging at me.

I looked back at him, completely at a loss for words, as Kelly went back to her desk, still laughing.

Mitch shot her one long glare before starting down the hall.

I trailed behind him worriedly, a million questions running through my head.

I wanted to ask him how he knew Kelly and Betty, how long he'd known them, and just everything else, but anxiety was stopping me from saying anything.

Mitch paused outside a door with a gold nameplate that simply said 'Betty Smith' before turning to me.

"Remember kid, same logic here as when facing a poisonous snake or spider: they're more scared of you than you are of them. Wait, maybe that doesn't apply here, she ain't scared of anything. Eh, it'll be fine. No sudden movements?" he suggested with another slightly helpless shrug.

"I can hear you out there," a voice twanged through the door. "You better get yourself in here and explain the situation before I call the police on you again."

Mitch's lips twitched and he glanced at the door quickly.

"It was one time and mostly a misunderstanding. Betty!" he cried in a warm voice as he pushed the door open suddenly. "It's been too long, you look great. Age has been kind to you."

The dark-haired woman seated behind a grand but cluttered desk in the centre of the room narrowed her eyes at him.

She didn't look at all like I'd expected her to. She was in jeans and a t-shirt with a brightly coloured blazer draped over the back of her chair. A brown folder was open in front of her but she closed it as we entered the room and pushed it to one side.

"Yeah, because I had the good sense to get out of the sun before it could damage my skin like it's done to yours," she said, leaning back in her chair and swirling the disposable coffee cup in her hand. "Now, why don't you come in and explain yourself so I can help sort out this nightmare you've brought to my door? And, no, I'm not talking about you, darling. Why don't you come in and take a seat? Can I get you anything? A drink, some food? Do you need a change of clothes?"

I looked back at her in confusion, not quite sure how to respond to her kindness.

"Umm... I'm good thanks," I said awkwardly.

"Come sit down at least whilst Mitchell explains everything to me?" she asked, her voice hardening as she glanced at him again.

I crossed the room and sank into one of the surprisingly comfortable brown leather chairs in front of the desk. She smiled broadly at me before tapping on the phone on her desk.

"Kelly, could you bring in a selection of drinks and cereal bars?" she said into the phone then looked back at me. "I know you said you didn't want anything, but I've found it's always better to have some food out in case you do get hungry."

I smiled uncertainly at her.

"Sure thing," Kelly said over the speaker.

"Great. Now, Mitch, sit down and start talking. What are you doing kidnapping people again?"

CHAPTER SIX

"So you see, it wasn't a kidnapping. The kid came willingly, plus they treat her like shit in her home," Mitch said around the chunk of cereal bar in his mouth.

I nodded emphatically in agreement.

"Plus, you know I'll take care of her. Zaq was never injured too much and now he's retired with a wife and a kid on the way! And, he's got a nice job at that big fancy museum down the road," Mitch wheedled with a hopeful smile.

"You don't have to tell me that, I was at the wedding too! But I was also there when he got shot in the leg and had to miss one of his exams," Betty snapped.

"Ah, but you got that rearranged for us and he aced it in the end. You said it yourself, you didn't expect him to do that good."

"I did not," she cried looking personally affronted. "I always expected him to do well."

"But not to get damn near full marks. Highest out of all the kids you look after, right? I must be doing something right," Mitch grinned, sensing that he had won her over.

It seemed like she was never really against him though. She'd been too quick to give in.

Betty sighed heavily, her gaze falling on me.

"And you really want to go with him? You know you'll still have to study and it might be dangerous where you're going?" Betty asked.

"She's already outrun some of the Sterlings anyway," Mitch added, his voice rising teasingly.

Betty's eyes bounced between us.

"They were some of Sterling's people?" Betty asked, her body strangely still. "In this country?"

"Oh, yeah," Mitch said with a tilt of his head. "They followed me from Italy."

Betty's eyes flickered to the window and then to her screen.

"Have you brought them to my doorstep again?" she asked, finally moving again and tapping on the phone again. "Kelly, I don't want any more visitors today. We might have some trouble, some of the Sterlings have been spotted in this country again."

A guttural word was growled through the phone and I wasn't sure what language it was, but I was pretty sure it was a curse.

"I'll tell Dan downstairs to keep an eye out for them,"

she said finally.

"Thanks," Betty said before looking back at Mitch. "So, have you brought them to my doorstep?"

"Shouldn't have. Changed the car along the way, doubled back, took scenic routes and wasn't followed as far as I can tell, but you know the drill. You got a back-door out of this place?" Mitch asked.

"Of course I do. Did you really think I started working in an office and immediately forget everything I learnt out there? I'll have Kelly take you out that way," she said with a nod. "Now, we need to get this mess cleared up before you can leave."

Mitch nodded grimly.

"We have to be on the road soon anyway. If we don't get to the next location before them, there'll be nothing left for us."

"Well then, we better get started." Betty pulled her keyboard closer and started typing. "Damn this two-factor authentication. Every time I log in, I need to do this damn thing on my phone."

Her phone lit up and she poked at it briefly before glancing back at the screen.

I waited patiently despite desperately wanting to get up and go around to her computer screen to find out what she was doing.

"Do you want Mitch in here for these questions or would you rather him wait outside?" she asked me.

"Oh, ummm…" I glanced at him and he smiled kindly.

"I don't mind, kid. I can wait outside," he offered.

"No, I think it's okay. I don't mind if you stay," I decided.

"Alright, what's your surname, Grace?" she asked after a period of typing.

"Grace Holliday," I answered quickly.

That wasn't my surname, I had no clue where it came from.

"And you were placed at... Nina and Arthur West's house four months ago?" she read.

"That's right," I lied.

"You told Mitch that they weren't very good to you. Can you elaborate on that some more, please?"

"Oh yeah, just they didn't always have food for us, weren't particularly nice, there were a lot of other kids there," I listed, not sure where the words were coming from but they felt right.

A flash of guilt went through me for a moment at the thought of getting someone in trouble but I pushed it away.

"They've got... four other foster kids there, is that right?" Betty asked, glancing at me.

I nodded.

"And do they usually have food for the rest of the kids? Treat them okay?" she asked, her tone entirely non-judgemental.

"Yeah, I think we just clash. They don't really like that I'm a vegetarian, I think," I said with an awkward shrug.

"Oh," Betty said, her gaze flying towards the tray of food and drink perched on the corner of her desk. "I am so sorry, I didn't even think to ask."

I watched in confusion as she poked the phone again.

"Kelly, can you bring in some non-dairy milk, please? We still have a few bottles in the fridge, don't we?" she asked.

There was a pause before the phone beeped again.

"Yeah, we've got a couple of options. I'll bring them in now," Kelly replied.

"Oh… you don't need to do that," I said awkwardly, not liking putting people out even in my own imagination.

"Don't be silly, we don't mind! I know some people don't like to drink dairy milk, especially vegetarians. I should have really asked already," Betty smiled as the door behind us opened and Kelly walked in with a tray of labelled glass bottles.

I watched uncomfortably as she crossed the room and placed it on the table, winking at me.

"Thank you," Betty said as she started to leave.

"Not a problem. Also, I spoke to Dan. He knows the situation now," Kelly said before ducking out of the door.

"Oh, wonderful. Okay, I just need to reactivate your status as a foster carer and ask Grace a couple of questions. Do you mind heading out to the hall for this bit?" Betty asked with a smile at Mitch.

"Not at all, give me a shout if you need anything. Do you need me to do the interview again or we good from last time?" he asked, standing and plucking another cereal bar from the tray.

Betty scanned the computer screen.

"Should still be good, but I'll let you know?" she asked.

"Not a problem. I'll be just down the hall if you need anything," he said, shooting me a grin before exiting the room.

Anxiety churned in my stomach and I turned back to Betty, unsure of what to expect.

"You don't need to look so scared," she said with a gentle smile. "I bet you've had dozens of interviews with social workers before." "Is that what you are?" I asked before I could stop myself. "I mean… it just said 'Child Protection' on the door, but I wasn't sure."

A small smile started on her face.

"Yes and no. I trained as a social worker and that is part of my job now, but I work for an external agency. We handle the more… difficult cases. The complex ones that need a little more hands-on support. It's my job to deal with the more legally or ethically dicey cases, and you definitely fall into my caseload now," she explained.

"Is that what I am now?"

Her head cocked to the side causing her dark brown hair to spill over her shoulder.

"You've gone on the run with an older man you've only just met. You're not exactly an easy case anymore," she said, her eyebrow rising at me.

"Umm..." I said, unable to think of anything to say in response to that. She made it sound almost... inappropriate. "But it's not like that. We aren't in a relationship or anything."

Betty laughed easily.

"I know, darling. Mitch is a good man, despite all the trouble I gave him. But, looking at it with no knowledge of him, it wouldn't look good."

"Oh," I said quietly.

In real life, I would have considered that and been worried about it but in my fantasy, it didn't matter.

"Yeah, and soon he'll want to take you abroad. How do you think that's going to look in the press? An older man takes a young, at-risk teenage girl abroad to chase nothing more than rumours. Granted, he's good so you'll find what you're looking for nine times out of ten, but still."

My mouth went completely dry and, for a moment, I debated opening my eyes and coming out of the daydream but Betty burst into laughter.

"I'm messing with you! That's where I come in, I'm here to make sure that it's all legal so you won't get any hassle!"

"Is that... okay?" I asked uncertainly.

"Of course, this isn't the first time I've had to do it.

Barely even the first time I've had to do it this month," she muttered, looking back at her screen. "Are you sure that this is what you want to do? It's going to be dangerous and it's a lot of physical work, running, climbing. You're not scared of heights, are you?"

She paused, her fingers stilling over the keyboard as she eyed me carefully.

"No, Mitch asked me that too. Why is it such a big deal?"

Betty chuckled softly and shook her head.

"Of course, he asked too. We knew a kid back when we were in the Sterlings together, Roger. He was new to the whole thing. Not a fan of heights, but he didn't tell us beforehand."

"What happened?" I asked, brushing over everything else she said.

I'd ask more about it later but for now, I just wanted to know about Roger.

"He died, sweetie. He froze crossing a canyon out in some desert somewhere. We couldn't get to him quickly enough and he couldn't hold on any longer."

She looked down, her hand moving quickly on the table, tracing a shape that I barely noticed.

"Oh," I said softly.

"Yeah, pretty rough way to go."

I nodded, unsure of what else to say and preoccupied with the mental image of him falling to his death.

But surely, in this fantasy I couldn't be hurt. I'd just wake up, right?

"You know you've still got to study, right? And that it's going to be a lot of independent work, reading out of textbooks, listening to lessons, that kind of thing?" she asked after a pause, going back to her questioning.

"Yeah, Mitch said."

"And you're okay with that? Do you get carsick?"

"Umm… a little but normally it isn't too bad."

She nodded, typing rapidly.

"Okay, so for travelling, you'll mainly need audio-books and videos. What about reading on planes, boats, or helicopters?" she asked. "Any of that make you ill?"

I thought back, trying to remember the last time I'd been on any of those.

"I'm fine on planes and boats, I think. Not sure about helicopters; never been on one before."

She nodded.

"It's not too dissimilar to a plane. Once you get used to it, you should be fine. And what kind of learner are you?" she asked, her fingers poised over the keyboard again as she waited for my answer.

"Umm… I don't know," I said with a bit of a shrug.

"Okay, how do you like to learn? Do you like to have it all written out prettily with mind maps and diagrams, do you like to have someone explain it to you? Or do you prefer to read it from a book?"

"Read from a book," I answered immediately.

"Ah, an independent learner, good. So, I'll make sure you get all of the information you need. You're in the middle of doing your GCSEs, right? Just completed the first year?"

"Umm, yeah," I said, sitting up a little taller.

Her eyes bounced back and forth as she read from the screen.

"Okay, you've done pretty well, clearly struggling more in a few subjects. It seems like maths, French and physical education aren't going too well for you. What's going on there?" she asked.

My heart dropped into my stomach. It felt as though I was getting my grades in real life and I had nothing to say.

"Generally, when a person isn't doing that well, it's due to one of four factors. You're not enjoying them, you've got a bad teacher, you're bored of what you're studying, or you are actually struggling. Which is it of those?" she asked, her voice interested.

"Um, it varies, I think. I really don't like my French and P.E. teachers so I don't think that helps and we never actually do anything interesting in the lessons. Plus, it's never any good sports, just hockey and netball!" I said, the words rushing out of my mouth.

"And you're not a fan of hockey and netball?"

"No, it's so boring. You have to just stand on the court or field and wait for the ball to come near you!"

Betty nodded.

"And what about French?" she asked. "Same issue? Not learning anything good?"

"Yeah! We just go over vocab and tenses again and again and the teacher thinks that it's going to magically teach us how to speak French properly!"

"It's pretty useful to know to get a basic understanding before you try to speak in full sentences, isn't it?"

Her tone wasn't dismissive or belittling. It sounded like she actually wanted to hear my thoughts on it.

"I guess," I allowed, "but, we never get to go any further than that. We just spend the entire class having to memorise the words!"

A sigh slipped out of Betty's lips.

"That is one of the worst things about school in this country, and in most countries, I guess. They don't teach you how to learn or how to apply the information. It's strictly a test of memory, which rarely comes in handy in the real world," she said, her voice surprisingly passionate. "What about maths? Bad teacher?"

"No," I said. "He's fine…"

"Okay, so what's the problem there?"

"It's boring," I said quietly, looking down. "I find most of it really interesting but then once I've finished all the questions, I just need to sit there and wait for everyone else to be done."

It was the truth. In real life, it always went that way. I would find it interesting when he was explaining how to work stuff out. Then, he'd either go on about it for so long that I'd get bored and tune him out or we'd get to do questions. I usually finished before the others and then had to wait for ages for everyone else to catch up.

He always told me off for not paying attention too; and when I said that I'd finished all the questions, he told me to just look through my work and double-check my answers, which was so boring. I'd already done the questions once, I didn't want to have to do them again.

"So, you get bored of it easily which means that you rush through your work, don't check your answers and then lose interest in the topic?" she guessed with alarming accuracy and a tilt of her head.

I nodded, peeking up at her worriedly and not sure how she'd react to it.

"Well, being out in the field will be more interesting to you, I'm sure, but you'll need to learn to check your maths and all of your answers. In school, if you get a question wrong, the worst thing that can happen is you lose some marks. Do you know what could happen out there?" she asked.

I shook my head, fascination flaring in me.

It felt a little like I was being told off but she was being so nice about it so it didn't bother me too much.

"It sounds very dramatic, but it could mean that you die. Or, in my case, you could lose a toe."

My mouth dropped open.

"You lost a toe?" I asked.

"I did. Made a silly mistake, miscalculated how much weight something could take and next thing I know, it had to be amputated."

"Why? What happened?"

"Stupidity on my part mostly, but you learn quickly out there. You have to."

I nodded, desperate to hear more but not wanting to be rude or to pry.

I wasn't sure how a miscalculation could ever lead to needing an amputation or what that miscalculation could be, but I wanted to know.

"Any other questions?" she asked with a gentle smile.

I bit my lip.

I had so many other questions but I felt weird asking them. It felt like a really personal thing and I barely knew Betty.

Finally, I shook my head.

"Do you have anything you want to ask about Mitch?" she asked.

My heart leapt.

Yes, so many things.

"How long was he working with the Sterlings? You said that's how you two met, right?"

She chuckled lightly.

"I don't actually know the answer to that. He was an established member of the team by the time I joined, but yes, that's how we met. Even then, he took people under his wing. I think that's why they hated him so much," she said with a smile and a shake of her head.

"Really?" I asked.

"Oh, yeah. Looking out for others isn't exactly the

kind of thing they like. I honestly don't know how they do it but they have an almost endless supply of new recruits so anytime one dies, they're able to get someone to fill their spot without much trouble."

It felt like my heart slowed for a moment as I processed that.

"Do they die often?"

"Yeah, pretty often. It comes with the job," she said before catching herself. "But, Mitch will look after you. He had a kid, Zaq. He came to him under pretty similar circumstances and he made sure he was alright."

I sat up straighter.

"Yeah, you two mentioned him earlier. Who is he?" I asked.

"Another reckless kid who Mitch took under his wing. But, he joined in a pretty different way. He was working in a harbour after he ran away from his foster family and heard Mitch talking too loudly whilst trying to impress someone. That little terror hid on his boat and Mitch didn't realise until he was far enough out in the sea that getting rid of him would have been a death sentence."

Betty smiled fondly and I found myself feeling strangely jealous.

I wanted someone to talk about me like that.

"That kid had a talent for getting himself into terrible situations. Mitch decided to keep him on after that, obviously, but not a month went by that he didn't do something that made me want to strangle him."

"Really?" I asked, truly intrigued by him.

"Oh yeah, he was reckless as hell and too intelligent so he generally knew when a risk would pay off. There were a few times when it didn't, like that time he got shot right before one of his A level exams and the time I got a call from a hospital in Thailand after he'd lost Mitch in a bet. Even I don't know that full story and I just don't want to. I truly don't know why he would use Mitch as a wager, but… most of the time, his risks paid off."

My tongue darted out to wet my lips and longing filled me as I listened to Betty speak.

It sounded terrifying but so fun to live the life that Zaq had lived. I wanted it and I could have it, at least in my dream.

"Anything else?" she asked gently.

"Ummm… Is there anything I need to do? Like, do I need to speak to my foster parents and let them know I'm okay?" I asked, a faint hint of worry entering me as vague faces crossed my mind.

I wasn't sure how I knew, but they were the faces of Nina and Arthur West.

"Nope, I can sort all that. It shouldn't be too difficult because they haven't gotten the police involved, so I can simply call them and let them know that you've been reassigned to a different home," she said with a smile.

Sadness washed through me.

"They didn't even report that I was missing?" I asked,

looking down so that Betty wouldn't see the tears that threatened my eyes.

It was stupid. I didn't know them and they were made up! But I still felt so rejected.

They didn't even notice that I was gone.

"I'm sorry," Betty said softly.

I sniffed and shook my head.

"It's fine," I lied.

She started talking again, her tone soothing, but loneliness burnt in my stomach, leaving an empty pit of nothingness. Anger started to wash over me. The point of my daydream wasn't to make me feel worse, it was meant to be an escape. I didn't have to stay there. I didn't have to feel like that.

I blinked, wrenching my eyes open and staring down at the empty page of French homework as faint dizziness made the lines swim across the page.

I sighed and reached for my pen.

CHAPTER SEVEN

I stared down at the almost empty quiz before me, my mind startlingly blank. I'd revised all of the words in the vocab test yesterday, I knew I had, but now... I couldn't remember anything.

The classroom was filled with the endless scratching of pens on paper as everyone except for me scribbled furiously. Even Duncan, who sat across from me and consistently failed every single quiz, was writing even if his face was scrunched up in confusion.

I had to at least try. I couldn't do worse than him for a second week in a row. He was a sweet guy and all, but he seemed to take genuine pleasure in making Madame Noel angry.

He looked up, feeling my gaze on him, and rolled his eyes in an exaggerated gesture before smiling and looking down at his work again.

"Five more minutes," Madame Noel called from the front of the classroom in a heavily accented voice.

Panic flared within me and I looked down at my quiz.

I had to do something. I had to try and work out some of the words.

I guessed the first two words, felt slightly better about the next few before coming to the fifth word and being completely stumped. I didn't even know what letter the word started with, and why would I ever even need to know the French word for swimming pool? It couldn't just be 'le swimming', could it?

No, that didn't feel right. It definitely wasn't that.

My gaze wandered over to the paper in front of Ella, who sat next to me. I didn't want to cheat, not really, but I really did not want to spend another break sitting in the cramped classroom, repeating the quiz.

Piscine! I realised, just as my eyes found Ella's answer.

A hint of shame speared my chest but I forced myself to keep writing. Even if I had to guess the next few, I would not leave any words blank.

And I didn't.

The rest of my answers were guesses and I couldn't help but feel that, if he were real, Mitch would be disappointed in me. He'd stressed how important school was. I wasn't sure why he'd been so insistent on it. Maybe it was just because I wanted to do well and he was part of my imagination so he did too. I wanted to make something of myself, prove myself to others. Plus, I needed to do well. There was no other way.

My mom had been very open about that. If I dropped out of school or couldn't get into university, she'd kick me out. Cut me off. She'd said that many times, but I wasn't sure if she'd actually do it. I knew she'd be thrilled if it happened though. She would mention it constantly. Always pointing out that I had failed and that I would never do anything with my life. She already said that sometimes and it hadn't even happened yet.

"Alright, pens down now!" our teacher shouted.

My eyes widened and I quickly finished the last word I'd been halfway through before she shouted again.

"When I say now, I mean now! Not in a minute, not once you've finished writing the word. Now!"

I dropped my pen and lifted my hands above my head, as everyone else was doing, watching Madame Noel as her eyes narrowed.

"Phoebe Wright! Are you suddenly exempt from the rules? Did I miss the meeting when that was agreed?" she shouted.

I lowered my hands slower, watching as the teacher slowly stalked towards her prey.

I winced, feeling terrible for Phoebe. Madame Noel just loved picking on her. Phoebe was timid. She wanted to do well, but it was never enough for the teacher.

"Sorry, Madame Noel. I was just trying to finish the last word. I knew it, but I couldn't remember if there was an extra 'e' at the end or not!" she said quickly, her words breathy with fear.

The teacher didn't care though, a small smile grew on her face as she neared her.

"I'm sorry, did I say 'finish the word you're writing' or did I tell everyone to stop?" she asked, a predatory look on her face.

"To stop," Phoebe almost whispered.

"That's right, and why do you think the rules don't apply to you? Do you suddenly believe you're special for some misguided reason?"

I couldn't stop staring. I wanted to stand up and shout at Madame Noel to leave her alone, but I couldn't do anything.

"I don't think I'm exempt from the rules," she whispered.

"So, you actively chose not to follow them?" her voice sharp and ringing through the classroom.

I knew that the people in the classrooms around us would have been able to hear what Madame Noel was saying but they'd never do anything about it. I'd had her for three years; they hadn't done anything about it before.

Phoebe couldn't meet her gaze, she stared pointedly at the table as tears gathered in her eyes. She nodded, unable to speak.

"Your planner. Now," Madame Noel demanded, holding her hand out.

With trembling hands, Phoebe reached into her bag and retrieved her planner, holding it out to the teacher who took it and marched to the front of the classroom.

She sat down, turned to the correct page and began writing furiously.

The room was silent and tense as we watched Madame Noel write what I knew would be a scathing note to Phoebe's parents, probably informing them that she would be in detention until the end of the term.

Finally, she pushed away from her chair again and returned to Phoebe's desk, a smug smile on her face.

"Go sit outside. You will retake your test after school today, and you better use this time to revise your vocabulary because if you fail one more test this term, you will be in detention every lunch and after school every day next year too."

I swallowed.

It was not an empty threat, and I knew it.

Tears slowly trickled down Phoebe's face as she packed her bag and trudged out of the classroom, refusing to meet anyone's gaze. Fury built in me and I stared at Madame Noel's triumphant expression.

She'd enjoyed it, I realised. She enjoyed tearing Phoebe down for trying to finish her test. It was so unnecessary and cruel, but she loved it.

Hatred rushed through me as she stalked back to the front of the classroom and tapped a few keys on her keyboard, bringing up the answers on the board.

"Swap papers with the person sitting next to you and begin marking now!" she commanded.

Ella thrust her paper into my hands and snatched mine off the table, reaching for her pencil case to select her red pen.

It was unnecessary. Madame Noel didn't request that we use a red pen to mark but Ella seemed to delight in it. It was probably because she always got full marks but, whatever the reason, it annoyed me.

I barely needed to glance up at the board to mark her paper. Once again, she had not made a single error but, I realised with sinking suspicion, I had made many.

"One more minute," the teacher called.

I suppressed a sigh as I wrote the number twenty on Ella's paper and glanced over at mine. Ella moved quickly, her hand shooting out to cover the number that she'd written.

Barely able to stop myself from rolling my eyes at her, I met her smug gaze.

She wanted to wait until the teacher told us to hand our papers back but there was no need. We had both finished marking, she was just delaying the inevitable.

I couldn't even work out what I'd gotten because Ella's arm was covering half of them but, based on the number of wrong answers on the left side alone, I would be spending another break time in the classroom.

"Hand them back!"

Ella placed the paper back in front of me with a flourish, snatching hers back and gasping in mock surprise.

"Full marks?" she cried loudly enough for most of the

class to shoot her flat, unimpressed looks, but she didn't care. "You did good too, Gracie! So close to passing!"

Her tone was condescending, and again, loud enough for everyone to hear.

I didn't bother responding. Instead, I stared down at the bright red thirteen that she'd both circled and underlined.

One below the pass.

"Alright. I'm going to call out the grades from highest to lowest and I want you to raise your hands when I reach yours, understood?" Madame Noel asked without waiting for an answer. "Twenty?"

I sat silently, watching as a couple of people, Ella included, raised their hands smugly.

"Nineteen?"

A few more people lifted their hands.

I waited anxiously for her to reach my grade and eventually she called, "Fourteen?"

She glanced around at the other kids who had just scrapped passing grades.

"Close, you should aim to do better next time," she demanded. "Thirteen."

Briefly, I debated not raising my hand and lying about my grade, but Ella's expectant smile made me do it anyway.

Madame Noel sighed loudly.

"Four people joining me for break today. Who else? Twelve!"

I looked down, watching out of the corner of my eyes to see when Duncan's hand would go up.

Madame Noel kept calling numbers, getting lower and lower and I found my anxiety increasing as she did.

He was sitting silently, a smile on his face, not breaking eye contact with the teacher as she continued speaking, until finally...

"Zero," she called, her eyes narrowed.

Slowly, almost proudly, he lifted his hand.

Whispers erupted throughout the classroom and I found my lips lifting into a smile.

"Zero, Mr Habshaw?" she asked, her voice taking on a dangerous edge.

"Seems that way," he said with a shrug. "Damn, I really thought I would do better this time. I studied and everything."

A few people giggled and Madame Noel sent them a glare.

I bit my lip, not sure how she was going to react to the fact that he clearly didn't care.

"Did you really?" she asked, her tone slipping dangerously low.

"I did," he lied, not even trying to sound regretful. "Maybe I should go back to not studying at all. I did better then."

Madame Noel's shoulders rose and fell slowly as she moved closer to his desk.

"And why are you studying French, Mr Habshaw,

if you clearly do not care about the language?" she demanded.

My eyes bounced back to Duncan's face, which was the picture of innocence.

"Well, you see," he started in a condescending yet informative tone, "at this school, it's required that we study a language to be able to do our GCSEs here, and because it doesn't have an option for Klingon or Dothraki or any other languages I actually care about. I had to settle for French."

More laughter circled the room as the colour drained from Madame Noel's face.

"Gather your things," she ordered. "You can go explain to Mr Pritch why you felt the need to disrupt my class."

I felt a smile rise on my face at that. Mr Pritch was our head of year but he was also in charge of the rugby team, which Duncan was the Captain of, so he wouldn't be in much trouble.

"Sure," Duncan said lightly, taking his time to pack his bags as the teacher turned her back on him and stalked back to the front of the classroom.

"Open your textbooks to the chapter you were working on last week and continue!" Madame Noel shouted, her hands clenched into fists.

Duncan slowly strode out of the room, pausing to grin back at us before letting the door slam shut behind him. His voice could be heard through the door, chatting easily with Phoebe. A small smile came over my face as I heard her laugh, before I pulled my textbook towards me and started flipping through it.

My eyes glossed over quickly as I stared at it, debating just giving up on it for today and reading back over the words that would be in my vocab resit in forty minutes. There was no point in reading the new chapter as we probably didn't have enough time left in the term for a test and I wouldn't have any other opportunity to revise.

I turned back a couple of pages, ignoring Ella's self-righteous sigh at my actions, and started reading.

But my mind didn't want to stay on my French work, it wanted to explore. The fantasy of Mitch hovered just at the edge of my consciousness, tempting me. I wanted to slip back into the daydream, but at the same time, I was reluctant. I didn't want to go back to where I'd left it. I knew it was ridiculous, but I was scared of crying in the fantasy and accidentally crying in real life and having Madame Noel pounce on me.

But... surely some time had passed in the fantasy since I was there last. Even if it hadn't been that long in real life, it could have been longer in there. Time might not work the same way there... right?

Breathing in slowly, I let myself slip into the other world.

The chair was no longer solid and cold beneath me, but now it was the squishy leather passenger seat of Mitch's car where I was slumped, glaring at the empty coffee cup in between us.

"Wanna talk about it?" Mitch asked, not taking his eyes off the road.

I blinked away the fleeting dizziness and glanced up at the road before me. It wasn't as busy as I had been expecting, we were clearly on the outskirts of the city.

I shook my head before realising that he probably couldn't see me because he was focusing on driving.

"No," I said quietly.

"You sure? I might get it," Mitch said, his tone unexpectedly soft. "I know what it's like to feel a little forgotten."

"It's fine," I said, really not wanting to get into the conversation as tears threatened to build in my eyes again. "So, where are we going now?"

A smile built on Mitch's face.

"Well, first we're going to stop for petrol and snacks, then Edinburgh. Via Sheffield," he added quickly.

"Why Edinburgh?" I asked. "Are we looking for something specific there?"

"Indeed we are. If my guess is correct, there should be something pretty special waiting for us there. Oh, yeah, that's a fair point," he said as he pulled into a petrol station and stopped the car at a pump.

I watched him cautiously as he turned off the engine before glancing at me.

Panic fluttered within me briefly at the serious look on his face.

"Tell me, kid... How do you feel about desecrating a graveyard?"

I paused, making sure that I'd heard him correctly, but I was pretty sure that I had.

"Umm... fine, I guess?"

"Ah, good. You'd be surprised how often we have to do that in this line of work. It's never a case of getting to go somewhere nice and just find what you need carefully buried in the sand. Nope, it's always in a grave or at the bottom of the damn ocean. Man, you would be surprised how often I've had to dig up a corpse." He sighed and shook his head before looking back at me. "Have you still got that phone I gave you before?"

"Umm..." I tapped my pockets, feeling the familiar lump of the phone in my left pocket. "Got it!"

"Great, go in and get us some snacks then pay for petrol, will you? It's better if I stay out here, the cameras in the forecourt are always shit. It's," he checked out the window, "pump number seven. And can you get us some candy? I got a real sweet tooth so anything gummy. Oh, ideally some stuff that's suitable for veggies so you can eat it all without having to worry about what's in it."

A smile started to appear on my face but I started to scramble out of the door before he spotted it.

"Oh, wait, kid! You gotta get changed too! Grab some clothes out of the boot. There should be a bathroom in there." He pushed the door open before I could respond.

I had no real memory of it, but somehow I knew that we had gone shopping for some clothes before leaving London. I pushed the door open and started towards the boot, scanning the mostly empty forecourt as I did. People were going about their day, doing nothing particularly suspicious.

I watched the man at the pump next to us out of the corner of my eye as I pulled the boot open.

The bags in there were strangely familiar. They tugged at the back of my memory, like I'd seen them before, but I pushed that aside and started rooting around in them. I was still wearing the clothes I'd worn to the pub which felt like a lifetime ago.

"Once we're a little further out of the city, I'll find us a gym or leisure centre where we can use the showers," Mitch said as he started filling the car.

"Cool," I replied absentmindedly as I dug through the bags, looking for something to wear but I was over-whelmed with options.

There was everything in the bags: underwear, a coat, jumpers, a pair of trainers, walking boots and even more. I ripped the tags off a waterproof-looking back-pack and started shoving clothes inside. They were all my size and, based on the style, I knew that I'd picked them out, even if I couldn't really remember it.

"Oh, kid, can you grab some drinks? You need to have at least two big bottles of water, I ain't having Betty call me up to yell at me for getting you dehydrated. It's happened before and I never want it to happen again."

He shook his head gravely as I laughed.

"Really? She'd call you up over that?" I asked, still giggling.

"When Zaq was younger, not long after I started taking care of him, he got hospitalised briefly for dehydration. Man, I don't even know how she found out, but boy did I get a very loud and very angry phone call about it. Bright and early the next morning, we were enrolled in a nutrition and dietary needs course." He rolled his eyes at me dramatically. "But I'm not going to make the same mistake twice, so make sure you get enough water, okay? And some other fun drinks. Don't get me wrong, water is necessary and all, but damn is it boring."

I laughed and zipped the bag shut.

"I'll try to grab enough to make sure I don't get hospitalised," I replied with a smirk.

"Good. If you ain't sure what to get, hold it up to the window and I'll let you know," he said, craning his head to check how much petrol he'd added.

"Okay," I said, shouldering the bag and starting towards the station just as a bell chimed and woke me from my fantasy.

CHAPTER EIGHT

Breathing out a heavy sigh, I looked around the classroom again. There were a handful of us still sitting at our desks, having been made to stay behind at break to resit the vocab test. It had gone a little bit better for me, but we still had ten minutes left of the break.

Part of me wanted to risk getting up and handing my test in early, but I knew if I did that, I'd have to stand at the front of the room whilst the teacher marked the test and commented loudly on everything I'd gotten wrong.

At least if I waited until the end, I wouldn't get the test back until the beginning of my next French class which wasn't for a couple of days, and then I wouldn't have any more until after the summer.

It was definitely the better option, even if it meant I would be worrying about whether or not I passed for a little longer. At least I had slightly more time to delve back into the dream. It wasn't long enough to get to Edinburgh, probably, but it was better than nothing.

I pulled my top over my head, pausing to grab onto the sink as a wave of dizziness threatened me, stronger than it had been the last time I'd slipped into my fantasy. I swayed, tightening my grip and silently begging not to fall on my ass.

The floor was disgusting. It smelt, and looked like it hadn't been cleaned in weeks. It was… well, exactly what I expected for a petrol station bathroom and it was not the best place to get changed.

My hand shot out again, catching my bag just in time as it slipped from the broken hook on the back of the door, and I sighed. Still holding it, I grabbed a handful of tissues to wipe the stagnant water off the back of the sink, trying my best not to let any of the murky liquid touch my skin, and propped the bag there before looking into the streak-covered mirror.

The new clothes looked good on me, even if they were just black sports leggings and a top. They fit me well and the trainers were surprisingly comfy.

Mitch had insisted on that, I somehow knew. In all the other shops, he'd avoided people as much as possible but there, he'd marched straight up to someone and asked for help.

I paused, my hand freezing as I stuffed my clothes back into the bag and pulled out my makeup remover.

How did I know that? I hadn't imagined that bit, so it couldn't have happened. But it felt like it did and I knew that he would have done that.

He'd said that I needed some shoes that wouldn't rub, provided enough support, were waterproof, and the sole was thick enough not to be pierced easily. The sales assistant had looked concerned at that, but Mitch had played it off well.

But how did I know that? I hadn't been there for that.

Pushing back the wave of uncertainty, I washed the heavy eye makeup off my face and slathered on some moisturiser before shoving it all back into the bag. Glancing around to make sure I hadn't missed anything, I zipped the back up again and looped my arms through the strap before pushing the heavy door open.

"Took you long enough," a man's snide voice said.

I blinked and stared up at the man who was waiting on the other side of the door, his arms crossed and a glare on his face.

My initial impulse was to apologise, but I didn't want to. I shouldn't have to, I hadn't even taken that long!

"There's another petrol station across the street," I said in as sweet a voice as I could manage, my heart hammering in my chest. "If you needed the bathroom that desperately, I'm sure you could have gone there."

I slipped past him before he had a chance to respond, not quite out of earshot before I heard him mutter, "Little bitch. Someone ought to teach her a lesson."

My body tensed, but the door slammed shut behind him, signalling my safety.

It was dumb. I knew it was just a fantasy, but still.

I wanted to get to Edinburgh and become a treasure hunter, not get beaten up in a petrol station toilet.

I shook my head and hurried to the drink fridges. I needed some bottles of water and some other 'fun drinks', whatever that meant.

Staring up at the shelves of drinks, I felt a hint of worry wash through me. There were so many options. Too many. Water was easy enough, even though there were a lot of different brands, but Mitch had said we had to have two big bottles each so I just grabbed the biggest ones they had that still had sports tops. They would be the easiest to drink in the car.

The fun drinks worried me though. I had no clue what he meant by that. I assumed that he meant weird flavoured drinks but that could be anything.

Clutching the four bottles in my arms, I glared up at the drinks. I started to reach for one at random before one of the bottles began to slip and I had to grab at them again. Annoyance flared in me, despite having put myself in the situation, and I looked around just as someone walked past carrying a basket.

An audible sigh slipped from my lips as I realised that I could have just got a basket instead of having to juggle everything.

I slouched over to the pile of shopping baskets, aware of the cashiers' drowsy eyes following me as I moved towards the door, and awkwardly let the bottles loudly tumble into the basket on top. I picked it up, smiling uncomfortably at the person behind the counter who was still watching me, and returned to the drink aisle, staring up at the drinks.

Anxiety bubbled in me and I bit my lip, reaching out at random. Spinach, beetroot, apple and grape smoothie. Not bad, but probably would taste like dirt. I dropped it into the basket before shuffling along to the next section of drinks. Again, I went with the tried and tested method of reaching out randomly and grabbing a drink, some strange fruit flavoured cola, and putting it in the basket before glancing back at the window.

I couldn't see Mitch from where I was standing, he must have gotten back into the car, but I could just about see the top of it over the shelves of candy and chocolate bars that lined the window. I turned back towards the fridge and shuffled along again, reaching out for the next drink, an energy drink. I grabbed the pastel orange can and stared at it, confusion coming over my face.

Mitch didn't exactly strike me as someone who would drink an energy drink, much less one that was simply 'butterfly' flavour, but it sounded weird, so I dropped it into the increasingly heavy basket anyway. The thin metal handles of the basket were starting to cut into my hands painfully, making me regret all of my choices.

We had enough drinks, I decided, and even if we didn't we could stop somewhere else along the way. Mitch had said we'd be stopping outside of Sheffield.

That was only a few hours probably, we would have enough until then, surely.

I shuffled towards the rows of sweets and candy that lined the window, stretching up on my toes to peek over them and make sure that Mitch was still there.

A small smile grew on my face when I spotted him and relief washed through me. Not that I'd really expected him to leave me at some random petrol station but... I half expected it. He was staring at something on his phone, but before long, he looked up, his eyes meeting mine, and he grinned.

I smiled back and looked down at the candy before me. He'd said he wanted some gummy candy, ideally something that was vegetarian. That meant no gelatine. I dropped the basket on the ground, my screaming shoulder muscles thanking me, and slowly paced along the row.

Occasionally, I felt the cashier's eyes on me again, but luckily the petrol station was busy enough that they didn't bother me at all. Still, I felt a hint of anxiety as I tread back and forth along the shelves, not wanting to keep Mitch waiting for too long. It already felt like I'd been in the shop for too long. I needed to hurry up.

My slightly frantic gaze landed on an unassuming pack of strawberry laces with 'Gelatine-free!' written on the front. With a grin, I scooped them up, my eyes scanning the other sweets by the same brand. They all were vegetarian, I realised with a grin. But I couldn't get five packets of sweets, that felt like too much.

I grabbed one of each bag, standing up on my tiptoes again and waving slightly to get Mitch's attention. He looked up, his head cocking to one side.

Which ones? I mouthed, dropping most of the sweets onto the shelf in front of me and holding up two packs.

Mitch's eyes narrowed and he leaned forwards to get a better look at the sweets. I waited, aware of people's eyes on me but ignoring them until finally, he pointed with both hands. I bit my lip to hold back a surprised laugh before dropping both packs in the basket at my feet and holding up two more options.

Again, Mitch pointed with both hands, but that time I couldn't help the giggle that slipped from my mouth. Dramatically, I rolled my eyes and made a show of dropping the sweets into my basket before not even bothering to ask him if he wanted the other bag too.

I hefted the basket up again, having to use both hands to carry the basket, and wandered along the aisle, grabbing some dried mango, a few bags of crisps, and a chocolate bar as well. Mitch hadn't told me to buy them, and they were somewhat of an impulse decision, but they all looked really good.

I joined the end of the queue, waiting impatiently for my turn and finally heaving the basket onto the counter when I'd gotten to the front.

"Any fuel?" the woman behind the counter asked flatly as she scanned the excessive pile of snacks.

"Yeah, pump seven please," I said with a glance to double-check.

She poked the screen a few times before returning to scanning the drinks.

"Want a bag?"

Dumbly, I looked down at the growing pile of stuff I'd bought.

"Um, yeah. Please," I added.

The woman grabbed a bag and started loading it.

"Gunna need a couple. They're five pence each, that okay?" she asked, barely looking up at me.

"Yeah, of course."

I almost wondered what would happen if I said no. Would she say 'well then you can have it for free'? No, I doubted it. People probably tried that on her every day.

"You going on a road trip or something?" she asked, finally packing the last bottle of water.

"Something like that."

"Is that your dad out there?" she asked, looking up at Mitch with a spark of interest in her eyes.

"Yeah," I lied.

"Unlucky. He's cute."

I stood there awkwardly, not sure what to say in response to that, but luckily she didn't seem to need a reply. She tapped the screen a few more times before looking back at me.

"That's seventy-four pounds and twenty-three pence."

"Oh yeah," I said, scrabbling to pull the phone out of my pocket and tapping it on the card reader.

My heart squeezed with anxiety as I waited for it to beep to tell me it had been accepted.

"That's all gone through," the woman said, pushing the bags towards me.

"Oh, thank you," I said, rushing to grab them.

The plastic strained around the bottles as I edged out the door, weighed down by the bags. The sun was momentarily blinding but I was quickly under the canopy again.

Worry prickled within me as I neared Mitch's car. I'd gotten more than we needed, that much was for sure. What if he got annoyed at me? He really could leave me at the petrol station.

What if he was tight on money? I knew he said he was a treasure hunter, but I honestly wasn't sure how much one could even make doing that. Surely with the travel, hotels and constant switching of cars, it would be an expensive job?

With a tense smile, I pulled the door open, the plastic bags cutting into my fingers.

A laugh erupted from the car.

"Oh, kid," he chuckled. "I am glad you involved yourself in my business. I was so worried you were going to come out with a single bag and no candy."

I smiled uncertainly, worry still ravaging me, and shuffled.

"Well, what are you waiting for? Get it! Pass me those bags, I'll put them behind our seats for easy reach. Did you get all the candy you held up? Did you get that's what I meant? The more the merrier!" he asked, his voice full of mirth.

"Yeah, I thought that's what you were going for so I just got them all. I mean, we don't need to eat them all today, right?" I asked, loading the bags onto my seat slowly as Mitch hauled them onto the seats behind us.

"Of course, we don't! Also, and this should go without saying, we do not eat like this every day. It's a treat. Normally, it's a balanced diet when possible. At least one piece of fruit or veg with each meal, if not more!" he insisted.

I nodded quickly.

"I also got some dried mango, if that helps?"

He chuckled quietly again.

"It does. Damn, I love mango. Alright, get in and let's go!"

I climbed in quickly, clicking my seatbelt on and smiling to myself as the radio started up again.

"What kinda thing do you want to listen to, kid? You're in charge!" Mitch said, pulling back out onto the road. "Grab my phone out of the middle there. We can do podcasts, music, or some of your lessons if Betty's sent them over already. Your choice!"

I reached for the phone, but a bell jolted me back into reality before I wrapped my fingers around it.

Taking a deep breath to steady myself, I blinked and glanced around the classroom. Most of us were still there, having learnt the hard way that it was better to wait until the end of break to hand in our tests.

"Well, what are you doing still sitting there?" Madame Noel demanded. "Put your tests on the table and get out! Do you not think I have classes too? I had to waste my break staring at you lot, I don't want to do it for any longer! Go!"

I rushed to pack up my bag and joined the queue of people placing our papers on the disgruntled teacher's desk.

She didn't even bother to look up as we left, her eyes already scanning the top test with a look of disgust on her face.

"How do you think you did?" Phoebe whispered once we were out in the corridor, falling in step with me.

"Mmm, not much better. You?" I replied, edging past the younger students who were waiting outside her door for the next class.

"Bad. She's going to kick me out of class again on Friday, I bet. I cannot wait until we finish our GCSEs and I never need to see her again!" she said quietly.

I turned the corner and pushed open the door to the staircase.

"Oh yeah? Are you not planning to stay here for sixth form?" I asked.

"Yeah, but I'm not taking French, I'm not that stupid. I'm not going to do anything that means I need to be in the language block. Hopefully, I'll only have to see her in assemblies and then I can hide behind you. Wait, you are planning to stay here for sixth form, right?" she asked, panic creeping into her voice.

"Yeah, don't worry. I'm not going anywhere," I said, trying to keep the sadness out of my words. "Well, unless I don't get the grades to get into here."

I laughed but Phoebe didn't.

"Don't say that!" she gasped. "You're going to get in. You're predicted mostly B's, right?"

"I mean, I think so. Apart from French, obviously. What are you predicted?"

"Mostly A's. I probably won't manage some of them though. Like, how are you even meant to get an A in PE? I joined the netball team like she asked, but I swear Miss Dennis still hates me," she sighed heavily and I laughed softly. "And obviously, I'm going to fail French. How are we meant to learn with her being so terrible?"

Phoebe glanced over her shoulder to make sure Madame Noel wasn't nearby and I found myself checking too, but luckily, the courtyard behind us was almost empty.

Phoebe sighed and pushed the door into the humanities building open. I ducked inside, a chill coming over my skin immediately.

"I might just ask my parents to send me to France this summer. My uncle has a place over there where I could probably stay. You should come too!" she offered, smiling.

I bit my lip, disappointment flaring in my stomach preemptively.

"That would be fun but… I don't think I can," I said, causing Phoebe's face to drop.

"Oh…" she said softly, looking down.

"I mean, I don't think my mom would be too happy about it. You know what she's like," I added quickly. "Plus, we're meant to be going to Scotland for a few weeks so…"

"That should be fun at least," she said, her tone convincing no one.

"Yeah…"

Phoebe smiled at me supportively and we continued climbing the stairs towards the Religious Studies class-room silently.

"Did you do the homework for RS, by the way?" she asked as we neared the top.

"What? 'Watch a show or movie that makes you happy to be alive'? I mean, he didn't really expect us to do that… Did he?" I asked, a little bit of panic bubbling in my stomach.

"I mean, maybe! Mr Ray did say that we'd discuss what we watched today! But, then again… we might just have movie time again. Do you reckon we'll be watching

Disney films again? Did we finish the last one?"

I thought back to the last lesson.

"I don't think so. Maybe our homework will be 'go home and finish the movie' again," I said.

Phoebe laughed before stopping outside Mr Ray's classroom and pausing to gather herself before pushing the door open.

The room was dimmed, with the lights turned off and feeble sunlight peeking in the cracks between the blinds. Everyone turned to look at us as we entered and I felt my face heat up.

"Girls, come on in," Mr Ray said with an easy smile.

"Sorry we're late," Phoebe and I chorused as one.

"That's alright! Come take your seats!"

He pointed to two empty seats in the front row of tables and we slipped into them quickly.

I stashed my bag under the desk, not even bothering to get my notebook out. It would be pointless, it was clear we were going to be watching movies anyway.

"Alright," Mr Ray said, pushing his sleeves back and picking up two DVD covers off his desk. "What are we feeling today? Classic Disney or some of the newer stuff?"

CHAPTER NINE

"Kid," a gentle voice said, breaking through my sleepiness.

I slowly opened my eyes, the world swimming around me, and blinked hard.

"I fell asleep?" I asked dumbly.

"Looks like it," Mitch said with a wry smile.

I rubbed the sleep out of my eyes and looked around. I wanted to ask where we were but I stopped myself, taking longer to stare out the windows instead. Huge towering piles of warped metal reached towards the sky in every direction, glinting in the bright sun. Neat rows of cars stretched out in between them and ours had joined the end of a queue.

"Is this where we're switching the cars?" I asked finally.

A genuine smile grew on his face as he gestured with his head for us to get out of the car before reaching for the door handle.

I scrambled after him, climbing out quickly and staring up at the hulking piles of semi-crushed cars. A strange, sharp, metallic tang filled the air, crossed with the acrid stench of pollution and fumes. A deep, rhythmic banging was coming from somewhere in the distance but I ignored it, hurrying around the car to join Mitch.

He leant back against the hood of the car, raising one hand in greeting at the guy walking towards us.

He looked exactly how I'd expected him to. His white hair was long enough to blow in the gentle breeze as he walked and his tanned shoulders poked out from under his vest top. He was well built despite his age, and it was clear he'd been working in this field for a long time. He just had that energy around him.

"Well, fancy seeing you here, Mitch!" he called as he neared. "Who's the kid? Not yours, is she?"

"Not biologically," Mitch said with a grin. "Or, at least, I don't think she is. Something you're not telling me, kiddo?"

I looked up, surprised that he was talking to me. I was far too used to being with my mom when she spoke to people. I was expected to stand to one side politely, only joining in when absolutely necessary or when I was spoken to. Being included so casually in the conversation felt a little... unsettling.

"Not as far as I'm aware?" I said with a shrug.

The man laughed, leaning against the back of the car

in front of ours, and grinned at Mitch again.

"She's my latest foster kid. I needed someone little to be able to crawl through tight spaces now that Zaq's gone. Grace, meet Greg," Mitch said, cocking his head towards the man in introduction.

"Nice to meet you," I said, feeling a little shy.

"You too, kid," he said with a nod before looking back to Mitch. "What happened to Zaq? Last I heard he'd gotten himself a real job, rather than spending his time skulking around with you."

Mitch laughed.

"That's right, he's got a proper job, he goes to meetings. All the boring stuff!" Mitch said proudly.

He was beaming, obviously thrilled that Zaq was doing well for himself. It made my heart pang a little, but I wasn't too sure why. I think it was just the idea of some being so proud of their kid, even if Zaq wasn't biologically his, made me happy yet envious and a little sad.

"Ah, well, you've obviously prepared him well for the real world. No clue how you did that! Bodes well for you, kid. If you ever get bored of chasing rumours halfway round the globe, you can settle down and do something with a solid paycheque!" Greg laughed a little too hard at that and I saw Mitch's smile harden slightly.

"That reminds me, did you manage to get that car I wanted?" he asked in a lighthearted tone.

The smile on Greg's face took on a strange quality as

he pointed with his chin to a car at the end of the row next to ours.

"What's that?" Mitch demanded, scandalised.

I glanced between the sleek-looking black car and Mitch, not quite understanding the confusion.

I didn't know much, or anything really, about cars but it looked fine. It seemed like a nice car, nothing too off-putting about it.

"That's your car," Greg replied with a smirk.

Mitch gaped at him before walking towards the car and stopping just before it.

"This is a throwaway assignment, why would you give me this thing?" he asked, sounding genuinely upset.

"You asked for a car with boot space, I got you a car with boot space. I don't get what the big deal is," he said with a wicked grin that made me think he knew exactly what the problem was.

Mitch sighed loudly, finally reaching out and touching the car ever so slightly.

"She's got boot space?" he asked, sounding wistful. Longing, almost.

"Three hundred and thirty-four litres," Greg confirmed with a nod. "That's including the space under the bonnet too though. Should be enough."

Mitch sighed again and opened the bonnet, looking as if he were searching for a reason to reject the car, before closing in softly and moving to the back of it.

"And you found one without a spoiler?" he breathed,

running his hand along the back of the car.

"Of course! I know how you feel about them."

Mitch finished his inspection of the car and rounded on Greg again, who was trying to smile innocently.

"This is a throwaway assignment! Why would you give me this thing?" Mitch demanded, sounding genuinely sad.

Greg let out a cackle and held the keys out to Mitch, letting them dangle in the air between the two of them.

"Because I know how much it's going to hurt you," he giggled.

Mitch looked around indignantly.

"Why can't I have that one?" he asked, pointing at a beat-up looking jeep next to us.

"Ah, sorry, that one is already promised to another treasure hunter," Greg joked.

"You're evil," Mitch said flatly. "My first Porsche and I need to dump it? What's the problem with it? Why are you giving it to me?"

"Very little. It runs well actually, unlike that Ford I gave you a couple of years back. Not that many miles on it and it's got no rust."

Greg's explanation went straight over my head, but Mitch nodded as if he understood it.

"Okay, so why are you giving it to me?" he asked again.

"I'm not giving it to you, you're paying for it. Or, at least, whoever your current client is will pay for it. Standard price. Let's call this… revenge," Greg smirked.

"Revenge?" I asked as Mitch narrowed his eyes at Greg.

"That's right. Revenge for this asshole leaving me on a damn deserted island with just a catamaran to get me halfway across the damn ocean."

"What's wrong with that?" I asked, looking between the two of them.

"Have you ever tried to steer one by yourself?" he demanded.

I shook my head.

"Can't say I have."

"It's a fucking nightmare!"

"Hey, language. She's a kid," Mitch interjected.

"And it leaves you a target for pirates and thieves!"

"And you told me you always wanted to steer one. I was just trying to help," Mitch insisted with a grin.

"You're full of…" Greg broke off and glanced at me. "Crap. You did it to get back at me!"

Mitch smirked.

"You asked for a boat, I gave you a boat."

"And you asked for a car, so I gave you a car," Greg retorted quickly.

Mitch pursed his lips and I could tell that he wanted to swear at him but, for my sake, he didn't.

"Fine," he said eventually. "Thanks for the car. I'll text you the location once I dump it."

"I know you will," Greg replied with a less evil-looking grin. "Right, I'll get out of here so that you can load up the car and I can pretend I didn't see nothing."

He pushed away from the car he'd been leaning against and started to walk away.

"Take care of yourself!" Mitch called to him.

Greg lifted a hand in answer but didn't look back.

"Nice to meet you," I called, feeling weird not saying anything.

Greg did turn back at that.

"You too, kiddo! Look after the old guy and make sure he doesn't do anything too reckless."

"I'll try!"

I turned back to Mitch as he opened the boot of our car and the boot of the Porsche.

"Some stuff is going to have to go in the front for sure," he muttered. "Kid, will you come give me a hand? Clothes and whatnot go in the front of the car, shovels and equipment in the back."

I nodded and stepped forwards to help him.

"Sorry to interrupt, have you already had dinner?" a familiar voice asked.

It took me a moment to realise that it wasn't anyone in the scrap yard talking to me.

"Oh, yeah," I said, blinking hurriedly and looking up from the book I'd been pretending to read, trying to ignore the way that my room swam around me.

"Oh? Did you have anything nice?" my dad asked, leaning against my door frame with a gentle smile on his face.

"Just some pasta," I lied, having had to think surprisingly hard about it and realising I hadn't eaten. "If I knew you were going to be home so early, I would have made extra."

"Ah, don't worry about it! You're the kid, I should have made dinner for you!"

I shrugged.

"I don't mind," I said honestly.

"I know, but still."

I smiled at him, hating how sad and worried he looked.

"Is mom still..." I asked, not needing to finish the question.

"Asleep on the sofa? Yeah, she is. I'll make her some food and wake her up with it."

"Might be better to just let her sleep?" I said, thinking about how angry Mom sometimes got when she was woken up.

My dad sighed as he considered it.

"Probably a bad idea," he said. "I don't think she had any lunch and you know how she gets when she doesn't eat enough."

"Mmm," was all I said.

"Are you still hungry? Can I make you anything?" Dad asked hopefully.

"Mmmm... I think I'm okay," I said with a smile.

He cocked his head to the side, a devious smile coming over his face.

"What about if I order from that pizza place you like?" he offered, raising his eyebrows at me. "Would you still not be hungry?"

"The one that does those really good brownies?" I asked.

His smile grew, knowing that he was onto something.

"That's the one! I think I still have the app. Do you want the usual, cheese pizza, garlic bread, and brownies? Any drink?"

I paused, considering it.

I was actually hungry, but I just really didn't want a family meal. They were always so tense and usually broke out into arguments before too long.

But the idea of those brownies made my stomach rumble.

"Yes please, but I think I'm good without a drink," I said.

"Ah, I'll get you one anyway. You can always take it to school with you tomorrow!" my dad said with a smile. "I'll order it now and sneak it up when it gets here so your mom doesn't drag you downstairs for dinner. Make sure you hide the boxes and take them out when you go to school tomorrow. If you get caught, I'm not covering for you!"

He was lying, he always did.

"Thanks, Dad," I said with a smile.

"You got it, darling. Enjoy the rest of the book."

He closed my door softly and I waited until I heard

him pad back down the corridor before letting my eyes flutter shut again.

"You okay, kid?" Mitch called as I stumbled slightly and leaned against the car for support against the wave of dizziness that crashed into me.

"Yeah, fine," I said as loudly as I could manage, blinking quickly to banish the white spots that swam in my vision.

"You sure?" he asked, rushing towards me and grabbing my elbow to steady me.

"Yeah, it's okay. I'm feeling better already."

It was only a bit of a lie.

"What happened?" he asked, his expression concerned.

"It's fine, just low blood sugar or something, I think. It just happens sometimes."

That was true but normally, it was when I hadn't eaten properly or had missed a few meals.

"Does that happen often?"

"Not really. Just when I'm not eating properly. I feel better now," I said with an awkward smile.

It felt weird to have him looking at me with so much worry. It made me a little uncomfortable, it felt wrong. Only my dad had ever looked at me like that before.

"Do we need to go to a doctor to get some blood tests done?" he asked, still looking at me.

"No, no, it's okay! Plus, we have to go to Edinburgh, right?"

"Your health is more important than that," he said, sounding like he meant it which confused me.

"Honestly, I'm fine," I insisted. "Can I help you load the new car?"

He examined me closely before nodding.

"I'm going to trust you for now, but if it keeps happening, we're going to a doctor."

I opened my mouth to complain but he held his hand up and cut me off.

"Nope," he said. "I'm not arguing with you on this. Your health is more important than any assignment and if you start getting dizzy or fainting when we're out there, you could get seriously injured or die."

I looked down guiltily.

It wasn't anything to do with my health. It was just something that happened sometimes when I started daydreaming. I didn't need to speak to a doctor about it, I didn't even know what I would say.

"Okay," I agreed finally.

"Great," Mitch said, smiling widely which made me feel even worse. "You stay there for now. I'm going to grab that smoothie and I want you to drink it all. It probably tastes like dirt but it should have enough sugar in it to make you feel better. I don't want to hear any complaints but we're going to start eating better and more consistently, you hear me."

I nodded, trying to fight the smile that threatened my lips.

"What?" he asked finally.

"Nothing... It's just... I thought the smoothie would probably taste like dirt too," I admitted, looking down and not sure how he'd take it.

Surprisingly, he threw his head back and laughed.

"Kid!" he cried whilst still chuckling. "Why did you get it then?"

I shrugged, not bothering to hide my smile.

"I wasn't sure what you liked!"

"Well, if it tastes like dirt, I ain't a fan! No smoothie should be so heavy on the vegetables! And, did you read the back of that bottle? It's got beetroot in! Why would a smoothie have beetroot in it unless they were actively trying to make it taste like dirt?" he demanded as he pulled the door open and started digging around in the bag.

"So, what you're saying is you want me to always get you smoothies and snacks with beetroots whenever possible?" I asked, trying to sound as innocent as possible and not giggle.

He glared at me and fished the bottle out.

"What I'm saying is if you get me a drink with beetroot in, I'm going to make you have it! Now, drink your dirt." He held the smoothie out to me with a grin.

I took it from him reluctantly.

"Can I at least come and have a look at what you're packing?" I asked.

He examined me closely as I opened the bottle and

took a sip to prove that I would drink it.

"Okay, but if you need to sit down or feel faint again, you have to, alright?"

I nodded and followed him around to the back of the car.

It only had my new clothes and a couple of backpacks inside, nothing that looked like it could be used to desecrate a graveyard, as Mitch had said. I watched closely, wanting to ask questions but forcing myself to wait.

"We're going to need to find somewhere to stash some of your clothes," he muttered, almost to himself.

"Where do you keep yours?" I asked.

"You're looking at them," he said, hefting one of the beaten-up bags out of the boot and depositing them in the front boot of the Porsche. "Keep drinking!"

"Is that it?" I asked, after taking another sip.

I was grateful that I couldn't taste it because it smelt like a garden and not the nice freshly cut grass smell but the swampy, overgrown kind of garden.

"Nah, I keep some stuff in some leisure centres across the country. You'd be surprised how long you can use a locker in them with just a small bribe," he grinned as he took the final bag of my clothes out of the car, threw them into the Porsche and slammed the first boot shut.

I looked into the empty boot, confusion running through me.

"Is that everything? Where's your treasure hunting stuff?" I asked, a little disappointed.

"What treasure hunting stuff?" he asked with a laugh. "You expecting me to just lug around shovels, weapons and that kinda thing?"

"I mean… yeah, kind of?"

He laughed again and returned to the seemingly empty boot.

"You mean… like this?"

He lifted the carpet of the boot with a flourish and stepped out the way for me to get a better look.

A smile slowly grew on my face.

Squeezed in around the spare tyre was the treasure hunting equipment I'd been looking for. Shovels and pickaxes lined the space, barely fitting in, whilst two black hard cases were carefully placed under them.

"What are they?" I asked, pointing at them.

"One of them is my laptop. Top of the range, or at least it was a couple of years back but the second they bring out a new one that can handle all my software, I'm getting it. The other one is a little hard to explain. It's a machine that scans the ground and produces a picture of what's underneath. Perfect for grave robbin'."

He grinned at me toothily.

I looked between them, excitement growing in me.

We were going to do it. We were going to find treasure.

"Where are the weapons?" I asked, taking another gulp of the smoothie as I watched Mitch carefully place the stuff into the boot of the new car, making sure that it was jammed in so that it wouldn't rattle around or do any damage.

He looked at me, his expression devious.

"Well, I can't exactly drive around with guns just sitting in the boot! Have you ever tried to explain that to the police? I tried the classic 'oh, they're just really realistic props' but they rarely buy that! They're in the tyre. Plus, a couple of good, easy to grab locations in the car. Finish that smoothie and help me pull the seats up, will you?"

CHAPTER TEN

I leant back against the cold brick wall of the green-room where we had our drama class, my eyes fixed on the definitely illegal recording of a play we'd be studying next year. It wasn't bad. It was a dramatisation of the Salem witch trials, which I always found fascinating, but the sound kept dipping out and we could hear the endless rustling and whispering of the audience.

I was pretty certain that Mrs Martell had recorded it herself. I'm sure I heard her shush someone at some point. She seemed like the type who would do that. I'm not sure what it was, but she just had that energy about her.

I let my head fall back as another annoying burst of whispers tore out of the speakers, blocking out whatever the actors were saying. It was so hard to pay attention when I could barely hear what was going on.

With a wave of dizziness, colour washed across my vision. Flashes of rolling green fields, hills topped with lusciously full trees and the faintest glimpse of the ocean in the distance, danced just beyond my awareness. It was dark and stormy, nothing like the sea I'd been on in the boat with Mitch before.

Finally, the flashes of colour solidified, slowing down until I was staring at a slightly disappointing looking church. It was shorter than I thought it would be with no spire. I always preferred churches with spires, they looked so much cooler.

The stained glass was pretty cool though.

I blinked roughly and sat up straighter.

I didn't want to zone out. Not in Drama class, I enjoyed it too much. But... we were just watching a play and we'd probably watch it again at the beginning of next term, so it didn't matter too much if I stopped paying attention.

"What do you think, kid?" I heard Mitch ask distantly.

I hesitated, torn between my fantasy world and the real world.

"It's not what I expected," I replied after a pause.

"No? Were you expecting some grand, Notre Dame-type cathedral?" he asked with a grin.

"A little, yeah. I mean, I've been to Edinburgh a couple of times now and the rest of the buildings are so nice and old looking. This looks weirdly modern, you know?" I said, staring up at it.

"Well, that makes sense. It is. The church was

destroyed a good few times," Mitch explained. "There was a revolution and multiple fires. They ended up restoring it in the nineteen-hundreds, that's probably why it looks so new."

I cocked my head and stared up at it.

"It would look cooler if it had a spire," I said finally.

"There used to be one!"

I looked at him in surprise but he was staring up at the church, waiting patiently for the chattering tour group to move past us.

They did, slowly, and I wanted to hurry them along, but I forced myself to wait.

"Oh yeah," he started up again as if he hadn't even stopped. "Back before it was renovated, it had a tower and everything but they made a mistake."

"What happened?" I asked, fascinated.

History class was never this interesting. If it was, I would have paid more attention.

"An explosion. They used to use the tower as a gunpowder store."

"What?"

"Oh, yeah. It's fairly safe, as far as explosives go. Decomposes pretty slowly and it can be stored for a long period of time, if you store it correctly in a nice and dry place but... clearly, they didn't."

There was a little too much understanding in his voice.

"Wait," I said as realisation hit me. "Have you used

gunpowder before?"

Mitch laughed loudly, but his eyes darted around at the people who were now staring at us.

"Of course, kid! You know I work in special effects!" he lied easily and just loudly enough for the people around us to stop staring quite so worriedly.

"Sorry," I muttered as soon as they'd moved on.

"That's alright, I think we covered it pretty well. Shall we do a quick lap of the graveyard and then we'll go find a spa or something to dump some of our clothes and get cleaned up?"

"Sure," I said quickly, my eyes darting around the surprisingly large graveyard, actually paying attention to it for the first time.

The small path we were standing on reached the church before splitting in two to circle the building. Small offshoots of the path, cracked by tree roots and from age, stretched out towards the grand gravestones. We started down one of the offshoots, looking at the graves.

There weren't as many as I expected on this side of the church but they were much bigger than the tombstones in my nearby church back home. The grass was bright and well maintained too. Someone clearly cared for the land and the people buried there, even if they were long gone.

"See those ones built into the wall?" Mitch pointed towards the back wall with his head.

I followed his gesture, my eyes widening as I noticed the incredible things built into the side walls. I couldn't quite call them tombstones. They were giant, even taller and longer than I was. They looked like a strange combination or cross between a grave and a monument.

I walked towards them without really even noticing.

Daisies had appeared on the grass before them, left-over offerings from long-dead families, but I didn't pay them much attention. I was too captivated by the decorations on the tombs. Some had lions, family crests or just plaques written in Latin, but one in particular called to me.

The base was fairly plain. Made of bricks that had been worn and darkened by the rain, all details on the base had been destroyed but along the top, a smaller slab somehow had not been as damaged by the weather.

Latin words were etched into the far sides but I understood very few of them. One stood out though.

'Mortal'.

"Why is there a skull and crossbones on this grave?" I asked quietly, aware of the people wandering around behind us.

I didn't want to speak too loudly, just in case it was relevant to the mission. I didn't want to be the one to ruin everything.

"It's actually not what you think!" Mitch explained cheerfully. "The symbol was used a very long time ago, back in the Roman empire, but it stopped being used over time and then it had a resurgence in popularity, not actually by pirates at first but by the Catholic church. More specifically, it was the Knights Templar, which actually makes sense because they were heavily linked to piracy."

"Really?" I asked, genuinely surprised.

I'd never heard that the church was linked to piracy before, and it sounded so strange, but Mitch sounded confident. I completely trusted that he was telling the truth.

"Listen to the nice man, Janey," a woman beside me said, crouching down beside her toddler and pointing up at Mitch.

Mitch hesitated for only a moment before launching right back into his lesson.

"So, once the order of the Templars had been disbanded, a lot of them were very skilled mariners, and they started using the skull and crossbones as their flag."

I felt my eyebrows draw together.

That didn't feel like a full explanation.

"Why though?" I asked after a pause where Mitch looked cagily at the woman and the toddler standing next to us.

He sighed.

"I don't think this is the best story for your kid to hear," he said to her finally.

"She'll be fine," the woman said snootily. "Janey is very gifted and mature for her age."

Mitch raised one eyebrow slightly.

"If you say so. There are two different stories as to how the symbol began being used for pirates. The first one is that after the Templar was disbanded, the Grand Master, who was the person in charge of them, was burnt alive by the rest of the Catholic church. Some of the surviving Templars went looking for his body, but only found the femurs and his skull and, because they were mariners, they basically fled. They became pirates and what was left of the Grand Master became their flag."

The woman beside me quickly ushered her kid away, shooting Mitch dark looks.

"You sure you don't want to stay? The next story is even better!" Mitch called after her before chuckling. "Ah, that was mean, but I tried to warn her!"

"What's the next story?" I asked with a grin.

"The next one is actually more interesting, if you ask me. There was a Lord of Sidon, who was alive back in the Templar days and he was actually a Templar himself. He got married but she died when she was pretty young still, but this was back in the day so it was pretty common. Anyway, he ordered the Templars to help him find her body on the evening of the burial and dig her up. I know, pretty nasty but it does get worse. When he was excavating the grave, he reported hearing God telling him to bury her again and return in nine months because she was going to have his son."

"What?" I cried. "But she was dead? How could she have his kid?"

"Exactly! She couldn't, she was a corpse. But, he made them bury her again and they returned in nine months, just like the voice told him, and when they dug her up again… there was a skull resting on his bride's leg bones!"

"Really?"

"According to the legend! Apparently, this time, the voice said to him that he had to look after the skull and it would protect him in all his ventures!"

"Was he a pirate then?" I asked, trying to connect the stories.

Mitch cocked his head.

"Well… that isn't part of the legend, but the port of Sidon was known across the globe as a haven for pirates so it's a little uncertain if they're connected or if the Lord became a pirate or if the Templars that became pirates took his good luck charm to watch over them too. It was hundreds of years ago though so the facts are a little spotty."

"That's so interesting!" I said honestly, staring at the tombstones again.

"Isn't it?" he said earnestly.

"So, why are they on these graves?" I looked around surreptitiously. "Are they pirates?"

"Eh, not necessarily. Sometimes it's used just to symbolise death, like the ones that say that."

He pointed at some words that were etched into the bottom of a tombstone a few along from us.

I walked towards them, reading as the words came into focus.

"Memento mori? What does that mean?" I asked.

"It's an old Latin saying. It means 'remember, you must die'."

A shudder went through me.

"It sounds like a threat," I said, very aware of the hairs on my arms standing on edge.

"Eh," Mitch said with a shrug. "Less of a threat and more of a reminder. The saying and thought exists across a lot of cultures and religions, but I think it mostly boils down to making sure you're living a good life and one worth living, you know?"

I nodded but ice slithered down my spine.

I wasn't living a good life. I wasn't doing anything particularly good with it. I was just existing. I knew that I was just a kid, but surely I could be doing something better.

What was I doing with my life? I was spending my time zoning out, not paying any attention in class, and barely doing any work or homework. I was doing nothing. I would be nothing. My teacher had said for years that the work we were doing that year laid the foundation for what we did in the future, what we became. If we slacked now, we would become nothing.

I was limiting myself, spending my days hiding in

fantasies and daydreams just because the real world wasn't enough for me.

"Oh crap," Mitch said suddenly, glancing at his watch.

A faint hint of vertigo hit me and I focused on him again, my surroundings swimming ever so slightly as I came back from wherever I'd been.

"We need to get to the other side to have a look at where we have to dig tonight and then we have to get back to the car. I only put an hour on the parking!" he said, turning and starting across the grass towards the path.

I hurried after him, trying to push the thoughts out of my mind.

I'd worked hard for my GCSEs. I could slack a little bit. The next week barely mattered and it would be the summer holidays soon. Some people weren't even coming to class... I'd start paying attention again at the beginning of the new year.

"What's that?" I said, slowing as we passed a weird flat metal cage with a slab of stone on top.

"That?" Mitch asked, pointing at it. "That's a mortsafe."

He continued walking and I raced after him.

"What's a mortsafe?"

"They were invented to stop grave robbers. They'd put a body in there and drive a spike through the head before locking it up and putting the slab on top so that people couldn't steal it."

My mouth dropped open.

"How long did they keep the body in there? Like, was it a permanent thing? It seems kind of gross to keep a body out in the open for so long. Wouldn't it smell?" I asked, glancing back at the grim contraption.

"I assume so, they normally do," Mitch said with a shrug. "But they usually weren't kept in there for too long. Only six weeks or so for them to get nice and decayed so that no one wanted them anymore. Okay, come have a look at this."

I look at the monument, taking in the snake in the centre. It was wrapped around a pot or an urn of some kind but it stared out towards me, its beady eyes seeming to look directly at mine.

I tore my gaze away from it and looked at the words on the plinth it rested on.

"Non omnis moriar?" I tried to read.

"Not bad pronunciation," Mitch said kindly but I felt like he was lying. "Do you know what it means?"

I shook my head. I couldn't even begin to guess.

"That's okay, we'll add Latin to the rotation of classes. I think I probably still have some of the lessons that Zaq studied somewhere, I'll fish them out. It means 'not all of me will die'."

"That's... ominous," I said finally as Mitch began leading me across the graveyard again. "Is it a clue or something?"

"It's a quote. From a poet way back in Roman times.

I don't reckon it's a clue, just something interesting. This, however…"

He came to a stop on the dry mud path and looked into one of the mausoleums with a grin on his face.

Confusion flared within me.

"This?" I asked.

"This."

I looked at the strange building. It looked so shockingly ordinary. Nothing about it stood out. It was short and stout with absolutely no decorations or grandeur. There was an empty archway rather than a door, anyone could just walk in.

"Are you sure you don't mean that one?" I asked, pointing at the much more elaborate one next to it.

The building was rounded with a fancy crest above the dark grey doors. It even had a dome! I mean, there might have been weeds and plants growing out of the top of it and between some of the bricks, but it looked so much more like something that would be hiding pirate treasure.

"George MacKenzie's tomb?" he asked, looking scandalised.

I shrugged.

"Maybe?"

"No! He had nothing to do with anything fun. Sure, he was a real bad guy, but that grave has been desecrated too many times to have anything of use. This, this is the one we want."

He marched inside past the metal gate that had been propped in the doorway, not doing anything to block people from entering.

I slipped in after him, glancing back at the tour group who were coming up along the path outside.

Mitch was turning slowly, scanning the walls, floor and finally, the metal bars that blocked out some of the sunlight.

"What are you looking for?" I asked.

"Signs that people have been here recently. Have a look at the floor, can you see anything suspicious?"

I looked down immediately at the dark pebbles, examining them for any traces of footprints or scuffs.

I wanted to say 'no' immediately, but I could feel Mitch's gaze on me. I needed to do better. I had to find something, whatever he'd noticed. I stopped mid-turn, something catching my attention. It wasn't really anything, just something a little... different.

"Are you here on a field trip?" a loud voice asked.

I whipped around, staring at the smiling man in a white shirt that loudly pronounced he was a tour guide.

"Kind of. I homeschool my daughter and you know what it's like. It's always better to show someone a place you're trying to teach them about," Mitch said in a jovial tone.

"Ah, of course," the guide said. "But if you're looking for the tomb of Bloody MacKenzie, I'm afraid you've overshot just a bit. You know, I can give you the tour for just nineteen pounds each!"

He grinned at us hopefully.

"Well, that does sound lovely!" Mitch cried with a smile. "You know, I got so mixed up there, I thought this was his tomb! I was going to say, it was nothing like what I expected!"

Mitch grinned at me, but he widened his eyes slightly.

He wanted me to do something, to get us out of it. It was a test.

"Oh, that sounds so interesting! Hey, do you know anything about the mortsafes?" I asked, making a show of how fascinated I was. "That is what you said they were called, right, dad?"

"That's right! See, I knew taking you here would help! Trust me, I tried to teach her this stuff at home but it went in one ear and out the other! I think it's because she's always glued to that phone of hers," he said and I slipped it from my pocket, pretending to be outraged.

"Hey, I am not! I've paid attention all the way around this place!" I cried, waiting for him to pull his wallet out, a plan forming in my mind.

"You have, you have," he grumbled with a roll of his eyes.

"Ah," the tour guide chuckled. "Well, hopefully, I can make the tour more interesting than whatever is on your phone! That'll be thirty-eight pounds, please."

Mitch started to pull out his wallet to pay him and I brought my phone up, pretending to just be checking my texts.

"Wait, did you get the parking for one hour or two?" I asked, arranging my features into a look of confusion.

"One. Why, kiddo? What time is it?" he asked, looking at me.

"Dad! It's almost four!"

Mitch gasped, looking appropriately shocked.

"Oh, no! We need to get back to the car! If I get one more ticket, your mom is going to kill me! Let's go!" he cried before looking at the disappointed guide. "I am so sorry, we'll have to come back another day! Alex, come on!"

He rushed towards the door of the mausoleum as the tour guide stepped out of the way sadly.

"You always do this!" I chided him, feeling bad. "I wanted to go on that tour! Can we come back next week?"

The tour guide perked up slightly at my words even as we rushed past him and started across the grass.

"We'll have to see what your mom says! Which way did we park? Was it down here?" he asked, keeping the charade up.

"Yeah, come on!"

We rushed over the grass and out the gates of the graveyard, still in character. It wasn't until we were halfway down the street that Mitch started to slow.

"That was pretty good, kid," he said with a grin.

"Thanks! But, you called me Alex, why?" I asked.

A tiny bit of fear nibbled at my stomach. I was

worried that he'd forgotten my name. Maybe Alex was some other kid he'd looked after before, like Zaq.

"Well, I couldn't exactly use your real name, could I?" he said with a laugh. "It's always better to use fake names with people you don't know or trust. Then, it's harder for them to trace you. I mean, sure, they still can give physical descriptions but we can change that up when needed. So, what did you see, Grace?"

I smiled at his use of my name even though part of me thought he'd done it just because he knew what I was worried about.

"Well, it could be nothing..." I started unsurely. "But did you see the back wall? Under all the weeds and plants."

A small grin started on his face.

"Why, yes, I did. Wanna see what's under that plastering tonight?"

CHAPTER ELEVEN

The water slipped gently across my skin as I paddled slowly down the length of the pool, taking my time to enjoy the sensations. The spa was empty apart from me and Mitch, who was in one of the saunas or maybe even napping in the quiet relaxation room. I had debated going in there too, but it was a little too quiet for me.

The whole room had been specifically designed to promote relaxation and mindfulness, from the padded, comfy looking loungers to the dim fairy lights built into the ceiling that looked like stars in the night sky. A fire crackled softly on one wall, which always relaxed me, but there was no other sound.

It set me on edge. Even a few minutes in the room had made my skin crawl and my breathing speed up. Mitch had sighed and left the room pretty quickly too, telling me he was going to find somewhere warmer for a nap and to wake him if I needed anything.

I didn't want to though. I wasn't sure if he'd gotten any sleep the night before and he started yawning before we even checked into the hotel. We'd gotten a few weird looks at that, but I think booking separate rooms had helped convince the people working that there wasn't anything weird going on. Also, the fact he had IDs for both of us with matching surnames.

I'd meant to ask him where he'd managed to get his hands not just on a fake ID for me, but one that looked so realistic. It made sense though. He probably burnt through fake IDs pretty quickly, so would need to be good at finding or making new ones.

I glanced out the window toward the rooftop pool, not quite sure if I actually wanted to go swimming out there or not. It looked really nice and there were even places to sit built into the edge of the pool so I could look out over the city but...

I looked around the pool area I was in again.

There was no one else there. No one to tell me off for being a kid in a grown-up area. Or... maybe it wasn't a grown-up area. I'd just always assumed that kids weren't welcome in spas and no one had told me otherwise.

A smile came over my face and I swam towards the stairs, not even stopping to grab my robe in my rush to get to the other pool.

Even though it was late June, the breeze caused goosebumps to erupt on my skin and I quickly climbed into the heated outdoor pool. A sigh slipped through my lips as the warm water quickly heated me again.

The water was shallow enough to wade, but still I padded through the water towards the metal seats and sunk into one. A spray of water hit my foot and I jolted it out of the way, looking down at the dark footprints that had been painted onto the floor of the pool.

I edged my feet onto them again, sighing contentedly as the high-pressured water massaged my soles. I couldn't stop myself from leaning back and letting my eyes flutter shut, the warm afternoon sun gently baking me as I sunk further into the water.

It felt like an eternity had passed before a soft splashing alerted me to someone's presence. My head shot up and I blinked hard to try and clear the blue colour from my vision. Relief washed through me as I spotted Mitch wading towards me, the water splashing against his scarred body.

"So you fell asleep too, kid?" he called.

"Yeah, not for long though I don't think," I said as he dropped onto the seat near me.

"I feel like a right dumbass," he said, slicking a wet hand through his hair. "I didn't even have my gun on me. I should have gone down to my room when I started to get sleepy."

"It was fine though. No one even came in."

"Mmm," he replied, unconvinced. "Anyway, we need to talk about tonight."

My heart started racing immediately.

"What do you mean?"

"We need to go over the plan and what you're going to do. Probably not the best idea to do it here, even if they were nice enough to let us stash some of our clothes here for a few months." He glanced up at a camera that I hadn't even noticed. "Are you done in the spa? Shall we get changed and then we can go down to my room and work out where we're going for dinner?"

His tone was light, very different to before, and I knew it was intentional.

"Sure, I'm starting to get hungry anyway," I said, mimicking his tone and smiling.

He nodded and started back towards the door to the inside of the spa.

I followed him, only a little reluctantly.

It had been so nice and relaxing in the spa and, although part of me craved the adventure and the excitement of what was to come, I had really enjoyed the calm. I felt so much more at ease. It was as if all of the stress of my GCSEs had somehow dissipated.

"Oh my!" a woman exclaimed as she turned the corner and almost walked straight into Mitch.

"Sorry 'bout that," Mitch said, stepping aside so that she had room to pass.

Her eyes scanned his chest, taking in the long gash that spanned the length of his side and what was clearly a scar from a bullet on his abs.

"Oh gosh," she whispered, her eyes fixed on the scars.

It was a good thing she couldn't see his back where there were two more bullet holes and a handful of other miscellaneous scars.

"Oh, yeah," Mitch said, looking down at his body. "Appendicitis, liver transplant and... what's this one kid?"

"Lung transplant," I added solemnly.

"That's the one. I always forget about that!" he chuckled cheerfully. "I'm real unhealthy!"

The woman looked startled and hurried away from us without saying anything more.

Mitch continued to laugh under his breath as we made our way towards the changing rooms before stopping outside.

"Alright, kid," he said, with a casual look around the corridor. "Remember what to do?"

I nodded.

Stash the extra clothes in a bag in one of the lockers, make sure there's nothing identifiable in there, and then text Mitch with the locker number and code that I used. Shouldn't be too hard but still, a thrill of excitement went through me.

"Okay, good. Meet me in my room after and we'll order some food and go over the plan. Do you remember the room number?" he asked.

"One hundred and sixty-four," I recited.

"Good. And you know what to do if you see people you recognise?"

Sterling's people.

"Yup," I replied.

Run and scream.

He nodded, satisfied.

"Okay, kid. See you downstairs."

Mitch turned and wandered into the men's changing rooms.

I ducked into the women's changing rooms, glancing around to see if anyone else was in there. Anxiety skittered in my stomach as I realised that there was someone in the showers where I would have to go.

I really didn't like the idea of being ambushed in the shower or in the middle of getting changed, but in the back of my mind I knew that I'd be able to just blink and leave the world if I needed to.

Crossing to my locker, I typed in the combination I'd used before with shaking fingers and pulled out my backpack. Rooting around until I found the plastic bag within, I listened carefully.

The person in the shower was humming a tune softly, one I didn't recognise. I wasn't sure if that made me feel better or worse. Pausing, the plastic bag containing my shampoo and conditioner clutched in my hands, I debated skipping the shower. I could just get dressed quickly and rush down to Mitch's room. I could probably shower there and I knew I'd feel safer there.

But it felt weird. If I did that, I'd feel like a wimp. Mitch might change his mind about me being able to come with him if he realised I was too scared to be alone for even five minutes.

I could do this.

I could shower quick, keep an eye on the door and my surroundings and then go down to his room and learn the plan for tonight. I had to.

I took a deep breath, glanced back towards the showers, and stuffed some clothes and my towel into the bag. I grabbed the phone Mitch had given me, almost as an afterthought, cursing myself out for being dumb.

If anything did happen, I'd need it to call him.

My hands trembling slightly in fear, I crossed towards the showers, eyeing the opaque closed door behind which humming could be heard. It was louder now but I still didn't recognise the tune.

Ducking into one of the other cubicles, my heart hammering in my chest, I waited and listened. Water still splashed from the occupied cubicle and she hadn't even stopped humming. Part of me wanted to crouch down and make sure that it wasn't some kind of ploy to make me feel more comfortable. Maybe there were five of Sterling's people crammed into that tiny cubicle, just waiting for me to let my guard down enough to attack.

It felt wrong but I had to know. I leant down on the clammy tiled floor and peeked under the light blue wall, spotting a pair of feet. I stood immediately, feeling guilty and not wanting to see anything more.

I was getting paranoid. There was no one there. I just

needed to shower and get dressed quickly.

I grabbed the shampoo and conditioner out of the plastic bag and hooked it by the door, pausing to listen before turning the water on and stepping under it. The boiling hot water scalded my skin and caused me to jump back, my breath hissing out of my lips. Tentatively, I reached a hand to test the temperature of the water and, finding it less skin-meltingly hot, stepped back underneath it.

Washing quickly and stopping every few seconds to listen carefully, I was done before long. I turned the water off and finally stripped out of my swimming costume, wanting to be naked for as little time as possible, just in case the Sterlings were there.

Mitch had instructed me on what to wear for tonight. I had to wear dark colours to blend into the barely lit graveyard but also I'd need to wear a hoodie or something that I could discard if it got too dusty when we were digging up the grave. I needed to be able to move well and run if required, so I settled on black leggings, a black slightly oversized top and a plain black hoodie.

It felt a little as if I had just googled 'burglar costume' but I could imagine someone wearing it for non-nefarious purposes. It wasn't that abnormal to dress head to toe in black, I'd look like I just preferred to wear dark colours hopefully.

The other shower stopped and I froze, waiting anxiously just in case, but the woman continued moving around in her cubicle. My heart pounded in my ears and I realised I had to make a decision, leave now and stash my bag or just hide until she was gone.

The second option felt wrong. She would have heard me in the showers too, so it would be strange if I didn't go out soon. Or maybe she'd just assume I had anxiety and wouldn't think too much of it.

No, I had to go out. I couldn't keep Mitch waiting too long, he might leave without me.

Slipping the shampoo, conditioner and wet towel back into the plastic bag, I hauled my shoulders back almost painfully. I needed to look relaxed, confident and like I fit in. If I did, then the woman wouldn't look twice at me.

Pushing the door open, I marched out into the changing room and quickly realised that I hadn't needed to faff for so long or even worry. The woman was already gone.

My face burning with embarrassment, I unlocked the locker again and pulled the backpack out, making sure that I hadn't left anything in it. There were a couple of changes of clothes in it but nothing else. I grabbed my trainers out and slipped them on before shoving the bag back into the locker and sending Mitch the locker number and code.

I'd just started out the door when fear gripped me and my steps faltered.

What if I'd mistyped?

What if I somehow sent him the wrong number and then we came back in a couple of years and I couldn't get any clothes out? Would I just be stuck without anything because I messed up and didn't think to double-check that I'd typed the code correctly?

Sighing, I turned back into the changing rooms and traipsed over to the locker, typing in the code once more. Anxiety bounced in my stomach as I waited for the light to flash. Green. I hadn't mistyped, I was just being dumb.

I shook my head to myself and left the room again. This was my fantasy. I didn't need to worry about something as trivial as whether or not I'd written four numbers correctly. It would be fine.

I breathed out an annoyed sigh as I hammered the lift button, hoping that I hadn't taken so long that Mitch had gotten bored and left me there. My phone buzzed and I fumbled to pull it out of my pocket, my sweaty hands making it much more difficult than it needed to be.

Got it, Mitch had written. Followed by, *Dinner order?*

I chewed my lip as my stomach growled.

I wasn't even sure if I would be able to taste anything in this world. I hadn't been able to before. But then, things were feeling more real. I had felt the pool water against my skin, the sun on my face and the lift moving around me. Maybe it would be possible now?

Not sure, I typed back. *What's on the menu?*

I glanced up at the changing floor numbers before looking back down at my phone.

I'm almost at your floor, can I have a look at the menu when I get there? I asked.

Anxiety bubbled in my stomach and I almost wanted to text him again to say that he could just order me whatever and I'd be happy with it but the speech bubble appeared to show that he was typing.

Sure, kid, read his response.

I chewed my lip again, my teeth digging in even harder as I tried to work out if he was mad at me. He could be annoyed that I hadn't just decided on something, but I didn't know what room service offered! I couldn't just choose something because if they didn't have it, he might get even more annoyed.

My fingers twitched over the screen and I forced myself to lock my phone and put it in my pocket as the lift came to a stop.

If he was annoyed at me, it was fine. He probably wouldn't abandon me in Edinburgh... right?

I stepped out into the corridor and scanned the numbers quickly, hurrying to his door before knocking softly.

He pulled the door open before long, his hair wet and dripping but a bright smile on his face.

"Damn, kid. You really were almost here, your text only just came through. Come in, come in," he said, turning and leading me into the room.

Technology and tools were scattered everywhere. Pickaxes and shovels were placed on a towel on the bed, guns, knives and other weird-looking weapons were on the table in front of the mirror and two iPads and a laptop were on the small circular table by the window.

Mitch crossed to the table and sunk down into one of the chairs, squinting at the satellite image on the computer screen.

"Sit, look at the menu," he instructed distractedly. "Scan the thing at the bottom to open the website then you can order dinner. Do you mind ordering for me too? I already know what I want and you can pay with the card that's linked to the phone."

I nodded, my eyes already scanning the menu before landing on the vegetarian burger.

Two different types of cheese and a hash brown? Done.

I scanned the picture and ordered it before looking up at Mitch.

"What did you want me to order for you?" I asked.

"There was a risotto there that looked good," he said, surprising me.

I'd expected him to go for steak or something similar.

I scrolled down the list until I found it.

"Roast vegetable risotto?" I asked.

"That's it! What are you having?"

"The veggie burger!" I said with an excited smile.

"Oh, that sounded good, but you gotta get some

vegetables with it too. Remember what I said about us eating more fruit and veg?" he asked, looking up over the computer briefly at me. "Have a look in the sides, there were a few options there."

I scrolled down to the section he mentioned.

"Oh," I gasped, spotting something delicious. "Honey roasted carrots!"

My mom used to make them sometimes. Back before she started drinking so much.

I looked up at Mitch hopefully, worried that he'd say I couldn't get them, but he was too busy looking at the screen. It took him a minute to notice my gaze, but when he did, he smiled.

"Get them, kid. Let me know when you've ordered, I want to talk to you about the plan for tonight."

I swallowed, fear spiking in my stomach and making me queasy.

My palms were slick with sweat as I confirmed the order and put the phone down, my foot wanting to bounce to get rid of some of my nervous energy.

"Okay, all sorted?" he asked, looking up from the screen again.

I nodded.

"Great. So, I've been looking into the laws surrounding listed buildings in Scotland and it turns out that the monuments are most likely listed. I thought they might be, but now I'm pretty sure. Do you know what that means?"

"Mmm, kind of. It means that they're like, old and protected, right?" I said, pulling on some trace of a memory that I wasn't sure where I'd found it. "It's a crime to tamper with them, isn't it? Oh…"

I trailed off, realising that what we were going to do would probably count as tampering.

"I see you've spotted the problem," he said, smiling slightly and nodding. "It is a crime and if we were to get caught, we'd be able to get out of it, but it might mean spending some time in a police station."

I swallowed, fear warring with the knowledge that I'd definitely be able to get out of any trouble we got into.

"So… that being said, you're welcome to stay here and I can swing by and pick you up on the way out of the city," he offered.

"I still want to come with," I said immediately.

He laughed.

"Kid, think about it. It could be risky."

I was already shaking my head before he'd finished talking.

"It's worth it," I insisted.

A smile grew on Mitch's face and he nodded slowly.

"Alright. Let me hide all this stuff," he gestured at the tools and weapons, "so we don't scare the poor person who brings us our food, and I'll tell you what the plan is for tonight."

CHAPTER TWELVE

My heart pounded as we walked up the cobblestone path and I couldn't stop myself from peering over my shoulder every few steps as if Sterling's people might appear out of the shadows with guns. Mitch had said that we'd be safe for now though which did make me feel better but the fact that he'd made us pack the car up again and that I'd seen him slipping a gun into his holster didn't help.

It was just a precaution, apparently. But he had said you could never be too sure. The Sterlings are like bed bugs, Mitch had said, popping up wherever they're wanted least and being irritating as hell.

Mitch carefully hitched his bag a little higher on his shoulder and I winced at the muffled clanking that came from inside. We'd wrapped everything in towels to try and prevent them from making as much noise as possible but it still felt deafening in the night air.

"See anyone?" Mitch asked under his breath as we

entered the Kirkyard.

"No," I breathed back, scanning the dark graveyard intently.

The lamps were sparse, bathing some parts of the space in light but the edges were cloaked in shadows. Even so, I was pretty sure we were alone.

"Do they not lock the gates or anything to stop people from coming in at night?" I muttered, my eyes sweeping our surroundings.

"Nah, they're pretty relaxed about that kind of thing here. As long as we don't make too much noise, we should be fine."

My steps faltered and I needed to rush to catch up.

"Aren't we going to smash down a wall?" I asked.

Mitch snorted softly.

"Such an inelegant solution," he muttered. "We're going to sort out the weeds, pry the plaster off, and go from there."

I nodded slightly, my hair falling in front of my face, the colour startling me for a moment before I remembered it was a wig. It felt unnatural, the shade too dark for my skin, but Mitch had insisted that it wasn't that bad, despite how bad I knew it looked.

My own hair had been plaited tightly, Mitch's work, and was bundled up under the scratchy wig. It was horrifically warm too. The hot air felt muggy and too humid. My hands were sweating inside my two pairs of plastic gloves and I was really regretting wearing the hoodie that Mitch had suggested.

I understood the purpose of the precautions, of course I did. The wig was to cover my own hair so that firstly, people didn't recognise me and secondly, so that I didn't leave any evidence there, same with the gloves, but it felt excessive. Surely, one pair was enough.

At first, it had been fun and exciting, but with each step it became more and more obvious how illegal our actions were. I had to keep reminding myself that it was just a dream. Nothing bad could happen.

As we sauntered quickly but casually towards our target, it felt like something terrible was about to happen. My heart fluttered in my chest and my hands trembled. Sterling's people could appear at any moment and pounce. I wasn't ready. I didn't even have a gun! Not that I knew how to use one but still, it might make me feel better just to have one.

It wouldn't, not really. It was just more pressure and the thought of holding something in my hands that could easily end someone's life was… terrifying.

"When we reach the mausoleum," Mitch muttered under his breath, pulling the collar of his leather jacket slightly higher against an imagined chill, "I want you to go inside and hide against the wall next to the door whilst I get everything set up, understood?"

"Yes," I breathed back.

He nodded ever so slightly, his black hair (also a wig) bouncing with the movement.

He'd already told me what to do back at the hotel. I was meant to hide out of sight whilst he went to find the big sheet of plywood he said he'd seen propped in the doorway of another mausoleum. I couldn't recall seeing it, but he'd been certain. Apparently, it was fairly normal for some of them to be blocked off like that which sounded pretty weird to me. Surely, they needed more than just some wood to keep people from going inside. Mitch had said that it wasn't even attached to anything, just propped in the doorway. That wouldn't stop anyone!

We started along the path towards our goal, my heart racing in my ears, and I glanced around once more. The graveyard was empty, silent apart from the wisps of music that snaked out of the surrounding buildings.

I clenched my hands into my fists, staring back at the approaching structure.

This is what I wanted. I'd made up the entire world just so that I could become a treasure hunter. I couldn't chicken out now.

I darted into the stone building, throwing myself against the wall and waiting for someone to spot me. But, nothing happened. No voices shouted that I was somewhere I shouldn't be, Sterling's people weren't already waiting for me there. The world was silent apart from the steady pace of Mitch's footsteps pacing away from me.

I didn't dare move, my eyes fixed on the duffle bag

that Mitch had tucked just inside the door, as I heard footsteps approach. My hands clenched into fists, even though I knew it was most likely just Mitch, and a sigh slipped out of my mouth when he finally appeared in the doorway.

What would I have done if it were someone else? I'd never even punched anyone, not really! I mean, I'd been to karate classes when I was a kid but this felt far too real. I'd never punched anyone without gloves on!

"You okay, kid?" he breathed as he struggled to prop the weathered sheet of wood into position before hissing in pain and snatching one hand back. "Lousy piece of crap. A damn splinter."

I stepped forwards, my legs finally working.

"Can I help?" I whispered.

He shook his head, managing to balance the sheet in a way that blocked us from view.

"There we go," he said before looking down at his palm and picking at it. "Got the little bugger!"

He grinned at me before turning towards the wall.

I followed him towards it, squinting in the low light.

"This is going to be a bit of a nightmare," Mitch warned me, glancing up at the metal bars above us. "This damn place don't have a roof. I mean… I get why they did it. The houses around here will be able to see right into this place, but it makes things more tricky for us. We can't use a torch. Too obvious. Sky's pretty clear though. Should be able to make do with just the moon."

I glanced up at the visible sky distrustingly.

Mitch might have said that it was pretty clear, but the clouds floating lazily across it made me worried.

"Okay, kid. Do you want to be the one to hold the weeds back or do you want to chisel away the plaster?"

I glanced at the thick vines that curtained the back wall. Holding them back sounded a little boring, but I'd only ever used a chisel a couple of times in school and that never went well for me. The table mirror we'd been forced to make in Woodwork was forever wonky and lopsided.

My dad still displayed it proudly, of course, but I'd heard my mom telling him to just bin it.

"I'll hold the weeds," I decided.

"You sure?" Mitch asked, carefully unzipping his bag and retrieving the chisel. "This is way more fun."

I shook my head, not wanting to say anything more.

"Alright, I'll try real hard not to stab you in the hand."

Mitch grinned at me before walking towards the wall and pulling the leather sheath off the chisel.

I rushed to follow him, trying not to think about whether or not I'd be able to feel pain in this fantasy, and gathered as many of the weeds as I could in my hands. I pulled them gently to the side, standing back against the wall so that Mitch had more space to work.

Carefully, he slid the tip of the chisel under the loose edge, putting one hand against the plaster to catch it as he slowly levered it off. The small but sharp crack made me jump and my head whipped towards the doorway.

"It's okay," Mitch whispered quietly as he lowered the hand-sized slab to the floor before straightening and sliding the tool back into place.

The process was painfully slow and made my skin crawl, not just because of the bugs that repeatedly landed on my hands and arms. It took everything in me not to shake them off, push Mitch out the way and grab the folded pickaxe that I knew was in his bag. That would have done the job in minutes.

More than once we had to pause as a cloud drifted in front of the moon, plunging the mausoleum into near total darkness, and each time I wanted to scream. We were taking too long.

"There it is," Mitch breathed, talking for the first time in a while.

I leaned forwards, trying to see around him just as another cloud went in front of the moon.

"What is it?" I whispered, not willing to wait to find out.

"I don't know yet, but I've done this enough to know that we've found what we're looking for."

I glanced up at the hazy moon.

"Do we have to wait for the moon to come back out or can you keep going?" I asked impatiently.

Mitch chuckled under his breath.

"That ain't a good idea. Anything could be in this

thing and I really wouldn't be surprised if there was a trap."

I edged slightly further away, my back bumping against the rough stone bricks.

"What kind of trap?"

"Eh, could be anything. I'm not entirely sure about the age because, obviously, this thing was created in the... probably seventeenth century? I reckon it was repaired after some time in the eighteenth or nineteenth, maybe later, so this thing could have been put in anytime in those centuries or maybe after so..." he paused, seeming to be thinking hard. "It could be anything from a simple spring-gun or some kind of explosive but, of course, the plastering on this thing was pretty crappy, so it's possible that whatever was inside it has rusted to the point of no return."

"Does that happen often?" I asked as the cloud finally moved out of the way and I could see the wall again.

Mitch had managed to remove most of the plaster and I could just about see the corner of a hole behind it but the rest was still covered.

"Eh, quite often. A lot of the things I work with are a minimum of a couple hundred years old, normally a few centuries or older. They didn't always have the time or material to make sure everything got sealed off from the elements, and you know how rain causes metals to rust and wood to bloat and... Ah, there we go."

Mitch was silent for a moment as he pried more plaster away from the hole, revealing a small, varnished dark wood box that was jammed into the space.

"Just a little more and we'll be able to start working on the traps. God, there was this hellish one we accidentally triggered on Suakin Island about ten, fifteen years back. It was meant to shoot wooden spears at anyone who triggered it but it had been destroyed by rain over the years and the spears pretty much crumbled into splinters which then were baked by the sun and honestly, I think they did more damage than the spears would have."

My mouth fell open.

"What happened?" I gasped.

"Well, I noticed the holes in the wall about half a second before they fired so I was able to get in front of the kid and turn my back so it wasn't too bad. I don't think Zaq enjoyed picking a hundred odd shards of wood out my back though. So much for the Port of Good Hope. That Ptolemy was either an idiot or had a great sense of irony because that place was nothing but a pain. Ah ha! This should do it!"

There was another soft crack and a puff of dust erupted outwards, catching in my lungs. I hugged the vines as tightly as I could with one hand and brought the other to my mouth to smother the cough that was threatening to escape.

"Sorry, kid!" Mitch whispered with a grimace. "Should have warned you to hold your breath. I'll remember next time!"

My eyes watered as my chest strained with the effort to hold back a cough. Panic at the thought of coughing or sneezing and drawing attention to us was almost strong enough for me to leave the fantasy but I knew all that awaited me in the real world was my empty bedroom. I swallowed the cough down and blinked a few times to clear my vision before focusing on the wooden box.

"Ah, look at this thing. I bet you that's a release switch underneath there," Mitch said, leaning closer. "See under the box?"

He moved back slightly so that I could see.

There was a crumbling small sheet of wood that had been stained white. It would have blended into the bottom of the brick if it hadn't been so worn and rain damaged.

"Yeah?" I said.

"So, the way release switches work is there's a mechanism under there that activates when a weight is taken off it. I assume this one activated a while ago though because normally they use metal springs and the likes so it should be entirely corroded. Hopefully."

I paused at the uncertainty in his tone.

"Hopefully? What do release switches normally do when they are triggered?" I asked.

"Ah, I assume this one was designed to injure whoever steals whatever is in the box so... we'll find out. Step back and hold your breath."

I did as he instructed, moving as far back as I could whilst still holding the vines out of the way, and squeezed my lips together tightly.

He gently nudged the edge of the wooden base with his chisel.

I waited anxiously for something dramatic to happen.

"Huh," he said quietly.

"What?" I asked quickly.

He cocked his head and leaned in again.

"I reckon it's triggered already. See how it's slightly higher at the front?" He pointed with the chisel. "That means something isn't right. We'll need to squish it down just a bit to be able to get the box out. It's jammed in there, see?"

I squinted at the box.

It did appear to be jammed into the brick-shaped hole, but Mitch was right. If the base came down a little, he'd be able to get it out.

He stepped away from the wall and turned towards me.

"Alright. What I'm going to do is lift the front edge a little more and shine a light in there. Nothing too bright, but enough to just get a peek at what's happening. I want you to move back as far as possible and hold your breath again, okay?"

I nodded.

"I might need you to grab tools from the bag whilst I'm doing this. If you're not sure what I mean by anything, just ask," he said with an easy smile as he walked towards his bag and crouched down in front of it.

I nodded again, but worry spread through me. He was so relaxed, too relaxed really. If I were talking about traps and bombs and other stuff that could kill me, I would not be so unbothered.

I watched as he slipped the chisel back into its sheath and started rooting around in the bag. He pulled out a couple of knives, sliding them out of their leather covers to check something before finally settling on one that was entirely flat from the tip to the end of the handle.

He grinned at it widely before moving back toward the wall.

"Okay, ready?" he asked, waiting for me to nod before slowly sliding the blade under the box.

My body froze and tension thrummed within me as Mitch slowly started to press down until the box moved away from the roof of the hole. The shiny, slightly tacky looking coating on the box was covered in dust and lightly dented from where it had been resting against the brick for so long but apart from that, it didn't look damaged.

"Ah, fuck. I need another tool. Can you have a look in the bag? You're looking for something that kinda looks like if tweezers and pliers had a baby that was a giant," Mitch said, looking back at me.

I hurried towards the bag, his instructions playing over in my head as panic gripped me. What if I took too long or gave him the wrong thing and everything exploded and he died?

What if I died? I mean, I'd been told or had heard somewhere that if I died in a dream, I could die in real life but this wasn't exactly a dream. Sure, I was in bed and resting in real life but I was in control. I had to survive... right?

My hands closed around rubber handles and I pulled the tool out. It looked like tweezers but longer and wider with wooden grips. The tips were angled slightly and opened as my hands tightened on the handles.

"Is this it?" I hissed, turning towards him.

"You got 'em! Bring them here!"

I did as he asked, holding them out to him before realising that one of his hands was holding the knife and I wasn't sure if he'd be able to use the tweezer thing single handed.

"Hold them for just a second, okay?" he asked as he reached into his pocket for a small flashlight.

He held it in his mouth and twisted the base causing it to tick softly before pulling it back out and pointing it towards the hole.

The light was dim, barely even there, but in the dark night, it was blinding. He lifted the knife slightly, pushing the top of the box back up into the top of the hole again.

"Hmm," he muttered softly. "That looks like it's rusted through. Shouldn't be a problem."

He flicked the flashlight off again and shoved it back into his pocket.

Even with his reassurances, I was worried but I knew I had to trust him. It was either that or leaving and I didn't want to do that. I had nowhere else to go, not really.

"Okay, kid," he started, looking up at me again. "Do you want to hold the knife or get the box out?"

I stared wide-eyed at him.

Both sounded terrifying. If I slipped holding the knife, the trap could explode, even though Mitch seemed pretty sure that it was safe, but if I slipped or my hand shook when I using the tool, I could set it off anyway. But, that's why I was here in this fantasy. I wanted to do something scary and fun.

"The knife," I decided.

Surely it was easier to just hold a knife still?

"Good call."

He cocked his head towards it, changing his grip so he was supporting it with just two fingers and making space for me total hold.

I slipped my hand around the strangely shaped knife, the flat edges feeling weird in my palm.

"When I start to move the box," he started, taking the tool from me, "the weight is going to change on the knife so you'll need to keep an eye on it and readjust when needed. If you're not sure or need me to help, just say and I will."

I nodded, not taking my eyes off the knife as my heart started to speed up.

Mitch slowly began to slip the tips of the tweezers into place before loosening his grip so that the tool gripped the box.

"Ready?" he asked.

I nodded again, too scared to speak.

Painfully slow, he started to pull. The box inched forwards, the weight coming off the back of the knife as it did. I felt like I couldn't breathe as Mitch gently wrapped his fingers around the box and abandoned the tool.

Whatever coating the box had on it made things more difficult. It was tacky, almost gummy. It kept catching on the knife, and every time my heart leapt into my throat.

"So close," Mitch promised. "Just a little bit… ah!"

He grinned triumphantly as the box slid free.

"What about this?" I asked as he set the box softly on the floor behind us.

"Don't worry, I got it," he said with a smile, reaching out for the knife.

A bang sounded so loudly that I opened my eyes and sat up, staring around my room in terror as my heart galloped.

"What the fuck?" my mom screamed from downstairs.

CHAPTER THIRTEEN

"That bitch!" Mom screamed.

My body tensed as fear speared my heart and I strained to hear more, needing to know if she was talking about me.

My dad's quiet rumbling voice sounded, but I couldn't pick out any of his words.

"She knows! She knows to make sure the dishwasher is on!" she cried, her words slurred.

Tears started to form in the corners of my eyes and I pressed my fist against my lips, trying to hold back all sound as my dad said something else.

I could have sworn I'd turned it on after I made food. Did I not?

"I don't care that she's been at school today! Do you not think that I've had a busy day too? Do you think that I sit around on my ass all day?" she demanded.

A shaking breath slipped from my lips as my hands trembled.

"I don't care how late it is! She doesn't deserve to sleep! She should come down here and clean up the mess she made!"

A door slammed and I jumped, terrified tears slipping from my eyes and trailing down the sides of my face.

I knew she probably wouldn't hurt me but when she got like this, she was terrifying. My breath came shallowly and quickly as I heard footsteps starting on the stairs.

"No! Get out of my way!" she screamed. "You always do this. You always protect her. She's not a baby anymore and you're meant to be on my side! You're my husband, that means you support me, not her!"

"I know, I do," my dad said, his voice now audible as they argued from the stairway. "Here, let me make you dinner! Or, I can order you something! What do you want? I'll get you anything!"

More tears slipped free as I waited for Mom's response, desperately trying to pull myself together in case she came in.

"I want your daughter not to take me for granted and to stop treating this house like a fucking hotel!"

She always called me his daughter when she was annoyed at me. It was like I was such a disappointment to her that she couldn't even bear to accept that she was my mom.

Maybe I was.

"I know, I'll talk to her in the morning," he lied.

He wouldn't. He tried to shield me from Mom, not that it worked.

"Ha!" she barked out. "Fat lot of good that'll do! That child can't remember a simple fucking instruction even if it's written in front of her!"

"I'll talk to her," Dad repeated, firmer this time. "Let's go downstairs. Why don't you put on that movie you wanted to watch and I'll make something for you to eat?"

There was another bang from the stairs before footsteps started to retreat downwards. Loud, stomping ones.

I slipped out of my bed, rubbing my face to erase all traces of tears even as my hands shook. I peered out into the hall through the crack in my door, checking to see if my mom was still out there before pulling the door open a little wider.

My dad stood on the stairs, still in his work suit, his shoulders slumped.

"Dad," I hissed as loudly as I dared.

He spun around, glancing down the stairs before racing towards me as silently as he could.

"Darling, what are you still doing up?" he whispered, reaching quickly and wrapping his arms around me.

"I'm sorry," I whispered, trying not to let any more tears fall. "I thought I'd turned it on."

"Oh, it's not your fault, sweetheart. You know how

she gets when she hasn't eaten all day and has been drinking."

I clutched at him tightly, guilt wracking me despite his words. I wanted to apologise more. To tell him I was sorry for not turning on the dishwasher, for not making sure Mom had eaten and for not hiding her half-empty wine bottle whilst she was asleep so she wouldn't finish it when she woke up. It was more than that though. I wanted to apologise for being a terrible daughter and a bad person, but I couldn't get the words out.

I wanted to but I couldn't. If I started to say them, they'd feel too real.

My dad pulled back slightly and smiled at me.

"I should go downstairs, kiddo. Make sure your mom gets some food in her before she falls asleep again."

I nodded, not quite trusting my words.

"Go back to sleep, okay?" he said.

I nodded again, swallowing hard before saying, "Good luck down there."

He smiled at me, his eyes crinkling around the edges.

"Don't worry about me. I can handle your mom."

Over his shoulder, my eyes found the badly plastered holes in the wall on the stairs. At least there were no new ones tonight? She must not have hit the wall too hard.

It wasn't that I didn't believe him, I just worried.

I nodded and pulled away.

"Let me know if you need a hand with anything?" I said, knowing that he wouldn't.

"Of course. Get some sleep, you have school in the morning."

I nodded and slipped back into my room as my dad walked reluctantly back down the corridor, stopping to shoot me a tired grin over his shoulder. I let the door slip shut behind me, plunging me into darkness as I leaned back against the door and slid to the floor.

My hands clutched my knees to my chest, digging my blunt fingernails in as tightly as I could. The fear suddenly hit me again, and my chest tightened as burning tears threatened to overwhelm me once more.

I felt powerless, scared, and hopeless. I hated living there, unable to ever do anything right and having to be careful not to set my mom off every time I spoke or did anything. The smallest mistake sent her reeling and in a horrible mood for days. There was no escape.

I was trapped.

I dropped my head back against the door, silent sobs shaking my body. I had at least three more years stuck in the house until I could go to university and never look back.

If I got in, that is.

I wasn't sure I was going to be able to and the idea of that made my tears stream faster. Everything was so scary and fast and overwhelming and I just didn't want to deal with any of it. I didn't want to deal with anything! I wanted to go back to my fantasy where I was safe and with someone who didn't scream at me whenever I made a simple mistake.

Letting out a slower, trembling breath I realised I could just go back to my fantasy. There was nothing stopping me.

My eyes slowly shut and I breathed out, opening them again once a wave of vertigo hit me. My hand tightened around the flat knife, the edges biting into my hand as I fought not to move it at all.

"Okay, slowly let go," Mitch instructed.

I forced my fingers to open as the world stopped spinning quite so quickly.

Mitch took hold of the knife, carefully edging me out the way.

"What do we do now?" I asked. "Should I grab a rock or something to weigh it down?"

Mitch sent me a grin that felt so reminiscent of my dad that my stomach dropped.

"Nah, that rarely works. It might work for one this old, but with the newer ones, they are so carefully calibrated that we'd need to get the weight and the distribution perfect otherwise… boom."

"So, what do we do?"

"You move back to the other wall and I'm going to test a theory."

I started edging back before he's even spoken, almost tripping over the box as I did.

"Which is?" I asked.

"That this trap has already fired. The springs look

rusted and there's a residue that's stained the bottom of the box, but we're about to find out."

Ever so slowly, Mitch lifted the knife away from the box. I held my breath, panic making me lightheaded.

"There we go," Mitch whispered victoriously. "Guess I've learnt something in my twenty or thirty or whatever years on the job."

He turned towards me with a grin which I returned cautiously, guilt still worming into my heart.

I looked down at the unassuming box between us.

"Now, what? Do we take it and run or…"

"Gotta open it here," Mitch replied, moving towards the box and crouching.

"Why?"

"Dumb mistake I made when I was a kid. I found an artefact similar to this one, threw it in my bag, and left. Turns out it was a decoy and it exploded the back carriage of a train. I was damn lucky I chose that moment to go get food."

I eyed the box suspiciously.

"It was a bomb?"

"Oh yeah. I didn't think something that old would have so much firepower, but now I know better. I don't reckon this one is a bomb though, it's too light. Want to come have a look?" he asked.

I nodded, moving closer before shooting a look towards the doorway.

The graveyard seemed quiet, not that I could see

much around the wooden sheet Mitch had propped in the doorway, but it felt like we were safe.

I dropped to my knees, the dry mud feeling strangely warm through my leggings, and stared at the box.

"So, see how dusty the box is?" Mitch asked, running the knife across it in demonstration.

"Yeah?"

"That's because it's coated in wax to seal it and protect whatever is inside. It's a good idea but it also means that small particles, like dust, stick to it easier."

Mitch scored a line in the top of the box before starting to pry the wax off.

I watched carefully, trying to memorise everything he said and did so that I could be more useful next time instead of just watching.

"How much of the wax do we need to get off?" I asked.

Mitch cocked his head slightly, glancing over my shoulder and eyeing the doorway before responding.

"Not much. Just enough to work out how this box opens. I reckon the top just swings up."

I nodded, continuing to watch him work silently.

He methodically cut into the wax, prying it up and peeling as much as would come off before throwing it into the duffle bag.

"Why are you putting the wax in the bag? Surely it'll make things in there sticky," I asked.

"Gotta leave this place looking as clean and not suspicious as possible. The vines should be thick enough that no one really looks too hard at this but when they do, they should just assume it's vandals and plaster it back up," he said without looking up.

"What about the trap?"

"Eh, people are dumb. It should be safe. I reckon whoever they call in will just remove it without even working out what it was meant to do. There we go!"

Mitch peeled a chunk of wax back, revealing the entirety of the top of the box and some of the edge. I started to lean forwards, trying to see more and wanting to know what was inside.

"Careful not to lean over the box. If there's a spring dart or something in there, you do not want it to hit you," he warned.

I moved back immediately, having not even considered the possibility of being shot in the face with something from that small box. It didn't look like it was big enough to hold a dart or anything like that. It was only about the height of my middle finger, surely that wouldn't be big enough.

Mitch carefully wedged the tip of his knife under the lip of the box, his eyes darting up to check on me, before he slowly began to lever it up. A sharp, splintering crack tore through the air and I winced, my eyes hunting for the source of the sound, certain that it was Sterling's people and that they'd started firing at us.

"Sorry, should have warned you they nailed the lid

down," Mitch whispered after a while.

I rested one hand on my racing heart in an attempt to still it.

"I thought we'd been caught!" I whispered back.

Mitch grinned at me apologetically.

"Not just yet, but look at this."

He pried the lid up further and tilted the box towards me.

Hesitantly, I leaned forwards to get a closer look at whatever was inside, confusion washing through me.

"A key?" I asked, staring at the elaborate, but somewhat disappointing golden key that rested in the bottom of the box.

"A key," Mitch said with a grin.

"Is that it?"

"It's all we need."

A stone skipped along a path behind us and the grin dropped from Mitch's face.

He lifted one finger to his lips, gesturing for me to be silent, before reaching out and tucking the key into the inner pocket of his jacket. Slowly, he lifted the box, placing it into the duffle bag and zipping it shut as quietly as possible.

I couldn't move, I was frozen in fear as I strained to hear more.

There was movement outside, that much was certain. Quiet, muffled footsteps sounded occasionally as someone, more than one person, walked across the grass.

I wanted to ask Mitch what to do, but I knew that any noise could shatter the silence and we would be attacked.

Mitch's eyes found mine again and he brought his finger to his lips again before gesturing for me to stand. I started to move as slowly as I could, each rustle of my clothes horrifically magnified until I was standing.

Mitch padded towards the door, bringing his face to the small space so he could peer out. One hand tucked the duffle carefully over his shoulder as the other reached for the gun he had holstered.

"It's not them," he breathed, causing a sigh to slip out of my mouth as he let go of the gun again. "As soon as this couple leaves, we go too. Stay vigilant. Just because we haven't seen them yet doesn't mean they aren't here."

I nodded, slightly comforted by the fact that they weren't there yet, but still terrified by the concept of them appearing.

It's my fantasy, I tried to convince myself. I get to decide if they show up or not.

"Okay, on the count of three, we're going to go. Walk straight to the car and if I say run, run. Don't stop for anything or anyone. One, two, three!"

He lifted the plywood sheet out of the way, propping it on the outside of the mausoleum and marching quickly.

I hurried to keep up, keeping my head forwards, but I couldn't stop my eyes from roaming. The graveyard was empty. A little too empty. There was absolutely no one there and no noise. Even the music from the surrounding houses had stopped.

I was painfully aware of eyes on me. I wasn't sure where they were, but they pricked into my skin, making me itch.

"Mitch," I breathed. "I don't think we're alone."

We reached the path on the other side of the grass, turning towards the gates and speeding up.

"We aren't."

It took all of my strength not to burst into a run as footsteps started behind me.

They weren't close but they were moving faster than us. They'd catch up.

"When we turn the corner, run. Get to the car and get in as fast as possible."

I nodded, my heart stuttering in my chest.

The corner wasn't far, but it felt like an eternity before we reached it. I burst forwards, sprinting down the street and almost knocking a woman over. I was past her before I even heard her shout, blindly sprinting towards the car we'd left earlier, aware of Mitch running ahead of me.

He was faster than me. He was faster and he was going to leave me there.

I pushed myself to move even quicker, hearing another shout behind me as someone else ran into the woman but I couldn't look back.

In front of me, the car beeped and Mitch ripped the

door open. I flung myself towards the door, my sweaty hands slipping on the door handle as I finally let myself glance back.

"Fuck," I muttered, looking back at the door and hauling it open.

They were too close, they were going to reach us before we could escape.

I threw myself into the seat, slamming the door behind me.

"Strap in!" Mitch shouted, not waiting for me to follow his instructions before he pulled the car out of the spot, narrowly missing an oncoming car.

I grappled with the seatbelt, my hands shaking and barely able to get it in.

"Are they following us?" I asked, my breath coming in pants as I turned and looked over my shoulder before checking the mirrors.

"Yep," Mitch said grimly. "Those assholes. How did they find me this time?"

I sunk back in my seat, my heart racing and sweat caking my entire body.

"What do we do?" I cried, my voice high pitched with fear.

"We lose them. We ain't going back to the hotel, I got a plane waiting for us near enough, but we need to get rid of them before then."

Mitch weaved through the streets, overtaking cars, his eyes bouncing between his mirrors.

"Get rid of them? How?" I asked, my voice still squeaky.

"We need to lose them, get them stuck in the city or lost. Grab my phone for me, will you?"

I looked around the car frantically, my eyes landing on the smartphone in the cup holder.

"Got it!" I shouted, fear making my hands weak.

"Find the app Red, Yellow, Green."

I scrolled through the many pages, landing on one that had the icon of a traffic light.

"Okay," I said as I clicked on it and waited impatiently for it to load. "Now, what?"

A map appeared on the screen, showing our location and the streets around us.

"Click on the menu button on the top left and find the bit that says 'User's programmes" and select the third one down."

I did as he said.

"Green ahead, red behind?" I read, wanting to make sure before I selected the programme, just in case I accidentally broke something.

"That's it! Click it and then when the popup appears click 'Execute'," Mitch instructed, skilfully weaving through the city.

I did as he said, my sweaty fingers leaving a smear on the screen.

"Okay, done."

"Great!" Mitch said with a grin as he glanced in the

mirror again. "Now I want you to go to messages and start a new one to someone called 'Pilot Lauren'."

I closed the app, glancing in the mirrors at the cars that were following us closely, before opening his messages and typing in her name.

"Okay, what do you want me to say?"

"Coming in hot, Sterling's on my ass, and I got a stowaway." He paused for a moment as he swerved around a car, narrowly missing it, and sped through a yellow light. "Should be at the farm in about… thirty minutes. Will lose them by then. Got that?"

I finished typing and scanned back over it quickly to make sure I hadn't missed anything.

"Think so."

"Great," Mitch replied, accelerating even faster as we started to get into a slightly less busy area. "How many cars do you see following us?"

My eyes snapped to the wing mirror.

Two cars weaved in and out of the traffic behind us, mimicking our movements, but there was another one. It was slightly further back but catching up quickly. They were all different models and colours but they were defi-nitely all following us.

"Three."

"Good. You caught the grey Audi at the back?" Mitch asked with a glance in the mirror.

I nodded before realising he was focusing on driving.

"Yeah," I said before his phone buzzed in my hands.

"The pilot's responded. They said 'okay, will warm up the engines. Location?' What do you want me to say?"

"Hold on," Mitch said before cutting in front of a car and swerving down a side street. "Say 'no clue, will know once we're in the air, but prep for long distance'."

I typed it back and hit send, glancing in the mirrors again.

"Long distance?" I asked, a tiny bit of anxiety gnawing at my stomach. "How far do you think we'll be going?"

CHAPTER FOURTEEN

I stared blankly at the board at the front of the class-room, trying to focus on what Mr Parsons was saying, but my mind didn't want to stay on one topic for too long. I was exhausted. I'd barely managed to get any sleep and, when I did, I woke up stiff and uncomfortable after passing out against my bedroom door. Even if I had been able to sleep properly, I'd probably still be tired. I always was.

There was a constant, ever-present fog of weariness that infiltrated every aspect of my life. Well, almost every aspect. I'd never actually noticed it when I was with Mitch, but that made sense. It was a fantasy, nothing more than a dream. Why would I be tired?

"Okay, turn to page thirty-two!" Mr Parsons instructed the four people who were still listening to him.

He'd separated the class out into those who he thought would probably do well in their GCSEs and therefore might study Maths at A levels and those who wouldn't. Most of us were at the back of the classroom but there were a few people who were undecided, myself included.

I wasn't really sure how I would do or what I wanted to do, so I settled for sitting next to Phoebe and staring at the teacher, hoping something would sink in.

My mind threatened to wander away again though, teasing me with a taste of that familiar dizziness that always accompanied my daydreams nowadays. I wasn't worried about it anymore, I almost yearned for it. But, I had to focus.

I needed to think about my future. The teachers were right. It was important.

But... I had left Mitch in the midst of our escape from Sterling's people. I wanted to know what the key was for and how he planned to get away. The desire to know more itched. It pulled at my concentration and tempted me.

I fought back halfheartedly. I did want to stay in the real world but...

"There we go!" Mitch cried victoriously. "Latch Farm airfield and without even getting into a gun fight!"

I glanced at the mirrors, double-checking to make sure we weren't being followed, before my eyes fell on the plane idling on the runway ahead of us. It wasn't a huge plane, but my heart thrummed with excitement.

Two people waited on the tarmac in front of the

plane, chatting as we pulled closer.

"Well, look what the cat dragged in," one of them called, putting her hands on her hips as we climbed out of the car. "Been a minute since I saw you last, Mitch."

He smirked at her, slamming the door shut and retrieving his bag from the boot.

"Well, don't you look great? Red hair this time, huh?" he asked, nodding towards her.

She grinned and tossed her long ponytail over her shoulder. The vibrant, deep red shade caught the midday sunlight, shining beautifully.

I was immediately jealous. I wanted long, flowing red hair. She clearly dyed it, and it was so pretty.

"Of course. Told you I'd work my way through the rainbow next!" she said with a grin.

"It looks great," he replied genuinely before turning towards the guy who was standing in front of us. "Oscar, been a while, how have you been?"

The light-haired, extremely attractive man gave Mitch a smile.

"I'm still alive," he joked in a deep, gravely voice. "How about you? You look like you're just about hanging in there?"

Mitch snorted and threw the keys to him which he caught in one hand.

"I'm barely clinging to life, clearly," he replied in a flat tone. "Crap, I didn't introduce you. Lauren, Oscar, this is Grace, my latest stowaway."

They both looked at me and I tried not to cringe away from the attention.

"Nice to meet you," Lauren said with a smile.

"Good luck keeping up with this old codger," Oscar teased.

"Nice to meet you both," I answered with an awkward sidelong glance at Mitch.

He smiled supportively at me before looking at Oscar again.

"Did you bring a spare licence plate with you?" he asked. "There weren't too many cameras along the route, but you never know when Sterling's twats have hacked the ANPR system."

"No, because this is the first time I've ever pretended to steal a car," Oscar said, rolling his eyes and hooking a thumb into the backpack on his shoulder. "I got everything I need, as always. Couple different licence plates, Chemgene to get rid of all of your leftover DNA and an incinerator already burning somewhere."

Mitch shook his head with a slight smile.

"Thanks, mate. You know where you're dropping the car when you're done?" he asked.

"Of course. Already memorised the route."

"I don't know why I doubt you."

"Me either. Next time you're in the country give me a little more notice, we can grab a drink," Oscar offered with another handsome smile.

I almost wanted to give up on that fantasy then and

there just to start a new one where I was the same age as him. He looked mid-twenties. That wasn't too old.

"Sounds good. Take care of her?" Mitch asked, sounding slightly desperate.

Panic shot through me and my head whipped around to Mitch as the fear that he was leaving me with Oscar gripped me. I wouldn't have minded spending a little more time with Oscar, even if the age difference made me uncomfortable, but the idea of Mitch leaving me behind made me breathless.

He wasn't looking at me though, his eyes were fixed on the car, longing evident on his face.

I smirked at the realisation that he didn't want to leave the car behind.

"I'll take good care of her, I promise."

Mitch heaved a heavy sigh and looked back towards Lauren.

"Alright," he said reluctantly. "Let's get in the air."

I looked away from Mitch to examine the plane cautiously.

It was much smaller than any plane I had ever been on, but it looked cool. It was silver with a pointed nose that felt far too long for the rest of the plane.

"It's an Embraer Phenom one-hundred," Lauren said with a grin. "Tiny little thing, but big enough for the three of us."

I smiled back at her distractedly, worry starting to edge its way back into my heart.

The plane looked like a strong breeze might knock it over. I couldn't imagine it hurtling through the sky.

"Need a hand with your bags?" Oscar asked us, breaking through my worries.

"If you don't mind?" Mitch replied. "Got some in the front and back."

Oscar nodded, moving silently towards the boot and opening it. The muscles in his arms strained as he picked up some bags and started to bring them towards the hatch Lauren had opened under one of the engines. I blinked, realising I was staring at him instead of helping and rushed towards Mitch.

"Can I help?" I asked quickly, my face heating up.

"Sure thing, kiddo. Bring these to Lauren, will you?" he said, passing two backpacks to me.

I nodded, lifting one onto my shoulder, and traipsing towards Lauren. I handed them over with a smile before joining Mitch by the car again.

"Anything else?" I asked him, watching as he pulled up the carpeting in the boot.

"Nah, that should be it. Feel free to go in and get comfy, we've got quite the journey ahead of us."

I nodded and turned towards the plane.

I still didn't trust it, but I trusted Mitch and he didn't seem to have a problem with it. I climbed the stairs carefully, not feeling comfortable with how much they bounced under my weight, before stopping just inside the cabin and staring around.

It was even smaller inside and the cockpit led straight into the rest of the plane without even a wall separating it. Four white leather seats with built-in seatbelts pointed at each other. One side had a table between them, but the other didn't.

I hesitated, looking between the two sides. Should I sit facing the pilot or away from them? Did I want to have a table in front of me or would Mitch need it? And did the door at the back of the plane lead to a toilet because, if not, I had some concerns.

The plane bounced slightly as Mitch climbed the stairs behind me.

"Get comfy, these two take a while to say goodbye," he said, gesturing out the door behind him at Lauren and Oscar who were locked in a passionate embrace.

His hand cupped her cheek as he kissed her deeply.

"Urm, which side do you want?" I asked, tearing my eyes away from them as jealousy flared in my stomach.

I didn't want to be kissing him specifically, despite how hot he was. I think I just wanted someone to kiss me with as much fervency.

Maybe, one day.

"Mind if I take the table?" he asked, lifting the black case that I knew held his computer. "I gotta work out where we're going."

"Oh, sure," I said, quickly slipping into the other seat facing the back of the plane and doing the seatbelt up.

Mitch buckled the briefcase into the chair next to me before sitting on the other side of the table so he was at a diagonal to me.

He craned his head to look around me out the window.

"Are they still going at it?" he asked before answering his own question. "Yup. Man, they do this every time."

He leaned back in his chair and looked at the ceiling with a heavy sigh, a small smile playing on his lips. He clearly didn't mind it too much.

"Okay, kid, once they've finished doing what they're doing, we'll head out of here. When we're in the air, we can start to work out where we're going next and head that way. We'll likely have to stop somewhere to refuel because this thing can't make it too far, but we can shop for anything we need for the next location whilst Lauren is coordinating that," he explained.

Even if I had felt okay about flying in the tiny tin can before Mitch's speech, I certainly didn't after. The knowledge that the plane couldn't make it very far was something I could have done without.

"Does it make sense to start flying if we don't know where we're going? Like, what if we get up there and realise we're going the wrong direction and have to turn around, but run out of fuel?" I asked, my voice coming out a lot more high pitched than I meant it to.

Mitch shrugged.

"I mean, that is a possibility but there are airfields

close enough that it shouldn't be a problem and, if for some reason it is, we have parachutes, but we won't need them. Plus, that's a better option than sitting around and waiting for Sterling's people to hunt us down."

I swallowed, hating the idea of having to use a parachute, but hating the idea of finding out what Sterling's people would do to us more.

"What would they do?" I forced myself to ask. "If they did find us?"

Mitch cocked his head considering it.

"Well, there'd be a firefight and the plane would probably be damaged so we wouldn't be able to fly and my client would owe someone a lot of money," he started before pausing.

"And then?" I prompted.

"Well… if they managed to successfully capture us alive, they'd find the key and potentially torture us to find out where we were headed and what the next step is. Then, they'd either lock us up, abandon us somewhere, or take us with them to help them find the items we're looking for. I think I'm too useful to them for them to kill me. Unless, of course, Kurt is still leading this group in which case they'd kill us both and then take the key. That man hates me."

My mouth dropped open and I was at a loss for how to respond to him.

Sterling's people had felt like such an… abstract concept. I'd seen them in passing, heard about them like they were a boogey monster, but having Mitch calmly explain what they would do to use drove home just how real they were.

"Ready to go?" Lauren asked, bounding up the stairs behind us, her cheeks slightly flushed.

I nodded quickly.

"All ready. Mind heading south until I work it out?" Mitch asked.

"Alright, you know the drill; don't do anything dumb 'til we're cruising," she said, slamming the door shut with a heavy thud.

My breath started to come quickly as the engines quickly started, drowning out Lauren's hushed voice. Panic grew within me.

The plane was too small, the stakes too big, and we still didn't know where we were going.

It was a terrible idea.

The engines whined loudly, the noise only growing as we sped along the runway. I knew I was hyperventilating, but I couldn't stop myself. Nothing was helping, I couldn't get my breathing under control.

My eyes found Mitch who was watching me.

Copy, he mouthed before taking a deep, exaggerated breath.

I did as instructed, my instincts shouting at me to ignore him and continue to gulp in air.

He blew the air out, the noise drowned by the scream of the engines, but he still smiled at me supportively.

I continued to copy him, my hands digging into the armrests as the plane jolted into the air and I mentally tried to work out how much damage crashing into the ground at this speed would do to me.

But, thankfully, I didn't find out. The plane lifted into the air easily, rising to an altitude where the noise of the engines quietened almost too much.

"You okay?" Mitch asked once the fasten seatbelt light switched off.

I nodded tightly, not able to talk just yet.

"Don't worry, kid, I get it. I used to be scared of flying too. First ten or maybe even twenty flights I took, I cried the whole way. You do get used to it though. I actually quite enjoy them nowadays. There's something so peaceful about it," he said with a grin.

I smiled at him, my jaw locked tightly.

I wasn't sure what to say. I wasn't scared of flying, normally I was completely fine, it was the plane. That's what made me panic. That and the fact that the cockpit was attached to the rest of the plane. I don't know why that made me so anxious but it really did.

"So, want to have a look at the key?" he asked, loosening his seatbelt so that he could retrieve it.

I nodded before pausing.

"Am I okay to touch it? I won't break it, will I?" I asked.

"Nah," he said, holding it out towards me.

I leant forwards, stopped by my seatbelt, but just

about managed to close my fingers around it.

I sunk back in my seat, staring at the key. It was less disappointing now but I still expected more somehow. It was a dull, aged golden colour, and about the length of a pen, but that was it. I'd expected it to be more decorated or for something to be etched into it, but I couldn't see anything.

"Am I missing something? It's just a key, right?" I asked. "Could you not have just picked the lock?"

As soon as the words came out, I panicked. The question sounded so rude, but I just meant that it didn't look like a particularly complex key.

Mitch cocked his head and held his hand out for the key which I passed back to him immediately.

He examined the key, running his fingers along it and narrowing his eyes.

"I could have," he allowed. "I mean, this only has a couple of bits, barely any wards. It's pretty easy. But, I think the biggest reason is I don't know where we're going next. I mean, I have some suspicions but this key holds the answer."

"What are your suspicions?" I asked quickly, already fascinated.

My fear of flying was forgotten already, I was distracted by the mystery at hand.

"Mm," he said quietly, "could be a couple different places. I'm hoping it's somewhere nice and easy like France or Switzerland, but I doubt that. Turkey or

Greece is looking more realistic at the moment, perhaps Jerusalem. Somewhere linked to Christianity."

"Why?" I asked.

"Combination of a couple of things," he replied. "There was a very old reference to Dante in the last place I went to before coming to England."

"Dante?"

"Yes, La Divina Commedia." He looked up at me but I was still clueless. "Have you heard of Dante's Inferno? You know, 'abandon all hope ye who enter here' and all that?"

It was vaguely familiar, but I wasn't sure where I'd heard it.

"I think so?"

Mitch shook his head in mock exasperation.

"What are they teaching you in school? It's widely thought to be one of the greatest works of all time and you weren't taught about it?" he demanded.

"Don't think so," I said with an apologetic shrug.

"I'm not surprised, but I am disappointed in the school system. La Divina Commedia or the Divine Comedy is a poem written by Dante Alighieri back in the thirteen hundreds. It's a snapshot into how the world viewed the afterlife and explains the different sections, starting with Hell, Purgatory and then Heaven whilst discussing sin, virtue, truth and theology," Mitch explained, his eyes lighting up as he spoke.

I couldn't help but think if he were a teacher, he

would be my favourite. His enthusiasm reminded me of Mr Ray.

"Anyway, Dante had a huge impact on religion and culture as a whole and although he described his Hell or the Inferno, he didn't explain the specifics of it. There was an artist, Manetti, who actually did a series of woodcuts of how he imagined Hell to look, based on Dante's work, which of course was picked up by Galileo who favoured him due to the political situation of the time but that's neither here nor there. The floor of the abandoned castle I broke into before leaving Italy was actually a mosaic rendition of Manetti's overview of Hell."

My mind raced as I tried to keep up with what Mitch was saying but I felt like I was falling behind.

I wanted to ask him to repeat it but I was too embarrassed.

"Okay?" I said quietly, more to myself than him.

"I was so sad to blow that up," Mitch said with a sigh. "Such a beautiful building, it just needed a little love and care and it could have been restored so easily."

"Then, why did you?" I asked.

Mitch sighed heavily.

"It's the price of the job. Sometimes you have to ruin something beautiful to protect it and yourself. I just destroyed the room, but if Sterling's people had found it, they would have ripped the whole mansion apart. At least my way, most of it is still standing," he said sadly.

I opened myself to speak but Mitch gasped, looking down at the key.

A high pitched squeal came from it as he gently twisted the circular end of the key.

"Oh, ho. This really isn't just a key," he said as it slowly separated from the shaft.

I watched as he placed the end of the key on the table and glanced into the hollow shaft.

"Well, what do we have here?"

CHAPTER FIFTEEN

I must have fallen asleep at some point on the jet because I awoke to Mitch dropping into the seat in front of me.

"What do you know about the history of leprosy?" he asked, his eyes shining with excitement.

"Nothing," I said, blinking the sleep out of my eyes and looking around the jet.

The scrap of yellowed, old paper that Mitch had retrieved from the shaft of the key was still on the table but now, it was squished between two pieces of glass. His computer had been pushed back and his notebook was tossed down on the keyboard. An empty, crumpled can of energy drink lay next to it.

"What about leper colonies? Lazar houses?" he prompted, sounding incredulous.

I shook my head wordlessly.

His mouth dropped open in mock distress.

"What about leprosy? Hansen's disease? Nothing about

the transmission? Have you never even read the Bible?"

"Nope," I said. "It's mentioned in the Bible?"

He dropped his head back against the seat heavily.

"Alright, that does it. As soon as we land, I'm calling Betty. We're having health and disease, infectious disease, and epidemiology added to your syllabus. Classical studies too!"

I nodded, fascinated by the concept of all of those.

"Are they necessary to learn to be a treasure hunter?" I asked, kind of hoping they were.

"Of course! You'd be surprised how often people hide gold and other good stuff when they think there's a pandemic or the world is ending. Oh, wait! How's your knowledge of religion and previously predicted end times?"

"Umm... not good?" I said, truly having never considered it.

Mitch shook his head and leant across the aisle to grab his notebook, flicking to the back page and scribbling something down.

"Going to need to do something about that. Religious fanatics have some great relics and artefacts," he said with a grin. "Anyway, as I was saying, the history of leprosy!"

He stopped talking and cocked his head at me.

Wariness washed through me, accompanied by a gentle amount of panic.

"What?" I asked.

"You were sleeping," he said like he'd only just real-ised. "Do you need to go back to sleep? How many hours have you had recently? Not enough, right? Oh, damn. I need to do better. Alright, we're stopping in France in an hour or so. Go back to sleep, and I'll walk you through it then."

"What?" I asked, completely taken aback. "I'm fine! I'm awake! I want to know now!"

Mitch examined me carefully.

"Alright, but you're getting an early night tonight, you hear me?" he said, his eyes still narrowed.

I nodded, unable to help the grin that grew on my face.

He continued to watch me for a moment before letting out a heavy sigh and beginning his explanation.

"So, turns out I was wrong. I thought we'd be headed to a church or cathedral or some other religious build-ing, but boy was I wrong! Spinalonga. Dante's gate. The clues were there from the beginning and I missed every single one of them!" Mitch slapped his knee and leaned back again with a grin.

I had no clue how any of it was connected even though it was my brain making it up. I must have heard scraps of information from television shows or movies and stored them away. Either that, or it was all nonsense and Spinalonga didn't even exist. I wasn't sure.

"I don't get it," I admitted finally. "How are they connected?"

I was worried that Mitch would get annoyed or angry at my question, but he just grinned even wider, happy to explain what he'd worked out.

"So, I knew it was somehow connected to Dante before because of that place in Italy, but I didn't know anything more than that until this." He stood briefly to grab the pressed piece of paper and held it out to me.

I took it, the glass covering the paper making it surprisingly heavy, and examined it closely.

The scrap of paper had clearly been ripped off of a larger piece, the bottom edge was jagged and torn. The writing was elaborate, cursive, and hard to read, but I squinted at it nonetheless.

"Know what that is?" he asked.

I shook my head, not even sure where to start working it out.

"That is a ship's log. Well, part of one. Detailing the delivery of Hydnocarpus wightianus oil to an island. Spinalonga. It must be."

"Why?" I asked.

"Hydnocarpus wightianus oil or chaulmoogra oil was grown in India and used as a treatment of leprosy," he said.

"Okay?" I said slowly, things were becoming somewhat clearer in my head but I was still lost. "But, how does that connect to Spinalonga? You said something about Dante's gate?"

His face lit up.

"Yes, I did! So, I'm going to assume you know nothing about the island?"

"No, sorry," I said with a shake of my head.

"Don't apologise, kid!" he cried. "I don't think many people your age would know about it. Or even my age, actually..."

He trailed off, looking thoughtful for a moment.

"So... Spinalonga?" I prompted finally.

"Yes! So, the island was one of the last active leper colonies in Europe! I think there are a few still going in the world to this day, but none in Europe anymore, according to my research. Leprosy as a disease has existed pretty much forever. I mean, they've found significant evidence of it in skeletal remains from five hundred AD but there are descriptions of it even further back," he explained, his eyes alight as he spoke.

"What even is leprosy? I mean, I think I've heard someone say something about it making your fingers fall off, right?" I said, scraping the depths of my memory to find that scrap of information.

Mitch grinned at me.

"It can! It's known as a long-term infection which causes nerve damage, rashes, and a bunch of other bad symptoms. But, because people with it often lose feeling in their fingers and toes, they can get injured or get an infection, not notice, and then end up losing parts of those extremities because of it. Sometimes they don't even realise they've lost it until they spot the missing part lying around!" he explained a little too happily.

"Oh," I said quietly, trying to ignore the horrifying concept of losing a finger or a toe and not realising it.

"Yeah, pretty horrifying disease really."

"How do people get it?"

I just wanted to know if we were risking catching the disease by going to the island. Surely, we weren't. The island was probably abandoned now... right?

"That's an interesting question with a pretty varied answer. I think they traced an outbreak back in the medieval times to the trade of red squirrel fur, but generally, it's transmitted through extensive contact with someone who has the disease. I think it's something like ninety percent of those who get the bacteria don't even end up developing leprosy, but for those who do, the incubation period can be massively different. I mean, some people can have the disease for up to twenty years before it makes itself known."

I shuddered at that idea.

"You can have leprosy for twenty years before knowing it?" I asked, my tone horrified.

Mitch nodded, looking grim.

"Yeah, I think that's one of the reasons it's so stigmatised to this day. That, and how visible the disease is. People get pretty twitchy and cruel whenever someone has an obvious or visible sign of being different. And, you know, the Bible isn't too kind about it, like a lot of other things. If I remember correctly, it's described as a 'physical embodiment of sin and uncleanness' but I might be paraphrasing. Either way, people are dicks when it comes to the disease."

"But it isn't even that contagious?" I asked.

"Nope, and nowadays it's treated pretty easily. Just six months to two years of medication and then people with leprosy are no longer contagious and are only at a really low risk of relapse."

"Huh."

"Yeah, it's pretty simple! I think medication is generally given for free by the World Health Organisation too nowadays, but that doesn't stop people with the illness from being shunned and cast out. I like to think it's better now, but it's probably still pretty bad. Back at the beginning of the twentieth century, it was definitely worse though."

"Really?" I asked.

As horrific as Mitch's explanation was, it was also fascinating. I'd never learnt about it in school so I thought leprosy was an old disease. One that didn't exist anymore, like the plague.

"Yup. People were shipped off to Spinalonga and other leper colonies around the world and any trace of them was erased from history as much as possible. I mean, they had their property and assets taken, their citizenship revoked, and their names erased from the registries of their hometowns."

"Oh, wow. What happened when they got to

Spinalonga? Was it just an empty island or were there, like, hospitals and stuff for them there?" I asked hopefully, trying to push the image of a completely bare island from my mind.

Mitch gave me an almost sympathetic look.

"Kind of," he said carefully. "Well, once Epaminondas Remountakis arrived on the island some were built but before that, it was more of a… empty island where people waited for death. I mean, there were some houses and settlements there. Quite a lot was left over from the earlier days on the island where it was a military base and then a trade settlement but… they didn't have running water for the first thirty years or so."

"Why not?"

"It's a cold answer, but not enough people cared. Greece as a whole was struggling financially and was involved in quite a few different wars at the time so looking after people who they tried to pretend didn't exist wasn't exactly a high priority. I mean, they didn't even give the people there enough supplies to grow their own food so they were stuck relying on people from the nearby village who had set up a daily market on the island. But, of course, they weren't given enough money to afford adequate food or medicine."

"That's horrible. So, they were basically just expected to just suffer?" I said, disgusted.

"I mean, yeah. But, Spinalonga wasn't the only place with horrific conditions like that. Pretty much every leper colony was a dark place and every government liked to pretend they didn't exist. At least some people tried to help on Spinalonga and when Epaminondas Remountakis and some other highly educated individuals arrived on the island, things took a turn for the better."

"Oh, really?" I asked, my heart feeling a little lighter.

"Yeah. Epaminondas Remountakis started the Fraternity of the Sick and spent the rest of his life making things better for the people on the island. You know, sorting out the water situation, fixing up the houses, and making sure they had access to food, medicine, and entertainment. From what I've read, it became less of a prison and more of a community where kids who were born there could go to school and leave once their parents were cured."

A smile came over my face.

"I'm glad. But wait, where does Dante come into this?" I asked, finally remembering how we got onto the topic. "Also, why would whoever left the key in Scotland go to Spinalonga if they probably didn't have the money to pay for the oil?"

Mitch leant back in his seat, his eyes distant as he thought quickly.

"I mean, the first question is easy enough to answer. There was a tunnel onto the island for the lepers to use that is known as Dante's gate, but I assume that the sailors who left the ship's log and delivered supplies to the

Spinalonga must have had a reason for doing so. Probably a contract from someone who knew someone on the island. Rich people got leprosy too, so it would be possible that some wealthy merchant's kid or wife was sent to the island so they did what they could to make sure they were okay," he said finally.

"They'd be split up from their families?" I asked.

"Yup, pretty brutal situation all around. I'm sure some people tried to help those who'd been taken but generally, they just tried to forget that person existed."

I nodded, my mind distracted.

"That makes sense. So you reckon it's linked to some rich family or something? Like, that's how the sailors got access to Spinalonga?" I asked.

"Maybe. It could have been a few different things though. Maybe the sailors were just really good people who didn't like that people were suffering on the island with no help. They might have heard whispers of what was going on there or had personal connections to the people there or... more often than not in this job, it's linked to an underground ring."

I stared up at Mitch, taken aback.

"An underground ring?" I asked.

"Yeah. A hidden agenda, secret society, a good-hearted or maybe evil group of people doing something they're not meant to," Mitch suggested lightly.

"Do you come across a lot of them?"

Mitch laughed uproariously.

"Oh man, if I had a pound for every group I came across, I wouldn't have to keep doing this job! I mean, I would, I love it, but I wouldn't have to," he said, finally, wiping his eyes.

"Huh," I said quietly.

Maybe there were groups like that in my world, like in reality. It made sense, really. There were always hidden agendas, people doing things they shouldn't or going against what people think they should be doing. It would make sense.

"We'll probably find out more once we get the treasure before we have to hand it over to my client."

I nodded.

"When do you think the treasure was put on Spinalonga? I mean, do you think that whatever we're looking for was on the island before the leper colony set up there? Or could it have been before then?" I asked eventually.

Mitch's face stretched up into a smile.

"Good catch. It could have been. Truly, we have no idea how old the key is, when it was put in the Kirkyard or when it was used last. I mean, the key might have been passed down through families and then the ship log could have just been put in it at the beginning of the twentieth century, replacing whatever they used before then as a clue but we'll see when we get to the island," Mitch said.

I nodded.

"So, are we flying right onto the island? How big is it? Is there an airport?" I asked, aware that I was bombarding him with questions.

"I wish we could, but alas, there is no airport there. Closest is Crete. Heraklion airport. Luckily, they allow private planes to land there and there's a hotel very close to Spinalonga," Mitch said with a self-satisfied grin that I didn't quite understand.

"Oh, yeah?" I asked uncertainly.

"Oh, yeah. A luxury hotel. You ever stayed in a room with a private pool attached to it? And four other public pools on the property?"

I shook my head.

The idea of a private pool attached to my hotel room felt so... luxurious. There was no other term for it.

"Oh, you're in for a treat. Just wait until you try the food too! It's so good. We're going to have a great time."

"Do we have time to relax and try the food and everything?" I asked somewhat reluctantly. "Do we not just have to get to Spinalonga and then leave again?"

Mitch smirked.

"I mean, technically yes, but we need to scope out the island, make sure that Sterling's assholes aren't already there and waiting for us, work out transport, safe ways to get in and out, and so much more. We're going to be there for about a week before we can go to the island, I estimate. As long as we're there alone, we got time to be cautious, but if Sterling's people appear... we might need to speed things up a little. Should be fine though."

"So… we get a week at a luxury hotel?" I asked, just needing to be sure because it sounded so incredible.

"We absolutely do. And, don't get me wrong, we got some work to do whilst we're there. Monitoring the island, making sure that we've not been followed, and you've got some school work to do but… a lot of that can be done from next to the pool. We've got to blend in and not draw too much attention to ourselves because, if this goes tits up, they're going to be looking at hotel guests, so we need to be perfectly normal and not stand out in any way. Everything we do needs to make us seem not like the type to go… treasure hunting, got it?"

I nodded.

"So, how do we do that? How do we blend in?"

Mitch grinned at me.

"Well, first step is clothing. We gotta look the part which is why it's good we'll be stopping to refuel soon enough. We're going to go out and grab a new wardrobe for both of us whilst Lauren sorts out the plane. Then it'll be a case of lounging around the pool, playing into our characters, and making sure that no one suspects anything. Hopefully, I'll be able to get us a room or two that overlooks the island so we can set up monitoring equipment from there. You know, some telescopes and whatnot. I think they're still doing tours of the island too, so I'll get us booked on those which should be helpful. Gives us a nice, legitimate reason to be there and have a look around."

I nodded.

That made sense. It would be good to see the island and try to work out what the key could open or if there was anything that stood out as suspicious. I wasn't even sure what that would be, but I liked to think that Mitch would be able to spot something. I mean, he'd been working as a treasure hunter for years, he had to be able to.

"Alright, any other questions?" he asked.

About a million, but I couldn't quite form them into actual questions that would make sense. Plus, I didn't want to annoy him. I'd already asked a bunch of questions, too many. I didn't want him to get sick of me.

I shook my head.

"Awesome. We should probably grab a computer for you when we land too. Gotta get started on those lessons," Mitch said. "You can use my iPad for now if you want whilst I book us some rooms. They better have some space."

"What if they don't?" I asked quickly.

The idea of lounging around a pool, eating glorious food and just experiencing the hotel sounded so, so good. I didn't want that to be snatched out from under me so soon.

But, surely, in my own fantasy that wouldn't happen. It couldn't. I mean, I could just make there be some spare rooms, right?

Mitch grinned at me as he stood, stretched and settled in the other seat.

"Well then, there might be a server issue at the hotel. What a shame it would be if someone's room was cancelled and rebooked under our name."

CHAPTER SIXTEEN

"Act like a brat," Mitch muttered as he turned towards me, pretending to look back at the plane out the window.

I glanced at him in shock before my eyes snapped to the man who had rushed forwards to help us with our bags.

I didn't want to come off as rude, but I trusted Mitch. He was still looking out the window as the guy approached us. His white clean outfit bore the symbol of the hotel we were staying at and he was marching towards us.

"Dad," I said in a loud, flat voice. "The guy from the hotel is here."

Mitch turned towards him, his face lighting up.

"Oh, they did send someone!" he said with an accent that wasn't entirely his own, thrusting his bags at the man who grabbed them from him. "I was so worried that, because we hadn't come through on a commercial flight, we'd be waiting hours. Do you remember when we went to that tiny place in the Maldives? Man, we were waiting hours. I almost had to get that guy fired!"

Mitch took my bag from me and started towards the airport doors without waiting for the man who chased after him.

I wanted to rush to catch up with him too, but he'd said to act like a brat so I forced myself to dawdle, walking slowly and pouting slightly.

"Mr Taylor? The car is just this way," the man called to Mitch, who was marching towards what was definitely the wrong car, and gestured towards a pristine white car.

Mitch turned back towards him, the look of surprise on his face.

"Silly me! I just assumed it would be this car!" he said, his hand already stretched out for the wrong car's door handle.

He turned and strode towards the correct car, looking back to where I was waiting under the canopy of the door.

It took a surprisingly high amount of willpower for me not to move immediately towards him but instead, I stayed back, squinting in the bright sun. I was not well dressed for the climate, which I realised was intentional. Mitch had told me to wear black leggings and a black hoodie and I belatedly realised that it was to make it so I looked like I was refusing to fit in.

"Are you coming, Alice?" he called, looking expectantly at me.

I cocked my head to the side, before looking up at the canopy above me, then back to Mitch and sighing heavily.

"I guess so," I muttered, just loud enough for him and the person from the hotel to hear me.

I slunk over to the car, reluctantly dragging my feet, and climbed inside.

Mitch slammed the door shut behind me before jogging around to the other side and climbing in as the hotel worker struggled with our bags.

"Am I doing okay?" I muttered as I pretended to struggle with my seatbelt.

"Doing good, kid, but ham it up more. Pretend you hate me and hate that I dragged you here," he replied in his normal voice before jumping back into his other accent as the guy climbed into the front seat. "Man, the weather here is ridiculous! Is it always this hot? Look at how blue the sky is, Alice!"

I ducked my head to glare out the window, crossing my arms with a heavy sigh as the car peeled away from the curb.

"Wow, so blue," I grumbled flatly. "How long is the journey?"

"Now, now, Alice. What did I say? We're going to have one holiday without a fight, aren't we?" Mitch chided gently.

I wanted to apologise. I never wanted Mitch to chide me or tell me off, even as part of an act, but we needed to sell it.

"You said that," I muttered. "I never agreed to it."

"Alice," he sighed, sounding genuinely sad. "Just because your mom isn't here doesn't mean—"

"It's your fault she isn't here," I snapped, cutting him off despite how guilty I felt.

"Alice," he said again, sounding slightly more begging.

"No, it is!" I said, raising my voice. "You're the one who divorced her, not the other way around."

He sighed, his shoulders slumping.

"You'll understand when you're older," he muttered after a pause, staring pensively out the window.

My heart went out to him but I forced myself to sigh loudly, dragging the noise out.

"I doubt it," I said snidely.

Mitch sighed again, giving me a subtle thumbs-up so that the driver wouldn't see, and I grinned out the window.

The world that rushed by was fascinating. I'd never been to Greece before, but it was stunning. The streets were more colourful than I was used to and the people seemed more friendly, but the journey was over too fast. Before long, we were pulling up in front of the large, glass-fronted building.

The man rushed around the car to open the door for

me and it was difficult to stop myself from staring. I had to play the part of a bratty kid who was used to holidays like this. I needed to be bored.

"Thanks," I muttered grouchily as the guy shut the car door behind me.

He smiled at me politely, but I forced myself to ignore it and turn to look at Mitch instead.

"How long is it going to take you to check us in?" I said loudly, trying not to cringe at how rude I sounded.

"Shouldn't be too long," he said, smiling uncomfortably at the couple who were walking past, looking at me in surprise. "Go in there and grab a seat. Just relax until I've finished sorting everything out."

I rolled my eyes at him, worried that I was playing it up too much, and stormed into the cool, air-conditioned building behind us.

The scattered circles of low armchairs were mostly empty but still, I walked to the furthest one before sinking into it and wishing I hadn't left my phone in my bag. I gazed back towards my bag longingly, but the man who had driven us from the airport was loading into a golf cart for us. I couldn't go and ask him for my phone. That felt weird.

I glanced around instead, my eyes scanning the lobby.

There were no signs of Sterling's people there. Or, at least, I didn't think there was. I wasn't sure what exactly to be looking out for. Before, in the pub, they'd been in black combat clothes, but there was no one dressed like that in the lobby. That would be too obvious though; they would have gotten changed, surely.

The couple checking in before Mitch could work for them. They looked fairly young, fairly fit. It wouldn't surprise me.

Mitch turned around, his eyes also scanning the room before landing on me and, even from a distance, I saw his shoulders slump noticeable. It was an act, an excuse for him to be looking around the room, but he pulled it off well.

I tried to let my eyes linger on him before flicking towards the people in front of him and back again, trying to communicate my worries to him. He raised a hand to ruffle his hair and nodded just noticeably, before looking forwards again.

Out of the corner of my eye, I saw a man walking towards me, dressed in the same crisp white uniform as the man who picked us up from the airport.

"Excuse me, miss?" he asked, waiting for me to look at him. "Can I get you a drink?"

I just wanted some water, but that didn't feel right for the character I was pretending to be.

"Can I just get a glass of champagne?" I asked, barely looking at the man and feeling horrible for acting so dismissive. "Just whichever one you have about."

He didn't even hesitate or ask to see my ID despite the fact I was clearly underage.

"Of course," he said, rushing away again.

I was a little surprised at how easy that had been, but now worry turned in my stomach. I'd never had champagne. Well, I had. I'd tried a sip of it but never more than that.

I'd need to find a way to get rid of it without it being too obvious about it. Maybe Mitch could help.

The man rushed back towards me just as the couple in front of Mitch walked away and he approached the check-in desk.

"Here you go," he said, holding his silver tray with a single long-stemmed flute of champagne out towards me.

I took it, the stem of the glass feeling too fragile in my hands and smiled at him tightly before taking a sip of the tart, fizzy liquid.

I should have just asked for water.

"Thank you," I said with a tight smile.

He nodded at me before rushing away again.

I watched from a distance as Mitch spoke to the woman at the check-in desk who smiled at him, taking tiny sips of my champagne. I regretted my choices immediately, but it felt too late to ask for champagne and also a glass of water. That would just be weird... right?

I didn't have a chance to mull that over enough to come to a decision, because Mitch stepped away from the desk and was looking around the room. I knew that he'd seen me and the glass that I was holding, but I quickly and pointedly looked away so that I didn't see his reaction.

"Alice," he called, having walked towards me.

I took another sip of my drink, pretending to stare out of the window down at the stunning view.

The sea stretched out in the distance with Spinalonga jutting out of the water like a fortress. The various blue-roofed white villas and pools were scattered before the building leading down to the sea. Even that was stunning. It was the most beautiful and pure blue I'd ever seen before in my life, dotted with white sailboats.

It was pretty and so much nicer than anywhere I would have been able to go in real life.

My heart squeezed slightly at that realisation. I wanted that luxury. I wanted to experience it for real, not just in what was essentially a dream.

"Alice," Mitch said from just in front of me in a gentle voice. "Are you ready to go to our rooms?"

I blinked, realising where I was and smiled at him tightly.

"I guess," I drawled but my voice was filled with suppressed emotion.

"Come on," he said softly, tilting his head towards the door behind him.

The golf cart they'd loaded our bags onto was now gone and another idled in its place, the driver looking at us.

I pulled myself up, glancing at the view one last time before looking back at Mitch.

"Let's go then," I sighed.

"What are you drinking?" he asked casually.

"Champagne."

His steps faltered and he shot me a look of barely suppressed approval.

A flash of happiness burnt through me at that. He was impressed by me. By the decision I had made. I knew I shouldn't have gone for water. Champagne was what Alice the brat would have ordered.

"You're drinking?" he asked, his voice rising slightly. "I thought you agreed to only having a drink with dinner whilst you're here with me?"

His tone was demanding, as if he expected a fight.

"You took too long!" I said, matching his tone and exceeding it.

"No more. Give me that," he ordered, reaching out for the glass.

I hesitated, knowing exactly what I should do. I didn't want to, but I knew what Alice would have done.

I brought the glass to my lips, taking several big gulps, before handing him the empty glass with what was more of a wince than the smug grin I was going for. The champagne had burned the back of my throat, coating it with acrid liquid and stopping my grin from being quite as wild as I wanted it to be.

Mitch sighed loudly, placing the glass on a nearby

table, before grabbing my arm and leading me towards the door as my eyes stung from the drink. I forced myself to smile happily and shoot the boy who was sitting by the door reading a book a grin as Mitch dragged me outside.

I barely got the chance to see the boy's reaction, but I saw enough to know that his eyes followed me from the lobby.

"Mr and Miss Taylor?" a woman who worked for the hotel asked with a polite smile, clearly taking in Mitch's grasp on my arm, but not saying anything.

It wasn't particularly tight, but I knew it looked bad. I yanked my arm away from him and cut in before he could say anything.

"Are you going to take us to our room?" I demanded obnoxiously.

"Yes," the woman replied in a flawlessly polite tone.

"Good. I left my phone in my bag and someone took it there already, I hope."

"Alice," Mitch warned in a tone that told me to keep going.

I narrowed my eyes at him before smiling at the woman.

She didn't even falter. She was perfectly professional which made me a little sad. She must have dealt with people like me before.

"If you'd like to take a seat, I'll take you to your suite," the woman said, gesturing towards the golf cart.

I had to hide the surprise that went through me.

Even the golf cart looked perfect. The seats were the exact blue of the stitching on the logo of the hotel, the rest of the cart white. There was no visible dirt or dust. It was clear that a lot of work went into making the hotel look perfect.

Mitch climbed into the row of seats just behind the woman who was driving, but I hesitated. Normally, I would have climbed onto the seat next to him without hesitation but... Alice wouldn't have.

I sighed loudly and slowly walked towards the back of the cart, hauling myself onto the rear-facing seats and dropping down heavily.

My eyes found the boy through the glass front. I wanted to look away immediately, to blush under his gaze, but I didn't need to here. My lips slowly rose as I took in his dark, floppy hair and chiselled face.

He looked to be about my age and he was still watching me. He smiled hesitantly as the cart started to move away.

I watched him until we turned, blocking him from view, my mind mulling over this new possibility. He was cute, that much was obvious, but I was here with Mitch. Surely, I couldn't do anything about that cute guy who seemed into me... right?

But, maybe I could. Like, surely Alice the brat would flirt with him if she saw him again... right?

We pulled up in front of a two-story white villa whilst I mulled it over and tried to justify attempting to flirt

with him, but the sight of the place where we'd be staying for however long it took us to scope out the island
and go over there pushed all thoughts of the guy out of
my head.

I fought to stop my mouth from dropping open as
I climbed down from the golf cart and walked towards
it, stopping to let a tiny lizard cross the orange tiles in
front of us.

"This is where we're staying?" I asked, trying to keep
the wonder out of my mouth.

"It is. I know it's not quite the place you went on holiday with your mom a few weeks ago, but it's still nice,
right?" Mitch asked, injecting just the right amount of
desperation into his voice.

"I guess."

Mitch grinned at me before tapping his keycard
against the scanner on the door and pushing it open.

"Thank you," he called to the woman who had been
waiting to make sure we could get into the room as she
waved at us and drove away.

He pushed the door open fully and gestured for me
to step inside.

Our pretty much brand new suitcases, intentionally scuffed by us on the flight with sandpaper so they'd
appear well used, waited by the door, but I barely
noticed them as I stared around the room.

"Wow," I breathed.

The room, or villa I should say, was huge. And I

was just looking around the downstairs! The lounge stretched out, long and thin, with large grey sofas in front of the glass french windows. I stumbled forwards, looking towards the windows. The wispy white curtains had been pushed back, revealing the private infinity pool beyond which gave way to treetops and, eventually, the sea.

The villa felt so private, so isolated, in the best way possible.

I opened my mouth to speak, but Mitch got there first.

"What do you think of the place, Alice?" he asked.

Confusion washed through me, but I recovered quickly. If he were calling me Alice, he must be doing it for a reason.

"It's fine. Where are the bedrooms?" I asked loudly.

Mitch sighed, having finished surveying the room, and started to root around in his duffle bag. He pulled out something that could easily be mistaken for a phone and started slowly pointing it around the room, watching the screen intently.

"There's only one room, I thought I told you this. It's upstairs and one of us will be staying on the pull-out sofa."

He was looking for cameras and listening devices, I realised.

"Well," I said, sneering at the sofa. "I hope you'll be comfortable on it."

I turned on my heel and stalked towards the stairs before marching up them.

The bedroom was somehow more impressive than the room downstairs. The huge bed in the centre looked spacious and comfortable and it took everything I had not to throw myself onto it and fall asleep immediately.

Despite what I had said downstairs, I expected Mitch to take the bed. He'd paid for the room. Or, at least, his client had. He deserved the proper bed, not me.

The attached bathroom was pretty impressive too. It stretched almost the full length of the villa with a huge sink, a bath opposite, and right at the end of the room, a shower. A sigh of longing almost slipped out of my mouth as I stared up at the giant, square shower head. I could already tell that the water pressure would be great.

I wandered back into the room, smiling at Mitch but not saying anything as I walked towards the attached balcony. Two seats and a small circular wooden table sat in the middle of the balcony, overlooking the pool and the sea.

Spinalonga was right in the middle, the balcony giving us a great view of it. I wanted to ask Mitch for his binoculars, to stare at the island and check it for motion. He'd said that people went on tours there, but I couldn't see anything from how far away it was. Instead, I settled for leaning against the wooden wall of the balcony and squinting in the bright sun.

The island looked tiny but I knew, up close, that

would be very different. A wall surrounded much of it, and huge husks of buildings were placed seemingly randomly on it. I wasn't sure which part was Dante's gate or where the lepers would have entered the island from. Maybe the right side of the island where it kind of sloped down into the sea. That could have been a port? There were some ships just off there too so that would make sense.

The door opened slightly more behind me and Mitch sunk into one of the chairs.

I looked back at him and he gestured for me to take a seat too.

I did so, waiting for him to speak.

"All clear. No cameras or devices here. We should be good to talk pretty freely, but maybe not too loudly," he said, craning his head to look over the balcony.

I nodded, still not feeling comfortable talking.

"So, what do you really think of this place?"

CHAPTER SEVENTEEN

"I'm going to miss you so much!" Phoebe cried, throwing her arms around me, her shoulder smacking me in the chin. "Promise me you'll text me when you're in Scotland?"

"Of course," I said, hugging her back. "There's not much to do whilst we're there so I'll be texting you, like, constantly."

"Good!"

"Don't feel like you have to reply right away though," I added quickly as she stepped back. "I know you're going to France in a few days, right?"

"Urgh, yes. My parents are sending me to go stay with my aunt or my cousin or someone and they've said they're going to have me fluent by the time I come back. I think they are vastly overestimating my skill. Apparently, they're going to make me order in French every night when we go out for dinner!"

"Oh, no," I laughed as Phoebe looked appropriately anguished.

"I know! We're going to be sticking to poulet and pomme de terres because that's all I can remember. I don't even like chicken!"

We both laughed before she glanced over my shoulder and sighed.

I turned around, spotting her mom pulling up behind us in her Land Rover.

"I should go," she said sadly.

I nodded and we walked over to her car slowly.

"Hi, girls! Good day?" her mom called, lowering the window to talk to us.

"It was fine," Phoebe said with a sigh.

"It was pretty good, thanks. How was yours?" I asked.

She smiled at me and pushed her long brown hair back from her face.

"It was good, thank you. You know how it is, clients to speak to, laws to uphold," she joked, making light of her job.

I knew that being a lawyer consisted of more than that, but she always made it sound pretty good.

I grinned back at her as Phoebe climbed into the car and pouted dramatically at me through the window.

"Did Phoebe tell you we're sending her away to Paris for the holidays?" her mom asked.

"Oh, yeah, she did. That sounds really nice," I said politely.

"She mentioned you're having some problems with that horrible teacher of yours too. You're welcome to join her?"

I wanted to say yes so badly that it hurt.

A summer away from my family, in Paris with Phoebe sounded spectacular, but I couldn't.

"I told you. She's going to Scotland with her mom, remember?" Phoebe said quietly, rolling her eyes at me.

"Ah, of course! Well, if you change your mind or get back early, just get Phoebe to text me and I'll book you a flight right away," her mom said with an easy smile that immediately sent guilt through me.

"Thank you," I said with a smile, trying to hide the worry.

I knew she probably was just offering to be nice, but I still appreciated it.

"Truly, it would probably do Phoebe some good to have someone else her own age there!"

"Mom," Phoebe groaned loudly.

"Sorry," she apologised with a smile, her eyes sparkling, before turning back to me. "Is your mum here to pick you up?"

I glanced down the row of cars automatically despite knowing that she wouldn't be there.

"No, don't think so."

A slight crease appeared in between Phoebe's mom's eyebrows.

"Do you want a lift home?" she offered.

"It's okay. I don't mind the walk."

"Are you sure?"

I mean, I wasn't really feeling walking home, but I knew that my mom would be annoyed if some other mom drove me home. It might reflect badly on her.

"I'm sure!"

It wasn't worth the inevitable argument.

"Okay," her mom said, unconvinced. "Well, we had better be getting off. I'll see you soon hopefully, Grace!"

"Bye! Bye, Phoebe!" I called.

"Text me!" she shouted back, as they started to pull away.

A smile grew on my face as I watched them leave before turning and starting to walk home.

The gentlest of breezes tousled my hair as I glanced up at the brilliantly blue sky. It wasn't even a conscious decision. Just one moment I was walking down the path outside my school, the next I was on the balcony in Elounda, leaning back in my chair as a soft dizziness touched me.

"Sun cream," Mitch said, dropping two bottles of factor fifty onto the table between us. "Put them on now."

I picked up the smaller bottle, turning it over before realising it was a specifically formulated for faces cream. I squirted some out into my hands before rubbing it into my skin.

"Make sure you get your ears too. Trust me, that can be an absolute nightmare," Mitch said before ducking inside once more.

I smiled and looked back at him.

"You've burnt your ears before?" I called.

"Just the lobes. Not sure how I managed to miss them, but they were agony. Do you drink coffee? I can't remember what you had in London."

I considered it for a moment.

I didn't, but I couldn't taste anything here so it didn't really matter if I said yes. Plus, I was tired. The caffeine in it might help. But then, if I couldn't taste anything, would the caffeine still affect me?

"No," I said hesitantly after a pause.

He popped his head around the glass door to give me a look as I poured some more suncream into my hands to start coating my legs.

"You sure about that?" he asked.

"Yeah..."

He chuckled softly.

"Well, you don't sound it. If you change your mind, help yourself to the coffee machine," he said, going back to it to pick up his coffee and bringing it outside.

He sunk into the chair again as I rubbed handfuls of the cream into my legs, standing and contorting to make sure I got everywhere that my shorts didn't cover. I wasn't really sure if getting burnt would have any kind of impact on me in real life or even the fantasy, but I didn't really want to risk it.

A knock came from the door behind me and I spun around, my heart rate skyrocketed. Mitch held one hand up to me, as if telling me to take it easy, before silently passing toward the door, peering through the peephole and pulling it open.

"Oh, breakfast!" he said loudly enough for me to hear as someone pushed a cart into the room piled high with silver cloches and tureens.

I sunk back into the chair, shuffling it around as subtly as I could so that I could watch the woman out of the corner of my eyes. Just because she was wearing the hotel uniform didn't mean that she definitely didn't work for Sterling. She could be undercover.

She pushed the cart further into the room before smiling at Mitch.

"Alice, come get some breakfast!" he called.

It took a lot of effort not to rush into the room and grab some of the food. It smelt so good and I was starving, but I knew that it wasn't what my character would have done.

"Alice!" Mitch called again as he took the receipt from the woman and signed it with a flourish.

I sat back in my chair, still watching but slowly rubbing suncream into my arms. I waited until I was completely finished with the suncream before slowly dragging myself out of the chair and stomping into the room.

"What?" I demanded as I entered.

Mitch had been chatting to the woman who was smiling prettily at him and leaning towards him, but he turned to me with a forced smile.

"This lovely woman has brought our breakfast. Doesn't it look nice?" he asked in a tone reminiscent of my mom's.

That kind of tone wanted me to agree and say nothing more but for once, I rebelled.

"Eh," I said, lifting one shoulder in a blithe shrug. "I'm not hungry."

It was a lie and my stomach chose that exact moment to gurgle loudly.

"You're going to have three meals a day whilst you're here, Alice," Mitch said in a firm, pleading tone.

I breathed in heavily and let it out loudly.

"Fine. I'll just have a croissant or some fruit or something. Thanks for bringing it, I guess," I said, barely looking at the woman.

"You're welcome," she replied in a cheery voice.

"I'll show you out," Mitch said to her with a charming smile before looking back at me. "Load up that plate."

I slowly and reluctantly grabbed a plate and started lifting the tureens and cloches, dropping them back loudly or placing them onto the low cabinet next to the cart as Mitch walked the woman to the door.

"So sorry about her," I heard him mutter. "She's going through a rough time."

"Don't worry. She seems like a lovely girl," the woman lied.

I leaned over the tray of scrambled eggs, sniffing the

sulphurous food and loudly said, "Ew."

Mitch glanced back at me, barely fighting a smile, before putting his hand on the door.

"Thanks again," he said before shutting it.

I looked down at the food, scooping up a large serving of some perfectly crisp latkes before moving towards a tray that had a sign stating 'vegetarian sausages' and grabbing a couple with the tongs.

Mitch whipped out the scanner he'd used the day before, passing it over the cart quickly before saying, "You know what, kid? You really missed your calling. You should go into acting."

I grinned up at him as he slipped the device back into his pocket, satisfied that there were no bugs on the cart, and grabbed a plate.

"Thanks," I said.

"Do you know brats like that or are you just an incredible actress?" he asked, loading his plate up with sausages, latkes and baked tomatoes.

I considered it for a moment as I poured myself a cup of water.

"I mean both really. Not that I think I'm an incredible actress," I added quickly. "I don't know. I guess I'm kind of basing it on people I know, like from school or something. Or, like, what I think would work best in the moment. Am I doing okay?"

"Kid, you're doing spectacular. I reckon bring up the divorce more though. That makes people uncomfortable, so they look away," he suggested. "They might listen in more but they won't look."

I nodded, waiting for him to grab a glass of water too before leading him outside.

"Yeah, good call. I'll do that. Have you got an idea for what happened to cause the divorce?" I asked as I sunk back into the surprisingly comfortable seats and took a sip of the bland water.

Water was never particularly flavourful but here, it truly tasted like nothing.

"I think so. What do you think of this backstory: your mom cheated on me, I found out and divorced her, but you blame me for breaking up the family? Maybe you have another sibling, younger brother or something, who refuses to spend time with me because of it."

I took a bite of the potatoes as I considered it.

A hint of salty, fried goodness burst in my mouth, surprising me so much that I gasped and choked on it.

"You okay, kid?" Mitch said, watching me with concern as I coughed and gulped down some water. "Is the story that good?"

I nodded as I shoved another forkful into my mouth, needing to know if I could actually taste it or if I was just going fully insane.

"Grace!" someone shouted from behind me.

I blinked, glancing down the sun-dappled path as dizziness threatened to sweep me off my feet, my eyes finally landing on Duncan who jogged down the path towards me.

Path of me wanted to blow him off, to disappear back to Elounda with Mitch and work out if I really could taste things there or not, but I forced myself to stay.

"Hey, Duncan," I said, trying not to sound disappointed.

He grinned at me goofily as he caught up.

"Did you not hear me before? I shouted your name like four times!" he said, nudging me with his elbow.

"Sorry, I was in a world of my own."

I smiled at him apologetically.

"Eh, that's fine. You know I like that about you." He grinned at me and hiked his backpack up over his shoulder a little higher. "So, are you coming to mine tonight?"

Confusion washed through me.

"Tonight?" I asked.

"Yeah! My parents are away, so I'm throwing a party. A bunch of people should be coming! It should be really fun…"

My smile wavered.

He always invited me to house parties, but I never really went to many. I don't think he expected me to anymore, but he still made sure to invite me. It was one of the benefits of being childhood friends with someone as popular as Duncan and I knew that, if I wanted to, I could have manipulated that into some semblance of popularity, but I didn't have the mental energy.

"Oh, that sounds really nice..." I started lamely.

"It should be!" Duncan continued, his unwavering enthusiasm high. "I've got like a bunch of cases of beer, basically every flavour of Bacardi Breezer, loads of mixers and vodka! That's still your go-to, right?"

I smiled slightly at that, remembering the last party of his that I'd actually gone to. Phoebe and I had snuck a case of Diet Coke and a bottle of vodka onto the garage roof outside his room and spent all night out there getting progressively more drunk. Duncan had found us at like three in the morning, flat out on our backs watching the stars.

He'd just laid down next to us and joined in, it was actually really nice.

"Yeah. I probably can't tonight though. I'm going away in the morning, so my mom will want a hand packing," I said, with a wince.

"Oh, where are you going? Scotland again?" he asked.

I nodded, stepping carefully over a huge crack in the pavement.

"Ah, that should be good though! Things are generally not too awful there, right?"

"Yeah, shouldn't be too bad."

"When do you get back? I'll throw another party!" he offered.

I chuckled slightly, knowing that no matter what I said, he'd respond positively.

"Not for a few weeks, I think."

"Awesome! I think my parents might be in Monaco then! If they are, I'm throwing the biggest welcome home party you've ever seen!"

I smiled distractedly at him, knowing that not many people would come to that party for me, but only just because Duncan was throwing it. Phoebe was away for the whole summer, I realised, dread filling my stomach. She wouldn't be able to go with me. I'd be alone there.

"That sounds good," I said carefully, squinting in the sun as we emerged from the shadowy path.

Duncan laughed easily as we came to a stop by the road and waited for a gap in the traffic.

"That's the most reluctant RSVP I've ever heard," he chortled.

I laughed a little at that, surprising myself.

"Sorry."

"That's okay, I know you don't always love the parties. But, you can always come over and just play video games or something if you want?"

I was silent as we rushed across the road, the cars barely slowing as they approached. I didn't want to respond or do anything to take my attention off the road. More than once, I'd been distracted and caught my toes on the curb on the other side. So far, I'd been lucky. No one from school had seen, but I knew it was only a matter of time.

"Yeah, that sounds good," I said with a smile once we

were safely on the grass on the other side of the road.

His face lit up with happiness.

"Awesome! I'll put it in my phone. Video game date with Grace, some point in a few weeks time," he said, pretending to type it into his phone.

I nudged him with my shoulder and he grinned at me toothily.

He always did stuff like that, but I knew he didn't mean anything by it. It was his personality, he was just silly.

He hesitated as I hopped the fence and glanced behind me, checking for animals.

"The field should be empty," I said, looking over my shoulder.

"Are you sure though? Do you not remember last time when you said it would be empty, and there was a cow in it?"

I laughed.

"That wasn't last time! That was like two years ago!"

Duncan narrowed his eyes, his hands tightening on the fence.

"Still…"

"It's empty, I promise."

He hesitated a moment longer before nodding resolutely and starting to climb.

"Okay, but if there is a cow in here again, I'm running," he said as he jumped down.

"Agreed."

We started to walk across the field in silence for a moment before it became too much for Duncan and he started talking again.

"How'd you think you did in exams? Well enough to stay at the school?" he asked.

"Probably," I replied with a slight shrug. "I mean, I've been getting mostly B's in my mocks so should do about the same. Apart from in French, that is."

Duncan laughed.

"Oh man, I can't wait to see the look on Madame Noel's face when I tell her I got an A star. She's going to scream," he giggled.

"Wait, why are you so sure you're going to do so well?"

He looked around dramatically, making sure there was no one around.

"Well... I may have gotten a tutor," he whispered.

My mouth dropped open.

"You did not!" I gasped.

He grinned at me but said nothing.

"You got a tutor?" I pressed.

"Keep your voice down!" he insisted jokily. "I don't want anyone to know! I need to have the satisfaction of telling Madame Noel exactly how well I did and making her think it was all me. It's the only thing keeping me going!"

"Why though?"

He grinned at me.

"Spite. The number of times she's told me I'm going to fail! I cannot wait to tell her I got full marks! Well, maybe not full marks, but good ones at least!"

"I have to be there when you tell her," I said with a laugh. "I cannot wait to see her face. Are you going to study French for A levels too?"

He considered it for a moment.

"I'm not really sure. I did want to do maths, further maths, sports sciences and something else. Maybe, like, philosophy? But, I could do French instead. Oh man, she'd be so pissed," he said, narrowing his eyes and grinning wickedly.

"She'd be furious," I confirmed.

"Okay, maybe I'll do that then." He paused for a moment, glancing towards my house and coming to a stop.

The garden was barely visible from where we were, but I knew that was on purpose. I couldn't have my mom think he'd walked me home, she'd immediately suspect something else was going on and we really were just friends. She knew that, of course, we'd been friends since primary school, but that wouldn't stop her from obsessing.

"I'll wait here for you to go into your house?" he offered, turning towards me and glancing hesitantly over my shoulder.

"Thanks," I said softly.

"Have a good trip?"

"Thanks. Hope staying here isn't too bad." I smiled up at him.

"It shouldn't be. I have Brad coming over for a few days so that should be good! But… text me?"

He smiled hopefully, waiting for my response.

"Yeah, I will."

He hesitated, looking uncharacteristically awkward, before holding out his arms for a hug.

I stepped towards him, wrapping my arms around his body as he squeezed me. It felt weird hugging him. We'd never really done that before apart from once when I'd been really drunk and hugged him as we left his party. But now, hugging him, whilst sober, felt strange. Not in a bad way, just different.

He held on for a little longer than I expected before pulling back.

"Cool. I'll wait here until you go inside," he said with a grin, pulling his bag higher again.

"Thanks," I said with a smile before starting to walk away from him.

I could feel his eyes on me as I walked towards my fence, shot him one last smile, and climbed over.

My body tensed noticeably as I walked towards the open french windows, knowing that if they were open, my mom was awake. I paused, just outside, and listened carefully. She was bustling around in the house, but I couldn't tell what she was doing or what kind of mood she was in.

Taking a deep breath, I pushed the curtains aside and stepped into the house, kicking my shoes off before padding softly towards the source of the noise.

"Grace!" my mom called as she spotted me, her hair pulled back in a bun and her eyes clear. "I've done all the washing. Make sure you get your suitcase packed tonight so we can leave nice and early tomorrow."

I nodded.

"Thanks, I'll go pack that now," I said with a forced smile.

"Good. And don't forget to bring some nice dresses for when we go out to dinner with your grandparents!"

"I will," I said, already slipped back into my fantasy world as I started up the stairs.

CHAPTER EIGHTEEN

I stretched my arms high above my head, writhing slightly as I stretched out my back. The sun lounger was surprisingly comfortable. It was padded and reclined at the perfect angle for me to be sitting slightly upright, able to see around the pool, but still be comfortable.

The chairs were pretty spread out too, which made me feel so much better. I didn't need to worry as much about pretending to be Alice; no one would be able to overhear us. I could just relax.

"Time to put more sunscreen on, kid," Mitch muttered quietly from beside me.

I blinked away some of the blueness from my vision.

Despite wearing sunglasses, the sun was cooking my eyes and making it a little hard to see. It was my fault. I had fallen asleep in it even after Mitch said I should probably move under an umbrella, but I was so comfortable and nicely warm that I hadn't wanted to move.

It was the perfect temperature and I was nicely full from breakfast. I blamed the hotel. It was too good. Everything about it was relaxing and what I wanted.

I sat up slowly, dizziness shooting through me. I wasn't sure if it was from dehydration or just the normal dizziness I felt when I started daydreaming now. It should have been worrying, I knew that logically, but I just didn't care.

Grabbing the suncream somewhat blindly, I started rubbing it into my skin.

"Make sure you're staying out of the sun a little more, kiddo. If you get burnt or worse, sunstroke, I'm leaving you here when I go to the island. Trust me, running around with that stuff is a recipe for disaster," he said under his breath.

"Why?" I asked a little too sharply, glancing up at the nearby umbrella.

I wasn't willing to risk it. I wanted to go to Spinalonga, I had to.

"You had sunstroke before?"

I shook my head.

I mean, I'd been burnt before, of course, but I couldn't remember ever having sunstroke.

"If you run around too much with it, which we'll probably be doing, you'll pass out and I'll have to carry you, which means that I'll have fewer hands to grab the treasure or fight anyone off. Could be a problem. Make sure you're drinking water too. Can't have you being dehydrated. Betty will murder me."

I chuckled quietly, dropping the now much lighter bottle of suncream on the low table between our two chairs and picking up my bottle of water, downing half of it in one go. I sat back down, grabbing the large floppy hat I'd discarded on the table before I'd fallen asleep and putting it back on my head as I surveyed the pool area.

It was huge and surprisingly quiet. I'd definitely seen some kids around the hotel before, but there weren't any at this pool. They must have been using the children's pool, I realised. Mitch had said that there was one.

There was barely anyone in this pool. Just one guy teaching a couple of people how to use the scuba tanks and a couple of older people swimming lengths. I watched them for a moment, debating joining them in the pool.

I did like swimming. There was a pool pretty close to my house so I went quite often. It was easier when we went to visit my grandparents though. One of the best things about their place was the fact they had an indoor pool. It was old-fashioned and not very big but they still had someone come in every so often to make sure it had all the chemicals and everything in it.

"Grace!" a sharp voice called, cutting through my fantasy.

I blinked, staring down at the pile of clothes I'd been folding without paying any attention to them.

"Yes, Mom?" I replied.

"Did you see the new swimming costumes I got you?" she asked, popping her head into my room.

"Oh, yeah. Thanks for that."

"Good. It's fine if you want to pack some of your usual ones for once Mom and Dad leave, but you can't wear any bikinis whilst they're there," she told me. "I will not have a repeat of last time."

I nodded, trying not to wince.

I'd made a mistake last time. I had worn a bikini while swimming. I didn't even think either of my grandparents had seen me walk from my room to the pool in it, but my mom had sat me down afterwards and told me how inappropriate they'd both said it was for me to wear something so skimpy.

It wasn't skimpy though. It was just a normal bikini.

Apparently, it made me look cheap. My grandmother had made a comment that evening about the lowering of standards for women these days and I knew it was directed at me.

I'd binned the bikini that night. It wasn't worth it.

It was one of her favourite things to say about me and all of her other grandkids. Everything we did was a reflection of how poorly we'd been brought up and how much things had slipped since the good old days when she was a kid.

I nodded.

"Thanks."

Mom smiled at me, seemingly happy that I'd just accepted her decision instead of trying to fight against it.

"Good. They mean well, Grace. They're just old and stuck in their ways," she said with a smile that made me feel a little guilty.

I nodded.

"I know. I've already packed the costumes."

"Great! Did you make sure to pack some nice dresses for when we go out for dinner?" she asked.

"Yeah, I think I've got a few."

"And they're not too short? Or low cut?"

"Nope."

"Okay, good. And you've got tights? And appropriate shoes?"

I suppressed a sigh.

"Got them."

"Alright. I'll leave you to pack. Your father should be home soon," she said, barely hiding her disgust. "Make sure you say goodbye to him tonight. He probably won't bother getting up in the morning before we go."

"I will," I said, despite the fact he always did get up before we left for Scotland.

He had every year since he stopped coming with us. Mom nodded once before turning and stalking out of the room.

I sighed and looked down at the pile of clothes before me.

I blinked, leaving my packing behind and opened my

eyes in Crete again. I was still looking at the pool and debating going in it, but now dizziness and self-consciousness washed through me. The bikini I was wearing was definitely what I would count as skimpy. If either of my grandparents saw me in it, they'd probably have a heart attack.

But, I didn't think I looked bad. I mean, it still wasn't as skimpy as most of the other bikinis people around the pool were wearing, so surely it was fine. I didn't look particularly good, that was for sure. I didn't have a good body, just an average one. No one really would look at me twice.

Apart from one person. There was someone who was shooting me surreptitious glances.

I looked down away from him immediately, staring at the phone I was holding. Mitch had bought it for me when we'd stopped to refuel, along with a smartwatch, laptop, and an iPad that I wasn't quite comfortable using yet. Apparently, they would make homeschooling and treasure hunting much easier but I was scared to even turn them on.

What if I broke them? He'd said that I probably wouldn't and, even if I did, it didn't matter as long as I was careful enough with them and it was an honest mistake, but I was still worried. I really didn't want to break them and for him to be disappointed in me.

I mean, I was wearing the watch. Mitch had insisted. He'd assured me it was waterproof and surprisingly hard to break. Plus, he said it was necessary because, in case anything happened and we were separated, he would still be able to contact me.

I blinked and tried to focus on the phone again. I was meant to be reading some stuff for my homeschooling, which I was doing before I'd fallen asleep, and not looking at the surprisingly cute boy who was definitely checking me out.

It was the boy from the foyer before, I was pretty certain of it. His hair was slicked back from the water which also had the sharp angles of his face look much sharper. He looked so hot.

And, he looked to be about my age, so surely I could go talk to him. I mean, it wouldn't be a problem, right? I wasn't Grace, I was pretending to be Alice who definitely would have gone to talk to the cute boy who was checking her out.

But, would Mitch be okay with that?

It felt wrong, I couldn't exactly go flirt with a boy in front of him. I mean, I didn't even know how to flirt with a boy but, with Mitch nearby, it would be a hundred times worse. It would be like flirting in front of my dad, I'd never be able to do that.

"You alright there, kid?"

I blinked, looking up at Mitch guiltily.

"Oh no. What are you up to?" he asked with an amused grin. "I'm going to go out on a limb and assume that you're not just really absorbed in that chapter of whatever it is you're reading."

I felt my face flush bright red.

"I mean, it is a pretty interesting chapter…" I tried to say, but it came out weakly.

It was an obvious lie.

"But not as interesting as that boy in the pool? Wasn't he in the lobby yesterday?"

My face turned even redder, if that was even possible.

I couldn't bring myself to speak as embarrassment wracked me.

"Well, Alice would probably go over there and talk to him," Mitch said, pretending to look back at the book in his hands.

I glanced at him.

"Shouldn't I stay here with you? In case something happens?" I asked.

"Eh, we're good for now and I'll shout if anything does go down. Alice wouldn't sit around with her dad all day, she'd go speak to that model-looking boy."

I hesitated, not quite sure what to say.

"You aren't the first kid I've looked after. Same rules apply to you as they did to the ones before. Don't do anything dumb or break the law in any traceable way, if you do want to… get to know someone a little better, use protection because sexual health clinics can be hard to find in foreign countries, and I don't think either of us want to be dealing with an unplanned pregnancy. Shout if you need help at all, no questions asked. Take your phone with you if you're going out of sight of me and keep your watch on at all times, okay?"

I nodded quickly, wanting to get away from this conversation as quickly as possible.

The idea of talking to Mitch about sex or anything like that was horrifying. I'd never so much as kissed a boy, but now he was talking about making sure I used protection and sexual health clinics. It made me want to run away and hide.

Like, I guess I was glad that he was being so open and accepting of it but… it was embarrassing as hell.

"Okay," I muttered. "I'm going to go swim."

"Good call, kid. You go swim," he snickered, seeing straight through my lie.

My face burnt as I sat up and dropped my hat and sunglasses on the lounger before standing and walking towards the pool where the boy was still swimming.

I tried not to watch him out of the corner of my eye as I climbed into the pool, gasping slightly at how unexpectedly cold the water was.

It was pretty nice, once I got used to it, and it felt wonderful against my skin as I started swimming lengths of the pool, pretending not to notice the boy's glances.

I wasn't sure how to approach him. I mean, that wasn't what I did. I didn't approach boys ever. But, Alice would have. It was much more her style to swim straight up to the boy and start talking to him even though that idea made me want to cringe.

I mean, I could at least start by shooting him a smile instead of keeping my eyes fixed on the water in front of me whenever we were swimming towards each other. He was swimming next to me so it made sense that I'd at least look at him, right?

Yes. That was how I was going to start it. I was going to smile at him and then just... play it by ear.

My heart thudded in my chest as I reached the end of the pool and turned slowly, facing back towards Mitch again. He was already swimming towards me, his eyes bouncing between the water in front of him and my face. I could do it. I could smile.

I felt my lips tick up into a slight smile as he approached, not taking my eyes off his face until something else stole my attention.

Someone was approaching Mitch. Some woman, in a white bikini which showed off their perfect tan, was slinking towards him. My body tensed and I started swimming towards him a little quicker, just in case.

If they were one of Sterling's people, we could be in trouble.

I reached the end of the pool, just within hearing distance as the woman reached him.

"Is this seat taken?" the woman asked in a low, sultry voice.

I hesitated, resting my arms on the edge of the pool and pretending to catch my breath whilst subtly watching them.

"My kid was sitting there, but she's wandered off somewhere," Mitch said, putting his book down and smiling at the woman.

"Well, I'm glad she did."

They were flirting, I realised with a start before turning and kicking away from the pool.

I didn't want to see that, it felt wrong. As much as I didn't want Mitch to see me flirting, I also didn't want to see him flirting. He was free to, of course. I just did not want to see it.

I sent the boy another smile as we passed each other and hesitated as I reached the other end of the pool. I didn't want to go back down the other end, not when the woman was still sitting on my chair and leaning towards Mitch like that. I wanted to give them some privacy.

Glancing back at them, I made my decision and swam to the edge of the pool, staying in the deeper end. I rested there for a moment, debating moving into the other pool to give him some more privacy.

It wasn't far. For some reason, there was another pool just overlooking the one I was in at the moment, but it was far enough away that I'd be out of earshot of whatever he and that woman were saying and he wouldn't be able to hear me. I'd seen some people swimming in it earlier, so it didn't feel too weird.

I paddled over to the nearest ladder, making sure to give the two people who were still in the middle of a diving lesson a wide berth.

Climbing the steps slowly, I shot Mitch a glance, which he returned, to let him know I was going before my eyes found the boy who was still swimming. His gaze met mine and I smiled slightly before cocking my head towards the other pool.

It felt so unnatural and weird, but his smile grew and he started swimming towards me.

I looked away before he could see my grin, and walked towards the other pool. I wasn't sure whether I should wait for him or look back, but I realised that Alice wouldn't have done either. She would have just expected him to follow her, which I was pretty sure he was.

I climbed the steps towards the other pool and walked across the wooden bridge, glancing down at Mitch and smiling when I realised he was still watching me. I climbed into the pool on the other side of the bridge, breathing out a sigh of relief as the cool water embraced my sun-baked body. I'd only been out of the water for moments, but it was enough to make me long for the cold again.

Out of the corner of my eye, I saw the boy walking across the bridge, pretending not to be watching me. I grinned and waded a little further into the water.

It was much more shallow than I'd expected. I really should have paid more attention to how deep it was before otherwise, I wouldn't have gone up there. It had been kids I'd seen in that pool before and they'd been swimming so it looked deeper.

I wouldn't be able to swim but I could definitely sit in it and look out towards Spinalonga.

I was glad about that though. I'd be able to keep a bit of an eye on Mitch in case anything happened and he could probably still see me, but we couldn't hear each other. I had my smart watch still on anyway so he'd be able to message me if he needed to.

I leaned back against the wall, letting the cool water lap at my chest and sighed happily.

"Hey," a slightly awkward voice said.

I looked up at the boy, letting a smile come over my face.

"Hey," I answered before looking back out over the beach and ocean.

"So, urm, come here often?" he asked, sitting down next to me.

"First time. You?"

"Nah, I've been here a couple of times," he said in a distinctly British accent.

He sounded posh, exactly the type of person I expected to be at this hotel.

"Nice."

Awkwardness hung in the air between us, but I wasn't really sure how to break it.

"You here with your family?" he asked after a moment.

"With my dad," I said, trying to inject some annoyance into the word 'dad'. "He's down there flirting with some woman."

"Ah," the boy said.

"Yeah. You here with your family?" I asked, trying to keep the conversation going.

"Kind of. Just with my older sister and Mom."

I nodded, aware that he was looking at me, but not sure what to say. I knew that if I looked at him, I would end up blushing, which didn't feel right.

"So, where are you from?" he asked.

"England, you?"

"Oh, me too! I'm from Winchester, where abouts do you live?"

"London," I said after a moment of trying to think of a posh place I could pretend I lived.

"Nice. Oh, shit, I realised I didn't tell you my name. I'm Christian."

He looked at me expectantly.

"Oh, I'm Alice," I said, silently celebrating the fact that I'd used the right name.

"Nice to meet you, Alice," he said, holding out his hand for me to shake.

I took it, feeling his warm, big hand envelop mine and smiling up into his dark brown eyes.

"It's nice to meet you, Christian," I said, trying to sound at least a little bit seductive.

His full lips slowly ticked up into a very attractive smile.

"How much longer are you here for?" he asked.

Out of the corner of my eye, I saw Mitch climbing the steps, holding my hat and sunglasses.

"Another week or so, I think," I said blithely.

Christian's smile widened.

"Good. Hopefully I'll see you around here more."

"Alice," Mitch called from the edge of the pool. "Are you ready for lunch?"

I let my gaze linger on Christian for a little longer before saying, "You will."

I stood, wading through the shallow water towards Mitch as I tried to ignore the sensation of Christian's gaze on my body.

It felt so weird, so different. I wasn't used to being that person, someone who would flirt so freely or who guys wanted to talk to or look at.

"Sure," I said to Mitch, fighting the urge to look back at Christian. "I'm starving."

CHAPTER NINETEEN

I rolled over, shoving my damp hair out the way, and closed my eyes again. It was starting to get light out, but it was still early. I didn't need to get up for another hour or so. I wanted more sleep.

My body still begged for it, but my mind refused.

I was too awake. Well, not awake, I was exhausted, but my mind was too alert. I was tense. I knew that if I did fall asleep, it wouldn't be long until my mom came in and woke me up so that we could get started on the journey. It was hard to sleep when I knew it would be broken.

Plus, dizziness hovered in my mind, just out of reach. The temptation to give up on sleep and go to Crete with Mitch and try to work out how we were going to break into an abandoned leper colony, laze in the sun, and flirt with that hot guy was too strong. Even now, I could feel the fantasy waiting so close to me and even though I knew sleep would be the smartest option, I couldn't.

I rolled over again, submitting to the temptation, and opened my eyes to a much brighter room. The thin, wispy curtains over the windows did little to block out the bright Cretan sun and the gentle whirl of the air-conditioning unit buzzed softly.

The sheets were softer too somehow. They were nicer than my ones back home, much comfier. I knew that if I were actually there right then, I'd have been able to get back to sleep. But now, with excitement buzzing in me, I just wanted to get up.

I sat up, pushed my hair back off my face and looked around the room. It was much nicer than my room back home too and I would have loved to live there but the startling lack of books wasn't right.

Everything about the room was light and airy and perfectly suited to a luxury hotel room somewhere like Crete, which almost made me wonder where my brain had gotten it from. If it were from an ad or something, I'd love to actually go there one day.

I slipped out of the huge bed and padded towards the window at the far end of the room. Pushing the curtains aside, I opened the french windows and stepped out onto the balcony. The warm orange tiles burnt my feet slightly as I crossed to the edge and rested my forearms on the wall, looking out over the resort.

A splashing from below me caught my attention and I looked down at Mitch who was dutifully swimming lengths of the small private pool. He continued swimming for a while before noticing my gaze and gesturing for me to join him. I nodded before turning and slipping back into the room, feeling the ice-cold air kiss my skin.

I rushed towards my suitcase which I'd tucked in the corner, just past the stairs, and grabbed some clothes for the day. I threw them on quickly, making sure that I looked good enough just in case I happened to run into Christian again, before brushing my teeth and rushing down the stairs.

I had felt bad when Mitch had insisted that I take the room instead of sleeping downstairs on the pullout sofa and I had refused. Kind of.

I'd tried but he wouldn't budge. He simply looked at me, then looked around the room before sighing and explaining exactly how easy it would be for someone to break into our room whilst we were sleeping. After he told me that, I didn't have it in me to fight that much. Of course, I was worried about him getting murdered in his sleep, but he'd assured me he was used to the risk.

I wasn't sure how I felt about that.

"Good morning, Alice," Mitch called from one of the seats outside, as I made my way through the lounge, where his bed had already been put away and his bedding folded neatly.

My eyes darted around the pool area as I made my way through the open door and sat down in the chair next to him.

"Morning," I said finally, having not noticed anything unusual.

"How did you sleep?" he continued in a perfectly pleasant tone.

"Fine," I snapped. "I would have slept better if I hadn't been woken up by you splashing around this morning."

Mitch smirked and gave me a subtle thumbs up.

"I'm sorry, Alice," he said in a tired tone that did not match his expression. "Can I get you a coffee to help?"

I sighed, my eyes darting towards one of the side walls as a splash came from the next pool over.

There was someone outside in the pool or on the patio of the room next to us, that's why he was acting like that and had called me Alice.

"Yes. You know how I have my coffee," I said dismissively.

He sighed loudly.

"Coming right up."

He gestured for me to follow him in and I nodded.

"Actually, I'll come with. Knowing you, you'll just mess it up like you mess up everything else," I said with as much venom as I could muster for how early it was in the morning.

I sent him an apologetic look but he just nodded at me, looking surprised and impressed.

"Sorry!" I cried softly as soon as the door was shut behind me. "That felt so mean!"

"Kid," Mitch said with a laugh, holding up a hand to stop me. "You did great."

I cringed but accepted his compliment.

He shook his head with a smile and started rooting through the coffee pods.

"Honestly, you did good," he insisted before glancing back at me. "I gotta say, I don't know how you have your coffee though. What do you want? We got a fancy machine here and a bunch of pods. I can do you a good deal on a latte, caramel latte, cappuccino, Americano, or a flat white, but I truly don't know why anyone would have that. Any of those catching your fancy?"

My mind reeled as Mitch started opening drawers on the cabinet the coffee machine was on.

I didn't drink coffee, not normally, but I kind of did want to try one. I didn't know what half the drinks Mitch had mentioned were though.

"Oh, got even more in here. Got some vegan ones, oat milk, coconut, or almond. Some iced coffees too and... orange juice. How does a coffee pod of orange juice work?" he asked, turning to me and holding out a small pod that had a picture of an orange slice on it.

I laughed, taking the pod and shaking it slightly.

It rattled worryingly, but I didn't have an answer for Mitch. I brought it up to my nose and sniffed it experimentally, but it just smelt faintly of coffee. I wasn't sure if that was from being in a drawer of coffee pods or if the smell came from the drink itself.

"Is it… is it orange juice and coffee, like, together?" I asked, holding it back out to Mitch.

He took it and looked down at the pod in fascination.

"You know, don't knock it until you try it. I've had it a few times. The flavour is unexpected but… not bad," he said, still staring at it. "But, I think this is just juice. Damn. I'll just have another latte then. What did you want, kid?"

"Um, a latte would be good," I said quickly, hoping that it would be. "Did you say there was a caramel latte?"

That sounded like it would be better. Sweeter at least.

"Mmm…" Mitch started pulling the drawers open again. "Yes! Got it here. One caramel latte coming up!"

I watched awkwardly as he fiddled around with the coffee machine, not quite sure what to do, before crossing over to the table and sinking into a seat. Steam poured out of the machine before coffee dripped down into the mug and Mitch placed it in front of me.

I sniffed the drink, the comforting sweet smell of coffee washing over me.

"So," Mitch said over the noise of his coffee being made. "Plan for the day…"

I sat up straighter, my attention on him immediately.

Would we be going to Spinalonga? Or something else fun?

"How's your stamina? I mean, I know that you can swim and you were pretty fast when I almost hit you with my car. Can you maintain that speed for long?" he asked, sitting down opposite me, his coffee in his hand.

"Um… only when I'm being chased?" I tried to joke before hastily adding, "I don't know really. I don't run much, apart from when we have to at school."

He nodded slightly and took a sip of his steaming drink, seemingly unbothered by the temperature.

"That makes sense. Probably the same for most kids your age, but we can work on that. We'll hit the gym today, not go too hard because being stiff and sore when you potentially have to run for your life is a terrible thing. Trust me, I learnt that the hard way. I wonder if they have a personal trainer at the gym here. I assume they will. My Greek is a little rusty, but I reckon we can work something out. Wait, you can't dive, can you?"

I paused, my cup lifted halfway to my lips.

"Like, diving in a pool or…" I asked, trailing off.

"Scuba."

"I never tried."

Mitch nodded, his eyes narrowed as he took another sip.

"How do you feel about learning?" he asked.

I considered it for a moment, taking the time to try some of the bitter yet almost sickly sweet coffee.

It sounded pretty fun, but also scary. The ocean was a terrifying place with sharks and other murderous animals. The thought of being trapped somewhere deep underwater, my oxygen slowly dwindling as some shark came towards me, made my heart squeeze in fear.

But, this was a dream. I couldn't get hurt in a dream, surely.

I was safe. I could feel that I was still at home, in bed. When I concentrated on it, I could feel my duvet resting on me, my pillow under my head, and I could almost see the light streaming through my closed eyelids.

Plus, in the dream, I'd probably be with Mitch, so I'd be okay. I'd be a pretty terrible treasure hunter if I couldn't scuba dive.

It felt necessary. We were about to dive in the dream I'd had before. We were on a boat somewhere similar to Crete, ready to go.

I needed to learn.

"I'd be open to learning," I said carefully.

Mitch grinned and nodded.

"I can sort that out. I wonder how much I'd need to bribe the diving people to let me borrow the equipment. I reckon if I tell them that we're both already certified and make some fairly real looking PADI documents, they won't mind too much. Then, I could take you out and teach you for real. There's got to be some not too horrible spots around here that we could use. It would be better to use a pool, of course, but we can't exactly say you're a diver then do that," he mused. "I mean, I managed to teach Zaq, I can teach you. That kid did not learn easily."

"Why not?" I asked, worry growing within me.

Mitch chuckled softly and shook his head.

"I mean, lots of reasons honestly. He wasn't a big fan of the ocean, didn't like swimming anywhere where he couldn't see what was going on under him, and didn't really get why you have to study so much to learn to dive."

I understood most of those things, truly. I didn't love the idea of something swimming under me and not being able to see it.

It made my skin crawl.

"You have to study to be able to dive?" I asked, choosing to focus on that instead of everything else he'd said.

"If you want to dive well, you do. The actual process of diving is easy enough, it's the other stuff you need to know. You gotta learn about buoyancy, warning signs of things like the bends or oxygen toxicity, how to communicate underwater, how to use dive computers and what not. It's a surprisingly large amount that you need to learn to be able to do very little."

I nodded, my mind swimming from everything he'd said.

It made sense but I'd never given it much thought. I didn't think it would be that difficult or require that much learning. I thought you could just put an oxygen tank on and be done with it, but… apparently not.

"But, I'll get that sorted this afternoon. First, breakfast, some time by the pool, and the gym. Are you ready to go down now?"

I opened my mouth to reply, but light burst in front

of my eyes and dizziness overcame me.

"Good morning, Grace! Time to get up and get ready to go. We're already running late!" my mother called.

I wrenched my eyes open, the brightness burning into my brain. My mom had turned the lights on in my room and it was blinding.

"Morning," I muttered, my voice gruff from sleep and my head still spinning slightly.

"Did you finish packing last night? Is this all you're taking?" she demanded, standing over the two suitcases I'd packed the night before.

"Yeah," I said, pushing myself up and rubbing the sleep and white spots from my vision.

My mom examined the bulging bags for a moment before sighing and turning away.

"Are you sure you have everything? I don't want a repeat of last time. My mother still brings up the fact that you didn't wear tights to dinner and how inappropriate that was."

I resisted the urge to sigh at her.

That hadn't happened last time, it had been years ago. I'd not worn tights with a dress to this fancy restaurant which apparently was super inappropriate, even though it was the middle of summer and I was, like, twelve, maybe thirteen. Surely, that was okay? I hadn't even considered that it would be a problem.

"I've packed tights," I said.

"Are you sure?"

"Yeah, I double checked."

My mom's nostrils flared at me.

"Don't say 'yeah', say 'yes'. I don't want to hear another lecture from my mother about how I've failed rearing you because you sound cheap," she snapped.

"Sorry," I muttered, just wanting our conversation to be done so that I could start getting ready.

"It's fine," she replied, her tone making it clear that it was not fine. "Have you packed your swimming costumes?"

"Yeah. Yes," I corrected myself quickly.

"And nice clothes for when we go out for dinner?"

"Yes."

"And some cardigans to cover yourself up?"

"Yes."

I knew better than to not pack those. My grandparents always judged me for showing too much skin, even if I didn't think it was that much. I barely wore anything low cut or revealing, and yet they made it sound like I was walking around basically naked.

They were never openly rude or mean, it was always just looks and little comments. It was enough to make me very cautious of what I wore around them.

"Good. Bring your bags down, we need to go out in five minutes. We're already running late and your father," she sneered as she said the word, "has been wasting time faffing with the car."

"Okay, I'll get up now," I said flatly.

She turned and left the room without saying anything more and I sagged, staring blankly at the duvet in front of me.

I was excited to go, kind of. Things weren't too bad there and Mom was normally in a bit of a better mood, but... there were also a lot of things I didn't like about being there. Hopefully, my grandparents wouldn't spend too much time with us when we were there and things would be better once they left. They always were.

I blinked heavily and started to stand, my imagination wandering back to Crete. Flashes of the world flickered through my mind as I started getting dressed mechanically, with only the faintest trace of dizziness. It was almost like every time I blinked, I jumped between my fantasy and reality, a foot in both worlds but not really present in either.

I caught glimpses of a fancy-looking gym, rows of gleaming and confusing-looking machines, weights, and a wall of windows overlooking the resort. A man, tall and overly muscular, talked to Mitch before pointing to various machines and showing me how to use them. Mitch worked out nearby, keeping an eye on me as if cautious to make sure I didn't do too much.

Even as I brushed my teeth and tied my hair up, I was aware of the phantom burn of a stitch starting in my side which made me chuckle slightly. I knew why I was feeling it. It was because, in my imagination, I was on the treadmill, the inclination turned up way too high, but I shouldn't have been feeling it really.

I shook my head, staring at my reflection, and pushed the imagined ache away.

"Grace! What is taking you so long? We need to go!" my mom snapped, her voice echoing down the hallway.

"Just a sec!" I called back, starting to leave the bathroom before stopping, my eyes finding the bottle of conditioner that I'd left in the shower.

A realisation crashed into me. I hadn't packed anything from the bathroom. My toothbrush, toothpaste, shampoo, conditioner, hair oil and everything else were still scattered around the room.

My eyes widened and I rushed along the hall and into my bedroom, grabbing my shower bag from my desk before throwing myself back through the door. I shoved the items almost at random into the waterproof bag and barely managed to zip it before rushing back into my room.

I stared helplessly at my bulging suitcases. It definitely would not fit in either of those but it could go in my backpack. That was barely full. I lifted the bag onto my bed and ripped the top open, shoving the toiletries bag deep inside and tightening it again.

I looked frantically around the room, searching for anything else that I might have missed, but I couldn't see anything obvious. It was fine. It would be fine. If there was anything that I really needed that I forgot, we could just go out to the shops.

I chewed on my lip nervously before shaking my head. I could hear my mom directing my dad around downstairs, I just needed to go down and be done.

I double-checked that I'd done up my backpack before swinging it onto my shoulders, ignoring the slight tweak in my back that it caused.

"Grace! Are you coming?" my mom shouted up the stairs.

"Coming now!" I called back, grabbing my suitcases and dragging them out of the room.

The wheels caught on the carpet, gouging deep tracks into it, but I ignored them, rushing towards the stairs and struggling down them, the suitcases heavy and unwieldy.

"Here, darling!" my dad called as I turned the bend, dropping a bag by the front door and rushing towards me.

"Steven," my mom snapped coldly. "Can you finish putting that bag in the car, please?"

Her tone made it clear that it was not a request.

Dad rolled his eyes slightly at me, helping me get the suitcases to the bottom of the stairs before turning back towards my mom.

"Right away, dear," he said to her before looking back at me. "Leave your bags there, I'll grab them in a minute. I've got a whole Tetris situation going on in the boot."

I chuckled lightly at him as he picked up the bag he'd

dropped and disappeared through the front door.

"Is that what you're wearing?" my mom asked sharply.

I looked down at my clothes. I was just wearing a t-shirt and leggings, nothing too questionable or so I thought. It was basically the exact outfit I'd worn in my dream with Mitch. He hadn't judged me for it.

"Yeah?"

"Grace, what did I tell you about saying 'yeah'?" she said, badly mimicking my voice as she said the word. "Fine. I'll just tell my parents that they're your travelling clothes and that you'd never normally wear something so casual out in public."

I ignored that, knowing that she was lying, but almost doing it for me.

Not fully, it was mostly for appearances.

"Want to help me squeeze the last couple of things into the car?" my dad asked me, reappearing in the house.

"Yes," I said, jumping on that immediately.

I grabbed the handle of one of my suitcases, but my dad shooed my hand aside with a grin and took it instead. I followed him from the house, the morning air surprisingly crisp for the middle of summer, and stopped at the back of our car. The boot was open and almost entirely full. I wasn't sure why, but my mom always liked to bring a lot of stuff when we went to my grandparents. They were pretty judgemental about things like repeated

outfits or not wearing the right shoes with a dress or…
well, most things.

"Oof," my dad huffed as he swung my first suitcase
up into the boot. "Is this all just books?"

My cheeks flushed slightly and I glanced back towards
the door, making sure my mom was out of earshot.

"Not entirely…"

He laughed, causing my mom to appear in the doorway, her arms crossed and her lips pursed.

"You sure you got enough?" he teased, loading the
second one in too.

"Probably, but if not, the internet exists," I shot back
with a grin.

He laughed and ruffled my hair.

"You sure you're going to be able to get signal up
there?" he joked.

"Eh," I shrugged. "Normally, you can get signal if
you hide on the roof just outside the room I stay in."

He narrowed his eyes at me a little.

"Good, but be careful out there. Don't go out if it's
raining and stay away from the edge."

"I know, I will, Dad."

He smiled at me before pulling me into a hug.

"Have a good holiday, Gracie."

CHAPTER TWENTY

The world crawled by outside my window, the journey seemingly endless despite the fact we'd only been in the car for an hour. My mind kept flitting towards Crete and Mitch, but it didn't want to stay there.

It was fun and interesting, don't get me wrong, but it wasn't appealing to me as much as normal. I think it was because we were just in our room at the resort, learning about diving which was really fascinating, and I did want to learn about it but every time I tried, I found myself withdrawing from the dream.

Fear was stopping me. I wasn't sure what it was about diving that made my heart clench with panic, but there was definitely something. It didn't matter anyway. I could feel the information soaking in which made it harder for me to want to stay there.

Plus, my heart longed for action and excitement, not for sitting around inside. I wanted to be out there doing stuff, running around rather than being trapped.

"How's it going, kid?" I heard Mitch ask, but he sounded far away.

I was only half in the world, dizziness pulling me away gently.

"Good," I replied faintly.

The next song came on, loud and obnoxious, but I knew my mom was enjoying it. She was tapping the steering wheel as she navigated the twisty roads slowly. Cars were lining up behind us, clearly getting frustrated by her glacial speed, but my mom continued along the road slowly, either unbothered or unaware.

I let out a breath, trying not to get frustrated, but the urge to throw the car door open and jump out was almost overwhelming. I just needed something, something to distract myself from the boring monotony.

I stared blankly down at the phone in my hands wanting to text someone, probably Phoebe, but it was too early. I didn't want to wake her even though I knew she was a morning person. Seven was too early even for her.

But, then what?

I couldn't just sit in the car and listen to the endless wall of noise streaming far too loudly from the speakers. I had already exhausted all of the apps on my phone, so what was I left with?

"Oh, for God's sake!" my mom cried as we pulled onto the motorway and traffic stretched on ahead of us endlessly.

The car ground to a stop as it joined the procession, my mom's fingers already starting to tap incessantly against the steering wheel again.

"Why are there so many cars out at this time? I know it's the first day of the holidays, but this is ridiculous!" she cried. "This is what we get for leaving so late. If we'd left when I wanted to, we would have avoided all of this!"

She revved the engine, as if her annoyance would somehow clear the traffic. It didn't, of course.

I understood her impatience, I didn't want to sit in the traffic either, but there was nothing we could do about it. Revving or ranting about how it was everyone else's fault did nothing to help.

I wished it did though. I wished there was a secret path or something we could do to get there faster. As much as I was dreading it a bit, I did want to get to my grandparent's house. Things were always stressful there, but they were also somehow easier.

My mom and I rarely fought when we were there. There were small blips of course, there always would be, but on the whole it was normally okay. Of course, things would be stressful at first, but as soon as my grandparents get bored of being around us and leave to stay in their other house, things would get better. We kind of did things separately most of the time when we were there but we'd have meals together and hang out sometimes. I usually just spent time going for walks, reading, swimming, watching TV, whatever I wanted.

I couldn't wait.

My head dropped back against the headrest and a soft, wistful sigh slipped out of my mouth as my mom tapped her nails against the steering wheel somehow more relentlessly than before.

I let my eyes flutter shut, not wanting to be in this world but also not wanting to go to Mitch's, which left me with nowhere.

I could go back to him, that wouldn't be too bad. I could sit in our room and continue to study, watch the videos he'd put on which explained the information better than the textbook and then see what happened after that but… I didn't want to. I knew that if I told him that I didn't, he wouldn't force me to, but he might be disappointed in me. He'd explained how important it was for me to learn, and I knew I needed to, but I was studying and learning when I wasn't even there so I didn't need to sit through it.

I wanted more.

I wanted more excitement. I wished that I could just close my eyes and skip through it all. Learn everything I needed to in the blink of an eye without wasting any time, but I couldn't. I didn't even want to, not really. It felt wrong. It felt like cheating and I wasn't even sure if I could do it.

I didn't need to though. I could leave that fantasy there, ticking away in the background, and come back to it when it was more fun. I didn't need to stick to just one fantasy. I could go anywhere.

But, where should I go? I wanted more excitement, more entertainment.

I felt the car spinning around me hazily as I let my mind wander, contemplating my next adventure. I could do anything. Do anything and go anywhere.

But, where did I want to go?

The car jolted forwards and I blinked my eyes open, the brightness blinding me for a moment as spots swam in front of my vision.

"This damn traffic!" my mom cried, slamming her fist against the wheel.

My head whipped around to face her.

That wasn't right. My mom didn't say things like 'damn' unless people could overhear her. She favoured stronger words, ones that would make her tell me off for being unladylike if I were to repeat them.

The window wasn't open. There was no reason for her to censor herself like that.

I looked around, my eyes scanning my surroundings and landing on the car in front of us.

Was it red before?

Excitement started to creep into my heart as I considered it. I wasn't sure, but I didn't think it was. I was in a new fantasy, I was almost certain of it. The trees on the other side of the road looked different now. They were greener before, but now they were tinged with reds and oranges, the leaves drying and falling from the branches as life slowly left them.

The building on our side of the road looked different too. There had been people working there before, but now it looked empty. The houses they were building seemed frozen in their incomplete state and I wasn't sure how I could tell, but something told me they'd been stuck like that for a long time. I couldn't put my finger on what made me think that. Something just seemed wrong.

My skin prickled as a creeping sensation trickled down my spine and that feeling of wrongness intensified.

Movement caught my eyes. Just a flash of something that I could barely see from where we were idling. Confusion washed over me as I stared at the shipping container someone had made into an office at the edge of the building site, not far from our car. I couldn't quite see into it, just a hint of the red-painted inner walls.

That seemed like a weird decision. Why would anyone go to the effort of painting the inside walls of an office in an abandoned building site? And from what I could see, the paint was bright and glossy. It looked fresh.

Maybe they were coming back to the site? Starting to work on the houses again soon?

The car crept forwards again ever so slightly and I

couldn't drag my eyes away from the office despite every part of my brain and body screaming at me to look away. From the new angle, I could see further into the office, but it didn't answer any of my questions.

The red paint wasn't just coating the walls. From what I could see, it covered the floor and ceiling too. The slightly viscous, chunky liquid coated almost every surface in the office.

A shadow crossed the doorway and my chest tightened. There was movement inside and it made my heart race even though I didn't know what was happening or why I was so scared. Even so, I wanted to scream, to tell my mom to pull onto the hard shoulder and drive as fast as we could away from there, to call the place, or just do anything, but I was frozen. I couldn't even blink as we pulled further forwards.

I could see into the office now. I could see the discarded piles of bones that had been sucked clean, but it didn't matter. Whoever or whatever had been in there before stepped out of the door, raising their blood-splattered face to the sky and letting the sky warm their skin.

I could almost feel the relief that the figure exuded as they stood motionless, simply relishing the feel of the sun's gentle caress but that bubble popped as their eyes opened and found mine. Their tongue, too long, stained a dark red and forked at the end, snaked out of their mouth and wiped the blood from their face. With the gore gone, I could finally see their features properly.

An involuntary shudder ripped through me.

They looked human, but barely. Their face was skeletal yet the skin hung from their bones loosely. Cheekbones jutted out sharply, but the flesh dangling from them was baggy. Their eyes, wide and gaping, lit up with excitement and expectation as their lips pulled back into a grotesque grin which showed too much of their pointed, blood-stained teeth.

They slowly lifted one hand to their lips, extending their snakelike tongue to clean the blood off their fingers. Their eyes fluttered shut in ecstasy and, even though I wasn't close enough to hear it, somehow I knew that they moaned throatily. They had enjoyed their feast.

My pulse danced frantically in my throat as their eyes opened again, still focused on me and the car rolled forwards as traffic started to clear. But it wasn't enough. We stopped again, still too close to the creature for my breathing to come easily.

Their gaze didn't leave me as slowly, the monster stepped forwards.

Their steps were clumsy and uncertain, staggering almost. They moved like a newborn deer, as if they weren't quite used to their body yet, but they quickly gained confidence. Their steps became longer, loping and utterly inhuman as they raced towards me, their hunger palpable.

There was too little distance between the monster and my open window. I hadn't even realised it was open before, I'd been too enthralled by the monster, but now my hand shot out to jab at the window controls and it rose at a leisurely pace. I looked around frantically for the lock on the door, but there was nothing.

I was going to die. It was going to reach me and tear the door open before devouring me like it had the bodies in the shipping container.

I glanced away from the approaching monster, staring at the unmoving row of cars in front of us. My mom could pull onto the hard shoulder and speed away, but there were cars on it too. It would buy us a few seconds, maybe a little more, but it wouldn't help.

We were going to die.

I squeezed my eyes shut as tightly as I could, fighting back a whimper, painfully aware of how close the monster was to us. I tried desperately, frantically, to escape, clutching at the faint dizziness that brushed my mind but it slipped from my grasp.

I opened my eyes again. We hadn't moved. That same red car idled in front of us and the monster was still hurtling across the building site towards us. I clenched my eyes shut again, my breath nothing more than sharp gasps.

I couldn't die. It was just a fantasy, a dream. Nothing more. I couldn't die in a dream, right?

I was the one in charge, I was in control of my fantasies. I could make the thing disappear if I wanted to.

I forced my eyes open, glancing at the monster in the mirror for just a second, before making myself take a deep, slow breath. I was in control. With my hands no longer shaking as badly as before, I let my eyes find the monster again and waited for it to disappear.

Nothing happened.

Desperation started to claw at my heart as I tried harder, willing the monster to vanish so hard that it almost hurt. The car in front of us jolted forwards and I let out a small relieved gasp, unable to look away from the monster. We were moving, we might be safe.

Well, not safe. Something told me that the monster, that aswang or vampire or draugr, whatever it was, would hunt me down until it found me. It would never be satisfied until it tasted my blood and felt my heart stop as it feasted on my flesh.

I would never be safe again. That thing was going to find me wherever I went. It was going to find me and murder me and I couldn't even escape the fantasy. I was going to die for real.

The car rolled to a stop again and a sob of fear escaped my mouth, but I pushed my fist against my lips to muffle the noise as a faint scream came from some-where behind us.

Someone had tried to escape. They'd noticed the monster and decided to take their chances on foot but it had caught them. It stopped, the screaming person held tightly in one hand, its eyes still on me.

"Grace?" a voice that could be my mother's asked. "Are you alright?"

I couldn't speak, too scared to even make a noise, as I watched the thing in the mirror. Its face stretched into a taunting smile as it looked at me, enjoying the fear and horror that was coursing through me.

"Grace?" my mom asked again, turning to look at me but I couldn't look away from the monster.

It seemed amused by my fear but the person in its grasp had finally had enough. They struggled and my mouth opened to shout something but I wasn't even sure what to say.

It didn't matter. The monster had grown bored or hungry. It lifted the woman into the air easily, one hand tangling in their hair and pulling her head roughly to the side before it sunk its face into her neck.

Its eyes fluttered shut briefly and her screams finally stopped as it feasted.

Far too soon, it opened its eyes, before pulling its head back. Sinew and viscera stretched from the body before snapping and spraying even more blood over the monster's face, but it didn't even flinch. It lifted the body, hefting it into the air.

I watched, frozen in horror, as the body flew through the air and crashed into the window on the back of our car, shattering it and sending blood everywhere.

"Oh, God!" my mom gasped, finally becoming aware of the monster.

Tears burned in my eyes. I wanted to rip the door open and run away too, but I was stuck. I knew it was useless. My limbs were heavy with terror and there was nothing I could do. It didn't matter. If I left the car, the beast would be on me in an instant but if I stayed, maybe I'd be safe.

I knew I was wrong but I clutched at that tiny flutter of hope anyway. Maybe, it wasn't that strong. Maybe it wouldn't be able to get through the sturdy metal of the car.

That hope was dashed as I watched the monster stroll towards the car. It didn't even bother running, it knew there was no escape. It just wanted to savour my fear.

Its smile was too confident. It knew the car posed no protection against it but still, it wanted to prove it to me. It wanted me to sob.

It reached the back of the car and plucked the body off it, dropping it carelessly onto the floor.

The creature's face split into a maniacal smile as it slammed its hands down on the boot, the squeal of metal splitting the air as it buckled under the monster's touch, proving that it would be useless to run or fight.

Tears flowed freely down my face but I couldn't look away from the mirror, knowing that if I did, I wouldn't know where it was. I couldn't breathe. My chest burnt, but I couldn't do anything to help it as the monster slowly walked around to the side of the car. Its nail scratched along the paintwork, cutting into it and piercing the metal beneath but I could barely hear the noise over the terrified screams coming from my mom.

I couldn't move. I couldn't fight. I couldn't do anything.

The certainty of death and suffering overpowered me, filling me with a hopelessness I'd never experienced. There was nothing I could do but stare into the monster's blown-out pupils as its hand slowly curled around my door handle and its face stretched into a wide smile, displaying bloody pointed teeth.

I was thrown forwards and the seatbelt cut painfully into my chest. The silence of the car was disorientating after the deafening noise just moments before.

Nausea threatened to overwhelm me and tears slipped from my eyes as my heart raced. My head snapped to the window, staring at the trees beside us, before my gaze darted to the mirror.

There was no one there. No monster, nothing.

The building site, now barely visible in the rear mirror, bustled with life and activity.

"Urgh!" my mom said, slamming her fist against the steering wheel again. "This traffic is ridiculous. I don't care what the satnav says, we're leaving the motorway at the next junction!"

I sagged back into my seat, wiping the tears away as subtly as I could and sucking in a shaky breath, my pulse still racing.

It was fine. I'd escaped. I was safe.

But, I knew that, in some fantasy, I was still there. Still alive, of course, I would be for days still, but wracked with agony. The monster would torture me, drinking in my screams and pain as it slowly feasted on my body.

A shudder went through me and I risked a glance at my mom. She was unaware of the fear that had my hands shaking even now as she fiddled with her phone, trying to find the next album to put on, but she felt my glance.

"What?" she asked, looking up at me.

Her eyes narrowed slightly as she took in my fearful expression and bloodshot eyes.

I swallowed thickly, squeezing my phone as tightly as I could to try and stop the trembling of my hands. How could I explain how close I had come to death?

"What's wrong?" she demanded.

"Nightmare," I muttered finally.

There was a pause before she snorted.

"A nightmare?" she asked, her words dripping with ridicule.

"Yeah."

"What was so horrible about this nightmare?"

I couldn't tell her. It was pointless. I knew she wouldn't understand and would just laugh at me instead.

"I don't really remember it now," I lied.

Her expression told me she didn't believe me, but she didn't care to press it any further. She looked back down at her phone, ignoring that the car in front of us had started moving as she searched for something to put on.

Someone behind us beeped, the noise sending my pulse racing again and my gaze scouring our surroundings but she just glared at the person in the mirror.

"Fuck off," she said venomously, finally selecting a song and moving the car forwards as she gestured rudely at the person behind us. "People have no manners these days."

She seemed entirely unaware of the irony of her words.

I pressed my hand against my chest, trying to steady my breathing. My heart pounded so hard I could feel it against my palm but, as I sucked in slow and steady breaths, fear started to drain out of me.

It was just a dream. A scary one, but still just a dream.

I was safe and I was in control.

"I'm not sitting around here for another second," my mom said.

She turned the steering wheel sharply, pulling into the empty hard shoulder and speeding past the rows of unmoving cars.

The next exit wasn't far, but time dragged slowly. I wanted to sink low into my seat and hide from everyone we passed but I couldn't.

Mom smiled victoriously as we pulled off the busy motorway, the satnav telling us off, and joined a smaller but equally busy road.

"Ha! This will be much quicker!" she said smugly as the journey time on the satnav increased significantly.

I let my eyes flutter shut again, not wanting to stay with my mom and hear her continue to go on about what a great decision she'd made.

A tiny flutter of fear gripped my heart as I let dizziness wash over me again but this time, my destination was clear.

"What did you think?" Mitch asked, pulling the respirator from his mouth and lifting the goggles up to his forehead.

I paddled gently, quickly taking in the warm water we were in, and spat the weird rubber mouthpiece out so that I could suck in a proper breath.

The water was shallow where we were, tucked in near a strip of sand at the bottom of a high cliff, and deliciously warm. My mind raced to catch up on what I missed, getting glimpses of the boat, a flash of fear as I fell backwards into the sea and the lingering sense of wonder I'd felt underwater.

"It was good!" I said, following Mitch further onto the beach.

He looked utterly at ease in the water, even with the heavy oxygen tank on his back. Something told me that he'd spent half his life in the water.

"Yeah?" Mitch asked.

From what I now remembered, it had been good. The world was so quiet underwater, just the soft rush of air and muffled sound of bubbles when I breathed. It felt like another world. One where I was weightless and moved so easily and freely. Fish had flitted past us, so close and entirely unbothered by our presence. It had been… wonderful.

"Yeah, it was great!"

I was a little sad that I'd missed it. The memories were good, but I wished I could have really experienced it for real.

"Awesome. Well, you did good kid. Shall we head back to the boat?"

CHAPTER TWENTY-ONE

My foot tapped against the floor, keeping in time with the music as I fought the ever-present urge to disappear back into my fantasy but fear stopped me. I could still feel the phantom sting of the monster's sharp, boney fingers digging into my skin as it held me.

I couldn't risk it. I couldn't risk going back there.

It was fine though, Mom was in a much better mood now that we'd crossed the border into Scotland, which made things easier. She'd even let us stop at a petrol station to grab some snacks.

She'd been happy, giddy almost, as she ambled down the sparse aisles of the shop. She'd picked up crisps, chocolates and multiple cans of soda, despite normally saying that people who snack are weak and undisciplined.

It was the slight change that always happened when we were in Scotland. I'm not sure if returning to where she grew up made her feel more like a kid or if it was the distance from our home and my dad but it was defi-nitely something.

She always got more tense around her parents but, once they were gone, it was better.

"I love this song!" my mom cried happily, her hand darting out to turn the volume up even louder.

I smiled slightly and looked away, my gaze roaming the rolling green hills surrounding us.

I loved Scotland. It was so much prettier than England, in my opinion. Everything felt so much more spaced out and the windy roads that edged along hills and cut through forests just felt emptier than back home.

My eyes followed a grassy mound that rose up in the distance. It was encircled by a weak-looking fence, barely standing, halfway up the hill. Faint interest washed through me as I eyed the radio towers and giant satellite dish on the top. It seemed weird that there would be one so far out in the middle of nowhere. There were barely any houses nearby, no shops or anything of note.

My mind wandered lazily, thinking of a million possibilities. It was probably nothing but it could be anything.

Dizziness speared my mind and I closed my eyes against it, fighting off the wave of nausea that came with it. Sucking in slow, deep breaths, I fought the urge to vomit. My hands tightened into fists as a chill crept over my skin.

Even as the queasiness wore off, that chill remained.

Carefully, I opened my eyes but it made no difference. It was dark wherever I was now. Whatever fantasy world I'd created, it was one without light. Or, maybe I was just in a darkened room.

There was a greenish glow coming from a small light on the wall somewhere beside me, but the light didn't reach far. It left the rest of the room untouched. Even so, I edged towards it hopefully. If there was a light there, maybe there was an exit.

Pain shot through my shin suddenly as something hard hit me and clattered loudly across the concrete floor, the noise echoing in the room.

"Hello?" a faint voice croaked.

It was weak, shaky and young.

I felt compelled to answer.

"Hello," I whispered back, stepping in the direction of the noise.

I managed two steps, my shin still stinging before stopping. Goosebumps rose on my arms and I felt the hair on the back of my neck stand up but I was sure why. Nothing had changed to make me feel so uneasy, but a faint smell had reached my nose. I couldn't quite work out what it was. It was musty, sweaty, but also sharp.

There was a hint of blood in the air.

"Who is it? How long have you been there?" the voice asked, growing higher pitched with fear.

Metal clacked somewhere in the same direction as the voice.

"I'm… I'm Grace. I just got here." I paused before asking, "Who are you?"

There was nothing for a moment before the girl snuffled quietly.

"You're not one of them," she said, her voice thick with unexpected tears.

I froze, glancing towards the light before staring back into the darkness.

"How do you know?" I asked, fear creeping along my spine.

"They don't care about my name. They just call me 'subject number four'."

The utter silence of the room seemed loud.

"There are others like you?" I asked, not even knowing who this girl was or why she was there.

She laughed hollowly before breaking off into hacking coughs that ended with her spitting something wet onto the floor.

"Not anymore. There were, or so I've heard. Before me, there was a boy, but he died so I didn't get to even meet him. I think this is the first time they've had two subjects in here at the same time. That's what you are, right?" she asked slowly.

I swallowed, wanting to say 'no,' but the word died on my lips.

Squeezing my hands into tight fists, I tried desperately

to remind myself that it was just a fantasy, not real at all.

I could leave at any point.

But that hadn't happened before. With that horrible monster thing, when I'd tried to leave, I'd been trapped there. It hadn't been until my mom had jolted me out of it that I'd even been able to escape. I couldn't rely on that happening again.

"I'm sorry, I'm talking too much. I remember how scared I was when I was first brought here. I'm Anna, by the way. You asked, but I didn't answer." She paused before asking, "Are you okay?"

Somehow, she sounded like she was worried about me, despite how frail she sounded. I should have been worried about her, not the other way around.

I nodded before realising she wouldn't be able to see me and swallowed again.

"I'm okay. Is there a light in here that I can turn on?" I asked, my voice sounding strained even to my ears.

I hated being in the dark, both in my fantasy and real life. I just hated not being able to see what was happening around me or if there was anyone else there. For all I knew, there were a bunch of those horrifying monsters waiting just out of reach to grab me and rip me apart.

Maybe Anna was one of those monsters.

"Yeah, it's over by the door."

I looked around, still unable to make out much in the dark room. I'd thought my eyes might adjust, but I still couldn't see anything.

"Were you unconscious when you came in?" Anna asked kindly. "It's over by the green light. There's a plastic box around the switch, but you can lift that pretty easily."

I moved cautiously towards the green light, trying not to walk into anything else, but my hands brushed against the cold tile wall without incident. I recoiled immediately, not expecting it to be as icy as it was, before forcing myself to sweep my hand across the wall.

I found the plastic box, my hands shaking as I tried to lift it but it wouldn't move.

"It's on a hinge," Anna said finally. "The front part pulls up."

I nodded to myself as my fingers found the small lip and I pulled it upwards, reaching blindly into the box.

The lights flashed on and I groaned softly as I forced my eyes shut against the too bright white glow that filled the room. Finally, I was able to peel them open and, at first, I couldn't see anything. The light reflected straight back at me from the white, smudge-covered walls, making it hard to focus on anything, but before long, my eyes adjusted.

The floor was a barren concrete. There was a drain in the middle and a metal chair lying on its side not too far from me. That must have been what I had bumped into. There were cameras in every corner, all of them pointing at the corner of the room I was trying not to look at.

I don't know why I was avoiding looking at Anna, but I was. I think it was a subconscious thing. I knew that if I did look at her, I'd never be able to forget the vision. It was a moment, a brief moment of weakness, where I debated closing my eyes and fleeing back to the car with my mom. I could still feel the car seat underneath me, the phone clutched in my hands, and I could almost hear the pounding radio.

But I couldn't run. I needed to look. I needed to know what was going on.

I shouldn't have looked.

Anna looked so much worse than she had in my imagination. The girl was thin, almost impossibly so, and young. She looked as if she were on the brink of starvation, her skin stretched tightly over her cheekbones, her eyes sunken and hollow. Her hair was sparse, unevenly sheared, but I couldn't look away from her wrists.

Thick manacles encircled her wrists, connected to the wall behind, with thick screws jutting out from handcuffs. Thin metal wires snaked out from the restraints, disappearing into her blood-crusted flesh.

Nausea threatened to overcome me and I stumbled backwards, leaning heavily against the ice-cold wall behind me.

"Sorry," Anna said with a wince. "I'm sure it can be pretty jarring to see me for the first time."

I shook my head, words not wanting to escape my

mouth but I forced them out anyway.

"Are they… are they drilled into your bone?" I asked, my eyes still fixed on the huge screws that protruded from the cuffs.

Anna lifted her hands slightly, the metal chains clanking loudly.

"Oh, yeah… they didn't use to be if that helps? They might not even use them on you, they just had a few near misses with me, but I can't exactly get far if I can't bring my arms and legs with me. I almost did get away though."

Despite her predicament, a wild smile appeared on her face.

"Why? What happened?" I asked, needing to know.

Anna's grin faltered and she looked down.

"Do you know why you're here?" she asked, not quite answering my question.

I shook my head, torn between lying and telling her the truth.

"When did they bring you in? Have you not had orientation?"

She sounded curious and a little surprised.

I hesitated.

I could tell her the truth. She wasn't real, a figment of my own imagination couldn't judge me.

"I… just appeared here," I said haltingly. "I don't know anything about this place."

Anna stared at me in confusion, her face entirely

blank.

Panic washed through me. Maybe I'd been wrong and she would judge me.

"You… just came here. By yourself? No one brought you here or forced you to come?" she asked finally.

"I guess not? It wasn't exactly on purpose."

"What happened?"

"I was just driving in the car with my mom and I saw something on a hill, like a satellite dish or something, and then I was here," I explained.

Anna nodded as if that made a lot of sense to her.

"Do you do that a lot?" Anna asked. "Be in one place and then get triggered and go somewhere else."

I hesitated again.

"Kind of. It's only started recently though. Normally, I can control it. Like, I'll go somewhere nice and do something fun but… earlier, something like this happened and I saw this… monster."

A shudder tore through me at the memory and I felt its hand gripping my wrist painfully tightly.

"What kind of monster?" Anna asked, bringing me back to reality.

Or, not reality. My fantasy.

"I don't know. It had… It had killed a bunch of people and it was eating their flesh, I think. It… it ran towards me. It wanted to kill me, and I couldn't escape."

Anna nodded sagely.

"That happens sometimes, but you normally wake up

after you die. Mostly. Sometimes, it gets a little foggy. What did the monster look like?"

"Umm… tall and kinda like a skeleton. Pale, too. Sharp teeth and its eyes were like… entirely black," I tried to describe it but knew that I'd done a bad job.

"Oh, yeah. That thing. I don't know the name for it, but they've killed me a few times. I mostly try to stay out of worlds with them now."

My mind stuttered then froze.

"You do it too?" I asked.

"Oh yeah. That's why I'm here. My parents sold me to this place a little while back. Sorry, I thought you knew."

"Wait… sold you?" I asked, taking another step towards her.

"Yeah. Not the best decision. For me at least, it was a pretty good one for them. They got a lot of money from it. Last I heard, they were able to move out of the shit hole I grew up in and both my sisters are now in a proper school so… at least there's that?" Anna ended wistfully and looked down.

"What are they doing to you here?" I asked, my voice hushed with horror.

Anna looked up, almost a little sympathetically.

"I don't know if I should tell you," she said, her cracked lips ticking up faintly. "Maybe it's best that you don't know more about this place? Then, it'll be harder for you to come back."

That made my heart seize with fear and I stumbled towards the girl a little.

"Please, I need to know."

Anna was silent for a moment, just staring at the floor in front of her.

"I can't tell you everything," she decided. "It's best that you don't know. If you know less about a place, your connection to it is weaker. You can't just flit in and out. You should… you shouldn't be here. They're experimenting on me. Trying to work out what I can do and how but… I think that's coming to an end."

"What do you mean?" I asked sharply, moving closer towards her.

"They've learnt everything they need to from me. I can't do anything else and they've improved all their tech and everything so… they don't need me. I'm not strong enough to keep doing full transmigration, I'll never have that ability no matter what they do to me."

I didn't understand what she was saying, but there was a glint in her eyes.

Something told me that this was intentional. She was lying about what she could do on purpose. It was her final act of rebellion, her last stand.

"But, what do you mean? What are they trying to do to you? I don't get it."

She looked up at me almost pityingly.

"A lot. They're trying to make more people like me. Trying to… harness my ability and the others before me.

Use it to their advantage."

"Why though?"

"Why does anyone do anything they do? Money, resources, to have power over others."

I swallowed, trying to ignore the goosebumps that crept along my arms.

"But what happens now? You said it's coming to an end with you. Will they let you go?" I asked almost desperately.

Anna laughed, the sound raw and hacking but filled with genuine surprise.

"No," she said finally, reaching to wipe the tears from her eyes, but being unable to lift the manacles high enough. She gave up and let her hands drop again. "I'll be dead soon. They don't let us go. They never do."

I didn't know what to say to that.

"Why?"

"They can't. I'd tell people what they've done to me here, even if I know they won't believe me. It's best for me to die."

"That's... that's horrible. There has to be a way for you to survive. I can help you get out of here!" I said, my tone hushed but desperate.

Anna sighed.

"Oh, Grace. I wish you could, but I'm fine with what's going to happen," she said with a gentle smile.

"How? How can you be okay with it? Are you not scared?"

Her smile was understanding and genuine.

"I don't think I'm scared of anything anymore. Do you know how long I've been doing this?"

I shook my head.

"Years. Almost all my life. I realised what I could do as a kid and they found me not long after that. I ran, hid, tried to stop using my gift but... It was only a matter of time. It's so hard living in your own messed-up world with no one who loves you and no way to protect the ones you love when you know you can escape to somewhere better. My sisters were happier when I was using my gift too. I could take the brunt of my parents' anger instead of them. They were... it was just safer."

"Then what?" I whispered.

"They found me. Well, kind of. I think their last subject must have died and they got desperate. I mean, with each one of us, they learn more about how to do this shit so if they don't have anyone who can do it, they're stuck, you know? So, I made the mistake of going to a new world, one I didn't know anything about, and they were somehow already there. I don't know how, but they're already in some worlds. They can travel to them easily so they were waiting for me."

Anna glared at her cuffs furiously.

I glanced up at the cameras on the walls pointing at us before asking, "Have you been here ever since?"

She nodded sharply.

"Yep. I basically spend all of my time here or in the

lab. Sometimes, I get to go to other worlds, but not so much anymore."

"Are you sure I can't help?" I asked, moving closer towards her.

Anna started to open her mouth before her head snapped towards the door.

The glass square, covered with metal mesh, had lit up. The corridor beyond it, once darkened, was now filled with light.

"Grace, you need to go now," she said, her voice low. "Stick to worlds you know are safe, try and resist the triggers and don't trust anyone. These people are everywhere. Go now!"

I hesitated, my heart pounding with urgency.

"Is there nothing I can do to help you?" I asked, panic gripping me.

"If they catch you here, it's over for both of us. They'll kill me immediately and trap you. Go now!"

I swallowed and nodded, not liking it, but accepting her words.

She wasn't real. She wasn't really going to die. She was just in my imagination, so she'd live on somewhere in my mind, no matter what happened.

I closed my eyes, reaching towards that familiar dizziness, but it was too slow. Anna growled, breaking me out of my concentration.

"Grace! Look at me," she commanded, her voice surprisingly strong.

I opened my eyes, staring deeply into her bloodshot green eyes as the sound of footsteps moved closer. My breathing quickened at the thought of the people on the other side of the door finding me.

"Go now," she whispered.

Dizziness overcame me instantly and I didn't even have time to blink before I was back in the car with my mom.

A gasp slipped from my mouth and I pushed myself back against the seat, staring out the window in front of me and needing to convince myself that I was really back there. Green hills surrounded us and there was no sign of the hill that had triggered my fantasy. I was safe.

My mom frowned and reached for the volume controls, turning the music down.

"What is going on with you today? First the nightmare and now whatever this is?" she asked, a hint of something close to concern warred with irritation in her voice.

"Nothing, just must not be feeling well. Didn't sleep well last night," I muttered, clutching my phone so tightly I was genuinely concerned about breaking it.

"Are you sure that's it? You're not... you're not on drugs, are you?" she demanded sharply.

I let out a stuttering laugh, my breathing still quicker than I'd like.

"No, I'm not on drugs."

"Good! Because my parents would never let me live

that down! I mean, can you imagine…"

I started to tune her out, trying to focus on my breathing and pushing the image of Anna from my mind.

It was silly. Just a dumb fantasy.

I was clearly just shaken from the dream earlier. That made sense. It was my panic-ridden brain just grasping at straws and trying to make me spiral further.

That happened sometimes. If I read or watched something that scared me too much, I always made it worse for myself. I'd get fixated on it, convince myself that it was real or that there was actually a person living in the attic above my room, watching my movements through some hidden hole.

That was the last one I'd spiralled on. My brain liked to make me panic like that.

That's what Anna was. She wasn't real, so I had nothing to fear.

"Can we stop soon?" I asked as soon as my mom paused to take a breath. "I need to use the bathroom."

CHAPTER TWENTY-TWO

How were we still driving?

I mean, honestly, how were we still going? Sure, my mom had stopped countless times for smoke breaks, to get more water and use the toilet, but still. It felt endless.

I'd dozed in and out of sleep for what seemed like hours, but when I checked the time on the console, only forty minutes had passed.

The urge to disappear into another world just grew stronger the longer I was in the car, despite how hellish the last two had been. It even stopped me from wanting to go back to Mitch's world even though I knew that was safe. Well, mostly safe. Sterling's people could be anywhere, waiting in the shadows, about to pounce.

Or the people Anna had spoken about. They still lingered in my mind. The scientists, the people experimenting on her, they could be there waiting. She'd said that I should stick to worlds that I know, that I was familiar with, but I wanted to explore.

I could feel them, tickling the back of my mind. Countless other worlds that I could visit, endless places where things were different. Where I could grab the steering wheel out of my mom's hands and send us careening into the black car in the middle lane that was keeping perfect time with us even though it should have been overtaking. Just anything to break the endless monotony.

I could do it.

In some other world, I could. I could yank the steering wheel and see what happened. I might get trapped there, but I couldn't die. Anna has said that if I were to do that, if I were to die, I could just wake up again. I trusted her, even if she was a weird figment of my imagination, brought on by mind-numbing boredom.

My hands twitched in my lap, begging to reach out for the wheel, but I just clutched my phone harder.

I was scared of death, you know? Even though I knew it wasn't happening in real life and there was a kind of morbid curiosity there, I was still scared of it. What if they were right? Like Mr Pritchard, our almost fanatic Religious Education teacher.

He'd told us before what happened after death if you were a non-believer, like me. He'd said we'd be damned to an eternity of suffering and misery, which honestly didn't sound that bad to me. I mean, he'd always been quick to add that it was just what the Bible said and that not everyone agreed with that or believed it but... there was something about his tone, and his cross necklace, that told me he believed we'd be going to hell.

What if I didn't though? What if I died in my imagination and, instead of it being hell, what if nothing happened? Maybe, that's all there is after death. Just an endless expanse of nothingness.

Would that be worse? I truly wasn't sure.

After considering that for a moment, a shiver went through me. It would be worse. I could barely be left alone with my thoughts now before they spiralled into mayhem, being left alone with them for the rest of all time? I'd go crazy.

Well.

That thought stopped me. Was I not already there? I mean, what even is the definition of crazy because I was pretty sure that a kid who spends most of their time trapped in their own fantasies, sometimes unable to leave, would come under that definition.

"Ah, good. Another service station!" my mom sighed happily, spotting one in the distance.

I barely managed to bite back my groan of frustration.

I was pretty sure we'd stopped at every single station in the last two hours. How? How could she want to stop at that one too?

Despite my fear, despite my reluctance, I found myself reaching towards that familiar, comforting dizziness. I couldn't stay in the real world any longer. If I did, I'd grab the wheel and direct us into oncoming traffic.

I wouldn't even reach for my dizziness, I'd do it in real life.

"You alright, kid? You've hardly touched your veggies," Mitch asked, gesturing towards my plate.

I looked down at the perfectly grilled slices of courgette, aubergine and other vegetables. Large flakes of salt decorated them and the smell that wafted off them made me glad that I could finally taste things in my fantasies. I wasn't sure if I was pulling the taste from my memory but it didn't matter, I was so glad that I was.

"Sorry, yeah. Just a bit distracted today. Tonight," I added quickly, spotting the setting sun through the floor-to-ceiling windows.

"Don't worry, we've had a busy day! How are you doing now? Not too stiff?"

Memories of the gym and scuba diving flitted through my mind again and I quickly took note of how my body felt.

"No, they're alright actually," I replied.

Mitch nodded.

"And how's school going? Still enjoying that new boarding school?" he asked, his tone suddenly much more tired yet needier than it was moments ago.

"It's fine, Dad," I sighed, as a waiter approached the table from behind me. "It's school, how good can it be, really?"

"But it's better than the last place, right? You hated that place."

He sounded so earnest that I almost wanted to cry.

I rolled my eyes and looked at the waiter, as if begging him to interrupt us.

"Can I get either of you another drink?" he asked with a lingering smile.

"Another whiskey would be great," Mitch said.

The waiter looked at me and anxiety flared within me.

I was happy with just my water, I didn't really want anything else, but the waiter was looking at me so expectantly.

"Can I get a cocktail?" I said. "I don't really care which one as long as it's strong."

The waiter smiled again and nodded before turning away from us.

There was a moment of silence as we waited for him to move far enough away for us to be able to talk normally. Luckily, the tables were well spaced out enough and the restaurant was quiet enough that Mitch was pretty sure we wouldn't be overheard as long as we spoke quietly.

"I have no problem with you drinking, it helps you fit in, but be careful about getting a hangover. This job is a lot harder when you're trying to fight that off," he warned quietly.

"I know, sorry. I panicked! I don't even want the

drink!" I whispered.

Mitch chuckled softly, shaking his head and looking down.

"Well, I'm glad I guess. You covered it well," he continued in a hushed voice before raising it slightly. "Ah, here he comes!"

I turned to look at the waiter approaching.

Part of me wanted to sigh and pretend he'd taken too long, despite it barely having taken any time, knowing that Alice would have done so, but I couldn't. It felt so mean and the waiter had been so fast.

"Thanks," I said with a brief smile as he placed the tall glass, filled with crushed ice and watery-looking brown liquid in front of me.

"No problem," he replied, looking into my eyes and smiling before placing a glass in front of Mitch who thanked him with a raised eyebrow.

The waiter rushed away again as Mitch lifted the glass to his lips, taking a sip around the huge circular ice cube inside it.

I eyed my drink suspiciously.

"Thoughts on what this is?" I asked worriedly.

"May I?" he asked, putting his drink down and gesturing towards mine.

"Be my guest."

I pushed the glass towards him a little, expecting him to take a sip but he just sniffed it.

"I'm going to go out on a limb and assume this is a

long island iced tea," he said, placing it back in front of me with a barely suppressed wince.

"Did you not want to try it?" I asked, picking it up cautiously.

"Oh, nope. Definitely not. I think everyone has a horror story or two that involves that drink and unfortunately, mine is still haunting me. It started with far too many long island ice teas and ended with me waking up handcuffed in the back of a police car just off the Norfolk Coast with a seemingly handmade knife made out of whalebone in my pocket and a barely patched bullet wound on my thigh. It was confusing for many reasons," he mused quietly, before taking a bite of his steak.

"Oh?" I asked, immediately wanting to know more.

"Well, I'm pretty sure I started drinking in Australia a couple of nights before that and truly the rest of the time is blank, but I think I've worked out that I made the knife myself. I had some splinters of it in my fingers and I can't think of any other reason why that would be the case. I'm impressed with myself though, I'd never made a blade before at that point and it was pretty well done."

Somehow that explanation made me even more curious.

"And you don't remember any of it?" I asked.

"Nope. I hacked some security footage to try and work out at least which airport I'd flown out of, but turns out I got a boat with a buddy to some other island with much worse security and a private jet from there. No clue who paid for it, but it wasn't on any of my cards. There is a strong possibility I jumped out of the plane at some point. Or maybe I was pushed. I have a murky memory of one of the police officers saying something about a parachute."

I realised that I had been staring at him with my mouth open and hastened to close it before asking, "Who shot you?"

Mitch ate silently for a moment as a couple was seated at a table a few across from ours.

He met my gaze for a second before looking back down at his food, rounding his shoulders as if he were exhausted from our conversation.

"Did I tell you my old buddy Oscar is going to be in town when we get back?" he asked in a forced, enthusiastic tone.

Oscar, the hot guy I'd met before, the one who had taken the car for us, had been the one who'd shot Mitch. I had to fight to not let my mouth drop open again.

"No," I said, trying not to sound as fascinated as I was.

Mitch's lips ticked up into a smile which he quickly hid by taking another bite of his steak.

I forced myself to reach out and grab the drink, trying desperately to slip back into the Alice persona despite wanting nothing more than to ask more questions and find out exactly what had happened between them.

The way they'd interacted had seemed so friendly and normal but he'd shot Mitch? If I'd been shot by someone, I don't think I would treat them like that.

I took a cautious sip of the drink, expecting it to be more aggressively alcoholic tasting but it went down surprisingly easily. The taste was… light. Easy to drink with a hint of coke. It was pretty good.

"So, what's in this anyway?" I asked, trying to sound snooty as I took another sip.

"Um… I don't really know. I think it's just all light spirits," Mitch said, before reaching for the drinks menu which he thumbed through unsurely. "Ah, there we are. Vodka, gin, white rum, tequila, Cointreau, lemon juice, sugar syrup and coke."

I lowered the glass slowly.

It sounded like a drink that would be made at one of the parties that Duncan threw.

They used to mix all of the spirits from his parent's alcohol cabinet together and then just call it 'mystery drink' but depending on the colour, they'd either call it 'red mystery drink', 'green mystery drink' or, more often than not, 'brown mystery drink'. It was always horrific, nothing like the delicious cocktail in my hand.

Despite how much I was enjoying it, I placed it slowly on the table, making a mental note not to drink any more of it.

"So, what do you want to do tomorrow, Alice?"

Mitch asked with a hesitant smile.

"I don't know," I said coldly, shutting him down immediately as I picked at my food.

"No?" he asked. "I thought we could take a trip to the island across the way, what do you think?"

I glanced towards the window where Spinalonga could just about be seen.

It was dark on the island but there were small spots of light, flickering slightly. I wasn't sure if they were fires that people who were on the island had lit or electric lights.

"Do we have to? What's so fun about that island? It won't be as good as the one Mom and Frank took me to last year," I said, looking away.

Mitch sighed softly.

"I know but... it still might be interesting? Apparently, it's an old leper colony, isn't that cool?"

I looked at him, forcing my face to scrunch up.

"Why would I want to go there?"

"It's history! It's important to learn about these things," Mitch explained calmly as the couple glanced across at us, barely hiding the fact they were talking about us.

"Why?" I asked flatly. "It's summer. Why do I need to learn things over the break?"

Mitch made himself take a deep breath, his shoulders rising and falling with the movement.

"It's important. You won't learn these kinds of things

in school! Plus, I've already booked a private tour."

I sighed loudly and placed my cutlery onto my plate, pushing it away from me and leaning back in my chair.

"Without even asking me first? Fine."

Mitch hurried to have a couple more bites before putting his knife and fork down too.

"Shall we ask to see the dessert menu?" he asked quickly. "You always used to like dessert, right?"

My stomach rumbled, despite the meal I'd just eaten and the fact that I'd been snacking all day in the car, but I crossed my arms.

I did want to see the dessert menu but, heartbreakingly, I knew Alice would turn it down.

"I don't eat dessert anymore," I said snootily.

Mitch looked down to hide his smirk.

"We could always share something," he insisted, seemingly seeing through my words to how much I wanted the dessert. "No harm in seeing what's on the menu, right?"

I pursed my lips before sighing.

"I guess."

Mitch smiled at me, his eyes glinting with laughter, before looking away and making eye contact with a waiter behind me who rushed over.

"All finished here?" they asked.

"Yes, thank you," Mitch said with a polite smile.

The waiter nodded and began collecting our plates.

"Is there anything else I can get for you?"

"We'd like to see the dessert menu, please."

"Of course, I'll bring that right over."

The waiter disappeared, leaving our table empty again.

Silence settled over us and I picked at the cloth napkin in my lap, trying to make it seem like I was uncomfortable and bored.

"So," Mitch started after far too long before his face lit up. "Wonderful! The service here is so fast! Nothing like last time we went out for a meal, right? Do you remember how bad it was at Nobi?"

I took the menu from the waiter with a slight smile, ignoring Mitch even though it made me feel horrible.

I scanned the page, my mouth threatening to water as I read the options, being drawn to the melt in the middle chocolate fondant with a summer berry compote and the creme brûlée. They both sounded so good, but I'd said I didn't eat dessert so I couldn't exactly say I wanted them.

"What do you think, Alice? Want to split a sheep's milk mousse with coconut and passionfruit?" Mitch suggested.

I looked up at him in horror.

That sounded like the worst thing he could have ever suggested. Just the sheer thought of it made me want to gag. I just couldn't imagine the taste or the texture of all of those things mixed together and I didn't want to.

"So... not that," Mitch said, looking up at me and

taking in my horrified expression. "How about... the creme brûlée?"

I felt my face light up, but there was nothing I could do to stop it.

Mitch laughed.

"Okay, creme brûlée it is. Anything else catch your eye?" he asked.

I hesitated, torn between wanting to mention the fondant, but also knowing that Alice wouldn't.

But maybe she would? Maybe she'd say it if she really wanted something... She'd make it more of a demand than a question.

That could work.

"I'm going to order the fondant," I said decisively after a moment.

Mitch's eyebrow twitched slightly, revealing his entertainment and he nodded.

"Great! I'll order the creme brûlée and you're welcome to have some of that if you want?"

I nodded slightly, trying not to seem too enthusiastic.

"Wonderful," Mitch said before closing his menu.

I copied him, sitting back and looking around the restaurant.

It was lovely, the kind of place we'd go to with my grandparents. One wall was made entirely of windows which overlooked one of the large pools, closed for the evening, and beyond that, the sea and Spinalonga. The tables were made of perfectly polished dark wood, which matched the bar and the decor on the walls.

It was very understated, coordinated, and well done. It was beautiful and made me feel a little out of place.

"Ah, yes," Mitch said as the waiter approached. "We'll have the creme brûlée and the chocolate fondant, thank you."

"Wonderful choices, I'll get those brought out for you shortly," the waiter said before nodding and disappearing again.

I went back to staring around the room, my gaze landing on Spinalonga through the window again.

The island was almost invisible in the dark, but that just made the lights seem more obvious. There were definitely fires or lights or something on the island but I was sure that Mitch had said it was abandoned.

"What's the deal with that island anyway?" I asked, trying and failing at sounding bored. "Do people still live there?"

Mitch must have known what I was talking about but still, he looked confused as his gaze followed mine.

"Ah! Spinalonga? Well, the person I spoke to today just said that it was an old leper colony and that it's abandoned now, so I guess not!"

"But, there are lights on there."

Mitch had looked away, glancing down at his phone, but now he looked up, examining the island.

"Huh, I guess so. I thought I saw some last night. They're probably just security lights triggered by animals or something. Apparently, there are a lot of cats around here," he said with a shrug, looking away again.

I nodded, pretending to be satisfied by his answer, but in reality confusion washed through me.

Mitch had said that he'd noticed it last night, that must have been intentional. Maybe he was trying to tell me that he was aware of the situation and was keeping an eye on it or maybe… I don't know. Maybe he was just playing along and nothing was weird about it.

We fell back into silence as we waited for our dessert to come and, even though I knew it was just for show, it made me uncomfortable. I was genuinely relieved when I saw Mitch smile at the waiter over my shoulder.

"The creme brûlée?" the waiter asked, holding out a plate.

A waft of caramel drifted towards me and I had to swallow to stop myself from drooling. It smelt so good. I was half tempted to change my mind and say that it was for me, but I'd already caught sight of the chocolate fondant. Somehow, that looked better.

"Just in the middle, please. Alice and I are going to share this one, aren't we?" Mitch asked, giving me a hopeful smile.

"Maybe," I replied in a disinterested tone.

"Great," the waiter said, placing the plate on the table. "And the fondant. Would you like that in the middle as well?"

"No, that one is just for me," I said.

I really wouldn't mind sharing with Mitch, but I knew that Alice would have.

The waiter smiled at me and set the plate down in front of me, not even fazed by my rudeness which made me a little sad. It must mean he was used to it.

"Fantastic, enjoy your dessert," he said. "Can I get you anything else? Another drink, perhaps?"

"That's all, thank you," Mitch answered for us both.

The waiter nodded before turning and walking away.

I picked up my fork intentionally slowly, trying not to rush as I stared at the delicious-looking chocolatey cake in front of me. It was topped in the berry compote with a fan of fresh strawberries to one side and a dusting of icing sugar on top.

I sunk my fork into it, cutting it open and letting the molten centre ooze out, biting back a moan. Scooping some up, I finally tasted it, the flavours bursting across my tongue.

The rich, deep flavour of chocolate was perfectly complemented by the sharp, tangy compote. The cake was moist, springy and exquisite. It was almost too good. I went back for another taste, unable to help myself despite wanting to offer Mitch some.

After a few more mouthfuls, I was able to pause.

"Would you like to try some?" I asked, trying to make it sound forced.

A practised look of surprise crossed Mitch's face.

"That would be lovely, thank you. Would you like to

try some creme brûlée? They brought another spoon,"
he said, nudging it towards me temptingly.

CHAPTER TWENTY-THREE

The walk back to our villa was wonderful. The warm, gentle breeze blowing off the ocean was tinged with salt and welcome. It pushed the hair back from my face and caressed my skin.

We could have chosen to use one of the golf carts that waited by the front of the restaurant, which would have gotten us back quicker, but we'd silently agreed to walk.

I was glad. We were walking in silence, partially because of the constant fear that someone would be eavesdropping but also because it was comfortable. I didn't mind it at all.

It felt a little strange though. The silence wasn't strained or filled with anxiety like it was when I was with my mom, it was just... nice. The soft whisper of the water somewhere nearby filled the air, disturbed only by the occasional buzz of the golf carts and susurration of the trees that had been planted around the resort.

Reluctantly, I blinked back into reality, focusing for

just long enough to look around. The roads were still windy and surrounded by greenery, which was enough for me to realise we were getting closer to my grandparent's house but still had a little while to go.

With a smile, I blinked back into Mitch's world, time barely passing since I'd been there last.

That was one thing I noticed. Time moved weirdly in my fantasies. Sometimes, it seemed to rush by. A whole day in the fantasy could be gone in an hour but other times, it moved so slowly. I didn't mind it, not really. I wasn't missing anything good, but it was still weird.

"How was your dinner?" Mitch asked after a while, his tone a little too enthusiastic.

I wasn't sure, but it felt like he was still being the person he'd been pretending to be before which meant I needed to pretend to be Alice.

"Fine," I said, pulling my phone out of my pocket and staring down at it blankly.

"Oh yeah? Did you enjoy dessert? That was real good, right?" he asked in a hopeful tone.

"I said it was fine," I said sharply. "How long is this walk anyway? I thought it was meant to be short."

Mitch looked around as if he were trying to work out where we were.

"I think..." He trailed off before pointing at a sign and exclaiming, "Ah, ha! Right there! Just down this path and we'll be at our house!"

"Villa," I muttered under my breath as if it mattered.

Mitch resolutely ignored me, but I noticed that he sped up.

Guilt spiked within me and I fought not to wince. Was he trying to get back to our villa quicker so that I'd stop acting like such a brat because, honestly? I understood that.

But at the same time, I felt bad. I had to keep acting that way, people might be listening in. Mitch had said that Sterlings people were everywhere so... I needed to keep up the facade, no matter how much I hated it.

Even so, I was relieved when we got back into our rooms. I waited silently whilst Mitch checked the security cameras and devices he'd hidden throughout the room before he turned and gave me a thumbs up.

My shoulders sagged slightly with relief.

"So, kid. What do you want to do now? Are you tired? Do you want to study more or prep for tomorrow?" he asked.

I started to open my mouth to reply without having made up my mind when something wrenched me back into reality.

"Are you listening, Grace?" my mom's voice demanded.

"Yes, of course," I lied, blinking the brightness out of my vision so that I could see the service station car park around us.

I wanted to cling to my fantasy and refuse to come back but I knew I had to stay in reality even as Mitch asked me what movie I wanted to watch.

I felt myself answer him, the voice barely an echo in my mind, not quite real but not quite fake, before my mom started speaking again.

"Fine. Hurry up and put all the rubbish around you in this bag."

I took the bag she thrust at me and started to load up our half-empty drinks and snack packets.

"What do you want me to do with the stuff we haven't eaten?" I asked, holding up a full bag of Twix bites.

Mom hesitated, looking at the chocolate with long-ing.

"Bin it," she said after a moment before correcting herself. "No, pass them here. I'll put it in my suitcase. That way, we can have some snacks in case Mom makes that horrible pasta dish again."

She gave me a tight smile before taking the chocolate and exiting the car.

The corners of my lips ticked up slightly before fall-ing again.

I knew exactly what pasta dish my mom was referring to. It was burnt into my memories. My grandmother had assured me that the cream-based dish was vegetar-ian but I was pretty certain that the sour, orange chunks were fish.

I wasn't sure though. The only thing I was sure about was that every ingredient was well past the use by date.

Both her and my grandad viewed them as more of a

suggestion. Something to be ignored, put in place only to trick those who are gullible enough to follow them and sure, sometimes they're probably not completely accurate but still.

I wasn't sure how she and my grandad were so okay with eating gone off food all the time. I could only assume that years of smoking, drinking, and poor diet meant that their taste buds were pretty much dead. It was the only thing that made sense to me.

The boot opened and I heard Mom wrestling with the suitcases before she started talking again.

"Grace, pass all the unopened food back through to me," she ordered.

I unhooked my seatbelt so that I could turn around more and started passing her the crisps and snacks we'd bought along the way.

"Do you want to run into the shop and get some more? Make sure you get some stuff that doesn't need to go in the fridge," she said, even though I knew that already.

We did the same thing every year.

Despite my generally strained relationship with her, she was always better around her parents. I think it was because we had a common enemy, you know? Her parents were terrible to her which I think made her want to be closer to me. She tried that at home sometimes too, when she and Dad fought, but it never really worked.

I think I liked him too much, it made it harder for my mom to make me side with her. That was less of a problem with my grandparents though. It's not that I didn't like them, of course, I loved them. I just didn't really know them.

Plus, my mom had been telling me horror stories about them and the way that they treated her and her siblings pretty much since I was born so… that made things difficult. It was hard to want to be close to them when I knew how they acted towards her when she was a kid.

It wasn't just when she was younger, it still happened now.

"Do you want anything specific?" I asked as I climbed out of the car, my legs stiff.

I stretched, wincing at the slight burn and tightness in my calves.

"Take my card and get some more Twix bites. Some crisps too, anything salt and vinegar, but not Pringles. And some bread!"

I nodded, reaching back into the car to grab it from her purse, before starting across the car park towards the service station and pausing to let a car pass.

The service station was surprisingly busy and I edged past people, trying to make sure I grabbed enough food whilst also not getting too much. If I got too much and it didn't all fit in the bags, she would get annoyed.

It had happened before. More than once.

I knew I shouldn't have been comparing it but it felt so different from when I was shopping for snacks for the journey with Mitch. I hadn't known what to get then either but, no matter what, Mitch had responded positively. I should have known what to get now, I knew what I liked and what Mom liked but she changed her mind a lot.

Nothing was safe.

I blinked, reaching out towards a bag of Maltesers, and suddenly I was sitting on the couch in Crete. Mitch was slumped next to me, a drink barely clutched in his hand as he dozed lightly. A snore slipped out of his open mouth.

I smiled, debating reaching out and taking his water from him before looking at the screen. I didn't need to look for long to know that we were watching my favourite movie.

A contented sigh slipped out of my mouth before—

"Excuse me, darling. Are you in the queue?" a friendly Scottish voice asked.

I stared blankly at the older woman for a moment before making myself smile.

"Yes, sorry. Just zoned out for a moment," I said, trying hard not to let myself sway as dizziness threatened to make me stumble.

"Ah, not a problem. Just didn't want to be cutting in front of you!" she said with an easy laugh.

"Thanks."

I smiled at them slightly before glancing out the window at the car. My mom was leaning against it, a cigarette in her hand as she stared intently at her phone. I wasn't sure if she hadn't seen me or was ignoring me but she didn't look up.

I looked away from her before looking back at the person in front of me just as they finished buying the items and stepped out of the way.

I smiled at the cashier politely as they started scanning my items.

"Anything else?" the cashier asked.

"No, thank you."

"Do you want a bag for that?"

"It's alright, thanks."

"Are you sure?" she asked, looking down at the pile of snacks and bread that I'd dropped on the counter.

I didn't quite remember grabbing the big bottles of water, but I was glad that I had. There was something strange about the water at my grandparent's place; it always tasted a little off. I must have just picked them up instinctively.

"No, it's okay. I've got a bag in the car," I explained.

"Ah, good. Alright, that'll be seventeen sixty," the cashier read from the till.

I tapped my mom's card on the reader before slipping it into my pocket and bundling the snacks and drinks into my arms.

"Thanks," I said before starting to walk away, the bag

of bread swinging precariously.

It bumped into my body with every step and I could feel it starting to slip from my grasp but I managed to reach the car without dropping it. I was glad. The car park ground was definitely not clean.

It smelt deliciously of petrol and the ground shimmered ever so slightly but even so, I would not want to eat bread that I'd dropped there. It was in a bag so it probably would have been protected from most of it, but I still wouldn't trust it.

"Start loading it into the suitcases. Make sure it's not too obvious though, I don't want to answer any questions from my mom about why we need so many snacks when she cooks us such perfectly good meals," my mom instructed, still staring at her phone.

I did as she ordered, shoving the food into the bags wherever I could before slamming the boot shut as Mom finished her cigarette and slipped her phone back into her pocket.

"We're about five minutes away," she said as we got back into the car.

"Okay," I replied, not sure quite what else to say.

We weren't, it was closer to ten but with Mom's driving, it would be even longer.

I wanted to slip back into my fantasy with Mitch, but I knew that I'd still be there watching Tangled on the sofa. I loved that movie, but I wanted more.

Fear started to nibble at my stomach as I thought

hard. I wanted to just let my mind wander and slip into any other fantasy, but I was worried. What if it was another scary one, like the one with Anna or that horrible monster thing?

No, I could control it. I could go somewhere fun, somewhere completely new and interesting and good. I didn't quite believe that but I forced myself to close my eyes and let out a slow, steady breath.

"Okay," a clear voice with an accent unlike any I'd ever heard before started. "It's very simple. I'm just going to turn down the gravity and then you need to make your way through the course."

I opened my eyes, immediately intrigued, and what I saw didn't disappoint. The space I was in was huge and littered with obstacles. Directly in front of me was what I could only describe as a car wash. Spinning pillars were covered with multicoloured ribbons and placed perilously close together meaning that we'd need to squeeze through them. I couldn't see anything beyond it other than the climbing wall that stretched up along the back wall but it didn't even look like the course ended there.

"And remember, whoever gets to the end first will get free drinks for them and their team for the rest of the evening!" the person went on to say, causing cheers to erupt from the people around me.

I joined in, my heart pounding with excitement even though I had no clue what was going on.

"Delph, are you ready?" a cute guy asked, his hand

touching my arm gently.

"Yes," I answered uncertainly as the person at the front of the crowd walked back and forth slowly.

"Good," he said, his lips spreading up into a smile. "Because if Gem and her crew win, I will be so annoyed."

I ripped my gaze away from his face to look at the small but powerfully built brown-haired girl that he'd glanced at.

"Oh?" I asked, hoping he'd explain more.

"Yeah. I'm still not over her beating me at Zero-G last week! If they beat us here too, I will never recover," he said dramatically.

Gem turned, as if having heard what the boy had said, and stuck her tongue out at him.

I felt a flare of jealousy shoot through me even though I didn't know any of those people. It felt wrong. The boy was mine; I knew that somehow.

"We need to take them down," he muttered to me, bringing his head closer. "Run through the washers, try not to get hit by any of them. Get there as fast as you can, once one person goes down it'll be carnage."

The smile on his face told me that he welcomed the struggle.

"Got it," I muttered, glancing once more at the people around me.

There was just a handful of us, maybe fifteen, and I wasn't sure how many were on my crew or how many crews there were. I wasn't even sure what the boy had meant when he said crew but the sleek, black jumpsuits that everyone around me was wearing made them look like they'd come straight out of a sci-fi film, and not a particularly good one. Maybe we were part of some kind of spaceship crew? That felt ridiculous. We were too young, but the thought did feel right.

Some of the people surrounding Gem, including the boy whose hand she was holding, were shooting us surreptitious looks which made me assume they were all on a different crew to us.

They didn't look particularly impressive, but there was a strange intensity about them. Even the small blonde girl at the front seemed to be radiating that strength and focus. It was weird.

"Crew Eight Nine Six will be victorious," the boy behind me whispered not particularly quietly before sending me a cheeky grin that made my stomach flop.

"Alright, crews, are you ready?" the man at the front cried.

Cheers erupted around me and I joined in without even thinking. It just felt natural. The excitement was palatable and I was already swept up in it. I could feel my heart pounding and my muscles screaming to rush forwards and throw myself into the fray without any regard for injury or pain. It didn't matter, I just wanted to have fun and win.

Over the cheers, I heard a shout from one of Gem's friends, "No retreat!"

"No surrender!" came the answering cry from the rest of them.

It sent a wave of fear through me.

They seemed so much more prepared, more ready, than the rest of us. Even though it seemed like the race or obstacle course was just for fun, I could tell that they were more experienced. I wasn't sure if they'd done it before or if they were just better, but there was something there that I couldn't quite identify.

I glanced down unsurely. I was wearing the same black jumpsuit as them, but mine definitely looked more worn. It felt bulky, like there was padding or armour sewn in, whereas theirs were much nicer and newer looking. I'd thought we were all wearing the same thing before but I was wrong. There were minuscule differences and I almost wanted to ask them where they'd gotten theirs from, but I knew it wasn't the time. I needed to focus. I needed to beat them.

"Final crew huddle, you have three minutes. Go!"

I whirled around as my crew gathered in a circle, shooting suspicious glances at the other two groups.

"Okay," one person, a girl, said. "Try and go in a single file through the washers, Delph at the front followed by Vela, Leus, Aust then I'll take the back. This course is weapon free this time so at least we don't have that to worry about because Gem and Cory are definitely better gunners than the rest of us. Once we get to the falling floor, Leus, you take the lead and get us across as quickly as possible. The lower gravity will be a challenge, but don't let it lull you into a false sense of security. This is still going to be hard and the floor will be a problem. The next two obstacles are a surprise, so we'll assess when we get there. Delph, get to the front, don't let go of Leus' hand and let's go!"

The rest of my crew let out a strange barking cheer before stepping back and looking at me.

I stared back, my head still reeling from the rapid briefing filled with so many words I didn't understand before the boy who'd been talking to me before nudged me.

"Come on, Delph, let's destroy the other teams," he said with a slightly concerning smile.

I nodded at him, taking my place at the front of the line and looking back at the boy I belatedly realised must be called Leus. I must be Delph. That was weird. It was the first time I hadn't been called my own name in a fantasy.

Or at least, I thought it was. I could have had a different name in the one with the monster, but I'd never know.

"We got this. It's just like on the base, but much more fun," he promised me before slipping his hand into mine. "And then we can get hammered and head back to our room."

My heart stuttered slightly at the flirtatious smile he sent me and I smiled back at him but inside, my mind was racing. I had no idea what this world was like or where I was or even if I was still on earth because the idea of being able to turn gravity down felt so alien, but I wanted to know more. I wanted to know who that boy was and what he'd meant by 'our room'.

Were we sharing a room? That felt... so adult and wrong but at the same time, I wanted to know more.

"Okay, gravity is being lowered, prepare yourself for the countdown," the presenter or whoever they were said into the microphone.

My breath caught in my chest as I felt myself straighten slightly without even meaning to.

It was a weird sensation. It felt a little like I was no longer tethered to the ground quite so strongly. My hair, which had been tied back in a ponytail, no longer fell straight down or rested on my back, it felt like it stuck straight out behind me. I turned my head from side to side slightly, trying not to draw attention to myself whilst also trying to suppress a giggle.

I bounced on the balls of my feet, feeling them lift from the ground far too easily.

"Okay, crews. Three, two, one..." the presenter started as he shifted back out of our path and threw his hands up in the air.

A buzzer sounded and I plunged forwards, excited screams echoing around me.

"I'll get out and open the gate, I guess," my mom sighed as we jerked to a stop.

I looked around at the familiar estate around us, my heart still fluttering with excitement.

CHAPTER TWENTY-FOUR

I stared at the elaborate white painted gates, my mind begging to be allowed to slip back into the fantasy where I could feel that I was rushing through the washers. I could almost feel Leus' hand clutching mine and I pushed forwards, the ribbons slapping against my armour. They didn't hurt, they were little more than a distraction but they worked.

I stumbled, laughter falling from my lips as I felt myself fall back into Leus. He went down heavily, his arms coming around me automatically.

"Forty years and they still haven't changed the code," my mom muttered under her breath as she climbed back into the car and slammed the door shut.

I wrenched my attention away from the other world, aware that I'd been staring blankly at the gate which was now dragging loudly along the gravel path.

"And remember," she continued without really even pausing, edging the car forwards along the long path up to the house. "They're old and they might say something cruel, but they don't mean it like that. They're from another generation where it was normal to be blunt, so if they say something hurtful, just thank them and ignore it."

She continued reeling off the usual list of rules and instructions that she always gave, but I'd stopped listening.

I longed to go back to the fantasy where I was fighting my way through an obstacle course, but I knew that it was silly. I needed to pay attention, to focus so that I could smile and wave at my grandparents as soon as they came into view. They probably wouldn't be waiting at the window, they rarely did despite the fact that I knew my mom had just spoken to them using the gate, but still, it wasn't worth risking it.

A couple of years ago, I'd been distracted. I hadn't looked up and they had been waiting at the window. The entire trip had been filled with snide comments about how I was too attached to my phone and didn't pay enough attention to what was going on around me. Well, until they'd gotten bored of our company and left us to go to their other house.

We weren't invited to that one and I can't say I missed them too much that time.

The tree-lined gravel path crunched under our wheels and the large house gradually came into view. I straightened my shoulders and forced a smile onto my face, eyeing the many windows and searching for my grandparents.

They weren't there, but I didn't let myself relax or my posture sag just in case.

"We'll leave the bags in the car for now and come get them later," my mom said as we pulled to a stop near my grandparent's car.

Not next to it, of course. They wouldn't allow that. We might accidentally scratch it and then they'd either have to drive around with a scratched car all day, which people would see and might judge them for, or they'd have to call someone to come fix it which I knew they'd also view as unacceptable. They'd have to wait around at home all day for the person.

That wasn't really a problem, they'd retired years ago and basically never left the house now, but the sheer inconvenience of it was too much for them.

"Okay," my mom muttered as she quickly slicked some lipstick onto her lips and wiped the nonexistent smudges of mascara from under her eyes. "Remember, big smiles, your exams went well and you're very excited to be here."

I nodded, trying to force more of a smile onto my face before I caught sight of myself in the mirror.

I looked manic.

I let my smile fade slightly until it looked less fake and wired and more natural, and started to climb out of the car.

My phone buzzed just as I slammed the door behind me and I glanced down at it. I'd expected the message to be from Phoebe, but it wasn't.

Hey! I just swung by your house to give you a present but your dad said you're already on the way to Scotland? Duncan had written.

I smiled softly and typed back, Yeah, sorry. Left ridiculously early this morning. You got me a present? You didn't need to do that.

"Grace," Mom called sharply, her smile wide and frantic as she traipsed across the gravel path towards the front door. "Phone away, please. We're here to see your grandparents, not to spend the whole time texting again."

I shot her a fake smile and slipped my phone into my pocket, speeding to catch up with her as she approached the huge bottle green painted door.

I'd always hated that door. It was a silly thing not to like, but I didn't. I wasn't sure how often it was painted but it was somehow always glossy and always slightly sticky. If I touched it at all, I left fingerprints in the paint which were always gone by the next time I came back.

Just looking at it made me remember the sensation of stickiness and made the urge to wash my hands rise within me.

We stopped in front of the door and my mom turned to me.

She looked me up and down for a moment before brushing some hair behind my ear and muttering, "That's the best I can do."

Without giving me a chance to react in any way, she turned and lifted the heavy golden door knocker. It clanged loudly, and I glanced at the smart doorbell that had been attached to the red brick next to the doorframe.

The door knocker was just for appearances, which didn't surprise me at all. A big and impressive door like theirs should have a door knocker, it would be expected. Like with my mom, all my grandparents cared about was how things looked and what people thought of them.

We waited awkwardly and I glanced at the doorbell again.

Surely, they knew we'd arrived. They'd answered my mom's call at the gate which meant that they knew a minute or so later we would be at the door, and yet, they made us wait.

"Should I—" I started to ask, still looking at the doorbell before the door opened suddenly, revealing my grandparents.

"Mom!" my mom called, rushing forwards to hug my grandmother who accepted the hug reluctantly. "Dad! It's great to see you both!"

"Yes, yes. Come in," my grandmother said, stepping back so that I could enter.

"It's great to see you," I echoed as enthusiastically as

I could, wrapping my hands around my grandmother's small frame.

My phone buzzed from my pocket and I hoped that she hadn't noticed as she patted my back once before pulling away, her eyes already scrutinising me as I turned to my granddad and embraced him too.

He hugged me a little tighter, shooting me a warmer smile, his eyes sparkling with mischief.

"We've left our bags in the car, for now. I hope you don't mind," my mom said, her voice still bright and happy.

It was fake though. I knew that and I'm pretty sure my grandparents did too.

"Yes, fine. We were just sitting down for some tea, I guess you'll join us?" my grandmother said.

"Oh, that would be great, Mom. I'll put another pot on," my mom said as we started across the foyer and towards the kitchen. "Make sure you take off your shoes, Grace."

I kept the fake smile pinned on my face as I kicked off my shoes and eyed the hallway surreptitiously.

For as long as I could remember, it had looked exactly the same. It was large and open, the staircase opposite the door carpeted in a deep crimson that was replaced every couple of years to prevent any signs of wear, and the most unsettling part of it was the paintings of my mom and my uncles that stared down at us.

They were each different sizes, my mom's the smallest by far, and had been done when they were each about eighteen. My mom had told me that hers was the smallest because they'd had to hire a different artist by the time she reached eighteen. Apparently, the artist who had done the portraits of my uncles had died or retired, but that felt like a lie. The reason changed each time I was told the story.

I suspected I knew the actual reason though. My grandparents didn't really like my mom that much. Before her, they'd had just boys and they liked it that way. At first, Mom had tried to be like her brothers, I'd seen the pictures. I'm sure that just embarrassed them though. I don't think my grandmother would have dealt with a tomboy very well.

She looked beautiful in the portrait though, I'd always thought so. Her blonde hair was shorter then, wavy too, and her smile was vibrant. She looked like she was just on the cusp of a laugh.

It made me kind of sad. I'd never seen her look like that.

I shook my head slightly and started to follow the others, glancing at the stone sculpture that sat on a small table in the centre of the foyer. It was surrounded by vases of flowers, but that didn't distract from the statue.

It was an interesting thing, for many reasons, and it never failed to make me smirk. It was carved out of one solid block of grey rough stone, about the size of my torso, and apparently, it was one of the earliest pieces of a now prominent artist but... that wasn't the best thing about it.

It was a vagina.

There is truly no easy way to say it and I was unsure if my grandparents knew what it was but... it was just a vagina.

I'd googled it once after one of my cousins had pointed it out, snickering, and the internet was divided. There was nothing from the guy who sculpted it to say that he meant it to be one, but everyone else seemed to be convinced. Some of his other pieces were pretty racy too, so it wouldn't be a surprise.

I longed to tell my grandparents what it was. Just to see the sheer shock and disgust that would come over my grandmother's face as she realised that the sculpture that she'd been proudly displaying to everyone who entered her house was something that she would see as obscene.

My grandfather would probably laugh. I think that he'd find it hilarious, but it was hard to tell with him. Sometimes he had a great sense of humour and would crack jokes and laugh at everything. Other times, he was scary.

I finally caught up with them as they entered the airy kitchen, the tiles icy beneath my feet.

The round table in front of the giant windows had been set for my grandparents. Two cups of tea, a teapot and some scones were waiting, the cups still billowing steam.

"Sit," was all my grandmother said as she seated herself delicately on one of the chairs and took a sip of tea.

I took a seat as my mom bustled around the kitchen, brewing another pot of tea for us even though neither of us liked tea. My mom was more of a coffee drinker and I didn't like either. I mean, tea smelt really nice, but the taste never lived up to it.

"So," my grandmother asked, turning her piercing green eyes towards me and raising one perfectly plucked blonde eyebrow. "Your exams went well?"

It felt like a statement rather than a question, as if my exams not going well was not an acceptable option. It wasn't, not really. My grandparents would never accept that.

They'd already told me the exact grades that all of my cousins had got, their tone hinting that they suspected that I'd never achieve the same. I might not, some of my cousins were really smart and I wasn't sure that I was.

I mean, I probably wasn't.

"Yes," I said with a smile. "I think they went pretty well."

My grandmother tutted and adjusted the crisp white shirt she had on under her tweed blazer.

"Well, I expect nothing less. Exams in this country are getting easier each year. They hand out As and A stars to anyone who manages to write their name correctly on the page," she said with a sniff.

My mother made eye contact with me over my grandmother's head and she shook her head at me pointedly.

"Mmm," I said noncommittally.

"Exactly. Honestly, no wonder this country is going to hell. People these days have no clue what they're doing," my grandmother continued, her tone clipped and her annoyance clear.

Luckily, my mom had finished brewing the tea and brought it over.

"Mom, I love what you've done with the garden," she said, glancing through the window at the flowers beyond. "It looks great!"

That was enough to distract her. My grandmother looked out over the garden, her expression unimpressed.

"Yes, the gardener didn't do too badly this year, although I don't enjoy how many tulips he's planted," she said, pursing her lips. "It makes the garden look cheap."

"I like them," my mom said as she poured a cup for herself and me.

I took the saucer and cup from her, accepting the dainty plate that she retrieved for me as well. It didn't matter, we wouldn't eat the delicious-looking scones in the centre of the table, no matter just how good they looked.

They would be fresh, I knew that. My grandparents had them delivered from the bakery in town midweek and they were always so good, but it wasn't worth it. If I had anything to eat now, I would spend the rest of the holiday putting up with comments about how it's nice to see a girl my size eating so much, even if I don't really need to be eating quite that much. It didn't matter that I was actually pretty thin, they just enjoyed finding something to pick at.

"You would," my grandmother said, shooting my mother a cold look before looking back at me. "Would you like a scone?"

My grandfather grinned at me as he reached for another one, his plate already littered with crumbs.

"Oh, no, thank you. I'm not particularly hungry," I replied, making my tone as polite as possible.

My grandmother raised an eyebrow at me, her gaze slowly moving up and down my outfit.

"I hope you didn't stop in the village to get some food on the way up?" she demanded, her tone sharp.

"No, no," my mother said soothingly. "We had a large breakfast before we left. Grace must still be full from that, right?"

Her look was almost pleading.

"Yes," I lied.

"Good. I don't know what you're wearing, but I wouldn't want anyone to see you in it. The clothing standard for people these days has fallen so disgracefully low," she said with a sad sigh.

I ignored the dig and chose instead to take a sip of

my disgusting tea.

"Ah, these are just Grace's travelling clothes! She only wears them on trips like this where she isn't going to see anyone or when she's working out privately in the house, don't you?" my mother said quickly.

"Yes, I would never wear these just out and about," I lied flatly.

"Wonderful. Why don't you run out to the car, Grace? You can bring the suitcases up to our rooms and change into something a little more appropriate?" she asked me.

"Oh, that sounds like a good idea!" I said, genuinely excited for an excuse to leave and be alone for a little while.

I wanted to go back to the fantasy, to where I was fighting my way across an unsteady platform, either side of me a gaping chasm. I could almost feel my crew mates clinging to the belt around my waist and my hair dripping from where we'd fallen into something earlier.

"Great! Are we in the usual bedrooms, Mom?"

My grandmother nodded.

"Yes, I had the housekeeper make the beds for you," she said.

"Oh, is Ada still working for you? I thought she'd stopped after she'd had her child," my mom asked, skilfully changing the subject to another one that she knew my grandmother was opinionated about.

She always enjoyed talking about the real, or

perceived, inadequacies of those around her.

I pushed away from the table and my mom sent me a short, covert smile before glancing back at my grandmother, her expression perfectly interested.

I smiled to myself as I walked from the room, ignoring my grandmother who had immediately started to complain about the fact that Ada had taken two whole months off around the birth of her child. Her argument was that the child had been in the hospital for the first three weeks anyway so Ada didn't even need to be there. Apparently, my grandmother had returned to work two days after having all of her children.

I wasn't sure I believed that, but I was happy to be out of the room. I wandered down the corridor slowly, trying not to dawdle too much but also wanting to take as long as possible.

My phone buzzed and I glanced around before pulling it out of my pocket. There were two messages, both from Duncan. The first one had come through about ten minutes before, but the other was new.

I know but I thought it might make the trip less painful. I guess I'll just need to save it until you get back, he'd written.

The next message was just a picture of a bottle of vodka held in his hand.

I grinned and looked around again, but I could hear my grandparents still in the kitchen with my mom.

Thanks, I typed. Feel free to drink it at the party though!

I tucked the phone into my pocket, still smiling and pulled the door open. Crossing the gravel drive once more, I stared at the car and realised belatedly that I hadn't asked for the keys from my mom.

The car locked automatically when we got out so I'd need them.

I sighed heavily and started to turn before the car beeped loudly. Confusion washed through me and I looked back at the house, spotting my mom standing at one of the windows, holding her keys in one hand and waving at me.

I waved back and mouthed, Thanks, before pulling the boot open and staring at the bags within.

I stood there for a minute, just staring at the bags blankly before shrugging and grabbing the nearest two. I'd need to take them all up anyway, there was no point in grabbing mine first.

I heaved the bags out, the weight straining my shoulders, and started toward the door again. There was no point in closing the boot. We were far enough away from the road that no one would see and the gate was locked anyway. The bars were spaced too closely together to be able to squeeze through and there were spikes on the top which would injure anyone climbing over.

I knew that from experience. One of my cousins had dared me to do it once and I could still remember the pain of the metal digging into the back of my thighs. I was pretty sure I was still scarred from it.

Dizziness tugged at my mind again and, with a smile, I dove back into it.

CHAPTER TWENTY-FIVE

My cheeks hurt from laughing as I hauled myself out of the water, the rest of my crew still splashing behind me. My gaze immediately fell on Gem and her crew who were already out of the water, huddled in a group and talking excitedly.

My heart sunk slightly but still, I turned and started to help the rest of my crew out of the pool. The gravity might be lowered but somehow that made swimming so much harder. The water didn't want to let go of us quite so easily which meant we were all exhausted by the time we dragged ourselves out of the water at the end.

Despite the loss, we were in high spirits. Once Aust, who was lagging behind, had been pulled out of the water and our time officially recorded, Leus had turned to me and threw his arms around my waist, lifting me into the air.

"You crushed it! I know you were nervous, but you did so great!" he cried as he spun me around.

"Truly," Vela said, reaching out to punch my shoulder lightly. "You did great. The way you managed to sort out that ridiculous phaser puzzle was spectacular!"

I smiled, a blush creeping over my cheeks as I looked down at Leus even though I had no real recollection of solving the puzzle.

I had glimpses of the memory. Just flashes of holding a weird-looking gun that shot a beam of light and perching on a tiny platform to point it at mirrors as my crew cheered me on but nothing more.

"Really! You did great!" Leus said, putting me back on the ground and placing a quick kiss on my lips.

I was taken aback, not quite sure how to react but the presenter interrupted us.

"Crew Eight Nine Six, congratulations on finishing the obstacle course! You are one of only one hundred and twenty teams to finish it in under two hours! If that crew hadn't been here today, I have no doubt you would have been victorious," he said with a glance at Gem and her crew. "Unfortunately, your time wasn't quite good enough to take the top spot but you did very well so your dinner will be covered tonight!"

My crew burst into cheers but my hand buzzed, confusing me.

I stared down at my empty hand blankly before my gaze travelled to the clunky screen on my left wrist. It was about the shape and size of my phone, but attached to a thick metal band that wrapped around my wrist. I couldn't see any kind of closure or any way to get it off which made my breath hitch in my throat.

My hand buzzed again and I blinked, reality hazily coming back into view as I slouched down the stairs at my grandparent's house, my phone clutched in my hand.

Did you get there okay? Phoebe had texted before sending a follow-up, Hope your mom isn't being too bad today.

I smiled slightly, glancing around before pausing and typing my response.

Yeah, got here like twenty minutes ago. She's not being too bad, just her usual levels of hell. My grandparents are just as bad as ever though.

I slipped my phone into my pocket and started down the stairs again, pausing at the bottom and straining my ears to catch a glimpse of the conversation which floated down the hall towards me.

"Honestly though. Don't you think it's about time that you cut your hair?" my grandmother was saying. "No woman over fifty should have hair longer than their shoulders."

"I'm not over fifty just yet, Mom," my mother replied in an upbeat yet tight tone.

My grandmother's sniff was loud enough that even I heard it.

"Well, maybe you should go back to the dermatologist then. You have so much sun damage."

I winced and turned away, starting towards the front door again.

I hated the way that my grandparents spoke to my mom but there was nothing I could do about it. Even if I were to go back in there and tried to change the subject or told my mom that she didn't look that bad, it wouldn't help. I knew that from experience.

I'd tried it before. I'd disagreed with my grandmother when she'd been complaining about something that my mom did, probably what she was wearing or something, and it was like I'd done something disgusting or massively out of line. Even my mom had sided with her.

It was tough. I could see how rude my grandmother was to her but she still desperately wanted her approval.

I paused mid-step and glanced back at the house, my eyebrows furrowing together. How was what my mom was doing any different to what I did? I sided with her even when she was being rude and tried not to antagonise her even when it wasn't my fault. I was so careful around her and why? So that she wouldn't explode or have a go at me? That never worked.

But it did make it easier. I'd stood up to her a few times before when I was a kid or when I'd been really tired and that had been hell. It wasn't worth it.

No, as soon as I was old enough to leave the house and not look back, I'd stop treating her like she was a bomb, primed and ready to explode. I wouldn't be like her. I would be better.

I hauled the last two bags out of the boot, having taken as long as possible with them, and closed it gently, hoping that no one would hear. If they didn't, I could pretend that I was still struggling with the bags so that I had an excuse not to go back down for even longer.

Actually, I could say that I was unpacking. I could start to hang up some of my clothes, pretend I was worried about them looking rumpled or getting wrinkles. They'd understand that worry, surely.

I tried to hide my grin just in case anyone had come to check on me and accused me of being up to no good. I started back across the drive, ignoring the buzz of my phone in my pocket until I was at the top of the stairs. I paused, listening carefully before putting the bags down.

There were no footsteps or voices.

I pulled my phone out of my pocket and read the text from Phoebe.

Oh, ew. Are they being dicks to you or just your mom?

Both, I sent back. *Apparently my outfit signals the downfall of clothing standards.*

I started to slip my phone back into my pocket before it vibrated again and I pulled it out.

Wait, what are you wearing that's so bad?

I looked down at my leggings and t-shirt.

Black leggings and shirt. I should change immediately, can't believe I ever let others see me in this, I typed back sarcastically.

Damn, was Phoebe's response.

I've literally been sent upstairs to hide from them but mostly to get changed into something more appropriate.

My mom's loud, desperate laugh floated up the stairs behind me and I hastened to grab the bags again and haul them to our rooms at the end of the corridor, as far as possible from my grandparent's room.

I'm pretty sure that was intentional. They wanted to limit contact with us wherever possible.

I dumped my mom's suitcase in her room before walking into my room and shutting the door softly behind me.

It was the same room I always stayed in when I was here. My mom was put in her childhood bedroom, I was in my uncle's. It was pretty strange. The wall was papered with pictures that had been torn out of magazines, a weird mix of scantily clad men and women, mostly posing with motorcycles, and I was never sure what to make of them. I think he just really liked bikes, but I was never too sure.

I sat down on the bed and checked my phone again.

You have not, Phoebe had written.

Oh yeah, was my response.

I stared down at the suitcases before me, knowing that I should start to unpack but...

Laughter erupted around me.

"Honestly though!" Col, the Captain of our crew, cried. "I thought for sure we were done for! I was absolutely certain that Leo was about to come through the door at any second and catch us in the gym!"

The laugh tumbled out of my mouth easily and I

leant back into Leus' arm.

"Wait, what were you even doing in the gym at that time?" I asked.

Col's face turned a deep shade of red, almost the same shade as her hair.

"I was... meeting someone," she said cagily.

"You were not!" Aust almost shouted, his bright pink cocktail sloshing onto the table below. "Who?"

We all looked at Col who was taking a slow and delicate sip of her drink.

"I just don't think that's relevant," she said, looking anywhere but at us.

I couldn't hold back the tipsy giggle that fell from my lips.

I felt wonderful. The world felt bright and fuzzy and I knew that I was grinning goofily but I didn't even care.

"It definitely is!" Vela wheedled. "Who was it?"

"Bootes?" Leus asked. "Or wait... Cans? Cet! It was Cet, right?"

I gasped happily and looked back at Col who had turned an even darker shade of red.

"Alright," she sighed finally. "How did you know?"

Drunken but delighted laughter exploded from us and I found myself almost doubled over the table, despite having no clue who any of those people were.

If they even were people, they didn't even sound like names but then, neither did ours.

As the laughter died down, a woman came to the

table, a silver tray tucked under one of her arms.

"Are there any empties I can clear off the table?" she asked with a smile that surprised me.

Some of her teeth had been filed into points.

Either that or they are that shape naturally.

I looked down at the table for the first time. We'd been told that our food was paid for and I had no idea how much time had passed since that moment. It had felt like seconds to me, but we'd clearly taken advantage of that. Half-eaten platters of food littered the table but they were outnumbered by the empty cups and pitchers that had been slotted into any clear space.

"Oh yeah," Col said quickly, jumping on the distraction. "I think we're done with some of these, right?"

She looked around the table where most of the others were chugging drinks to make space. My eyes widened and I grabbed my drink too, swallowing the deliciously fruity liquid as quickly as I could too before passing the empty cup over.

"Here," Col said as she accepted my cup and the many others that had been held out to her. "Thanks!"

"Not at all, doll. Can I get you lot anything else?" the waitress asked.

"Yes!" Vela cried immediately. "What was that green one that we had like three rounds ago? It tasted really fresh and fruity, but then the aftertaste made my tongue burn!"

A brief look of concern crossed the waitress' face but she hid it quickly.

"That sounds like the 'honey, give me another'! Do you want a pitcher or just a glass?"

"A pitcher! Wait, we need more though! Delph, you'll have another, right?" Vela asked, looking around at me with wide glassy eyes.

I bit back a giggle as I answered.

"Sure. I don't care what we have though, as long as it's strong!" I said, before reaching out and grabbing one of the semi-empty drinks in front of Leus.

I sipped it, unsure what had motivated me to do so, and shot him a cheeky smile that felt entirely foreign.

"Hey! That was mine! Can we get another pitcher of 'spicy yet delicious'?" he asked, his words slightly slurred as the arm around my shoulder slipped down to my waist.

I smiled up at him dopily, his blue eyes barely in focus.

I didn't know him, not really, but it felt so nice to have him touching me and holding me close.

"Of course, hun. Anything for the rest of you?"

I shook my head, still smiling up at Leus.

He ducked his head, nuzzling against my cheek before his lips found my ear.

"We should go up to our room soon," he whispered, desire dripping from his words.

My stomach clenched with anxiety and I knew my eyes were wide as he pulled back and looked deeply into them but still, I nodded.

It felt too grown up, too fast even though I clearly had a history with the boy. We were dating in this fantasy and we seemed so comfortable together, but part of me was still scared.

"That should be good. Thank you!" Col said to the waitress with a grin.

"Coming right up, sweetie," she replied, her gaze lingering a little too long on Col before she turned away from us.

"So?" Aust demanded the moment the waitress was gone. "Was it Cet?"

Col groaned loudly and dropped her head back.

"I was hoping you would have forgotten," she mumbled, sending another round of laughter through us.

"Nope! Tell us!" Vela cried.

Awareness of how loud and excited we were hit me suddenly and I glanced around the room over Col's head.

We'd been seated around a circular table, half of us crammed into the booth, the rest on chairs, but we weren't the only ones in the dimly lit room. Other groups laughed and talked loudly, seemingly not caring about how loud we were being and right at the other end of the room, I could see Gem's crew. Two of them were asleep, the little blonde one and one of the boys had fallen asleep slumped against each other, but the other three were still talking and drinking freely.

That made me feel a little less guilty and I was able to pay attention to what Col was saying just in time to hear, "So, we hooked up! Who cares?"

I burst into almost hysterical laughter as Vela cried, "Cet? Really though? Cet?"

"What's wrong with Cet?" Col asked, her tone making it clear that she knew exactly what was wrong with Cet.

"He's an asshole!" Leus said, his voice shaking with laughter.

"Plus he's tried to poach you from our crew like six times!" I added, unsure where the information was coming from but knowing that it was true.

"Yeah, well... he's hot," Col said with a grin.

"He is hot," Aust agreed with a sage nod.

"So... what's he like in bed?" Vela asked, leaning forwards, the single light above the tables casting weird shadows on her face.

I grinned at Col's flushed face and snuggled into Leus' chest, the movement feeling somehow both so natural and yet so weird.

I could feel his heart beating through the thin blue t-shirt he'd changed into once we'd finished the obstacle course. He was so warm, his body so solid against mine but it felt so nice.

His grip tightened on my waist and he placed a soft kiss on the top of my head, making happiness spread through me. I was somehow so sleepy and comfortable, but also wide awake. I felt like I'd never need to sleep again but, if I had the option, I'd cuddle up with Leus and never get up.

"I mean, it wasn't bed, it was in the changing rooms," Col muttered as she picked up an overly large wing from one of the platters in front of her.

I wasn't sure what animal it had come from, but I knew it wasn't a chicken.

"What?" Vela all but shouted, her tone incredulous. "You, miss prim and proper, slept with the Captain of the worst crew on the base in a changing room?"

Col looked like she wanted the ground to open up and swallow her, which would have been hard considering we were on a spaceship somewhere far away from any ground.

"I mean, they're not the worst crew on the base. They do pretty good on all of their missions…"

"That's not what she meant!" Aust argued, his words only just intelligible with how heavily he was slurring. "They're the worst! Personality-wise!"

"Well, I'm not exactly going to marry the man!" Col countered. "I just wanted a little… you know what I wanted!"

Vela cackled loudly and I found myself grinning too.

"You wanted a little bump and grind? A little bit of fun? What? Zero-G and missions weren't enough excitement for you?" Vela demanded with mock outrage. "You could have found a nice boy anywhere

here or on the last pleasure ship we were on and yet you had to choose Cet, the biggest asshole in the world!"

Col looked around desperately and I knew she was checking to see if the waitress was nearby.

"We're underage! The chances of me finding another guy who's also underage here are slim if not none!" she hissed. "Plus, I don't want a relationship, just a bit of fun so I don't care that Cet is a dick."

Vela shook her head, her lips pursed as she tried to hide her amusement.

"I mean, we run into that lot a fair bit," she said, nodding towards Gem and her crew. "Could always try and hook up with Cas."

Col's eyebrows drew together.

"Isn't he dating Aries?" she asked, turning to look at them entirely unsubtly.

I was fully aware that we were all staring at them too, but they didn't even turn towards us.

"I don't know actually. They basically never touch, but they're always around each other. I mean, do you see the way he looks at her?" Vela asked, cocking her head as she examined them.

As if on cue, the boy, who I assumed was Cas, leant towards Aries and said something softly. She laughed and his face lit up.

I might have never been in a real relationship, but even I could see that he loved her.

"Eh, not worth it either way. I bet the Council are

already eyeing that crew hard. I bet the second they graduate, they're going to be snatched up for all of the best missions," Col said with a sigh, turning back towards us.

I had no idea who the Council was or what that meant, but I found myself nodding.

"Oh, do you think those are our drinks?" Aust cried, pointing across the room and barely avoiding knocking over a bunch of glasses.

Vela laughed and slapped his arm gently.

"Gods, Aust, you're going to break everything!" she laughed.

He looked around the table blankly, his eyes unfocused and his movements a little too loose.

"I didn't hit anything!" he complained.

Col laughed softly.

"You didn't, but there's always next time," she said, her eyes sparkling with joy.

She seemed a lot more sober than the rest of us somehow and I was a little grateful for it. Even in my tipsy, if not drunk, state, I knew we'd be suffering in the morning. We needed someone to make sure we got home safely

"Nuhuh! I'm good! I barely break anything!" he insisted as the waitress approached our table again.

"I have the drinks!" she announced, lifting a jug off the little robot that had followed her over and now waited behind her like an obedient dog. "Where do you want these?"

I stared at the robot, having to fight the urge to reach out and pat it. It was silver and came up to about waist height. There were even little circular shapes on the screen on the front that looked like eyes.

I loved it.

"Oh," Aust cried and I ripped my gaze away from the robot to look at the pitcher waitress was holding.

It looked delicious. The bottom was a cloudy yellowish colour which then somehow transformed into a mouthwatering green before being topped off with a purple liquid. I had no idea what it tasted like but I wanted to know.

"Just in the centre, please. We can serve ourselves," Col answered for us.

"Of course," the waitress said, leaning over Col to put the drinks into the cleared centre of the table.

Col's eyes widened slightly at how seemingly deliberately close the waitress was to her and Vela barked out a laugh before turning it into an unconvincing cough.

We waited in silence for the waitress to finish putting our drinks down before she turned again, winked at Col and left. The robot trailed after her happily, and I found myself wanting to go and pet it.

"Well," Vela said, reaching for a pitcher and pouring a large glass for her and Aust before offering it to Leus and me. "Turns out you didn't need to go for Cet after all. You could have waited a week and hooked up with her."

Col blushed a deep shade of red again and glanced over her shoulder at the retreating waitress.

"Shut up and drink," she ordered.

"Yes, Captain," we all answered immediately, causing Col to groan and drop her head into her hands.

I had no idea where that had come from either, but happiness danced within me.

"Another?" Leus asked, holding the jug and reaching for my cup with the hand that had been around me.

"Sure," I smiled up at him. "But then we go upstairs?"

His eyes widened slightly and I knew that mine did too. The words had just fallen out without any thought and I hadn't even known I was going to say that! Not that I didn't want to go upstairs with him, I did a little even if it felt like a huge step.

I knew that, if I went upstairs with him, we'd probably sleep together or at least fool around. I wasn't sure how to feel about that, I'd never even kissed a boy in real life, not properly.

I did want to though, I just hadn't really even dated anyone, which made it difficult.

"I'll drink quickly," he said, his tone seductive as he filled our glasses and passed one to me.

"Me too," I said but my voice sounded uncertain.

"Grace," my mom's voice cut through the daydream and I blinked quickly to see her poking her head around my door. "Ah, thought I might find you up here. We're going to go out to dinner in about half an hour. Do you want to shower before we go?"

Her tone told me that the correct answer was yes.

"Oh, yeah, sure," I said, pushing all thoughts of Leus and his hand on my thigh out of my head. "I'll go now."

CHAPTER TWENTY-SIX

I chewed on a mouthful of the pretty good but small salad in front of me, picking around the pomegranate seeds. I wasn't sure who decided that pomegranate seeds belonged in salads, but I didn't like them. Apart from that, it was a pretty good salad. There were chunks of some house-made chicken substitute, spirals of deliciously sweet carrots, and shavings of cheese nestled amongst the lettuce. The dressing was creamy and delicious.

I ate slowly and carefully, making sure not to do anything that would make my mom or grandparents judge me too hard or accuse me of being unladylike, but it was hard. The lettuce was chopped roughly and with every bite, I felt a wave of panic that I would drop some onto my dress and stain it.

Despite my annoyance, I had changed into something more appropriate. I mean, it felt like I had to. We'd gone to the usual restaurant that we always went to with my grandparents. It was in some fancy hotel and they apparently knew the owners, so we were always expected to be on our best behaviour. I was never really sure if they actually did know the owners, but the waiters certainly knew us on sight.

The service was quick and very polite but a little weird. I mean, they always hastened to bring a new bottle of wine over for my grandmother whenever she finished one and never said anything about the glass that was in front of me.

Not that I drank wine, not really. It tasted of vinegar and made my mouth pucker, even if my grandmother described it as sweet. Apparently, I was at an appropriate age to begin liking wine, whether I liked it or not, so I needed to at least try.

I wasn't complaining though. Despite the taste, it did make the meals a little less painful.

"So, Stephen got a promotion?" my grandmother asked, picking at her food but barely eating any.

"Yes, he did actually," my mom was quick to say.

I wasn't sure if that was true or not, but it didn't matter. Dizziness had started to tickle the edge of my mind. I let it, not quite sure if I was going to go back to the weird ship I was on with Leus and my crew where I'd hopefully be waking up with a hangover, or if I were going back to Mitch.

My phone alarm rang loudly beside me and I rolled over, my eyes squeezed shut against the vertigo and brightness. For a moment, I honestly wasn't sure which world I was in, but then I forced an eye open and took in the familiar bright bedroom.

I swung my arm out semi-blindly, grabbing at my phone and turning on the alarm. I knew that Mitch would probably be downstairs, either having breakfast already or swimming, but I just wanted more sleep.

I let myself slip back into my doze, the room perfectly cool even though I was bundled up in the blankets. They were so soft and inviting, it was no wonder that I'd gone back there.

Also, I was a little glad I hadn't returned to Leus. It felt weird. I kind of wanted to but mostly, I didn't want to know what we'd done together. It felt... too adult. I wasn't ready for that yet.

I was ready to go downstairs and have fresh pastries out on the patio though; that didn't feel too grown up.

I groaned softly and rolled over, pulling the duvet with me before checking the time.

Nine am.

That was too early. I was on holiday, kind of. I should be sleeping in until at least eleven, if not later! But I still wanted to get up. I wanted to get started on the day and see what the plan was. Plus, the thought of those pastries was making my mouth water.

I sat up semi-reluctantly, adjusting my tank top and blinking as I stared around the room.

"Have you decided what A levels you'll be taking?"

my grandmother's voice cut through my fantasy.

"No, not yet," I said, immediately snapping back to reality.

"She's still got some time to work it out though, don't you?" my mom said, her tone overly supportive.

"Oh, yes. I don't need to decide until around Christmas time," I said.

"What are you considering?" my grandfather asked, sounding genuinely interested.

"Umm... I'm not actually sure yet. I was thinking maybe math and philosophy, but I'm not sure about the others," I said.

I really wasn't sure though. Some of it would depend on how things went with my GCSEs, and I truly didn't know how they were going to go. It might be that I did shockingly well in an unexpected subject; that would change things. The only one I was sure about was philosophy. I knew that Mr Ray taught it, and I wasn't really sure what the class would involve, but I wanted to find out.

"Philosophy?" my grandmother said, the tone making the word sound more like a slur or an insult than anything else. "That sounds like a terrible idea. It has no value in the world today. Esther took philosophy, and now she's a journalist."

I ignored the judgement that dripped from the word and glanced at my mom.

I liked Esther. She was one of my nicest cousins and

she seemed to genuinely enjoy her job, which is more than I could say for a lot of adults I knew, but that wasn't enough for my grandparents.

Being a journalist wasn't a flashy enough job, but nothing my cousins did would ever be enough for them. One was a doctor but still that wasn't enough because he went into paediatrics instead of being a surgeon, which was apparently much better.

I didn't get that though. Surely, working with kids and literally saving their lives was impressive enough?

I remained silent and stared down at my plate as the conversation continued on, my mother quickly and enthusiastically changing the subject before I had a chance to disagree with my grandmother. I'd eaten just over half. It wasn't enough and I was still hungry but if I ate anything more, I knew that my grandparents would comment on it.

I neatly placed my cutlery together on the plate and folded my hands in my lap, catching the not quite approving but not disapproving look that my grand-mother sent me before slipping back into the fantasy where I was getting dressed, my skin still sticky from the suncream I'd rubbed into it.

I glanced around the room quickly, making sure I hadn't forgotten anything before tucking my phone into my shorts pocket and racing down the stairs as quickly as I dared with feet slippery from the suncream.

I approached the windows quickly, knocking gently

so that Mitch would turn around. He did, a cup in one hand and an iPad in the other.

He waved at me with the hand that held his coffee and stood quickly, walking towards me with a grin.

He closed the door softly behind him before saying, "Morning, kiddo! Sorry, neighbours are out in their pool. I've been listening to their splashing for the last hour. I kept thinking it was going to wake you up!"

"Oh, yeah, sorry. I slept in a bit late," I said with an apologetic smile as I sat at the table and eyed the breakfast that had been brought in for us.

"Don't worry at all! I'm glad you did! You're a kid, you need your sleep. Want a coffee?" he asked as he drained his cup and put it under the machine again.

"Mmmm," I said as I considered it. "Yeah, please."

"Great! Caramel latte again?"

"Yes!"

"Good call! We're going to need to be sharp today, we've got big plans," he said, his tone a little ominous.

"We do?" I asked, trying to keep the concern out of my voice.

"Oh, yeah. I've booked us a private tour of Spinalonga first thing and then in the afternoon, we're going to go diving again. We'll be going as much as possible because I want you to get comfortable with it before we move on to the next place. Our next mission might be somewhere landlocked so getting as much practice as you can now is very important," he said, his expression serious.

I nodded.

The idea of going to Spinalonga excited me and I wanted to rush through breakfast to get there. It felt like the adventure was about to start for real.

"Cool! So… we're going to Spinalonga?" I asked.

"We are. We have to be down at the pier at eleven thirty, so we've got some time. Start eating! We'll probably be there over lunch and I don't want you to be hungry!" he insisted.

I grinned and started loading food onto my plate, eyeing the giant slab of hash brown and seemingly freshly baked bread. I wanted them both, but settled for having bread first; I wanted to start with something sweet. I grabbed the large pot of honey and began drizzling it over the hunk of bread I'd ripped off, biting into it and letting my eyes flutter shut with delight.

It was so good. I don't know what it was about the bread and honey, if it were how fresh it was or the fact that I was starving, but it was delicious.

"There you go, kid," Mitch said, placing a cup in front of me and sitting in the other chair.

"Thanks," I said around my mouthful before swallowing and asking, "so, do we need to, like, look out for anything on Spinalonga? Like, clues or something?"

I reached for more bread as Mitch considered my question, pouring even more honey on this time.

"Not really. I think just start by having a look around and see if anything stands out to you. I might pretend that I've confiscated your phone to give you a good excuse to dawdle and be looking around so much, what do you think?" he asked.

"Oh, yeah! That's a good idea!" I said excitedly.

"Great! You'll still have your watch, obviously, so if anything does happen, you can use that but I think this will work," he mused.

I grinned at him and finished my bread, licking some leftover honey off my fingers.

"Are you finished with your plate?" a woman asked in a gentle Scottish accent.

"Oh, yes. Thank you," I said, clutching my hands tightly in my lap as a wave of nausea hit me.

The waitress smiled at me and took the plate.

I glanced around the table, checking to make sure that no one had noticed that I wasn't paying any attention to the conversation, but they hadn't. I mean, it didn't really matter that much. My mom and grandparents strongly believed that kids shouldn't take part in conversations with adults unless they were directly spoken to.

I'd never asked why, but that hadn't stopped my grandmother from telling me her reasoning. Apparently, kids had nothing worthwhile to add to any conversation. It wasn't even worth listening to us.

"Would anyone like any dessert or a coffee?" a waiter asked, looking at my grandmother.

"A cappuccino, please," she said with a polite yet clipped smile.

"An espresso," my grandfather added.

"A cappuccino would be great," my mother added.

The waiter looked at me expectantly and I felt the others do the same.

I should have said no thank you, that's what they expected of me, but a flare of rebellion went through me.

"I'd like a latte, please," I said with a smile.

"Of course," the waiter said before hurrying away.

"Since when do you drink coffee?" my mom asked, her tone light but there was an edge to it.

"Oh, fairly recently. I had one at school and it was pretty good," I lied.

I wasn't actually sure if I would like a coffee in reality or if I would like it without caramel syrup, but it didn't feel right to ask for something like that here. It felt too immature, they would judge me for it.

"They serve coffee at schools now?" my grandmother asked sharply. "How ridiculous."

I felt irritation rush through me as my mother opened her mouth to say something, either to change the subject or agree with her, but I spoke first.

"Excuse me, I'm just going to pop to the bathroom," I said, phrasing it the exact way my mother had earlier when she'd left me alone with my grandparents.

They barely even looked at me, continuing the conversation as if I hadn't interrupted.

I slipped from the table without hesitating and

rushed across the restaurant as quickly as I could without looking like I was actually in a hurry to get away from my table.

Even with how uncomfortable I found eating there, I did enjoy going. It was a stunningly beautiful place. The hotel was a converted old manor building, but they'd done a lot of work on the restaurant to modernise it.

The roof had been draped with a cream-coloured tulle, which hid fairy lights that sparkled softly and made the whole room feel a little magical. Occasional paintings hung on the walls too. Romanticised versions of the landscape around us, some misty and mysterious looking, others shining under the sunlight.

It felt intimate, romantic and entirely the wrong place to go with your family. I was pretty sure we were the only family there too. Most of the other diners appeared to be couples of various ages, dressed in suits and formal clothes, their hair carefully styled and perfectly preened.

I was a little jealous. It would be a lovely place to go on a date.

I looked down and walked across the monogrammed carpet towards the bathroom, pushing the door open and breathing out a sigh of relief.

It was empty.

That bathroom was always my safe haven when I was there. It was so often empty because there was another one closer to the restaurant, but that's why I went to it.

People had to go out of their way to find it which meant I could normally stay there a little longer. If there were other people in there, I'd feel uncomfortable but there rarely were.

I looked around again before sinking into the weird fainting couch that lived in the bathroom. Normally, I wouldn't have sat on any kind of furniture in a bathroom other than the toilet, but it was always spotless in there which helped. It even smelt nice. There was a delicately floral perfume that always hung in the air.

I fished my phone out of my pocket and stared at it blankly for a moment.

I wasn't really sure what to do. I just wanted a bit of a break, a chance to breathe or be alone without my mom or my grandparents picking at me. I almost wanted to text Phoebe, but I wasn't sure what to say. I'd only be able to text her once or twice before going back to dinner too, so I felt bad.

I clicked on Instagram and scrolled through for a moment without paying much attention to what I was seeing. I didn't follow too many people on there anyway. A couple of people from school, a few celebrities and influencers, but that was about it.

A sigh slipped out of my mouth as I checked the time. I needed to go back. I had to return to the table and drink my potentially not horrible drink and smile politely as the others had conversations that I wasn't allowed to be a part of.

It wouldn't be that bad though. Mitch and I would be going to Spinalonga soon and I couldn't wait for that. I wondered what it was going to be like before blinking as a realisation came over me.

I could just google it. I had my phone in front of me and I was on the hotel wifi. I could just search the island and see if it actually existed or if my brain was just making it up.

A grin came over my face as I pulled up Safari and searched 'Spinalonga'.

It was a real place! An actual abandoned leper colony, just like Mitch had said. It really was in the middle of a bay opposite a hotel that looked a lot like the one we were staying at in my daydream. I must have seen it in a TV show or movie or something, because it looked almost exactly like I imagined it.

I smiled to myself before rising from the couch and stretching. I'd dawdled too long. I needed to go back before they got suspicious of what I was doing in the bathroom.

Knowing my mom, she would assume that I was talking to a boy or something scandalous and I really didn't want her to look through my phone again, even if there was nothing that bad to find on there.

I hadn't been talking to a boy, obviously, but she would still assume that I had. I don't know why but she just always assumed that I was when really, the only boy I ever spoke to was Duncan, and it wasn't like anything would ever happen between us.

He'd known me for too long. He'd seen me go through my awkward phase, which honestly I wasn't sure I was out of, and he would never be into me like that. He was probably into one of the pretty girls at school, like Ella, who took every opportunity to touch him or trail after him at parties. He'd told me a bunch of times that he wasn't into her, but I wasn't quite sure. I felt bad for him, though. He once pulled me out onto the roof and we hid there for like an hour just so that she'd get bored and stop looking for him.

I kind of felt bad for her too. It must be tough to be that unaware that someone isn't into you. Maybe she was aware. Maybe she just hoped that he'd change his mind but it didn't seem to be happening. Hopefully, for his sake, she'd get bored and move on to someone else soon.

I slipped my phone into my pocket, washed my hands, and slipped out of the bathroom. I stared at the stunning portraits on the wall as I walked down the hall towards the restaurant, admiring the paintings of the people who used to live in the hotel back when it was just a house.

Part of me wanted to imagine what it was like to live then. To have a giant house with staff and people to take care of me and cook for me and everything. I could just spend my days preparing for balls and speaking to suitors who would be lining up down the drive just for the chance to catch a glimpse of me.

But, no. The allure of exploring Spinalonga was too much for me. I didn't want to abandon that just for a throwaway daydream.

I returned to the table, smiling politely at my mom who was the only person who looked at me, and sat down again.

"You took your time," my grandmother said. "Your coffee will be cold."

I looked down at the tall mug which still billowed steam.

"There was a queue for the bathroom," I lied.

She raised an eyebrow before looking away, glancing at my granddad who didn't respond at all.

"What have you planned to do for the month?" my grandmother asked, her tone bordering on demanding.

"We've not booked anything just yet, you know we like to get here before we organise anything, but we were thinking horse riding, maybe hiking, seeing the sights. We might spend a day in Edinburgh again, that's always fun. Plus, Grace has some schoolwork she wanted to do over the summer, right?" my mom said.

I glanced at her blankly, trying to work out if I had mentioned anything to her about anything I had to do. I didn't think so. We hadn't been given any work, so it had to be a lie.

Realisation hit me. Mom had lied about me having work to do to give us an excuse to just be in the house, as if we needed a reason to just be relaxing during our holiday.

"Oh, yes. I want to get a head start on my schoolwork for next year," I lied.

My mom sent me a slight smile that warmed my heart, but my grandmother looked at me flatly. I knew she was going to say something judgemental, but I didn't want anything to dull the happiness I felt in that moment.

With a blink, I was back in Crete, standing on the pier and staring at the surprisingly small boat. A heavily tanned man in a button-down top and shorts stood in the boat, talking to Mitch.

I was the only one on the pier still, but the boat didn't look sturdy enough to get us across the water to Spinalonga. I knew that the water was fairly enclosed so there weren't really any waves or anything, but it still could be a little choppy.

I eyed the boat again but this time, Mitch turned to me.

"Come on, Alice. This trip is going to be fun!" he said in a tone similar to my mom's when she was talking to my grandparents.

It was that same forced enthusiasm and happiness.

I glanced at him worriedly and crossed my arms which made Mitch turn to the sailor and speak in a loud whisper.

"She's just annoyed because I banned her phone from the trip. You know how young people are today.

Do you have any kids?"

"Oh, yes," the man said. "A ten-year-old and a five-year-old."

"Oof!" Mitch said dramatically. "Brace yourself. I remember when Alice was ten. We used to have so much fun."

I looked away over the water, guilt churning in my stomach as the sailor tutted sympathetically.

"Do you remember how fun that was, Alice?" Mitch asked, his tone so kind and hopeful that it made my heart clench.

I couldn't ignore him. I just couldn't even though I knew that I probably should have.

I let my arms drop and climbed into the boat, dropping into the nearest seat and muttering, "It was fun."

CHAPTER TWENTY-SEVEN

We approached the light stone pier, the sun beating down on us and the gentle breeze blowing the hair back from my face. The island looked stunning up close.

The pier was little more than a flat outcrop of rocks with a short metal pillar sticking up with just one other boat moored there. It was a small thing, about the same size as ours, clearly owned by the woman who stood on the pier and waved as we approached.

She called out a greeting in Greek to the sailor before switching to a barely accented English.

"Hello!"

"Hi there!" Mitch called back over the noise of the engine.

I looked at her and smiled flatly before staring at the building that rose up from the island behind her.

It surprised me just how big everything looked. The space just beyond the pier looked almost too spacious and was dotted with short but dense light green trees.

The wall past them looked surprisingly well maintained. The light stone was unblemished even though it was topped with straggly weeds.

"Mitch?" the woman asked, stepping towards us.

I glanced at her as the sailor helped me and then Mitch out of the boat.

She was stunning. Dressed in trainers, light shorts and a t-shirt, she looked completely at home on the semi-abandoned island. Her dark, wavy hair had been pulled back into a ponytail and her smile was wide and welcoming. She almost looked like a treasure hunter from a movie.

"That's me!" Mitch said, reaching out and shaking her hand. "This is my daughter, Alice."

"Nice to meet you," I muttered, looking away again.

"Lovely to meet you both," the woman beamed. "I'm Vasia and I'll be leading your tour today."

"Fantastic! I can't wait to learn more about this beautiful place. I hear it has a rich history!" Mitch said enthusiastically.

"Well, I look forward to telling you all about it."

"I'll return in an hour and a half," the sailor called from behind us.

"Wonderful, thank you so much!" Mitch called back, waving as the boat began to pull away. "So, how do we get into this fortress? It is a fortress, right?"

He started marching across the space, further onto

the island, but I was torn. I looked back at the boat, watching it retreat and feeling anxiety build within me. It was our only way on and off the island. If something went wrong or if Sterling's people were here, we'd be trapped.

I mean, we could always swim but that felt like a horrible idea. We'd be sitting ducks in the water.

Or floating ducks.

Reluctantly, I turned and started to follow Mitch and Vasia towards the walls. The ground was less flat the further onto the island we went and it was covered in a smattering of sparse, short weeds.

As we started along the path, something caught my eyes, but luckily, Mitch was close enough that I heard him ask, "Is that a shop there?"

He pointed out to the right at the building that sat on the outside of the fortress.

"Ah, yes," Vasia said. "It's a self-service coffee shop so if you are thirsty, please, go get a drink."

Mitch turned back to me, smiling widely.

"Do you want to get a drink, Alice? It looks like it's a beautiful view!" he asked.

I looked into the coffee shop, pretending to mull it over.

It did seem like it would be lovely to sit under the canopy and look out over the unobstructed view of the water, but that wasn't the reason we were there.

"No, thank you," I said tightly. "I'd rather just get

this over and done with."

It was a lie but Mitch smiled at me indulgently before looking back at Vasia.

"Sorry. We agreed on no phones for this trip so that it's purely educational. I'm not sure Alice is too happy about it though," he said in a loud whisper.

I pursed my lips and looked away as if to hide my irritation.

It was a fight to keep my expression annoyed or even neutral. The island was stunning and I just wanted to stare.

"I think we'll just move on," he said, smiling at me.

I returned it reluctantly, trailing after Vasia and Mitch as they started up the stairs towards the entrance to the island. A booth had been placed next to the path, its dark walls covered in posters and caked with sand but today, the shutters were closed.

"Normally, the price would be eight euro per person to enter," Vasia said with a wave at the booth. "But, you are with me and this is a private tour, so it is free."

"Oh, wonderful!" Mitch cried.

They continued walking, quickly climbing the short ramp which directed them to the sloping path around the side of the fortress.

The wall there was slightly less refined. It looked like it had just been roughly carved from the rock. Scratch marks marred the walls and random shrubs and weeds burst forth from the cracks, some so large that they reached onto the path and we had to edge around them.

I let myself fall behind, taking my time and examining the place. The wall was jagged and uneven, but I wasn't sure if that was a bad thing or not. It meant that, if needed, we'd probably be able to climb it which would probably come in handy.

But, there were lights on the other side of the path, pointing at the wall. Maybe that would be a problem. If they were on and we were climbing down, we'd be too obvious.

We reached the top of the slope where a big but seemingly useless gate waited, the doors tied open. I'd expected the island to have giant wrought iron barriers, used for hundreds of years to stop people from trying to escape, but the gate in front of me was almost a disappointment.

The main frame of it was wooden and the bars were metal but it seemed so out of place. It looked like it had just been dropped onto the middle of the path but didn't belong there. It seemed to be only connected to one of the walls too. On the right, the wall was fairly flat and seemingly impossible to scale but the other was much rougher and barely connected to the wooden frame.

That wall looked like just a pile of bricks, so easy to climb that the gate was useless. That made me feel better. If we did go to the island after the gate was shut, which felt likely, it wouldn't be too difficult to get over.

I almost did want to climb that wall. There was a strange circular building much higher on the other side, with some overgrown grass and shrubs blocking what would be my path. I immediately wanted to go that way, to explore the weird building and find out its secrets, but I had to follow the others.

Mitch and Vasia had climbed the stairs just to the right of the gate and I clambered up after them, coming to a halt in what looked like the ruins of a church. A small white stone box with a cross on lay amongst the weeds. I stepped towards it but was stopped by a thin rope barrier.

I stared out towards the white box, squinting to read the words that had been etched into the top. I wasn't sure quite what it was but there was a date on it.

"Is that a grave marker?" Mitch asked, pointing at it.

"Yes," Vasia said. "It actually denotes—"

"I think we'll probably going to go straight to bed when we get back. It's been a long day of travelling, hasn't it, Grace?" my mom asked.

I blinked, dizziness almost overwhelming me, and let my head fall back against the headrest.

"Yes," I agreed, only half hearing what she had said.

Lights exploded in my vision, startlingly bright against the dusky world outside the car.

I stared out the window again, watching the rolling green world fly past, before blinking back into Spinalonga.

"That's so cool!" Mitch was saying. "Man, it must be so fun getting to learn about this place and wandering around it all day."

Vasia laughed softly.

"It is a pretty fun job. Shall we?" She gestured back towards the stairs we had climbed to the graveyard.

I'd missed what she said and couldn't even recall it but I assumed the slightly raised rectangular shapes around the place were graves.

I followed them down the stairs, stopping briefly to examine the map that had been attached to the brick wall below. It didn't have many details on the map, just some buildings of interest and a thin black line which showed our path. We appeared to be walking around the edge of the island, if the red dot showing our location was anything to go by, but there was a lot of space untouched by the path.

I glanced at Mitch who had continued walking, chatting freely with Vasia. I couldn't stop them to ask if we'd be able to go into the buildings away from the path, it would be wrong to interrupt them. Alice would never.

I looked back at the map before shaking my head slightly. I just needed to trust Mitch. He had been doing this forever, he knew what he was doing.

I longed to at least take a picture of the map though. That way, if we did get lost or if we needed to find out what a specific building was or its history, it would be easier. My hand reached for my pocket before stilling.

We'd left our phones at the hotel.

Well… I had, I wasn't sure about Mitch, but I wouldn't be surprised if he'd brought his. It seemed stupid not to.

I walked away from the map reluctantly, following the cracked path which was starting to be overrun by bushes with small white, yellow and red flowers. They made me smile a little. I knew the island had a dark and horrible history, but I still liked to think there was some beauty or happiness there, even back then.

We continued along the path, Mitch and Vasia far in front of me, pausing so that Vasia could point out another grave on the right, out amongst the seemingly wild plants. I wasn't sure who she said though, the name wasn't familiar at all, but I assumed they must have been important to have a grave far from the others. Either that or the opposite.

"Can we go up there?" I heard Mitch say excitedly from in front of me. "I want to see the fortress. That's what that is, right?"

I glanced at where he was pointing, a tiny flutter of anxiety and excitement starting in my stomach.

He'd pointed along what I thought originally must have been a long and not particularly steep set of stairs that doubled back along the path we'd taken from the pier but where ours had brought us through the gate, that one took us towards the strange circular building.

I fought the grin that wanted to appear on my face and looked at Vasia, worried that she'd refuse. It looked important, like it could have the treasure. Surely the biggest building on the island would have the most security and therefore, the treasure was most likely to be there... right?

Vasia hesitated for just a moment before saying, "Yes, but there is no barrier on these steps so go carefully."

Mitch beamed at her and started up the stairs excitedly.

I wasn't sure if he was just playing his part to perfection or if he were actually really excited to be going towards the building, but either way I clambered up behind Vasia.

The stairs were uneven and covered in dried grass but the view as we climbed was beautiful. Vasia had been right, there was no barrier or anything at the side to stop us from falling if we were to stumble, but that also meant that I had an uninterrupted view of the world below.

It was stunning. The remains of what I think was the church were somehow more impressive from above. The graves were less obvious but, when I focused on them, the sheer number was sobering.

But, that couldn't be it. There were a lot of graves but surely not every single person on the island who died there was buried in the graveyard. Had the church been there from the beginning or did it come later?

With a shudder, I realised there was no way of knowing. I could be walking on countless graves and I would never know.

"Oh, wow! Look at the fortress, Alice. It's so tall!" Mitch called back at me.

He was almost at the top of the stairs already but had stopped to look back at me and make sure I was okay. Or, maybe he was using that as an excuse to examine the bay and make sure that there was no sign of Sterling's people coming for us.

I turned away from the graveyard and stared up at the giant round fortress before continuing up the stairs, edging around the weird bushes. They looked almost like cacti, with strangely thick and rounded leaves but there were no spikes. Or maybe there were but they'd been worn away from years of people climbing the steps and brushing past them.

I reached the top, my view of the bay hidden by a crumbed, barely standing wall that was taller than I was but not by much. I was aware that, if I really wanted to see, I could have climbed onto the grassy edge next to the wall and peered over, but I didn't want to risk it.

I knew there was nothing on the other side but a sheer drop and, although I wasn't scared of heights, it worried me. My stomach felt a little tight as I stared at the wall. It was just a dream, of course, but I was high enough from the ground that if I fell, I'd be badly injured, if not worse. It wouldn't hurt me in real life, probably, but I couldn't just continue the dream after that. It would ruin Mitch's plans.

I wanted to find out the secrets of the island, discover

what treasures lay beneath the surface.

"Alice?" Mitch called. "Are you coming?"

I looked away from the wall to where he waited at a fork in the path just ahead of me.

"I guess," I muttered, hurrying towards him a little too fast.

"This side here is blocked off," he said, pointing to one of the paths that had a thin rope barrier across it. "But, apparently we can get in this way! Isn't this exciting? It feels like I'm back on Spinalonga in its heyday!"

He grinned and scampered towards Vasia who watched him with a slight smile on her face.

I followed them, the tall yellow-flowered weeds brushing against my legs as I started climbing again.

The island seemed to be full of stairs. It made sense, in a way. The whole place was built on a hill so it was either that or just making everything sloped but it made me glad that Mitch had insisted I didn't push myself too hard at the gym. If I had, the slight burning in my calves would be unbearable, I could tell.

We followed the precarious path as it looped around the fortress. Mitch and Vasia walked ahead with so much more confidence than I did, barely looking down over the short wall that would crumble if I were to fall on it. And then there'd be nothing stopping me from falling.

I swallowed and moved slower, staring at the ground and staying as far away from the not even knee-high wall, aware that they were waiting for me at the top. I could hear them talking softly and I rounded the corner at the top just in time to see Vasia laugh and lay her hand gently on Mitch's arm. She snatched it away when she saw me approach, but Mitch just smiled at me.

"Look how tall the fortress looks from here!" he said, turning towards the towering structure and looking up at it. "It's huge!"

Vasia turned quickly too without looking at me, as if she was worried about how I'd react to her flirting with Mitch, which made me a little sad. I didn't want her to worry even though I did understand. I was acting like a brat and I knew that Alice would probably have something snide or rude to say, but I didn't want to be like that. I would just pretend I didn't see it.

Mitch might have been flirting with her for a reason. I mean, if she thought he was into her then maybe she'd let us get away with exploring the island more? Or maybe he just wanted to flirt.

"Let's go up there!" Mitch cried before rushing towards yet another set of stairs that snaked around the side of the building.

I followed them slightly less cautiously this time, feeling more confident about the wall which was actually still standing and didn't look like all it would take was a strong breeze to send the rocks tumbling, and before long, we ducked under an archway which led us into the inside of the fortress.

I looked around, disappointment sinking within me.

I'd expected it to be a grand military base, filled with left-over canons and relics and stuff or something that hinted at its past but it was really just a shell of a building.

There wasn't even a roof. It was just a mostly roped off area of rocks that had fallen from the building and another set of stairs which took us into the rounded centre of the fortress. There wasn't even much to see there, but that didn't stop Mitch's excitement. He rushed across the grassy space and climbed the dangerously thin set of stairs that had been built into the wall, not even waiting for Vasia or me to follow him.

I wasn't sure if he was actually excited by the fortress or if it were an act but it seemed genuine. His excitement was contagious too. Every time he turned to look at me, a grin on his face, I had to fight to not smile too.

The car jolted to a stop and I blinked, staring at the world around me in confusion. I knew that we'd stopped at the gates to my grandparent's house and, from the front seat, I could hear the annoyed clicking of the button from my grandmother as she repeatedly pushed it even though the gate was already moving, but something felt a little off.

I shook my head slightly, trying to push that feeling and my dizziness aside. It was probably just that I was too used to being in Crete with Mitch. I was used to the sun beating down on us, not the dreariness of dusk in Scotland. It wasn't quite dark, but it definitely wasn't still light.

My stomach clenched and my hand tightened on my

phone as we sped down the path a little too fast for how dark it was. It always made me anxious when we drove down the drive at night. My grandparents didn't have any lights fitted out there, for some reason, and the thick trees that lined the path blocked out too much sunlight. We were essentially driving blind and hoping that my grandfather knew the route well.

I wanted to slip back into my fantasy, to Crete, but I was too tense. It felt like every muscle in my body was clenched as I held my breath and hoped he wouldn't hit a tree. He was going too quickly. If he did hit something, we'd be badly injured.

But, somehow, we made it to the house without incident.

I tried not to get out of the car too quickly as we pulled to a stop, but he had barely switched off the engine before I was out of the door. I breathed in the fresh air, a smile growing on my face despite the anxiety that was still coursing through me.

That was one of the things I liked about being there. It always smelt so good. It just smelt fresh. And not fresh like the air around where I lived that was always tinged with manure. It smelt like grass and plants and nature.

I missed it sometimes, which felt silly to admit. It wasn't my home, I shouldn't miss it. Not that I missed my actual home ever.

"Are you tired, Grace?" my mom asked pointedly as she climbed out of the car.

"Oh, yes. Exhausted," I was quick to say.

"It's been a long day and we were up early this morning," my mom told my grandmother, who didn't even respond.

She started towards the front door without even looking back at us.

I had a moment, a fleeting thought of what would happen if I didn't follow. If I turned and walked away from the house instead of traipsing after them obediently, what would they do? Probably nothing. I could see my grandmother just locking the front door and leaving me to sleep outside.

According to my mom, she used to do that sometimes when they were kids. If they came back later than she wanted them to, she'd lock the door and they'd either need to climb up the ivy on the side of the house, if it held them, or they'd sleep in the shed.

The last time we were there, after my grandparents had left and my mom had had too many glasses of wine to celebrate, she told me she used to keep a blanket out there, hidden so that my grandmother wouldn't find it and bin it. Apparently, that had really annoyed my grandparents when they finally worked it out. They'd said she didn't deserve it, even though it was the middle of winter.

I glanced towards the shed at the edge of the garden before sighing and following them towards the house.

CHAPTER TWENTY-EIGHT

I stretched out in my bed, the mattress uncomfortably hard under me. It always was, but I forgot about it each year and was always surprised somehow. I think it must have been the same mattress that my uncle had used when he was a kid and they just hadn't changed it in however many years but either way, it was lumpy and hard.

I rolled over again, wiggling to try and find a comfy spot where there wasn't a spring or whatever else there was digging into me, but I failed.

I sighed with irritation and pulled my duvet up higher, shivering in the cold room. There was always a faint breeze in the room, even with the windows shut. I wasn't sure where it was coming from or how but it was annoying. I could feel it against my skin almost constantly.

I rolled again, letting my mind slip back into the fantasy almost seamlessly and for a moment, I was disorientated. I'd expected us to still be on Spinalonga, but we weren't. I was in one of the restaurants, a pout on my face as I picked at my plate of perfectly grilled vegetables.

It was dark outside.

I stared out the window in confusion. How much time had passed? It had only been an hour or so in the real world. I'd showered as quickly as possible, having had to wait for the water to heat up, and had got ready for bed. I should have kept an eye on what was happening with Mitch whilst I was at it but I'd been distracted by texts from Phoebe. It was hard to keep bouncing in and out of my fantasy, it made me so dizzy I almost dropped my phone into the toilet.

She'd landed in Paris and was frantically texting me because her family insisted on only speaking to her in French. It had been hilarious and I felt sorry for her, but it had kept me away from the fantasy and now I'd missed the rest of the tour.

I still had some memories of it, when I thought about it hard. Flashes of a long tunnel, metal gates waiting just inside, and fear were the first thing to hit me. I remembered faintly being worried about the tunnel falling on us and crushing us or Mitch having to blow it up, like he did to the building in Italy. No, I'd been worried that Sterling's people were already there. That they'd already set the charges and were just waiting for the perfect opportunity to kill us.

They weren't though, obviously. It had just been the three of us on the island. Me, Mitch, and Vasia. They'd flirted a lot. I remembered being almost in awe of the easy way that Mitch flirted and how he managed to ask the most suspicious of questions but make it sound completely innocent. I mean, now that I was thinking about it, I could remember him asking about other entrances to the island and if anyone would be there after dark.

If anyone else had asked that, I knew that they would have been met with suspicion but somehow, Mitch had pulled it off. Vasia just laughed and said that there was another entrance somewhere but that no one used it because it was crumbled to nothingness. It was too dangerous.

I'd caught the expression on Mitch's face though. He planned to use it. Or at least look into it.

There was more too. I could just about remember flashes of colours. Buildings, surprisingly well-kept, with brightly coloured shutters, lined one of the streets but some of them had open doorways that we could duck into if needed. If we were being followed or shot at.

"You alright, kid?" Mitch asked, bringing his glass of whisky to his lips. "You've been pretty quiet this after-noon."

There was no one nearby, I could speak almost freely, but I still hesitated. I couldn't exactly tell him the truth.

"Oh, yeah," I said quickly. "I'm fine."

He surveyed me carefully and I quickly took another bite of the perfectly grilled courgette, trying to appear as normal as possible.

"You sure?"

I nodded quickly.

"Just… distracted," I lied, hoping it was enough.

"That makes sense," he said softly. "It's intense seeing a potential target for the first time, I know that. If you've changed your mind and want to stay somewhere safe when I go to where I need to, that's completely okay."

I shook my head.

"I still want to go," I said quickly.

Mitch laughed softly and finished his whiskey, the ice cubes clinking gently in his glass.

"We'll talk about it properly when we get back to the room," he replied in his normal voice before slipping into his more needy tone. "Do you want any dessert today, Alice?"

I forced the smile from my face and looked away from him, trying to arrange my expression to one of boredom.

"No. I didn't even want dinner but you insisted," I said, trying to sound as annoyed as possible.

"Can I get you another drink?" a waiter asked as he approached the table.

"No, thank you. I think we're done here actually. Are you going to finish your meal, Alice?" he asked me.

I scrunched my face up and shook my head, pushing

the plate away from me dismissively and grabbing my phone instead.

"I guess not. Can I just get the slip to sign, please?" Mitch asked.

I clicked on the Instagram app and scrolled through it mindlessly, pointedly ignoring Mitch as the waiter hurried away.

We sat in a tense silence until they returned moments later. I continued to ignore them, pretending to be entirely absorbed in my phone until Mitch handed something to the waiter and I felt his eyes land on me.

"Great. Shall we go back to our villa now?" Mitch asked me.

"Fine," I said, still not looking away from my phone even though there was really nothing interesting on Instagram.

I'd already seen everything on my feed and I truly just didn't care about anything else.

Mitch started to lead me out of the restaurant and I followed slowly, trying to look around the room slyly for Christian, but he wasn't there.

I was a little disappointed but at the same time, it didn't really matter. Even if he was, what would I do about it? Go over and talk to him and his family? Just the idea of that made my heartbeat quicken and I sped up, just in case. I couldn't think of anything more anxiety-producing than that. I would never have the courage to do it.

We emerged into the warm air and both slowed automatically. I slipped my phone into my pocket, preferring to walk back to our rooms without it. It was better to not have it. Then, I could focus on the world around us.

Couples walked by, hand in hand and in their own bubble. No one paid us any attention but I was glad. It made it feel more peaceful. I felt isolated but in the best way possible. It was relaxing. It almost felt like I could stand straight, like the weight on my shoulders wasn't slowly trying to crush me. I hadn't even noticed that before but now that it was gone, I did.

I found myself torn between wishing that the walk was longer and hoping that we'd get to the room quicker. I wanted to talk to Mitch about what he'd seen on Spinalonga and what the plan was but at the same time, I really enjoyed the walk.

It didn't matter. We were back at our door before long.

I waited for Mitch to open it and scan the room before walking over to the table and sitting down.

"We're safe. So, what did you think of the island?" he asked, joining me and pulling his iPad towards him.

"It was really interesting, not quite what I expected though," I said truthfully.

"No? How so?"

I cocked my head considering it for a moment.

"I expected it to all be ruins, like the church by the fortress, but the houses looked like they could have been built yesterday," I said finally.

Mitch nodded.

"You're right, they absolutely did. What does that tell you?"

My mind went blank but I forced it to start turning again.

"That the thing we're looking for is in the older bit, right?" I guessed slowly. "If it were in any of the houses or the newer looking church, people would have found it already... Right?"

Mitch grinned toothily at me.

"Bang on. So... where do you think it is? I'll give you a hint, I believe it is underground."

I wanted to immediately say I didn't know, but I took my time to think about it. The room was too quiet though. It made my anxiety rise until I began just thinking out loud.

"The fortress is too obvious, right? Like, people would have already looked there, wouldn't they? But it would need to be close, right? Like, if the treasure was put there when the fortress was still a fortress, it would need to be close enough that they could watch over it. That makes sense, I think. So... maybe in the church near there?"

Mitch grinned at me.

"I thought that too," he said, typing on his iPad. "I mean, keeping the entrance to the underground system nearby is only smart, right? That way, people in the fortress can keep an eye on it without it being too suspicious and they can access it with not too much difficulty so…"

I watched his face carefully as he trailed off, trying to work out what he was looking at on the iPad, but it was tilted away from me.

"Ah, here we go. I highlighted this place before. I had someone fly over the island last night to do some scans. I think we got away with it, but we'll see. Look at this, what do you see here?"

He turned the iPad towards me, watching my face carefully.

I stared down at the screen. It was a greyscale map of the area with some of the graves highlighted by a thin red line.

I looked between the highlighted ones and the non-highlighted ones, trying to see the difference but it was difficult. The graves were obvious. They were almost perfectly rectangular shapes, darker than the space around them but some were more evenly dark.

That was the difference. The ones that Mitch had highlighted were consistently dark but the ones that he hadn't were more spotty.

"Why are some darker than others?" I asked carefully.

I didn't need to look up to know that Mitch was grinning at me proudly. That made my heart clench with happiness.

"Because there's something other than bones in some of them," he said excitedly. "I reckon one of these graves holds the entrance to the underground cave system. There are probably more ways in, but I've had my person scan the shoreline and the only other way I can see is through a partially obstructed tunnel and I really don't want us to have to squeeze through there. Lauren barely made it."

"Lauren's here?" I asked.

Mitch chuckled lightly.

"Oh yeah, I've kept her close in case we run into any trouble and need a quick getaway. She's very used to that."

"So… are we going tonight?" I asked, my heart starting to race in excitement.

"Nah," Mitch said, turning the iPad back towards him. "Too obvious, plus we need to be in a better position for it. We need to prepare."

"What do we need to do?"

Mitch leant his head to one side causing it to crack loudly before leaning it to the other.

"I could do with hiring a boat, I think. A nice one with a little speed boat or a jet ski on the back. The boat would be better, a jet ski is less protected but it is more manoeuvrable so I would accept that too. We can rent it for the full day and camp out somewhere near the island, head over when it gets dark," he said, almost to himself. "We'll need to pack up here too."

I looked around the room, spotting his closed suitcase in the corner.

He'd kept it much neater than I had. My clothes were spilling out of the bag and taking over part of the room, I'd need to put them all away.

"Will we go straight from Spinalonga to the airport?" I asked.

I kind of hoped he'd say no. I wanted to spend more time relaxing by the pool and maybe flirt with Christian again but I didn't want to risk it if there was the chance it wasn't safe.

"It really depends on how things go when we're there. If Sterling's assholes haven't found us, then we'll come back here and lie low until an appropriate amount of time has passed but, if they have... well, we'll probably leave straight from Spinalonga. It's not worth risking it. I'll just call the hotel when we're on the plane and say that something came up at work or something. It's not the smoothest of exits, a little suspicious, but I'm sure it'll be fine."

I nodded, unsure which outcome I was hoping for.

Although just moments ago, I had wanted to stay on the island, now, the idea of staying at the hotel and waiting to see if anything kicked off on Spinalonga sounded painful. I knew that I'd spend every minute tense and waiting for the police to arrive and arrest us.

Maybe it would be better to leave straight away. But then, the idea of Sterling's people finding us was terrifying too. They were like something from a nightmare. Everything I'd heard about them painted them as cruel, ruthless people who wouldn't hesitate to murder me if it came down to it.

I really hoped I didn't die. I was enjoying the fantasy too much. If I did die, what would happen in it? Could I come back or would it be the end?

I couldn't just come back from the dead and I didn't want Mitch to have my death on his conscience. I needed to be careful, to be smart.

"So, what do we do tonight to prepare?" I asked. "Should I go pack up my stuff? Will we bring it with us on the boat tomorrow or is that too obvious?"

"Way too obvious," he said. "We'll leave it here. Lauren can come and pick it all up and, if we get to come back here, she'll drop it off again. I've already slipped her a spare key so you should probably get packed up. We'll need to bring some spare clothes for tomorrow too."

I stared at him in confusion.

"Wait, what? When did you give Lauren the spare key?" I asked incredulously.

Mitch chuckled under his breath.

"At dinner. Left it in a crumpled napkin and she and Oscar swept in and got it before the waiters had a chance to clean it away," he said nonchalantly. "They used the excuse of wanting our table. Why do you think I insisted on that specific table? I needed one out of the way and with a good view."

I stared at him blankly.

"I… don't know. I just thought you wanted to sit there," I said dumbly.

He laughed and pulled his phone out, reading the message before turning it towards me.

There was a message from Lauren that simply said 'Got it. You're paying for this ridiculous overpriced dinner.'

"She knows I'll pay for it. I always do when she's on assignment for me," he said with a shrug.

I nodded, still shocked that I hadn't even noticed before my mind caught up with what he'd said before.

"Wait, I need to pack a spare set of clothes?" I asked. "Why?"

"Yeah, just so that you can blend in more. You need to be all in black ideally. Well covered too. You're too pale, you'll stand out in the dark and that'll make you an easy target. Did we get any long-sleeved tops for you?" he asked.

I thought hard about the shop we had done when we stopped to refuel.

"Yeah, I think so."

"Okay, good. Pack one. Bring your trainers too, I'll pack them. I want us to look as normal as possible when we go onto the boat so I'm going to pack a bag and pretend it's picnic stuff. They'll provide that for us as part of the package with the boat so it'll just make me look more bumbling and useless, feel free to pounce on that," he said, barely looking up at me as he pulled up the notes app and started typing. "I'll need to bring the spades, some weapons too. Ah, I wish we had time for you to have some target practice, but it'll be fine. If you need to, just point and shoot. We'll need extra food too. I have some in my bag but you can never be too safe. I don't want the bag to be too heavy but we need to have all the usual stuff."

I watched him plan and mutter to himself, not having anything to contribute but also finding it fascinating to watch him. It felt like he was ten steps ahead of me, his mind always racing and strategising. It made me a little jealous. Well, not jealous but I wanted to be like that. I wanted to be quick and smart.

Maybe I could be? The fantasy was part of my mind, after all. It was coming from somewhere within me so I had to have the ability to think like that, didn't I?

I fought a yawn that caught me off guard, surprised by how tired my body was even though my mind felt wired.

"You should pack and sort out your stuff for tomorrow then get an early night," Mitch said, drumming his fingers on the table and staring into space. "Ah, money. We'll need to bribe them so that we don't have any staff on the boat. I can deal with it by myself, I lived on a boat for four years."

"You did?" I asked.

Somehow, I was still surprised every time I learned something new about Mitch. I wasn't sure why, I should have known better by then, but I still was. His life just sounded so cool and fun.

"Yup, I had to. It was a pretty safe way to live for a while. I had a fake ID that I used when entering marinas and I rarely had to pay for things. It was easy enough to live off of fish and I could trade for anything else I needed. It gave me some space and time for the people looking for me to give up… at least temporarily."

"Sterling's people?" I asked.

"Oh, no. That was a different time. There was a different band of idiots trying to kill me then, but I'm pretty sure their company has gone under. Most of them have been incorporated into the Sterlings, but their dumbass boss is gone at least." He grinned almost to himself before looking at me again. "Go on, you should probably get to bed. I'll wake up early and head down to the pier to bribe some people, but I'll set up all of the alarms and whatnot here so you'll be safe. I'll text you when I come back so you know it's safe to come downstairs."

I nodded, fear trickling into my stomach.

I hated the idea of being in the room by myself with Sterling's people potentially nearby.

"Can I come with you?" I asked, the words slipping out without my consent.

Mitch smiled at me softly.

"It would be easier if you didn't, kid. I can blend in better there without you and people sometimes get weird if you try and bribe them when there's a kid about. Plus, Alice would spend the morning in bed if she had the chance." He paused with an almost sad smile. "You'll be safe here though. I'll make sure the doors and windows are locked and I'll leave a gun on the stairs so you can defend yourself if you need to, but you won't. You'll be okay."

I hesitated before nodding.

I didn't want to insist on going with him. He made some good points but still, I didn't want to stay there alone. Maybe I'd be able to just avoid the fantasy for a while, step back in when I knew he was back.

But I knew I wouldn't be able to do that. I'd be constantly checking in to see if I had been murdered.

"Go on, up to bed. Leave your spare change of clothes out, I'll put them in my bag in the morning."

CHAPTER TWENTY-NINE

I was anxious before I even opened my eyes. Immediately, I was in Mitch's world, terrified and not wanting to move. I knew that I needed to get up and grab the gun that Mitch had left for me somewhere, but part of me didn't even want to do that. I was scared that, if I were to open my eyes, I'd see that Sterling's people were already there and waiting for me.

What would happen then? Would they torture me to try and find out what we were planning to do? I assumed that they would, but I wasn't sure.

I didn't want to find out but I couldn't just keep my eyes shut and wait in that limbo forever. That was so much worse.

Trying to stay as still as possible, in case someone was watching me, I slowly opened my eyes just a crack. Relief washed through me as I stared around my seemingly untouched hotel room.

It looked exactly as it had before I'd gone to sleep

the night before, which reassured me. But it didn't completely stop the anxiety that I felt. I knew that, at any moment, they could burst through the door or the window and I would be frozen in bed, unable to move and unable to defend myself.

I needed to get the gun.

I didn't know how to use it, but at least if I were holding it, I would have something. Something to defend myself with if needed. I hope that wasn't though. The idea of shooting a gun and potentially taking someone's life, even in a fantasy, was terrifying. To hold that much power in my hands felt a little overwhelming, even in theory.

And yet, not having it was worse.

I glanced around the room again before taking a deep breath and pushing my covers back. I scuttled towards the stairs as quickly as possible, seizing the surprisingly heavy pistol which Mitch had left lying on the top step, before rushing back to my bed. I sunk down, my back against the headboard, the gun clutched in my hands and waited. I wasn't sure exactly what I was waiting for, I just wanted to be prepared. Just in case.

My eyes flitted from the window to the top of the stairs and back again, sweeping the room and searching for any sign of anything suspicious. I tried to keep my breathing even but it was a challenge.

My hands tightened on the gun, clutching it to my chest before I realised how stupid that was.

The gun could kill me. If it were to go off and it hit me, I'd be injured, maybe even killed. But I couldn't just have it on the bed in front of me. What if they came through the window or surged up the stairs and I wasn't quick enough?

I lowered it hesitantly, torn between putting it down or continuing to hold it, when dizziness tore through me.

"Grace?" my mom called before knocking on the door gently.

"Yeah?" I called back, my voice a little scratchy from sleep.

The door opened and she ducked her head around it.

"Good morning, how did you sleep?"

It felt weird to have her ask me that. She never did back home. The only thing she said to me there in the morning was barked at me, generally asking me if I'd done all my homework or telling me that my shirt was wrinkled or my skirt too short. It was always followed by a lecture too, never just a simple question.

"Well, thank you," I lied. "How did you sleep?"

"Ah, about as well as I ever do here," she joked with a slight glance towards the door to make sure her parents couldn't overhear. "Mom and Dad are going out for breakfast, so I thought we could go too?"

We hadn't been invited, I noticed. Just my grandparents were going and my mom wanted us to go too. They probably didn't want us there.

I wouldn't be surprised if they were sick of us already.

"That sounds good," I said, sitting up and smiling at her.

She returned the smile and started to leave the room before looking back at me and saying, "We'll be going out in about twenty minutes. Make sure you wear a nice day dress and comb your hair. It's all over the place."

I waited for her to leave the room before sighing and sagging back down. I let my eyes flutter shut for just a second, checking in on Crete to make sure that Sterling's people hadn't arrived.

They hadn't. The hotel room was still completely motionless. My eyes flitted around the room, not quite focusing on anything, before landing on the gun in front of me.

I had placed it on the bed, clearly having decided that it would be better if I wasn't holding it. That made sense. I really didn't want to accidentally hurt myself or someone else.

I was glad that I had because my phone buzzed and I jumped so hard that if I had been holding the gun, I was pretty sure I would have either shot it or hit myself with it and both would have been bad.

I glanced around the room again before grabbing my phone and reading the message from Mitch.

All sorted with the boat, will be back at the room in ten.

Relief washed through me and I quickly typed back, *Okay.*

Ten minutes. I just needed to stay safe for ten minutes. That was manageable, surely.

I let my eyes shut again, blinking back into reality. I needed to get up and get ready for breakfast. As much as I truly cared about what was happening in Crete, I couldn't be late. If I were the one who was holding my grandparents up, I'd never hear the end of it.

With a groan, I climbed out of bed and looked around the room. My suitcases were stashed in the corner. I'd unpacked some of the clothes, just the stuff that would get wrinkled, but most was still in there.

I stretched slightly, trying to get rid of the crick in my back before walking over to it and rooting around for the right outfit. I wasn't sure what to wear, even with my mom's suggestion, and it wasn't long before anxiety forced me to slip back into my daydream and scan the room again.

I needed to pee. I really needed to pee but the idea of Sterling's people bursting into the room whilst I was on the toilet made my face flush. I grabbed my phone again and checked when Mitch had sent the text.

Only two minutes had passed. Barely any time.

But I could hold it for eight more minutes. I mean, it was a fantasy, I could just go to the toilet in real life and I'd be fine. Something stopped me from doing that though. I could feel my body mechanically choosing some clothes and starting to get dressed, but I chose to stay in Crete, shooting anxious looks around the room.

My phone buzzed again and I jolted, despite still holding it.

Going to swing by reception and ask them to organise some kind of picnic for today. Any request? Mitch had typed.

I took a deep and uneasy breath before typing back, *Nah, I'm okay with anything.*

There was a pause before I saw the three dots appear on the screen again, indicating that Mitch was typing.

I've asked them to make sure it's all veggie, don't want to risk them packing some meat in with your food and you not wanting to eat it.

I hesitated, guilt shooting through me.

He didn't need to do that. I hated that he was limiting what he was going to eat just because of me.

Although, he was right. Ideally, I didn't want my food touching any meat.

That's okay, you don't need to do that, I typed back before looking around the room again.

His response was quick again.

Kid, me not eating meat for a couple meals will hardly kill me. Back in eight-ish probably.

My stomach churned guiltily and I debated texting him back to try and insist that he changed the order but I stopped myself. He sounded sure and something made me think, if I continued to insist, he would just become more and more certain. I wouldn't be able to do anything, it would just make me feel even worse. I glanced around the room before jolting back into reality.

"Grace," my mother called, tapping on the door

again. "Are you decent?"

She never asked at home. I kind of liked it though. It meant I didn't have to scramble to grab some clothes or a bathrobe to cover myself.

I looked down quickly to check. I'd somehow chosen quite a nice dress. It was floral, summery enough that my grandparents wouldn't judge too much. Short but not too short. It was a good choice and I was a little surprised that I'd managed to do so whilst entirely in the other world.

"Yes," I said, crossing the room and pulling the door open.

"Ah, you look lovely! I assume you're going to wear tights?" my mom said, her tone making it clear that this was a demand, not a suggestion.

"Yes, of course," I said, walking to my suitcase and grabbing out a pair of skin-coloured ones.

"Good choice," she said condescendingly.

"Thanks. Did you want something?" I asked, trying not to sound rude, but desperately wanting to check on what was happening in Crete.

It hadn't been long, surely nothing could have gone wrong?

But even so, the urge to check was pulling at me. It was like an itch that I needed to scratch but I knew that, if I were to do so, it would just get worse.

"No, no, just wanted to make sure you were getting up!" she said lightly.

She was making sure I was dressed appropriately too, I knew it.

"Ah, okay," I replied.

There was an awkward pause and I wasn't quite sure what to say. I had nothing else to add and I needed to keep getting ready, to put my tights on and brush my hair, but I didn't really want to do that with her in the room. She was watching me strangely as well, almost as if she was aware of how awkward the situation was and wanted to do something about it but couldn't.

"Alright, I'll finish getting ready myself and meet you down there!" she said in an overly cheerful tone before leaving the room and closing the door gently behind her.

I felt my body relax, even though I hadn't even noticed it tense, and looked down at the pair of tights dangling from my hand before reaching out for that dizziness.

It came easily and I was immediately back in Crete. Once again, nothing had changed but my anxiety was still rising. It had been eight minutes since Mitch had texted me last and he still wasn't back.

Fear jumped within me as images assaulted my mind. Countless anonymous people, all dressed in black just like they have been back in the bar, grabbing Mitch, guns held tightly in their hands and even more attached to their uniforms. I could almost see them dragging him off somewhere.

They probably had a car waiting. Or a van maybe. It would be easier to transport him in a van, more space and blacked-out windows would make sense.

But surely, he would see them coming. He would be able to escape, wouldn't he? What if he couldn't? If he didn't see them coming and they managed to take him, would I just be trapped here forever? Or would someone come for me?

Lauren would come, wouldn't she? Mitch had said that she was nearby, waiting to be contacted by him again. I liked to think that, if something were to happen and Mitch were to be captured, she would help me. But she might be so distracted by what was going on with him that she might not. I might just be left in Crete, alone and waiting for someone to come and save me.

Maybe in this world, I could save myself.

My phone buzzed again but this time, I was slightly more prepared. I barely even jumped as I looked down at the phone, reading the message quickly.

Almost back now, I'll put all the traps and whatnot away then let you know.

Okay, I sent back.

I waited, my skin crawling with nervousness, for the door to open. In real life, I felt myself dragging a brush through my hair, pulling it back into a ponytail before sinking down in front of the mirror and grabbing my make-up bag. Mom hadn't said that I needed to put any on, but my grandparents always expected us to wear make-up and look presentable whenever we went out. Even if we were just going to the nearest shop or somewhere casual, they still expect it from us.

I'd made that mistake before, when I was just a kid. I must have been about thirteen when I went out for lunch with my mom. They had seen us when we came back to the house and immediately, they made a comment about my obvious lack of make-up. My grandfather had asked if I was ill whereas my grandmother had simply said that a certain type of person goes out without wearing make-up and I should be careful not to become that type of person.

I still wasn't quite sure what she meant by that and I'd never worn make-up before back then. My mom had taken me out that day to get some concealer, powder and mascara and I'd been expected to wear it ever since.

I blinked back into reality, ignoring the dizziness, and stared down at my make-up bag. I trusted myself to do a lot of things whilst not really paying attention and daydreaming, but I didn't quite trust myself to put my make-up on. I was pretty concerned that I would stab myself in the eye or something worse and I really didn't want to.

If it was bad and I had to go to hospital or something, I would never hear the end of it. That has happened before as well. I had slipped whilst climbing some rocks down by the beach and had caught my arm on something sharp on the way down. It hadn't stopped bleeding for ages and my mum had whisked me away to the nearest hospital.

I had needed stitches and everything, I still have the scar, but at dinner, my grandparents had both made comments about when they were kids, they would never go to hospital for something as minor as a small cut. It hadn't been a 'small cut', it had gone almost all the way from my wrist to my elbow but that didn't matter to them. They were still embarrassed by me.

I put on as little make-up as possible, rushing through it, before standing and glancing at my reflection. I looked alright, but I knew there would be something they weren't happy with. It didn't matter, I would never please them completely. There would always be something they hated about me.

I hesitated before jumping back to my daydream, getting there just in time for the door to beep softly and open. My hands found the gun immediately and I clutched it, despite knowing that it was probably Mitch.

I didn't want to risk it, just in case.

I waited, my breath coming in short bursts, as I strained my ears to pick up any sign of who it was.

It could have been a trap. It easily could have been someone else down there. Sterling's people could have stolen Mitch's phone and have been texting me from it, just to lure me into a false sense of security.

Carefully and as silently as possible I climbed out of the bed, edging towards the back wall so that I was facing the stairs. If it were them, I wanted to be prepared. I didn't want to be caught in bed and unable to fight.

"Gosh darn it!" I heard Mitch exclaim and I slumped against the wall as relief rushed through me. "It is such a mess down here!"

He was talking loudly, and I knew it was for me. He knew that I would be up here, terrified and waiting to know whether I was about to be attacked. He was doing it so that I wouldn't be scared.

I staggered towards the bed and dropped the gun on it carefully before wiping my sweating palms. I started around the bed, towards the stairs, listening carefully as Mitch bumbled around the room below.

After maybe a minute, I heard a heavy footstep on the stairs before he called up to me.

"Grace, it's just me. I've packed everything up down here so you can come down if you want."

I grinned before replying.

"Awesome, I'm just going to run to the bathroom before I do!"

I was still desperate and now that he was back, I couldn't stop myself from edging towards the bathroom.

"Okay, I'll order breakfast."

I slipped out of the daydream, as I rushed towards the bathroom, looking at myself one last time in the mirror before grabbing my phone and starting towards the door.

The corridor was silent and I wasn't sure whether to

go downstairs to find my mom or if she would still be in her room. I glanced towards her room before deciding there was no harm in checking.

I crossed the corridor and tapped on the door quietly.

"Come in," came her voice.

I pushed the heavy wooden door open and stepped into her room.

It looked the same as it always did. It had been her room when she was a child and it hadn't been changed since then, as far as I was aware. Her sun-bleached collection of dolls and stuffed toys still resided in one corner of the room. The light pink wallpaper was faded and dated but it made me smile a little.

"Ready to go?" my mom asked from where she sat at her vanity.

"Yes," I said.

She turned back towards the mirror, examining her lipstick for a moment before standing. She teetered slightly in her appropriately high heels, surveying her appearance before nodding.

"Alright, let's go let them know," she said.

She walked out of the room in front of me and I trailed behind her along the corridor and down the stairs. I was worried as she gripped the bannister tightly, the old wood creaking under her weight, but we made it down without incident.

"Mom," she called out, starting towards the kitchen.

"Are you ready to go?"

I glanced towards the front door, hesitating for a moment. I wasn't sure whether to just wait by the door or to follow her again but ultimately, I decided to go with her to the kitchen.

By the time I got there, she was standing in the middle of the kitchen looking around. Everything had been put away neatly. There was no sign that my grandparents had even been there apart from the teacups waiting by the sink.

"Could they still be upstairs?" I asked, not quite sure what else to say.

My mother blinked and looked back at me.

"They could be... I'll go check," she said before taking off down the hall again.

I followed slowly, not sure where else they would be. They might be in the lounge, watching television, but I poked my head in as we passed and it was empty.

I waited at the bottom of the stairs, listening carefully as my mum knocked on my grandparent's door, but there was no answer. I heard the door open, the hinges creaking loudly, before my mom marched back down the stairs.

She crossed to the windows at the front of the house without saying anything, her expression pinched. I watched as she stood there for a moment before joining her

"They've already gone," she said, her tone tight.

Confusion rushed through me and I glanced down at my phone, checking the time.

I was pretty sure that it hadn't been more than twenty minutes since my mom had come up to invite me to breakfast, but I wasn't certain. It hadn't felt like it had been that long though.

"I guess we'll just meet them there then," my mom said, the forced cheery tone returning. "They probably just wanted to make sure we got a good table."

"Yeah," I said noncommittally.

She smiled at me widely before reaching for the front door but I saw how much my grandparent's indifference towards her hurt. In a way, she was living in as much of a fantasy as I was but in hers, her parents loved her and cared for her.

Maybe we weren't that different, but at least I had my dad.

CHAPTER THIRTY

I glanced across the table at my grandmother, who definitely wasn't paying any attention to what my mom was saying. She had been talking happily ever since we had arrived and the poor waitstaff had grabbed another table to add on to the one my grandparents were sitting at.

It had felt intentional, the fact that they had got such a small table, and I knew it was. It was their silent way of telling us off for taking too long, even though I didn't think we had. My mom had ignored it.

She always did.

I hated it though. I saw straight through what they were doing and I knew it was just to hurt my mum. She wanted their approval, even now, but she'd never get it. It didn't matter what she did or what she made of her life, it would never be enough for them.

That thought sobered me because I knew it was true for me too. I would never be enough for my mom.

It didn't matter what I did or how well I did even, it still wouldn't be enough. But... I still wanted her to be proud of me, I still wanted her approval even though I knew it was pointless. I wanted her to smile at me with pride, to actually enjoy talking to me and spending time with me but... I wasn't sure that would ever happen.

I slipped back to Mitch almost without even realising.

"Morning, kid," he said as I reached the bottom of the stairs. "Are you feeling anything specific for breakfast? I was just going to order the usual variety."

"Yeah, that works for me!" I replied, looking around the room.

It didn't look very different from how it had the night before, but his duffel bag lay waiting on the table, clearly full. His suitcase was still unzipped though. It looked like he had only just finished stuffing things into it

"Sweet. I might ask them to bring more fruit than usual this time. We might be leaving tonight or tomorrow and I have not had nearly enough fresh melon." He paused and looked up at me, his expression strangely intense. "What are your thoughts on melon?"

I was somewhat taken aback by the combination of his expression and his question.

"Umm... I like it?"

Mitch heaved out an exaggeratedly over the top sigh of relief.

"Oh, phew! I was worried you were going to disagree with me on what is absolutely the best fruit. Have you ever had melon in a tropical country before?" he asked.

I shook my head.

"Oh, man!" he cried. "Then you have not lived. Imagine a melon from back home. But now make it so much sweeter and juicier and just all around better. Honestly, I would live on it if I could. And not just honeydew but watermelon too! Oh, maybe that's my favourite? I go back and forth between the two."

I laughed and sunk down into my usual chair, peering into the bag in front of me as Mitch continued scrolling through his phone, ordering us breakfast.

I couldn't really see much but I didn't want to reach out and pull the bag open. That felt invasive, weird.

"Excellent!" he exclaimed. "A platter of melon, three different types. Oh, glorious! Should I order two? No, one should be enough, right? It says it feeds four."

He looked at me over his phone, waiting for my answer.

"I think one should be enough probably," I said with a shrug.

"You're right, kid. I'll get a platter of fresh fruit too. Might as well enjoy the luxuries whilst we can. Although, one of my places has a stall that sells fresh fruit every morning just down the road. We should go there after this assignment," he said distractedly.

I looked up at him, my mind turning slowly. I have been so caught up on a mission that I hadn't even considered what we would do after we were done.

It felt too soon. I was having such a good time and although I did want to go to Spinalonga and find the treasure and whatever else we are looking for, I didn't want it to end. I didn't want to go back to normality, or at least whatever counted as normality with Mitch.

I knew it wouldn't be boring, of course, I was just enjoying the luxury. I loved being able to wake up and go for a leisurely swim, to relax by the pool for a bit and do some reading. I was even enjoying learning about all of the subjects that Mitch had insisted I start studying and, although I knew I would be able to continue doing that when we got to wherever we were going after this, I was sad that it was going to be over soon.

I blinked and looked around the table at my grandparents and Mom, running from my sadness again. We were eating in a strained silence, as usual. It seemed that my mum had finally run out of things to say, which made sense because nothing had happened since dinner last night. There was nothing new to talk about and I felt like we'd covered most of the other topics.

I looked down at my breakfast. Half a grapefruit, not even flecked with sugar. I wasn't sure why I'd ordered it, but my mum and grandmother also had grapefruit in front of them. I did a double take as I looked at mom's plate. Hers had sugar on it.

I was a little impressed. I knew that my grandmother wouldn't approve of it, she saw adding sugar to foods as a sign of weakness. I don't think she understood the food was meant to taste good, not just be sustenance. My mum adding sugar was an act of rebellion, no matter how small.

That thought made me smile slightly. That's how things worked with my mom's family. They didn't like to have big arguments, they preferred small stands. Small hills to die on.

But she was standing up for herself and, by extension, me.

Biting back a grin, I reached for the sugar bowl in the centre of the table, ignoring my grandmother's look of admonishment. I knew there would be a comment about it later, probably something about how I needed to go for a swim or a run to stop myself from looking flabby, which was ridiculous, but in that moment I didn't care.

My mum's eyes found mine as I liberally sprinkled sugar on top of the grapefruit half and the corner of her lips ticked up ever so slightly before being squashed back down.

I placed the sugar bowl back in the centre of the table and took a spoonful of my food. It was still sour, but less unbearably so.

Feeling a little happier, I let myself return to Mitch just as he lowered his phone and slipped it into his pocket.

"All ordered, should be here as soon as they're finished preparing it," he told me before hefting his bag off the table and placing it carefully on the sofa.

"Great, thanks. So, how did it go earlier? Did you manage to hire a boat?" I asked, excitement starting to build in my stomach.

Mitch grinned as he sunk into the seat opposite me.

"Oh, yeah. And I only had to bribe them half the amount I expected. Got scuba equipment sorted too, it should be loaded onto the boat by the time we get there, just in case we need it. So, all in all, a pretty successful morning!" he said.

I nodded, excitement building within me.

"When do we get the boat?" I asked, leaning towards him. "And what kind of boat is it?"

I don't know why I asked, I didn't know anything about boats. He could tell me the exact make and model and it wouldn't matter at all.

"It's just a catamaran, nothing too big or flashy but should be good for today. We have access to it from ten thirty but we should be late," he said, glancing at his watch. "I want them to think that we're just normal people who don't care for their schedules or being on time. So, we should get there at about... eleven eighteen. That seems like random enough time and I can pretend that I tried to get us there for eleven, but you held us up."

I nodded at him.

"What do we do until then? Do we need to prep or pack or anything?" I asked, glancing at the bag he'd placed on the sofa behind me.

"I did it last night. Got all the weapons, snacks, drinks and whatnot. Have you finished packing?"

"Yeah," I said quickly, barely needing to think about it. "I did it last night too."

"Great!" he cried with a smile. "And you've packed everything from the bathroom and checked under the bed for socks? Somehow I always find some there."

I smiled at him hesitantly, trying to remember if I had or not.

"I'm not actually sure," I said.

I thought I had but I couldn't be certain and I really didn't want to make a mistake. I wasn't sure what would happen if I left my toothbrush or shampoo or something behind. I doubted it would be that bad, but I didn't want to find out, just in case.

Mitch smiled at me gently before glancing towards his suitcase.

"Do you want to run up and double-check?" he asked. "I need to make things a little messy down here for when the food arrives anyway."

I had started to rise from my chair but that made me stop.

"Why?" I asked.

Mitch never left things messy normally. He always had everything tidied away before I even came down in the morning.

"Just so that, if the person bringing our food looks

into the room, they can't tell that we're potentially about to run away!" he said with a smile.

"Oh, that makes sense."

"Yeah! I won't leave too much. Maybe just a towel somewhere... maybe my hat too," he said as he glanced around the room distractedly. I stood and nodded to myself.

"Okay, I'll go make sure I've packed everything then," I said.

"Great," Mitch said softly before his eyes widened slightly and he looked at me. "Make sure you don't make the bed."

I felt my eyebrows scrunch together in confusion.

I didn't think anyone had ever told me not to make a bed before. I mean, not that I really made it anyway but still, it felt weird.

"Why?" I asked.

"Alice wouldn't," Mitch grinned. "In fact, she would probably leave it a mess on purpose."

I smiled back hesitantly.

"I'll see what I can do," is all I said before turning and walking up the stairs.

"What are your plans for the day?" came my grand-mother's cold voice.

It was more of a demand than a question and I found myself glancing at my mom before answering.

"I'm not sure actually," I said in the most polite tone I could manage.

"You wanted to go for a swim today, right?" my mom said.

Again, this was less of a question and more of a demand. I didn't mind too much though. Even though I knew my grandparents would judge me for my swimming costume choices no matter what, I liked going swimming there.

"Oh, yes. I did want to," I replied with a smile to her.

"Good," my grandmother replied snootily. "Children these days spend too much time sitting inside on their phones. When I was her age, I spent all of my time outside and riding my bike. When was the last time you even went on a bike?"

I had to think about that one. I did have a bike, somewhere. I had really enjoyed riding it when I was a kid, but I had outgrown it. I knew that I could ask for a new one, it would reflect badly on my mum for people to see me riding a bike that was too small so she'd get me one, but I just hadn't.

I didn't think I'd enjoy it anymore. When I was a kid, I used to go on bike rides with Duncan and my friends from the village where we lived but... we grew apart. I could no longer just bike over to someone's house and ask them if they wanted to go for a ride.

I didn't even really know them anymore.

"I'm not too sure, actually," I said, feeling unexpectedly sad.

"Just what I thought. No wonder this country is going

downhill. People don't get enough fresh air nowadays, they're too attached to their phones and televisions. It's ridiculous!"

Part of me wanted to point out that she and my grandad spent most of their time in the lounge, glued to the TV, but I knew it would go badly. It wasn't worth it.

Instead, I reached out for the familiar dizziness and returned to my room in Crete. I was crouching on the floor, staring under the bed. There was nothing under there, but I had made my bed. I needed to do something about that.

It felt mean. I knew that someone would come to change the sheets anyway, but it felt so rude to not even make the bed. Not that I made it home very often. My mom didn't care, she was too distracted by everything else.

I stood and pulled at the blanket, shaking it out so that it fell more naturally. It didn't look right though. It looked like I was intentionally trying to make it look messy. I was, but that wasn't the point.

I needed it to look better. I wanted it to look like I had just rolled out of bed and left it, not even thinking about how it looked.

I frowned and threw the blanket to one side before grabbing the pillows and punching them down so that they looked more like I'd just slept on them and not fluffed them after.

It still didn't quite look right but it was fine. It would do.

I looked around the bedroom one last time, feeling

strangely sad that we might be leaving it, before walking into the bathroom.

I had packed everything. The cabinet and shower were empty. I let out a soft sigh before leaving the bathroom, checking my suitcase was zipped up and going back downstairs.

Mitch has been busy in my absence. He had a small but crumpled pile of clothing on the sofa, a couple of bottles of suncream discarded on the side and his hat hanging on the back of the chair. It looked perfect.

He stood, surveying the room with a slight frown on his face and his hands on his hips but, when he saw me, he smiled.

"I know, I know," he said. "It's just for show, but I hate it. I'm going to pack it away the second our food gets here!"

I laughed and opened my mouth to say something but a quiet knock came from the door.

"Speak of the devil!" he cried, sending me a pointed look before walking to the door.

I slipped back into the Alice persona seamlessly, slouching across the room and kicking some of his shoes out the way. One skidded into the cabinet with the coffee machine one and made a surprisingly hollow thunk. I ignored the noise, despite wanting to wince, and continued my journey to the coffee machine.

I slid a cup into place, ignoring Mitch's exchange with the person who had brought us our food, and started brewing myself a caramel latte. I wanted to offer to make one for Mitch. It felt so mean not to, but I forced myself not to even turn.

I'd make one for him as soon as the person had left, I promised myself.

"Great! Thank you so much for bringing that. Alice and I are starving, aren't we, darling?" Mitch asked from near the door.

I ignored him, not even looking back at him.

It felt horrible.

The silence of the room was broken only by the stuttering hiss of the machine and I refused to look away from it. If I did, if I hesitated for even a second, I'd turn back to him and apologise, I knew it.

I didn't like being mean. It made my stomach feel uneasy.

"She probably can't hear me over that machine," Mitch said, but his tone made it clear that he was lying.

"Of course," the server replied smoothly.

The coffee machine clunked loudly, indicating that it was finished with the coffee pod and that I needed to add in the caramel milk pod, which I did as Mitch finished talking to the person and shut the door.

I glanced back at him over my shoulder, making eye contact.

He lifted a finger to his lips, asking me to remain silent, as he pulled the scanner out of his pocket. I waited for him to give me a thumbs up before speaking.

"Do you want a coffee?" I asked, before being dragged back into reality.

"Can I get you a coffee?" a woman asked.

I blinked and stared up into her brown eyes, trying to hide the dizziness that rushed through me.

"Hmm?" I said, still trying to get a hold of myself.

My hearing felt a little off. It was like I'd been swimming underwater and had only just come up. Everything felt too loud and distant.

"Would you like a coffee?" the waitress repeated.

"Oh. Yes, I'd love a caramel latte," I replied without thinking.

"Great! I'll be back with your coffees in just a moment," she said before rushing away from the table.

I glanced around surreptitiously, trying to work out if anyone had noticed my dizziness or that the waitress had needed to prompt me. My grandmother was glaring at me, but I wasn't sure if that was normal or not. It felt pretty normal.

"A caramel latte?" she questioned.

My eyes darted to my mom before I said, "Yes."

My grandmother sighed heavily before looking at my mother.

"Are you really not going to do anything about that?" she demanded.

My mom looked between the two of us for a moment, clearly torn before taking what seemed like a deep breath.

"Grace, I know that you're on holiday, but there is no need to overindulge," my mom told me.

"Exactly, first needlessly adding sugar to her fruit and now having syrup in a coffee?" my grandmother said, sounding genuinely concerned. "It's just too much."

I was surprised by the flash of anger that I felt. I'm not sure why it hit me, my grandmother had commented on my food choices many times before. I was used to it but now, I was annoyed by it.

But it wasn't worth arguing. I could just escape instead.

"Sit down!" Mitch said, gesturing towards the food. "Leave the coffee, I'll grab it when it's done. You need to eat!"

I smiled at him, sending a hesitant glance back at his brewing drink, before walking to the table and sitting in my usual seat as Mitch lifted the silver cloches and stored them on one of the empty shelves on the food cart.

"Oh, look at that melon," he cried before reaching out and grabbing a carefully cut triangle of golden fruit.

He bit into it, the juices trickling down his fingers and the expression on his face blissfully happy.

I reached out and chose a slice of watermelon, wanting to know if it really was as good as Mitch was making it seem or if he just really liked melon. The juices exploded in my mouth. It was somehow so refreshing, the flavour so delicate. It was delicious.

"So," Mitch said, watching me carefully. "Do I need to abandon you on some island somewhere or are we good?"

I grinned at him and reached out for a slice of honey-dew.

"It's delicious."

CHAPTER THIRTY-ONE

We ambled along the pier, Mitch walking in front of me, checking his watch frequently, whilst I moved slowly. I gazed around at the other boats, watching people working on them. Some were shouting orders to each other, clearly preparing the ships for the day, whilst others just lounged on the decks.

The sizes of the boats were not what I expected. Some were huge. I expected them to be just small fishing boats, little more than speed boats, but they were so much more. They were yachts, I think. Big hulking things made of a white shiny material.

I'd never been around boats before and it was almost overwhelming. There was just so much to look at and to see. There was movement everywhere and voices constantly overlapping.

"Ah, that one is ours!" Mitch cried, waving goofily at someone in the distance.

I tried to keep my expression neutral and unimpressed as I stared at the boat where two men were standing at the back and waving at us.

It wasn't the biggest there, but it wasn't far off.

"Doesn't it look great, Alice? Just like the one we rented in St Lucia that time!" Mitch continued excitedly, speeding up as he neared it.

I forced myself to keep walking slowly, despite wanting to rush as well.

His enthusiasm, even if it were fake, was contagious. It made me want to run along the pier and jump onto the small platform on the back of the boat which also held a jet ski.

A boy, about my age, caught my eye as I passed the boat he and his family were on. His lips curled up into a smile and I wanted to look away and hurry towards Mitch, but I forced myself to return the smile. It felt unnatural, wrong almost, but I liked how his gaze lingered on me as I passed.

Finally, I reached the boat.

One of the men was waiting on the small mock-wooden platform at the back for me. As I neared, he reached out, offering me his hand so that I could climb aboard without slipping.

I did so uncertainly. I'd expected the boat to rock more or to feel unsteady, but it wasn't actually too bad. It bobbed ever so softly as the waves lapped against the side but, other than that, it was fine.

I climbed the short set of stairs, gripping the burning metal railing tightly, just in case a wave suddenly hit the boat, and looked around the interior of the boat.

There was a big open space filled with low sofas, half of them covered by a canopy. Mitch's bag lay on the cushions in the shade, the dark duffle a contrast against the white cushions. I paused, staring at them in confusion for a moment. How did they manage to keep the cushions so spotless?

Surely, they must get stained or marked or something but they looked flawless. It was a little intimidating. I almost didn't want to sit on them, just in case I did ruin them somehow. However, I forced myself to sink onto the nearest seat and squinted up at the bright sun. I'd need to move before long. I didn't want to get burnt before tonight.

I could hear Mitch and the person who owned the boat conversing from behind the wheel nearby, but I ignored them just like Alice would have. I tossed my hair over my shoulder and reclined back on the sofa, enjoying the glorious experience.

The sun warmed my skin gently, lulling me into a calm and sleepy state as the boat rocked ever so slightly. It felt wonderful. It was so relaxing that I was genuinely concerned that I would fall asleep in the car with my mom.

I wondered distractedly how she would react. Would she let me sleep or would she be worried about me?

Neither, I somehow knew. It would make her suspicious. If I fell asleep at, I blinked back into reality to check the time on the dashboard, ten thirty in the morning, she would immediately assume that I had been up to no good the night before and that I hadn't slept.

I really didn't want her to think that again. The last time she had, she'd searched my room and roof outside my window. Thankfully, she hadn't realised that I could edge around the side and get to the back of the house from there where I could hide under the hallway window and not be seen.

I went out there quite a lot. It was quiet there, peaceful too. I could stay there for hours and my mom always gave up looking for me before long. I generally brought a book or my phone, because somehow the internet there was wonderful, and just relaxed for a while.

"All ready to cast off, Alice?" Mitch said.

I hadn't been asleep but it was close enough.

"Sure," I mumbled, starting to get up before realising that he had called me Alice and that meant I needed to be bratty. "Can you not do it yourself?"

"I could, but it's always more fun when we do it together. Do you remember how much fun we had last time we rented a boat?"

"No."

Mitch's face drooped so sadly that even the people who owned the boat, who had been climbing down the steps, paused and looked back. I fell back into the seat, pointedly looking away from Mitch whilst also watching them out of the corner of my eye.

"Are you sure you don't want a crew?" one of them asked Mitch, sending a not too subtle look in my direction.

"It might be easier with a few more people here," the other said.

"No, no. It'll be easier once we're out on the water. Sometimes, she just takes a while to warm up to me," Mitch said with a cross between a grimace and a smile.

"Are you sure? It's a big boat to helm by yourself," the first guy said.

I looked around worriedly, fearing that they were going to insist and ruin our plans completely. I needed to do something to give Mitch an excuse to hurry them off the ship.

My eyes landed on the cooler tucked down next to the table in the shade and the champagne bucket next to it. I glanced back at Mitch who was trying to reassure the men before standing with a heavy sigh.

"Are we going?" I demanded rudely. "Or can I start on that bottle of champagne, because if we're just going to sit in the harbour all day, I'm at least going to drink?"

There was a moment of silence before Mitch turned back towards me. He shot me a subtle smile before slipping straight back into his facade.

"Of course, I'm excited to get out onto the water too!" he said, rushing past me to pick up the bottle.

I made an indignant noise as he swept past me again and pressed it into one of the guy's hands.

I watched and the guy took it, but looked at Mitch in confusion.

"We're trying to rein in her drinking," he muttered quietly. "It would be better not to have too much alcohol around here."

I sighed loudly and stomped towards the wheel, as if I knew what I was doing and would steer the ship away from the pier with them on the boat if they didn't hurry up and leave.

I wouldn't, obviously. I didn't even know how to turn the engine on. I assumed there would be a key or an ignition somewhere, like with a car, but I really didn't know.

"Ah, I should deal with that," Mitch said loudly. "We'll make sure to get the boat back before ten thirty tonight."

"Nine!" one of the men corrected him hastily.

"Oh, yes! Of course," Mitch laughed easily. "We'll be back by nine."

"Way before nine," I muttered as loudly as possible so that they'd hear.

Footsteps sounded down the boat before they returned. I waited silently, my arms crossed over my chest as I stared at the complex controls, for Mitch to return.

"This should be fun, huh?" he said with a smile

as he lay his hand almost lovingly on the giant wheel. "They've already got everything sorted for us so all we need to do is take this beauty out onto the water! There's even food for us in the fridge below deck! I didn't need to bring any after all!"

I sighed loudly again.

"I told you so."

I looked away from him, even though I really wanted to watch as the boat roared to life and slowly surged forwards.

I wasn't sure what I expected. It was such a huge ship. I thought it would be more dramatic, but it just bobbed forwards gently as Mitch steered the boat skilfully towards the open water.

There was something strangely soothing about being on the boat. The slight bounce of the waves as the ship cut through them felt so natural. It felt so… relaxing.

"Alice, will you set an alarm on my phone for eight tonight so that we have enough time to take the boat back to the harbour, please?" Mitch asked, fishing his phone out of his pocket and handing it to me.

He kept his eyes on the sea in front of him, barely paying any attention to me, but his use of the name Alice was enough to let me know what he wanted from me.

"Sure," I sighed heavily, accepting the phone.

I unlocked it, and it opened to the notes app where a message to me was already typed.

Kid, it started, *keep acting like a brat until we get out into the water. I don't think that the Sterlings will have had a chance to bug the boat, but I'm not sure. Once we are anchored out there, I will scan it for everything, but until then we need to be careful. Even if there are no bugs, we still need to mostly stay in character. Because we are more isolated, it is easier for people to listen in so we will mostly communicate via text. It is safer that way. But, if you need anything, you can just ask or text me.*

I scanned the message twice, feeling the hair at the back of my neck prickle and stand on end. Suddenly, I didn't feel as relaxed. I felt more vulnerable.

I was a little relieved when my mom's voice pulled me from the daydream.

"Are you going to go for a swim straight away when we get in?" she asked.

I blinked and looked around, a little surprised that we were at the front gates of the house already. The drive home was but a blur in my memories.

"Oh, yeah, I think so," I said, already slipping back into my fantasy.

It seems like the best idea. I wanted to be as alone as possible for the next... however long the trip to Spinalonga would take. I wasn't actually sure what the plan was for once we were out on the boat.

Mitch had mentioned that we would be renting the boat for the full day and staying somewhere near the island so that we could head there when it got dark, but I wasn't sure what we would be doing all day or even what time it got dark.

How would we get the boat back before nine if we were going to be on the island?

I hesitated before typing out the question for Mitch. It would be suspicious if we were to disappear with the boat and then they found out that someone had broken into Spinalonga that same day, wouldn't it?

I hesitated and glanced down at the phone again. I wanted to ask Mitch so many more questions, more than just what was happening with the boat when we were done with it, but it didn't feel right. I was too aware that people might be listening in to what we had to say.

"Are you taking this back?" I demanded obnoxiously, holding the phone out to him.

"Oh, yes. Thank you for doing that, darling," Mitch hurried to say. "Did you turn the alarm on?"

I hesitated, wanting to give him an excuse to look at his phone and therefore see my question.

"What do you think?" I said waspishly.

I looked at Mitch in expectation as his eyes darted towards the phone before returning to me. He played the part perfectly, clearly deliberating over whether or not he thought Alice would have done so before making up his mind. He quickly unlocked the phone and I saw his eyes dart from side to side as he read my message before slipping it into his pocket.

"Urgh," I sighed loudly. "You never trust me! This is just like in St Tropez all over again."

"Alice," Mitch said, weariness evident in his voice.

"You stole someone's boat."

"And?" I snapped after half a second of panic because I hadn't expected him to say that. "Why even teach me how to sail a boat if you don't want me to use that?"

Amusement flared to life in Mitch's eyes but his expression stayed perfectly fatigued. He sighed heavily before glancing at me.

"Why don't you sit down?" he asked gently. "You said you had some books you wanted to read, right?"

"I guess," I said, dragging out the word before turning and storming towards the sofas at the back of the boat.

Part of me wanted to recline under the canopy, remembering Mitch's warning about sunstroke, but the idea of sitting out under the sun, the salty wind blowing in my hair as we cut through the waves, was just too good to consider the alternative.

I sunk down carefully onto the white cushions and pulled out my phone, staring at it blankly for a moment.

Cold water hit my leg and I glanced down at it in confusion. It was too cold to be from the sea and we were too high up surely. It took a few seconds before I realised where it was coming from.

With a blink, I was back in the real world, slowly sinking down into a freezing cold pool. My breath left me in an instant as my other foot touched the water. I stayed there, clinging to the strangely warm metal ladder and not quite finding the courage to move any further into the water.

I wasn't sure if it was always that cold and I had just forgotten or if it was especially cold that year but either way, it was glacial. I hesitated, fighting the urge to climb out of the pool and run up to my room where I'd at least be warm, before deciding to just get it over and done with. Reluctantly, I let go of the ladder and dropped into the water until I was completely covered.

I resurfaced with a gasp and pushed my hair back from my face. I was much more awake now and I started paddling before I could change my mind, already slipping back to Crete.

Barely any time passed in reality but I could tell it had in my fantasy. We were no longer just leaving the harbour, we were fully out in the bay. Spinalonga rose up in front of the boat as Mitch slowly brought it to a standstill. I stared at the textbook on my phone, not really taking anything in, as Mitch bustled around the boat.

He finally re-emerged from below deck and sunk into the seat opposite me, a contented smile on his face as he passed me an ice cold bottle of water.

"Did you find anything good to read?" he asked.

I continued watching him out of the corner of my eye as I said, "Kind of."

"Oh yeah?"

"Yeah."

There was an awkward silence for a moment before

Mitch shrugged, pulling his phone out and seemingly giving up on the conversation. I saw him typing and I waited somewhat nervously for him to finish the message and hopefully send it to me.

After a moment, my phone buzzed and I quickly clicked on the text he had sent me.

As far as I can tell, there are no bugs or anything so we are semi-safe to talk freely, but it would be best if we don't because there are too many ships out here for me to feel comfortable.

I quickly typed back, *Okay*, but he was already typing again.

Don't worry about the boat, I've already got it covered, Mitch had written. *Oscar will drop it back tonight if we are not on the ship at eight. I have already let them know that it might be a different person dropping off the boat. Please don't ask me any more questions on that one.*

Confusion washed over me. I truly could not think of any reason as to why someone else would be dropping the boat back or how Mitch had managed to convince them that that was normal. Although he'd asked me not to question what he'd said, I couldn't help it.

... what? I sent back, unsure how else to phrase it.

Mitch winced visibly and I waited a little nervously for his text to come through.

Ah... well, there's a pretty big swinger community here at the moment, most likely because of some stuff I posted online about it to get some excuses. I will have Oscar tell them that we are on another boat that decided to stay out a little longer.

I glanced up at him just in time to see his eyes widen and he started typing frantically.

Don't worry, I requested a kid-safe boat out here, manned by people who are not going to be taking part in the... Festivities. I will have Oscar say that you are on that boat, his follow up message read.

I fought back the urge to grin and started to type.

"Ah, I thought I heard you in here," my mom's voice said.

I quickly tried to refocus my eyes on reality and swam to the nearest side of the pool to her.

"Yeah, pretty much just got in," I replied with a smile.

She stayed near the door and I was glad. She was still wearing her ridiculous heels and I was genuinely quite worried that if she were to come any closer she would fall on the slick tiles.

"And you're wearing one of the costumes I got you!"

I glanced down, truly not knowing which swimming costume I was actually wearing. I hadn't been paying any attention when I picked it out and I was suddenly very hopeful that I was wearing one of the questions she had selected and not a bikini. I really didn't want to have to deal with my mum thinking I had purposefully gone against her wishes.

"Oh yeah," I said, feeling relief wash through me. "It fits great."

"Oh, fantastic."

My mum paused for a moment longer and I could

tell she was trying to work out what else to say to me. I wasn't sure what I could talk to her about either. It just felt so uncomfortable and weird, but we weren't the kind of people who just chatted. Eventually, the silence got too awkward for me and I ended up saying the first thing on my mind.

"Do you want to come swimming too?" I blurted out.

She smiled at me surprisingly softly but shook her head.

"No. Maybe slightly later on in the holiday I will but for now... I'll sit this one out."

I was pretty sure she was waiting for when her parents left. I could barely remember her ever coming swimming with me when we were at the house and never when her parents were there. It made sense really. Her mum liked to pick at everything. I feel like my mum being in a swimming costume around her would give her too much ammunition.

"Ah, okay," I said. "What are you going to do now?"

She looked away from me, shooting a glance out the window to the gardens beyond.

"I'm not sure," she replied. "I might go for a walk around the grounds. Get some fresh air."

She meant she was going to go chain-smoke as she walked around the gardens. She did that a lot whilst her parents were still here and I completely understood it. She had explained it to me once, when she had gotten drunk. Apparently, smoking relaxed her and made her less stressed and, seeing as being around her parents made her so stressed, it was probably a good thing that she had something to help.

Not that smoking was really ever a good thing in my opinion, but I was glad that she had something to help her cope. I couldn't really judge her, I was disappearing into fantasies to avoid the stress and she couldn't exactly do that. Or at least, maybe she could?

I'd never really thought about it too much. I think she needed to be too switched on around her parents, too ready to react to what they were saying and continue the conversation because they wouldn't. Even if she didn't need to be, I didn't think she would enjoy disappearing into daydreams. She seemed like the kind of person who would mock someone for that.

"That sounds like a good idea," I said with a smile.

"Yeah. I'm going to go do that. I'll have my phone if you need anything," she told me, but we both knew there was barely any signal on the grounds.

If I did need her, I would just have to text her and hope that the message went through whenever she found some signal.

"Great," I said.

She sent me a hesitant smile before turning and leaving the pool, shutting the door behind her, but I had already returned to my fantasy.

CHAPTER THIRTY-TWO

"Do you want to go for a bit of a ride on the jet ski?" Mitch asked, his question surprising me.

I have been so distracted, so absorbed in reading about the history of previously predicted end times, that I hadn't even seen him approach.

"Oh," I started before remembering that people might be listening in. "Sure."

Mitch sent me a wide grin before saying, "I'm going to bring a bag, just in case we decide to sneak onto that big island there! I feel like we'll be able to see so much more without a tour guide stopping us from going everywhere. I've even been reading up and researching the island. It would be pretty cool to break in, right?"

My heart started to race. I knew that it was just an act, he was just doing it so that if anyone was listening, it would be more convincing or it would seem more innocent, but I still had to fight not to clamour to go. I wanted to shout yes and immediately rushed to the back of the boat where the jet ski was but I hesitated, knowing that Alice wouldn't just agree.

"Do we have to?" I forced myself to ask, the words paining me. "I mean, we've already gone there once, do we really need to go again?"

Mitch's shoulders sagged disappointedly.

"There is so much on that island that we didn't get a chance to see! I've learnt so much more and I can't wait to show you everything." There was a pause before he quietly said, "You don't need to come if you don't want to."

The disappointment in his voice almost broke my heart. I knew that it wasn't real but still, I was so saddened by the idea of disappointing him.

I was kind of scared of going out on the jet ski too. It was getting dark out and the idea of zipping across the waves without being able to see what was in front of us was horrifying to me.

But I couldn't let it show. Alice wouldn't show fear and I was genuinely scared that, if I did, Mitch would tell me to stay on the boat.

"I'll come," I said with a heavy sigh. "As long as you bring some food or something."

I was trying to give him an excuse to bring his bag, knowing that we would need it, and judging by the way his face lit up, I had done well. I fought not to beam as pride washed through me. It was silly, he was a figment of my imagination, and yet it still felt so good to have someone be proud of me rather than disappointed for a change.

I was glad that I'd given him a reason though. I knew he wouldn't have just left it, but all his gear and my trainers were in the bag. I'd already changed into the spare set of clothes he'd insisted I packed and even though it was warm out, the long-sleeved t-shirt and leggings weren't actually too suffocating. The fabric was surprisingly breathable, but I would have put up with overheating a little bit if it meant I'd be harder for the Sterlings to spot.

"Of course!" Mitch said, jumping up with a huge smile. "I already have some food in the bag in case we get hungry, but let me just grab a few more bottles of water!"

He raced towards the mini fridge, fumbling with the bottles inside, before returning and tucking them into his duffel bag. He sent me another grin before fiddling with the straps and somehow slipping them onto his shoulders like a backpack.

"Oh, wait, no! Silly me, we need life jackets!" he cried before placing the bag back on the sofa and racing down the stairs at the back of the boat.

I waited, trying not to seem too excited or enthusiastic, for him to return. I have been looking forward to what we are about to do for so long now that it was approaching, I wasn't sure how to feel. I was so excited but also nervous and scared. I hoped the mission or whatever Mitch had called it was going to go smoothly and we wouldn't even run into the Sterlings, but something told me that we would.

"Here you go!" Mitch cried, thrusting a lifejacket into my arms and smiling again.

I started to put it on before pausing.

"Do you not need one?" I asked.

"No, no," he replied. "I'll be fine."

His tone was too light, too easy. It felt wrong. I continued strapping the lifejacket into place, considering it.

My eyes fell on his bag and suddenly it made a lot of sense. I wasn't sure if he would be able to have the backpack on if he also had to wear a life jacket. It felt like it would be too bulky, it wouldn't fit.

I chewed my lip anxiously. It felt dangerous to go out on a jet ski in the dusk, with the Sterlings potentially watching every move, and for Mitch not to be wearing a life jacket. If we were to fall into the water and he had his bag on, would he be dragged down to his death?

"Let's go!" he cried excitedly, before rushing back down the stairs.

I followed him slightly hesitantly, taking my time and glancing back at the rest of the boat. It felt strangely final to be walking away from it. Like we wouldn't be coming back.

I hated the idea of that. It had been so lovely and relaxing and the table under the canopy was still laden down with food. But... I did want to go explore Spinalonga. I wanted to find treasure and do everything else that Mitch normally did on assignments.

A splash caught my attention and I looked back at Mitch, to see him standing and gripping the handlebar of the jet ski which was somehow now in the water. I wasn't sure how he had got it from the back of the boat to the water but I didn't want to ask questions, just in case someone was listening in.

"Do you want to get on first, Alice? That way my bag won't be digging into you and I can reach around you to steer," Mitch asked.

Somehow, I knew there was more to it than just that. It was the same reason that he had given me the bedroom whilst he had taken the sofa. He was protecting me. If someone were to start shooting at us, they would hit Mitch first.

I hated that.

I wanted to argue, to let Mitch know that I knew his reason and I did not agree, but I forced myself to simply nod and climb onto the jet ski. It was just a fantasy, I reassured myself, even if he were to get injured he would be okay.

The jet ski bobbed under my weight, feeling a lot less stable than the boat had. I wasn't sure if it was just because of how small it was so the waves felt bigger or if it actually was a lot less secure. Relief shot through me as Mitch climbed onto the seat behind me.

My hands had instinctively gone to the handlebars, but now that Mitch was there, I wasn't sure where to put them. I stared down at the vehicle blankly before just deciding to rest them in front of me.

"Okay, ready to go?" Mitch asked.

"Yeah," I said, not sounding ready at all.

I heard him chuckle softly before he reached forwards and gripped the handlebars around me. It felt really weird to have him so close to me, he was almost like a father to me and it would have been weird for my dad to be so close to me too, but the jet ski jumped to life before I could think about it any further.

I jolted back against him, not expecting how suddenly it would move, before forcing myself to lean forwards again. We cut through the waves, bouncing and bobbing, causing water to splash me in the face. I was grateful that I was still wearing my sunglasses, despite the slowly setting sun, because otherwise, it would have really stung my eyes.

It felt weird being on the jet ski. It gave me a sense of almost déjà vu. It felt like… I knew that it was silly, but it reminded me of the first time I'd met Mitch. Not in the bar, before that. I'd gone to some other world or some other fantasy where I had been on a boat, surrounded by dark cliffs and lightly buffeted by a warm breeze.

But it wasn't the same. We weren't on a speedboat and the weather might have been similar, but there were no dark cliffs around us. Mitch looked kind of different too. He smiled more and he was more scarred.

It did remind me of that fantasy though.

Mitch took us on a meandering route towards the island, cutting backwards and forwards before finally bringing us close to the pier. I breathed a sigh of relief as we approached. Fear had started to sneak into my heart, causing my muscles to tense, as the sun slowly sunk lower and lower. It was getting harder to see, but I didn't dare take off my sunglasses, just in case the salty water blinded me even momentarily and the Sterlings attacked.

"We'll be going towards the target a slightly different way," he muttered into my ear. "I have jackets for us to put on once we get there too so we look more official and you'll need to change into your trainers."

I nodded slightly, wanting to say something in response but anxiety was stopping me from being able to speak.

It was all happening so fast and I was so excited, but also worried.

"When we get there, act like Alice still. We're going to walk towards an archway and once we're hidden by it, I'll give you the jacket to put on," Mitch explained.

I nodded again, my hands becoming slick.

Far too soon, Mitch pulled us to stop at the stone pier. He climbed off the jet ski and held it close so that I could get off easier. It felt a little strange to be standing on solid ground after being on the boat and then the jet ski for so long, despite not actually being there. I found myself swaying, feeling unsteady, even though it should've been easier.

I stumbled slightly and Mitch's hand shot out to catch me.

"You alright there, Alice? Still got your sea legs?" he joked.

I wanted to grin at him and thank him for steadying me but instead, I settled for snatching my hand away.

"I guess."

Mitch looked away from me, glancing around the area.

"Normally, I like to beach a jet ski but," he shrugged, "this one ain't mine. Give me a minute to tidy it up and we can go exploring. Are you excited?"

"Sure," I said flatly despite being genuinely excited.

I stepped away from the water slightly as I watched him tie the jet ski to one of the metal posts.

"There we go! That should do it. I wouldn't want this thing to get swept away to sea and leave us stranded here. Can you imagine the embarrassment of having to call a helicopter to rescue us when we're not even meant to be here?" he said, glancing up at the sky, as if looking for a helicopter.

I glanced up too, trying to keep my expression as bored and neutral as possible even though that idea made my stomach hurt. There was something so horrifying about the idea of not only being caught being somewhere we weren't meant to be, but also having to call someone to come and save us.

I knew that Mitch was just joking, most likely, but I still hated the idea so much that I couldn't think of an appropriate response to him.

"Alright, that should do it! Shall we get this way?" Mitch gestured towards a path that we hadn't gone down when we had come to the island before.

"Sure," I said with a shrug.

"Awesome! Let's go!" he said, taking off across the mostly flat stone area at a fast pace.

I knew that Alice would have dawdled or fallen behind but I couldn't bring myself to. I wanted to get further into the island as quickly as possible. I knew that I would feel safer once we were enclosed on all sides by stone walls.

We started through a tunnel which was so dark that Mitch muttered, "Grab my arm, kid. I can just about see where we are going."

I reached out semi-blindly, my hand slapping into his arm.

I gripped it as we edged further along the tunnel, letting go when I started being able to see the other end.

"Okay, stop here a second," Mitch said quietly.

I did as he said, waiting as he slung his bag from his shoulder and rooted around in it. He thrusted a folded wad of material at me and quickly slipped into a sleeveless vest himself.

I hastened to put mine on, my fingers finding a patch of embroidery on the chest but it was too dark to read what it said. I took the trainers he held out to me, slipping out of my flip-flops and leaning against the wall as I pulled the socks out of them and slipped them on.

Mitch waited for me to hand him the flip-flops back before holding his arm out to me and turning forwards.

"Okay, let's go. Follow my lead and keep your eyes peeled. If you see movement or anything suspicious, tap my arm and hide," he said in a hushed tone.

"Okay," I breathed.

He nodded and edged forward cautiously. I continued to follow him, my eyes fixed on the end of the tunnel but I occasionally peered over my shoulder into the darkness behind us. The island was silent, only the sounds of our footsteps and the gentle whisper of the sea could be heard. It felt like a trap though. The Sterlings could be hiding just out of the tunnel, ready to strike.

We emerged from the tunnel, coming out onto a surprisingly normal looking street with a towering tree in the centre. Anxiety flared within me as I eyed the shuttered windows and balconies on every strangely square house.

Some of them appeared to be abandoned, half-built. One even had a metal grate over the doorway and an unfinished roof but most of the others looked fine. Unlit lamps hung over the central path and I glanced up at them uneasily as we walked.

Part of me was scared that they could turn on at any moment, exposing us to anyone who happened to be looking. I mean, no one would be able to see us without a telescope, but I wasn't sure how many people would be looking out for us. It was possible that Sterling's people were watching us, even then, but that might have also been no one.

As we continued into the island, passing more and more buildings, things started to look a little different. It was obvious that the houses had had more work done on them. They looked more cheerful. The doors and shutters were painted bright colours, so vibrant they could be seen even in the dim light. The yellows, reds, greens and blues stood out so clearly from the clean white houses.

There were maps scattered around too. They were simple, made of a dark plastic, and drilled into the sides of the buildings, but Mitch passed them all without hesitation. He walked slowly, carefully, but with purpose.

Next to him, I felt like a newborn elephant. My steps were clumsy, loud and stomping, no matter how hard I tried to be silent. I knew he could hear them too. Every so often, when I stepped on a dried twig that I hadn't even seen, he winced, his head whipping from side to side as he checked to make sure no one else had heard us.

Me.

I was the problem. He was silent, making no more sound than a shadow.

Mitch stopped suddenly as we reached a fork in the path and I looked around, fearful that I hadn't been quiet enough and they'd found us, before he muttered, "This way."

He gestured towards the outer path, the one closer to the giant wall that surrounded the island.

I nodded and followed him, trying my best not to make any noise as we picked slowly over a rubble-covered path.

It kept surprising me. The island was such a strange mishmash of perfectly preserved, clean and clearly well cared for homes, covered in information posters about notable residents, and mostly decrepit buildings on the verge of collapse.

It worried me.

The semi-collapsed walls provided too many spaces for Sterling's people to duck behind.

"Have you seen your mother?" a voice asked, ripping me from my fantasy.

I turned, spotting my grandmother in the doorway and had to reach out for the edge of the pool as dizziness threatened to drown me.

"Yes, I think she went out for a walk," I replied, gripping the tile so tightly it hurt.

My grandmother sighed loudly.

"Of course, she did. The one time I actually need

something from her, she decides to wander off!" she complained loudly.

"Is there anything I can do to help?" I asked politely, fighting an almost overwhelming wave of nausea.

She regarded me, the expression on her face somewhere between doubt and suspicion.

"No," she said shortly.

"Okay, well… she said she has her phone on her. You could try calling it?"

"No. I guess I'll just wait until she gets back. If she ever comes back," she sighed loudly, turning and leaving the room.

I wanted to retort, to say something back like that my mom wouldn't just leave me there, but I felt like if I opened my mouth again, I'd vomit. I knew that if I threw up in the pool and they needed to call someone out to clean it, I'd never hear the end of it.

I pulled myself along the wall, not wanting to risk swimming or trying to pull myself out, before reaching the ladder and climbing it. I flopped onto the surprisingly warm tiles, gasping in air and trying to keep the contents of my breakfast in my stomach.

I wasn't sure why the dizziness was hitting me quite so hard. It didn't normally. Generally, when I went into or out of fantasies, I did feel some level of dizziness, but it was never that bad. I wasn't really sure what to do about it except just to stay lying on the tiles and hope it went away.

It did after a while. Eventually, the world stopped

spinning at such a dizzying rate and I was able to sit up. I looked around the pool area, not sure what to do now. I could go back in the water and risk feeling that sick and dizzy again or I could go back to my room and get changed. I couldn't exactly sneak out to the roof whilst my mom was on a walk, she might see me and then my safe space would be revealed.

I didn't think that she would look at the house, but I didn't want to risk it, even if I was pretty certain that she already knew about it and just lied to avoid spending more time with me.

Plus, I'd only been swimming for about forty minutes so I couldn't exactly stop then. It wasn't enough time. I already knew that, if I did decide to stop something and go to my room instead, I would hear about it later. My grandmother would have something to say about it. Probably some comment about how lazy young people are these days.

No. Despite the near miss of vomiting into the pool, I knew I had to return to Mitch. We were so close to our goal, I had to go back. Even if it meant that I would spend the rest of the day feeling sick and nauseous, it was worth it.

Even if it were to get so bad that I did throw up in the pool, it would still be worth it to find whatever treasure we were looking for.

"Careful, kid," Mitch said softly as I returned to the world.

I froze immediately.

He pointed down at a string, just a step in front of me and almost hidden by the tall dry grass.

"What is it?" I asked, feeling fear grip my heart immediately.

I tried to follow the string, to work out what it was connected to but I couldn't see fair enough in the dark.

"It's okay," Mitch told me softly. "It's probably just an alarm or something."

I knew that was a lie, but I wasn't sure how I knew that. It was a bomb. If I made one false move, we'd both die.

"Here, take my hand and step over it. It'll be fine," he continued in a soft and reassuring voice. "It's just like hopping over a crack in the pavement, you've done that before, right?"

I nodded, unable to take my eyes off the string that could kill us both, and reached out blindly. His hand found mine, so reassuringly steady under my trembling grasp.

My knees felt weak. I felt like they could collapse at any second and send me staggering into the wire, but I managed to lift my foot and carefully step over it.

"Good job, kid!" Mitch cried softly, letting go of my hand once we were a few paces away. "You just successfully avoided your first bomb! How do you feel?"

I knew that it was but still I found myself asking, "That was a bomb?"

He laughed softly.

"A little tiny one! Barely even worth worrying about."

My eyes darted around the island.

"Does that mean they're here?"

CHAPTER THIRTY-THREE

"Not necessarily. It means they've been here recently, but they might not be here now," he said softly. "All the more reason for us to get to our goal quicker."

I nodded, wanting to speed up but my legs still felt like jelly.

"Are they watching us?" I asked. "Do they have cameras here?"

He surveyed the area around us before saying, "Maybe, but if they knew we were here right now, they'd be here already too."

"How do you know they're not?" I asked, my tone bordering on hysterical.

The Sterlings terrified me.

If they were here, it meant we'd fight. We'd be shot at. We could be killed. Strangely, I didn't care that much about me dying. If I were to be shot and killed, I could either just come back anyway or... I don't know, do something else, but if Mitch were to be killed.

I wasn't sure if he could come back from that.

"I have people watching the island," he said, continuing forwards slowly. "No one has approached. Not even underwater. If they're watching us, they're waiting to see what we do."

I nodded and swallowed, too scared to speak.

His words reassured me, but at the same time, they worried me. I somehow hadn't realised how many people or how much work has gone into the mission. It was stupid, but it really surprised me. I thought it was just Mitch and me with Oscar and Lauren waiting somewhere nearby, ready to help if needed. But it sounded like there was so much more going on than that.

It made me feel bad though. I hadn't even noticed or considered that there would be more going on, that Mitch had planned anything else, but of course he had. It felt like he was always at least one step ahead of me, generally even more. It made sense that he would have planned or sorted every minute detail out.

"So, what do we do?" I asked, finally able to put my thoughts into words.

"We keep going," Mitch said. "Not much else we can do. I'll get some warning if people approach, but I think we have a little more time."

I nodded and rushed along behind him, not taking my eyes off the path.

It was getting darker though which made it harder.

I could barely see where we were going and more often than not had to rely on Mitch to lead me.

When we finally did start to approach the graveyard, we moved slower. Mitch's steps were somehow even quieter, his whole body tensed and prepared to strike. He was ready to attack in case the Sterlings appeared.

But they didn't. We reached the church ruins without incident, staying low to hide as much of our bodies behind the low wall as possible.

Mitch weaved through the graveyard towards one of the graves that we'd said looked suspicious on the map back in our room before stopping. He lifted a hand to his lips before tapping his backpack and miming digging. I nodded, understanding that he was telling me that he was going to get the shovel out of his backpack and start trying to uncover the door or whatever it was we were looking for.

He pointed at me and mimed for me to stay crouched and wait. I nodded again, watching as he carefully swung his backpack from his back, wincing at the soft bedding noise that it made. He rooted around in it for just a moment before pulling out a folded shovel.

Staying low and hunched over, he started to dig, pausing every few seconds to scan his surroundings. I did my best to do the same, my head turning rapidly as I tried to see everything at once. It was hard and it made anxiety thrum within me.

I was so on edge. I felt like there were a million

eyes on me, making my skin itch, but I hoped it was just psychological. It might be. It could be that I was so worried about the Sterlings being there that I was imagining it. I wasn't sure though.

My head whipped around as a hollow-sounding thunk came from the grave and I stared at it. There was just enough light left to see the grin appear on Mitch's face.

He moved quicker now, clearing the dirt and stones away, before gesturing for me to come closer. I did, leaning forwards to peer into the hole he had dug.

There was something there, along the right edge there was a hint of a rope. It looked old and was coated with dirt, practically disintegrated, but definitely a rope. And on the other side, there were hinges. They were rusted and dark, but I was pretty sure they were hinges.

I really hoped that it wasn't the top of a coffin. I knew it was unlikely but there was a worry at the back of my mind that Mitch was going to pull it open and there would just be a corpse inside.

Or, I guess it wouldn't be a corpse. It would probably be just a skeleton by now, but I still didn't want to see it.

Mitch rooted around in his backpack again, pulling a small crowbar and a tiny squeezy bottle from it. I watched in confusion as he leant over the trapdoor, squirting the bottle onto the hinges and leaving them glistening in the low light, before standing again.

I held my breath as Mitch tied a new rope onto the loop and wedged one side of his crowbar into the crack, using them both at the same time to lever the door up.

The hinges creaked softly, probably so quiet because of the oil Mitch had sprayed onto them, but swung open.

I peered down into the hole, but I couldn't see anything.

Mitch pulled a flashlight from the bag, packing everything back up as he looked around to make sure Sterling's people weren't approaching. I assumed they weren't because he turned the light on ever so slightly.

I stared down into the hole, taking in the rough stone steps, before looking back at Mitch. He met my gaze and gestured at me to stay where I was. I nodded again and he looked away, satisfied, before starting to climb into the hole.

An irrational fear gripped me. I knew it was silly, but part of me was worried that he would leave me waiting by the grave and never come back. I clutched the stone edge as he climbed down a few steps. I looked around again as beneath me, Mitch swung the torch from side to side before placing it on the floor and coming back up.

"Alright," Mitch said quietly before climbing out of the hole. "I want you to come down here and wait on the fourth step down. There are no traps, it's all safe."

I nodded and did as he asked, relief washing through

me before being replaced by excitement. Despite the balmy weather on the island, underground it was chilled. Everything felt a little too silent, the air a little too stale. My eyes bounced around the thin staircase we were on.

The stairs looked like they had been carved straight out of the light stone that the walls were made of. They were surprisingly smooth and worn but the walls were rougher and coated with cobwebs. I suppressed a shudder as movement caught my eye on the wall and I watched a small light brown spider moving horrifically quickly. It looked scary, despite only being about the size of my little fingernail. Its hairy body was so much larger than its legs and when it slipped into a web-crusted crack in the wall, I breathed a sigh of relief. That feeling didn't last long though. I turned away from the wall, staring down the staircase, as the sudden realisation that I was most likely surrounded on all sides by spiders hit me.

I couldn't even see the bottom. I could only see a few steps further down from the dim light that Mitch had placed behind me. Just above me, Mitch gently lowered his bag into the hole, letting it rest on the step next to the light before stepping in. He paused, whipping his phone out of his pocket and sending off a quick text before replacing it and starting to close the trap door above us.

Before that moment, I wouldn't have said that I'd

ever experienced claustrophobia. I didn't really understand it. I mean, I hadn't put much thought into it, but
I just assumed that no one really loved the idea of being
trapped in a small space. However, as the heavy stone
door closed above us, I felt it for the first time.

It felt like a rope was wrapping around my neck and
slowly tightening. Like the air was slowly being sucked
out of a room and there was nothing I could do and
no way I could fight it. It made me feel light-headed,
anxious and dizzy. So nauseous and frantically uncomfortable that I dipped out of the daydream for just long
enough to remind myself that I was safe. That, in reality, I was okay.

I was, of course. I wasn't actually trapped in a stone
tomb somewhere in Crete, I was in Scotland, at my
grandparents' house. Safe.

I just needed to remind myself of that a few times
before I felt okay to return to the claustrophobic and
scary dream.

"You okay, kid?" Mitch said softly, his voice echoing weirdly.

I blinked a few times to push the dizziness and white
spots away from my vision.

The door was shut above us. We were trapped.

The Sterlings could lock us down there and we'd
slowly starve to death, if we didn't suffocate first. We
were literally locked inside a grave and there was no
escape.

"Yeah," I said, my voice coming out a little tighter than I wanted it to.

I was safe, I reminded myself. I wasn't actually there.

"Ah… have I asked you before if you're claustrophobic?" Mitch asked, a bit of a grimace on his face.

"I don't think so," I said, sucking in a deep and slow breath.

"Huh. Probably should have, right?" he said.

I nodded.

He squeezed down the steps past me, stopping just in front of me and standing directly before me. He was bracing himself, I realised, getting ready to catch me if I were to pass out.

"I'm asking now. How do you feel about being underground or in tight spaces?" he asked gently.

I glanced over his head, looking down the stairs which seemed to go deep under the island.

I would not give up now. I wouldn't be the reason he turned back. This was my fantasy and I was in charge. I wouldn't be much of a treasure hunter if I couldn't even go underground.

"I don't mind them," I lied determinedly, taking another deep breath and forcing the nausea aside.

But, of course, he saw straight through me.

"Are you sure, kid? I can call Oscar to come and get you. He should be on his way to the island already anyway."

That surprised me.

"He is?"

"Of course! We can't just leave the door completely uncovered and obvious for anyone to see," Mitch said, making an awful lot of sense. "Oscar comes to help cover up afterwards and then some distraction. You know, trigger a few traps, set off a few tiny bombs. Nothing big enough to send any authorities our way, but just enough so that the Sterlings think they've got us. Just enough to distract them."

I shook my head determinedly.

"No, I want to come with you," I said.

Mitch smiled, a hint of pride in his eyes, as he reached past me to grab his bag and torch. He turned and started to step down the stairs again before pausing and looking back at me.

"How do you feel about cobwebs?"

The question was unexpected and I wasn't really sure what to say. I blinked and looked at Mitch uncertainly, aware of just how many cobwebs surrounded us.

"Umm... I mean, I don't love them?" I answered, fighting not to glance at them.

"But they don't creep you out too much?" he pressed.

I truly had never thought that much about them until I was under Spinalonga.

"I don't think so."

"Oh, fantastic! You'd be surprised how often the stuff is covered in cobwebs. Well, maybe not that surprised. It does make a lot of sense. Often, these places haven't been touched for years, sometimes centuries. They're abandoned. Left to rot and spiders," he said, his tone a little too cheerful.

I thought the urge to shudder again, barely managing not to. Maybe they did creep me out.

"Okay, kid. Follow my moves exactly. I don't believe there will be that many traps on the stairs. I mean, the people living on the island once used this passageway so they needed to make it possible to transverse without too much difficulty. They probably passed the path down from mother to daughter, father to son. Ah, the things parents can teach you," he mused happily.

There was a moment of silence as he started down the steps, moving slowly and carefully and he clipped the torch onto his shoulder strap as he did.

His words had made my mood a little more sombre than I'd expected. I wasn't sure what my parents had taught me, not really. I didn't really speak to my mum enough to learn anything from her, even when we were in Scotland. And as for my dad, I wasn't really sure either.

"Sorry," Mitch said softly, "that was ignorant of me. I know your parents aren't really around."

"It's fine," I replied, paying almost too much attention to where I was walking in an attempt to ignore all of the negative feelings that were threatening to overwhelm me.

"Not really. If it helps, I grew up in a similar situation to you. My parents, both treasure hunters too but not quite so ethical, stuck me in a care home pretty much as soon as I was born," he said, his tone light, almost too light.

"Really?" I asked.

I could hear the surprise in my voice, but I couldn't help it.

"Yep. My dad wanted kids but my mom never really did, and as soon as they had me, they realised that a baby didn't really work too great with their careers. I mean, can't exactly bring a kid scuba-diving or skydiving with you, can you? Ah, hold on one sec," he said, bringing his hand up to stop me.

He scrutinised a hole in the wall that I hadn't even noticed before stepping back and waving the crowbar in front of it.

Nothing happened.

"Oh, fantastic. Rotted to nothing!" he said cheerfully as he continued down the stairs. "They did come back for me though. Every year or so, in between assignments or missions, they'd come back for a few weeks or sometimes a few months, depending on who was looking for them, and try to teach me some stuff."

"Is that where you learnt to do all this?" I asked after a pause.

He chuckled softly.

"Kind of," he said. "When I was about eight or nine, they decided I was old enough to be useful to them. I mean, I dropped out of school and started getting in trouble with the law around that time, so I could have brought attention to them if they left me there. They taught me the basics, what to look for, which rumours to listen to, and which are intentionally trying to trick you but… I didn't stay with them for that long."

"You didn't?" I asked.

"Nah, even as a kid, I knew their views were… wrong. There was a lot they did and said that I wasn't happy with. I never really enjoyed treasure hunting when I was with them. For them, it was all about making the most money. They didn't care about information or the history of anything, unless it was relevant and could be sold or utilised in some way."

He shook his head sadly.

There was something so fascinating about him and his history. His parents seemed so self-absorbed, so similar to my mom almost. It gave me hope. It almost made me think that I might be able to do something with my life.

"Do you enjoy it now?" I asked.

I needed to know. I wasn't really sure why, but something had compelled me to ask. It was almost like I knew if he did, if he was truly happy, I could be too one day?

"Of course, I do! I wouldn't keep doing it if I didn't," he said, gesturing for me to stop before bending down to fiddle with a loose stone on the steps. "I have a lot of regrets for what I did when I was part of the Sterlings.

That lot kills too easily, they don't care about preservation or saving anything for future generations. They're happy to destroy and ruin and leave people entirely defenceless but… they also do a lot of things right. I learnt a lot with them."

I watched his back as he pulled the stone up and examined the device below, muttering under his breath.

"Do you… can I help?" I asked after a moment as he pulled a pair of tweezers from one of the pockets on his vest.

"Nah, you're good, kid. Ideally, I'd like to keep you as far away from any explosives as possible until you're happy and comfortable with them," he replied. "Especially one like this. It's been protected from the weather for a long time, unlike that one in Edinburgh. Some moisture might have found its way in but… it's most likely still in one piece."

I hesitated for a moment before asking, "Do you ever really get happy and comfortable with explosives?"

Mitch leant back and laughed.

"Alright, maybe happy wasn't the right word. You get more comfortable with them, but I generally think it's good to not completely let your guard down. That is a recipe for disaster and missing limbs."

"Missing limbs?" I asked, fighting the urge to clamber back up the stairs and far away from whatever explosive device Mitch was fiddling with.

"Yeah, it's fairly normal in this line of work. I've been

pretty lucky, the worst I've done is lose the tip of this finger and my little finger doesn't bend properly anymore," he said, holding his left hand up.

I looked at his hand in the torchlight. I'd never noticed it before, but the ring finger on his left hand was shorter than it should have been. It wasn't that obvious but once he'd pointed it out, I couldn't unsee it. He flexed his hand, curling it into a fist, but his little finger didn't cooperate. It bent slightly but not fully.

"What—" I started to ask.

"Oh, it's a long and nasty story. It's fine though, don't cause me too much hassle unless I gotta punch a lot of people with that hand for some reason, and then it likes to dislocate itself."

His tone was so easygoing but I couldn't help but stare at his hand in horror. I wanted to know what happened and how he could be so blasé about it, but I couldn't bring myself to ask.

He was silent for a little longer as he alternated between rooting around in his bag and doing something to the device on the floor. I watched, not quite able to see what he was doing around him and unsure what else to do or say. He'd said that he didn't need my help, but I felt so useless just standing there and watching.

"Alright, that should do it. Here, take my hand and hop over that step," he said, replacing the stone before standing and climbing down a couple of steps.

I took his outstretched hand and gingerly stretched

downwards, avoiding the step that he'd been working on.

"What did you do?" I asked, glancing back at it.

"Just primed it again, in case anyone follows us. Here, let me leave a marker. Lauren and Oscar shouldn't follow us down here and we won't be coming back this way, so we'll be fine, but still."

He squeezed past me and grabbed a stone from the floor. He scrapped it along the wall, clearing away some cobwebs and leaving behind a white cast on the rough walls.

It didn't feel like enough.

"Will that—" I started to ask.

"Be enough?" Mitch finished the sentence for me. "Oh, yeah. We've been working together for years; they know what to look out for."

I swallowed and continued following him down the stairs in silence, but I couldn't stop thinking about the bomb. What if it wasn't enough? What if they didn't see it or if they were rushing? Then what?

"What would happen," I asked, "if they did trigger it?"

Mitch grinned back at me.

"Don't worry, kid, I'm not like the Sterlings. It's just a flash bang. Granted, a very loud and powerful one, but nonlethal."

That made relief wash through me.

"Oh, good," I breathed.

"Yeah. I'd rather not kill people if I have the option. I mean, the Sterlings, as dickish as they all are, they're mostly just dumb kids. They prey on the young, vulnerable and intelligent but not wise. They offer a home, a job, and a community to the people who need it most. They don't deserve to die," he said softly.

I'd never thought about it like that.

I didn't really know anything about them but part of me understood why someone would sign up. I think, in real life, if someone offered me an escape like that, I probably would have taken it too.

"Ah, look at what we've got here," Mitch said, his voice dancing with excitement.

I looked around him at the brick wall at the bottom of the stairs. It was a dead end, nothing more.

"Did we choose the wrong grave?" I asked, feeling an undercurrent of fear start to thrum within me.

I really didn't want to go back to the surface. Oscar might have already re-covered the trap door and then we'd be stuck.

"Not at all," Mitch said and I could hear the happiness in his words. "It's a fake wall."

CHAPTER THIRTY-FOUR

"What?" I asked, peering at the wall before us. It looked real. It was made of the same light stone as the corridor that surrounded us. Nothing about it hinted that it was fake in any way.

"It's a fake wall," Mitch repeated. "I've come across them a bunch of times before. Normally, there's some pattern that you need to tap, hidden switches behind the stones. Once, I had to step on the right slabs on the floor at the same time. Lost one of my favourite tools that day, but it was one of the only things heavy enough to weigh it down. It was just after Zaq left, so I was stuck doing it alone. This one… I bet it's the stones. See how some protrude more than others?"

He looked back at me and leaned back so that I could see.

"Yeah?" I answered.

"That'll be it."

I watched as he examined the door closely, leaning

towards it but not touching anything. The anticipation was too much for me. There was nothing for me to do whilst he silently worked, there was nothing for me to even really look at.

The few protruding stones that I could see around him were completely unmarked. There was nothing obvious about them that even hinted at which ones we needed to press.

"How are we going to work it out?" I whispered after a moment.

Impatience was racing through me. I was excited, this was what I'd wanted to do, but at the same time, I just wanted to rush forwards and... I don't know, do something.

"I mean, I assume some of these stones once had some kind of marking on them. You see this one here?" he asked, leaning to one side and pointing at one near the centre.

I started at the completely ordinary-looking rock. "Yeah?"

"I think this once had something etched into it. You can just about see the outline of something but I think some of the rock has chipped away. We could just press the more worn stones, that would make sense, or..." He paused and shrugged his bag off his shoulder, pulling a strangely boxy-looking small camera with a thick case from it. "We could cheat."

He grinned up at me.

"What's that?" I asked, trying to peer over his shoulder as he switched it on and started moving it in slow, sweeping movements, pointing at the door.

"This is a scanner of sorts. It's a powerful little device, completely not meant for this purpose, but it can see through the stone to anything that's on the other side. And in this case... huh," Mitch said, looking up at the door again.

"What?" I asked, quickly looking between him and the door.

"Well, this is fun. I truly did not expect there to be another bomb here," he muttered.

"There's a bomb?" I asked, feeling my heart leap at his words.

"Yeah, it's probably not primed though. I mean, do you know how much effort it is to prepare a bomb and rush through a lowering door? It's hell. Every single time I have done it, I've just continued running and hoped for the best. That's only failed me a couple of times."

I stared at Mitch, not sure how to respond to that. I wanted to ask more about it, but I didn't want to distract him.

Not whilst he was trying to work out how not to set off another bomb.

"Mm," he muttered after a while, looking up at the door again.

"What?" I asked, wishing he would just tell me what

he was thinking.

"So, look at this," he said, seemingly unaware of all of the cobwebs as he leaned against the wall and held the device out to me.

I stared at it, trying to make sense of what I was seeing. As he moved it, I could see that some of the bricks had something behind them. They looked like they were attached to something, but I wasn't sure about anything other than that.

"Half of the stones are attached to something in the door. This mass here," he explained, bringing the camera to the centre where there was a darker shape. "But the rest, I think, are attached to these side bits. See, here and here?"

I watched the screen as he pointed the camera at a stone near the top and another near one side. They did seem to be attached to something that led to the edges of the door, but I wasn't sure why.

"So... do we have to press those ones?" I asked.

Mitch cocked his head slightly.

"I mean... it feels too obvious, right?" he said, glancing back at me, his eyes scanning the staircase behind me.

I checked over my shoulder too, making sure that there was no one silently sneaking down the stairs but they were empty.

"Obvious?" I repeated. "Why obvious?"

He grinned at me.

"We're under a church," he said, as if that were enough of an answer.

I stared at him blankly for a moment, but he just continued to smile at me. My brain works furiously, trying to work out what he could be referring to as he swept the camera back and forth over the wall before us.

He must have realised that I had no clue what he was talking about because finally, he spoke again.

"Father, son and holy spirit," he explained. "We need to push the stones that make up a cross."

My mouth fell open slightly.

No wonder he looked so uncertain about it. It did feel too obvious.

"Are you sure?" I asked.

He glanced at the scanner again before nodding.

"I'd say so. Alright, stand behind me and don't try to peek, okay?" he told me, shuffling slightly so that his body took up as much room as possible.

I nodded, moving so that I was behind him before completely ignoring his instructions and craning my head over his shoulder.

"Kid, what did I just say?" he said with a slight chuckle. "Duck your head down because if you get hit in the head with a stray rock, you're going to be in for a rough time!"

My eyes widened and I did what he said, huddling down behind him.

I really didn't want that to happen. If something did

happen to the door or if the stones Mitch was about to press weren't the right ones, it could explode. But then, I didn't want Mitch to be in front of me. He'd be right in the danger zone, he'd die surely.

Just as I realised that and lifted my head to say something, I felt Mitch start to move again.

"Okay, kid. Once the door opens, I assume it's going to lift up based on what I can see, we're going to rush through. Grab onto the back of my vest and move when I do. We'll stop just on the other side because there might be more traps or stuff there. Wait," he looked over his shoulder at me. "Do you want earplugs? This is going to be loud. I probably have a clean pair or two at the bottom of the bag."

I hesitated, poking my head up again to look at him.

"How loud is it going to be?" I asked.

"Well… in my experience with places this old, pretty damn loud. Back in the day, it was probably well-maintained and therefore silent but… No one has used it for years so the tech gets old and that makes it loud," he explained.

I bit my lip, debating it for a moment, before saying, "I'll be okay."

"Alright. Grab onto me now," he said.

I reached out, grasping the rough fabric as tightly as I could, and huddled down again. I felt Mitch move, probably reaching out towards the stone. The passageway was too quiet for a second before a loud noise came from in front of us, the sound of rock grating against rock.

"First one down and no explosion. Good start," Mitch muttered under his breath before straightening and reaching out with his foot to press the next one.

Again, nothing happened.

I was tempted to peer over Mitch's shoulder as I felt him reach out once more but I forced myself not to move. The only noise in the small passageway was the sound of stone scraping as Mitch pushed what felt like countless rocks.

Finally, he paused.

"Alright, kid. Last one. Are you ready to run?" he said.

My heart hammered in my chest and my sweating hands tightened on his vest.

Somehow, it felt so real. So much more real than when I was waiting for Mitch to uncover the trap door. This was it.

It felt... terrifying but I was exhilarated.

"Ready," I replied, my voice breathy.

"Okay. Three, two, one."

I heard the rasp of stone before there was a moment of silence. It stretched out, feeling like we were in a bubble that was about to pop at any moment but, when it did, dust showered from the ceiling and the noise was almost unbearable. I almost wanted to let go of Mitch to cover my ears, regretting that I'd refused the earplugs, as the deafening rumble of something moving in front of us.

The entire passageway shook so hard that I stumbled, fighting to keep my balance and struggling, but Mitch didn't even move.

Dust filled the air, falling from above and suffocating me, but I felt Mitch surge into action and I tightened my grip on him, blindly darting forwards.

My foot caught on the gouge in the floor where the door had rested and I stumbled against Mitch hard. He caught me, spinning to hold a hand up under the doorway and whirling me out of the way. I wasn't sure that it would have done much if the door were to come crashing down on me but he'd moved me out of the way before I had a chance to find out.

I coughed, still clutching Mitch's vest, as he turned towards the door. I felt him moving, but my eyes were crusted with dust so I couldn't see properly. I felt air rush at me though as Mitch fell still and the vague shape of the door crashed down again, cutting us away from the exit.

The silence that followed felt oppressive, somehow loud, and punctuated by my hacking coughs. I couldn't breathe. It felt like my lungs were coated in thick white dust, blocking any air from getting in.

"It's alright, give yourself a minute," Mitch said, turning back towards me. "Sorry, kid. I should have told you to hold your breath."

I forced my hands to release his vest and doubled over, catching myself on my knees as I coughed and fought to clear the dust from my lungs.

"You stay right there," he said in a gentle, soothing voice.

I wouldn't have been able to move anyway. I was breathless, trying desperately to fight the tightness in my chest.

"Grace," a voice asked and I looked around in confusion.

That wasn't Mitch.

"Was my mother looking for me?"

I blinked, the bright pool room startling me, and sucked in a mouthful of water. I coughed, paddling for the edge of the pool as I fought not to swallow even more.

My mom watched as I pulled myself out of the water and finally managed to clear the water from my lungs.

Even so, my chest felt tight as I stared at her.

"Um… Yeah, I think so. I told her she could probably call you if she wanted to," I said eventually.

My mom's eyes widened and she reached for her pocket, whipping her phone out and checking it.

"No missed calls," she muttered quietly. "Did she say why she wanted to speak to me?"

"No. She said it could wait till you got back though?"

My mother's face froze and she glanced over her shoulder.

"I should probably go find her. Did you want to go out for dinner soon?" she asked.

Confusion washed over me and my head whipped around to stare out the window.

Somehow, it was already starting to get dark. I wasn't sure how it had happened, but it was late. I had been swimming for hours.

"Yeah, that sounds like a good idea," I said, trying to hide my surprise.

"Great," my mom smiled back at me. "I'll go see what my parents want to do. You should probably get out and shower soon. All this chlorine is going to ruin your hair, it's already dry enough as is."

"Yeah, I'll go shower now," I said, fighting the urge to disappear back into my fantasy where I could almost hear Mitch talking to me.

I felt myself reply, feeling the phantom sensation of my lips moving.

"Did you bring a deep conditioning mask or do we need to go out and get you one in the morning?" my mom asked, bringing me back to reality.

"I brought one," I said, starting to stand and walking towards my towel.

"Good. Make sure to use it."

"I will," I said, trying not to sound irritated.

I was so used to it, but I still hated how much she cared about my appearance. It didn't matter if my hair looked dry, I already knew I had dry hair and I tried to fix it, but nothing really worked.

I did need to make sure that I didn't let it get too dry whilst I was in Scotland though. If it did or if my grandmother thought that it did, I knew that she'd have something to say about it. Knowing her, it would probably be something about me not knowing how to look after myself.

She enjoyed complaining about that. Apparently, my dry skin and sporadic acne were signs that I didn't know how to be a woman which, according to her, could only bode badly for my future.

She had told me that for years.

I wrapped the towel tightly around my body before following my mom from the room. She wandered off towards the kitchen, her body tensed and ready for the inevitable attack, whilst I started down the corridor towards the stairs.

As I climbed, I could feel myself slipping back to Mitch.

"Whoah, careful there. That is really unsteady," he warned, holding his hand out towards me.

I sucked in a sharp breath as I fought not to fall from where I was perched on a rotted wooden bridge. I grasped his hand as I stood still and blinked frantically, trying to force the dizziness out of my brain.

But I couldn't stand still. It was too precarious. The bridge I was standing on was between two outcrops of stone, but I couldn't really call it a bridge. It was more just a plank of wood with decaying rope on either side. I knew that if I were to so much as touch either of them, they would crumble to nothing.

There were holes in the wood too. Places where it had crumbled to nothing.

"You're alright," Mitch said softly. "Just step where I stepped."

I looked down at the bridge, trying to work out exactly where Mitch had walked, but I couldn't. I'd missed it, and now he was standing on the other side of the bridge with a hole in between us. He must have skirted around it, but I couldn't work out how. The wood looked too fragile. My eyes caught sight of the drop below me and I swayed, gripping Mitch's hand tightly.

I couldn't even see the bottom, just the light stone lining the endless ravine that seemed to cut deep into the earth.

"Grace," my mom said with a knock on the door and I immediately blinked back into reality.

"One second," I called back, looking around the bathroom.

I was standing in the shower, having turned off the water, combing a hair mask through my hair. I climbed out quickly and grabbed a towel, wrapping it around myself before opening the door just a crack.

My mom's face appeared in it.

"Mom and Dad are about to go out for dinner. Did you want to go with them?" she asked.

I hesitated for just a moment.

"Oh, I'm not ready yet," I said, stating the obvious, since I was naked and hadn't finished my shower. "I have a hair mask in still."

My mom nodded approvingly.

"Good. Alright, I'll tell them you don't want to go. We can always meet them there or just go somewhere else. What about that Italian place in town?" she asked.

I glossed over most of what she said, focusing on the Italian place.

I loved it there. It was one of the few places I could get a pizza without my mom judging me for it. Apparently, being artisan made up for it being a pizza. She didn't even judge me too much for ordering garlic mayonnaise.

"Tony's? Yeah, that would be great," I said with a genuine smile.

"Wonderful," my mom said. "I'll go tell them."

I felt my smile fall slightly, but I didn't force myself to keep it as I shut the door again.

I almost wanted to ask her not to blame it on me but I knew that it was pointless. She would never take the blame for anything that happened around her parents, it was just easier for her to blame me, but that just made them dislike me even more.

But... I did really like going to Tony's. It was a small place, kind of fancy but in the same way as the restaurants we went to with my grandparents were. As far as I was aware, they had never been and I didn't think they ever would. It was a shame, I feel like they would've liked the food there, it was really good. There was no point in trying to convince them though.

I pushed that thought from my mind as I methodically climbed back into the shower and began combing my fingers through my long hair, already disappearing to Crete.

Thankfully, when I was already on the other side of the bridge. I couldn't help but feel relieved about it even as I stared at the low tunnel Mitch had started through. It was little more than an archway cut into the tall light stone, rough and uneven on all sides.

I felt my stomach clench with claustrophobia, but I forced myself to follow him. Luckily, it wasn't that low. Mitch had to duck lightly so that he didn't hit his head but I could walk through easily. Even so, it felt tight. I was too painfully aware of the probably hundreds of pounds of stone on top of us that could come crashing down at any given moment.

I wasn't even sure how far underground we were. It had felt like we were climbing down the steps forever but I couldn't really trust time in my daydreams. It always felt a little…inconsistent. Either way, I was deep enough underground to know that if something happened and we got stuck, we would probably never be found.

"Whoah, whoah!" Mitch cried suddenly. "Stop."

I froze instantly, panic pounding in my ears.

I stood as still as I could as Mitch leant forwards slowly before he stopped moving again.

"Okay, kid. There's some kind of trap ahead so we're going to turn back and work out what to do out there," he said in a calm voice.

I let out a tight breath and did as he instructed, my knees shaking. What kind of trap would it be?

We'd already encountered bombs, would there be more?

Even through my fear, I felt the undercurrent of excitement. This was what I wanted when I dove into this fantasy. I wanted adventure, I wanted excitement. This was perfect.

It felt so real. Everything from the chill in the air from being underground to the musty scent of long undisturbed air made it feel like I was actually there. Despite being in the shower, combing my hands through my hair to rid it of knots, I could feel the solid stone beneath my feet. I could feel the hard wall of the passage against my arm as I bumped into it.

It felt real.

"Grace," a voice called.

I sighed, irritation washing through me. I knew that it was my mom again, but she'd only just spoken to me a minute ago. I almost wanted to ignore her, but I knew it wasn't worth it.

Reluctantly, I turned the water off and squeezed the excess water from my hair before stepping out of the shower again. I wrapped a towel around my hair and another around my body.

"Grace," my mom shouted again, her tone sharper this time.

She sounded far away and I knew she was in her room, shouting at me from across the corridor. She wouldn't be doing that if my grandparents were still there.

"Yeah?" I called, cracking the door open a bit as I began to gather my stuff to head into my room.

"Mom and Dad have gone out. Shall we go out in about ten minutes?" she asked.

I paused, clutching my still wet swimming costume to my chest, a slight smile forming on my face.

That should give me enough time to work out what the trap was with Mitch.

"Yeah, sounds great!"

CHAPTER THIRTY-FIVE

We emerged out of the stone tunnel again and Mitch turned back towards the trap thoughtfully. I watched him, impatience almost overwhelming me. I just wanted to know what he was thinking. Adrenaline was coursing through me, making it hard for me to just continue standing there.

"What do you think the trap is?" I asked after a full minute of silence.

"I'm not sure," he said softly, still looking at it. "I mean, there's a lot that it could be. We've already had a couple of bombs, it could be another. But then, they seem stupid to have a bomb down here. If it were to go off, it would completely destroy the path to the vault. They wouldn't risk that, this is the main entrance. But then, what?"

I fought the urge to shudder at the thought of a bomb exploding and leaving us trapped under so much rock. I wasn't even sure how far down we were but the small cavern we were in made it feel like we were deep under-ground.

"Could be another spear trap," Mitch continued. "There are some holes in the walls but I'm not sure if they're for gas or for the spears to get through. Could always be both."

I swallowed, remembering the story he'd told me about a spear trap before. He'd said that they had turned to splinters and done a lot of damage. That scared me. Seeing the splinters explode out of the wall would be terrifying, especially if they hit Mitch again like they had last time.

"Would they still be in one piece or would they be broken by now?" I asked, my voice louder than I expected and echoing around the cavern.

Mitch cocked his head slightly.

"I assume they'll mostly be in one piece. They're fairly protected down here, there's not too much moisture in the air and the sun can't reach them." He narrowed his eyes before looking at me. "Are you up to date with your tetanus shots?"

I did not see that question coming somehow.

"What?" I asked.

"The spears might be tipped with metal and that might have rusted by now. You should have had a booster around the age of... fourteen. Do you remember having it?" he asked.

I wracked my memory, trying to work it out.

I remembered having a vaccine in school in the last few years but I wasn't completely sure which one it was. It could have been the tetanus one but I wasn't certain.

"I don't know," I told him.

He nodded, his expression grim.

"Alright, you need to be really careful then. I know rust doesn't necessarily cause tetanus but it can give you it and when we get out of here, I'll call Betty as soon as possible to find out what vaccines you're not up to date on. We'll need to get them scheduled as soon as possible which is fine. It's better to be safe than sorry, because you never know when you'll have to rely on them," he said.

I nodded.

"That makes sense. So... what do we do now?" I asked.

"We'll put masks on, in case it is a nice little gas trap, and I'm going to grab a stone to throw at it to trigger it. I'm going to need you to wait out here, just in case it's a bad one, but listen carefully and do what I say," he said, already looking around for a stone. "Ah, there we go."

He spotted one and walked towards it, nudging it with his foot before picking it up. He dropped it again near me and swung his bag off his shoulder, rooting around until he found the masks. He passed one to me before securing his own around his face.

I watched him unsurely as I lifted mine into place, worry bubbling in my stomach. Part of me wanted to insist that I should be the one to trigger the trap, even though I knew Mitch would never agree to it. I could die in this fantasy and nothing bad to happen but I wasn't sure what would happen if Mitch would die. Would he be able to come back? Or would he just be gone forever?

I couldn't let that happen.

"Alright, wait out here until I tell you it's safe, alright?" he told me, his voice coming out muffled before he started towards the tunnel again, lugging the rock.

"Wait," I called, stumbling towards him, but I didn't know what else to say.

I couldn't see if Mitch was smiling, but the skin around his eyes crinkled as he glanced back at me.

"I've done this hundreds of times, kid. I'll be alright," he promised.

I didn't have a response. I couldn't put the sudden fear I felt into words. All I could do was watch as he walked down the tunnel, taking the only light source with him. Darkness started to consume me, making my skin prickle. If the Sterlings came in now, they could sneak in without me knowing and murder me before Mitch even looked back. I suspected they had night vision goggles or something like that.

The thought made a shiver race through me and I edged towards the entrance of the tunnel, watching Mitch anxiously.

My fear that I was about to watch him die overrode

my paranoia about standing in the dark, potentially surrounded, but I just couldn't look away. I needed to see.

He took a tiny step back before tossing the small boulder. I held my breath as I waited for the deafening sound of it landing on the floor but it came quickly, immediately followed by the scraping of metal.

I dropped to the floor instinctively as dust rained from the ceiling again. It felt like the world was shaking but this time, I held my breath. It was stupid, the dust couldn't get in through my mask but still, I was worried about it.

I blinked, staring ahead and fearful that Mitch was dead.

"Huh," I heard him say.

"What?" I replied, stumbling into the tunnel towards him.

"It was only spears," he said with an almost sad sigh. "Is it weird that I'm disappointed? I mean, come on people, do something inventive. Do you know how long it's been since I saw something new? It was easily three years ago, maybe longer. Such a disappointment."

I let out a shaky breath of relief.

"Is that how you're doing your hair?" my mom asked.

I blinked, staring up at her in the reflection of the mirror, almost catching my ear with my straighteners.

I lowered them slowly, forcing myself to smile at her as nausea gripped my stomach.

"Yeah," I said.

It felt like an obvious answer. I had already straightened most of my hair, I only had a small section left to do.

I wasn't even sure why I had straightened it, I normally just let it dry naturally or blow-dried it. My hairdryer was out in front of me though so I must've done that as well.

"Oh," my mum said, sounding clearly disappointed. "It looks better when you curl it. When will you be ready?"

"A couple more minutes."

She sighed heavily and glanced at her watch.

"Fine. I assume that's what you're wearing?"

I looked down at the dress I'd put on without really noticing it. It was a simple black one, surely she couldn't complain about it too much.

I'd been too busy in Crete. I wanted to go back there now, I could feel myself edging closer towards the spears.

"Yes," I said.

"Well... it looks nice on you."

My eyes widened and I looked up at her again, not expecting the compliment. "Thank you, you look nice too."

She did. She was wearing a dress, like she always did around my grandparents. It was a nice floral one, sleeveless and flared. The flowers were bright and summery, it was lovely.

My mom smiled at me, pushing the door open wider so that I could see her full outfit.

"Really pretty," I added.

She smiled at me, the expression genuine.

"Thank you. I'll wait for you downstairs, don't take too long."

She turned and stalked down the corridor.

I sagged slightly in relief, knowing that I shouldn't but immediately slipping back into the fantasy.

It was a terrible idea.

I was just about to step forwards, my foot hovering just above the slab, the spears waiting ominously for me to slip. I sucked in a tight breath, stepping backwards to give myself a moment for the dizziness to disappear. I stared at the spears, illuminated by the second torch Mitch had attached to his other shoulder and pointed back towards me, trying to steady myself.

Luckily, Mitch was too distracted by trying to squeeze past two spears that stuck out towards him. I watched as he edged forwards ever so carefully, his bag held in one hand. He just managed to make it through before glancing back at me.

"You alright, kid?" he asked.

I nodded and hurried forwards, the dizziness almost gone.

As terrifying as it was to edge forwards, feeling the slab underneath me bob slightly with each step, it was surprisingly easy. We got into a tense but manageable rhythm with Mitch glancing back over his shoulder every few steps to make sure that I was alright.

Part of me wanted to reassure him that I was fine and that he could just focus on moving forwards and not getting caught on any of the spears but I didn't want to speak. I was too busy holding my breath. I was worried that if I spoke or took too deep a breath, I would accidentally impale myself.

I took a careful, steady step forwards, my foot gently pressing down on the next slab. I watched out of the corner of my eye as the spears slowly retracted as my weight left the stone behind me.

"Almost there," Mitch breathed, causing a slight smile to come over my face.

We were so close, so almost out of the danger.

"Grace!" my mom called sharply. "What is taking so long?"

I blinked and scrambled up, making sure my straighteners were switched off before grabbing my phone and rushing out the door.

"Coming!" I shouted, rushing down the corridor before realising that I wasn't wearing shoes.

I turned and rushed towards my room, selecting a pair of flats before running back towards my mom.

"Sorry," I called as I reached the bottom of the stairs and slipped my shoes on.

"It's fine," she sighed. "Are you ready to go now?"

"Yes!" I said eagerly, knowing that as soon as we got into the car, my mom would start playing music again and I would be able to disappear back to Mitch.

I waited impatiently as my mom stepped into a pair of heels, not quite as tall as the ones she usually wore around my grandparents, before following her out of the house.

I crossed the drive quickly, fighting the urge to bounce on the balls of my feet as I waited for her to join me. I knew that it wasn't fair for me to be so impatient, she was struggling on the gravel, but I still felt it. I pulled the door open as soon as she unlocked the car and dove inside, clipping my seatbelt into place and waiting for her to do the same.

"Why are you in such a hurry?" she demanded.

"I'm just really hungry," I lied as innocently as I could.

She examined me closely for a moment before looking away.

"Are you sure that's it? You're not planning to meet anyone in town, are you?" she asked sharply.

"No, I don't know anyone here. I'm just really excited for pizza."

That part was true, I was excited to eat it. The pizzas at Tony's were so so good.

"Mmm," was all my mom said.

I knew that she didn't quite believe me and still suspected that I planned to meet a boy in town, but I truly had no clue how she thought I would do that.

I really didn't know anyone in the village. Whenever we were there, I was with her or at the house the whole time. There was no chance for me to meet anyone else.

She still expected me to though. Any time we went out or sometimes when I went for a run or a jog, she'd ask me if I was meeting anyone. Sometimes I was pretty sure she even followed me.

Of course, she always said she was just getting some fresh air or going out for a cigarette, but I didn't believe her. It seemed like too much of a coincidence that she just wanted to get some fresh air at the same time that I was outside or that she just happened to be in the same part of the grounds as me.

She slammed the door shut and inserted the key into the ignition as I fought the urge to flit immediately back to Spinalonga. I could feel it. We were so close to the end of the spears and I couldn't wait to squeeze through the last of them and see what awaited us next.

Would it be another bomb?

The car jolted back underneath me but I was half in the other world. I could feel the seat beneath me and the air con blasting me in the face, but I could also feel the creak of the slab under my feet and the way it bounced with each step I took.

Mitch had already reached the other side and he stood in front of me, smiling supportively. One of his hands was outstretched, ready to help me if I stumbled or slipped.

"Can you get out and do the gate?" my mum asked. "You know the code, don't you?"

"Yeah, I'm pretty sure I do," I replied, trying not to sound too dejected about being ripped from my fantasy again.

"Great."

I climbed out of the car, barely waiting for it to stop, and rushed towards the gate. I had to push the overgrown ivy out of the way to be able to access the keypad, but I managed to get the code right on my first try.

I tried not to walk too quickly back to the car, but my mom sent me a suspicious look as I strapped myself in again which made me think I failed. It didn't really matter though because we turned onto the road and her music became deafening again.

A smile came over my face as I returned to Mitch.

And there was a spear right in front of my face. I fought not to lose my balance as I stared right at the rusted point, just inches from me. If I were to sway or fall forwards, I had no doubt that it would imbed itself in my eyeball. That would kill me.

I forced out a tight breath through pursed lips, trying to keep my composure and not stumble. White lights burst hazily in front of my vision and I longed to reach out and grab the shaft of the nearest spear to steady myself but I resisted. Knowing how old the spears were helped minimise the temptation though. It would probably snap and then I'd impale myself on the spear that hovered just centimetres from my spine.

"Just a little further," Mitch urged.

I was so close, just a little further and I'd be out of the danger.

I edged my foot forwards, bumping into the next slab and looked down at it. So close, I just needed to squeeze past one more spear which was pointed directly at my tummy.

I held my breath, sucking in my stomach and leaning as far away as I could whilst also trying to avoid the spear that threatened to slice the back of my leg.

Finally, I was free! I staggered forwards, my hand clutching Mitch's for balance. Now that I was out of danger, my knees felt weak. I had to turn around to look at the spears again, trying to remind myself that I'd actually just done that, that they had been real.

Well. Not real. They were just a fantasy. But they were as real as anything else in the fantasy.

"Good job, kid! How are you feeling? Do you need to take a quick break?" Mitch asked, grinning at me.

I let go of Mitch and shook my hands a few times, trying to shake away some of the nerves. Adrenaline warred with excitement in me almost overpoweringly. It was distracting. It made me want to rush forwards, to throw myself at the next trap or bomb. But at the same time, I was scared. It was terrifying, but that added to the excitement.

I smiled back at Mitch toothily.

"Good!" I replied, my voice coming out louder and more excited than I'd expected. "Let's keep going!"

"Are you sure?" he said, his eyes scanning my face.

"Yeah!"

He chuckled slightly as he continued down the tunnel towards the opening.

"Ah, I remember the feeling well. The thrill that comes with the first successful mission," he sighed wistfully. "That never really goes away, you know? Like, every time you disarm a bomb or manoeuvre through a trap without injury, you still get that rush. I mean, sometimes it comes later but it's always there. It's one of the things that keeps me coming back. After doing a job like this for so long, how could I go back to regular life?"

I smiled, but it died on my lips.

Maybe he had a point. Even after doing something like this in a fantasy, how could I just go back to normal? I'd had a glimpse, a taste, of something so different, so exciting and fun. Could I really go back to my house and school and do my GCSEs and continue like normal? Like nothing had happened?

Or would I just spend the rest of my life in a constant state of wonder? After all, I knew what I could be doing now. I knew that this job was an option for some people, but it felt like there was no way I could chase it in reality. I couldn't exactly tell the careers advisor, who we were forced to speak to each year and who repeatedly tried to tell me that I should look into becoming a doctor or accountant despite having no interest in either area, that I wanted to become a treasure hunter.

I mean, was it even a legal job? I had to assume not. We were breaking and entering surely. Plus, in Edinburgh, that had been a crime too. We'd desecrated a listed building, stolen stuff from it.

It was all illegal.

But then, if this job did exist in real life, the Sterlings could too. They probably wouldn't be called that, but they had to be called something. They were probably private security or something like that for some rich person who had a penchant for artefacts. How would I find them and if I did, would I even want to join them? It would give me a chance to find treasure and experience this excitement, sure, but it also would be too… wrong.

No, I wasn't sure I could do that. I'd have to just settle for living half in my daydreams for the rest of my life. Maybe I could do that. I could spend half my time in reality, go to university and all that, half my time in my fantasy with Mitch, uncovering countless missing artefacts and treasures.

"Oh wow," I heard Mitch breathe.

I rushed forwards, exiting the tunnel and emerging into a much bigger chamber. My eyes widened as I looked around, trying to take it all in.

The space was huge, the ceiling somehow higher than

before and the far wall, on the other side of the gorge was painted beautifully. I glanced at Mitch, making sure it was safe, before stepping forwards to stare at the mural that someone had created.

It must have been depicting what life was like on the island, but it had been untouched for years. The colours were somehow still vibrant in the torch light. Vivid images of people talking, cooking and eating together. The streets of Spinalonga, not crumbling or strangely preserved. It looked… alive. The people were happy, they seemed accepted.

It was a community. A bright, thriving community.

I knew that it was probably an idealistic view of the island, but it filled me with such joy. I wanted to believe that the image before me was what it was like. That people there were happy and taken care of.

"Careful, kid," Mitch muttered, touching my arm gently to stop me from going too close to the deep gorge that split the cavern in half.

I stepped back immediately, glancing nervously at it.

"Now, what?" I said, finally looking around the rest of the chamber that we were in.

The chasm in between the two sides was wide, too wide to be able to jump over, but there were the remains of a bridge attached to the narrowest part.

I watched as Mitch walked towards it, nudging the rotted remains of the wood on our side with his toe. Part of it crumbled under his touch, sending planks crashing down the ravine.

It scared me how long it took for them to hit the ground with a hollow, echoing thunk.

"I thought that might happen," Mitch said softly. "For once, I hate that I was right."

My eyes followed the gorge to the wall on the left side. Even there, it didn't get any thinner. Something about that made me think that it wasn't natural. That the people who had lived on the island before us had created it. I wasn't even sure how they could have done that.

"Are you any good at rock climbing?" Mitch asked. "I feel like I've asked you that before."

"Um…" I quickly searched my memories, finding a hazy one from a childhood party, but I wasn't quite sure if it was real. "I'm not sure. I've not really done it too much."

In real life, I had but the memory of gouging my arm on the rock down near the beach made my blood run cold. I could still remember staring blankly at it as blood began to ooze out of the split skin and panic gripped my heart.

I was almost relieved when I heard my mom's frustrated sigh.

"Why does this always happen?"

CHAPTER THIRTY-SIX

I blinked out of the fantasy, just as I heard Mitch reply, and looked around.

"What's the matter?" I asked quickly.

"This damn car park!" my mom exclaimed, her frustration evident. "Everyone here parks like morons!"

I glanced around the car park, not seeing a single car that was over the lines, and said, "Mmm."

I could have slipped back into the fantasy where I knew Mitch was pulling a harness and a length of rope out of his backpack, but I didn't want to. I knew it was something I had to get over but the idea of climbing, wherever in the cavern we were going to do it, terrified me. Once I'd managed it the first time without injury, once I knew that my body was capable of it, it would be easier.

I wasn't sure if that was true or if I was just lying to myself but either way, it didn't matter. I stayed firmly in reality as my mom pulled into one of the many free spaces in the car park, ignoring the faint sensations from the fantasy world.

"That's not too bad," she said, pulling on the hand break and checking her lipstick in the mirror before switching off the engine.

"Yeah, it seems like a pretty good space," I replied.

I could feel myself walking in the fantasy, but I pushed it away even harder, trying not to get swept up in it again.

I started to get out of the car before pausing and inhaling deeply. The glorious scent of fresh pizza, cheese and garlic wafted towards me from Tony's and I couldn't help but hurry towards it. My mom did the same, rushing across the road and into the small, brightly lit restaurant.

I looked around at the familiar place, a smile on my face as I took in the pictures on the wall that had been there ever since we'd stumbled across the restaurant years before. Tony and his family smiled down at us from their original restaurant in Rome. In some, he was in the kitchen, in others serving customers and laughing with them.

It made me happy every time I saw the pictures. I could just tell he was doing what he wanted to do with his life. He seemed so happy, so fulfilled. Part of me wondered if I'd ever feel that way. The closest I ever got was when I was in Crete, but... that wasn't the same. It wasn't real.

"Okay, kid. I've got everything set up, are you ready to go?" Mitch's voice broke through my musings.

I returned to the cave deep under the surface of Spinalonga, my eyes landing on him immediately.

He was on the other side of the chasm, one torch attached to his shoulder and pointing straight at me, another on the floor and pointing upwards, lighting the cave. He was wearing a harness and I belatedly realised that I was too. It was attached to a rope that went all the way up to a metal hook and back to Mitch.

I couldn't see the hook properly but I really hoped that it was a new one that Mitch had somehow drilled into the stone and not something that had been there for however long.

He had. I had faint memories of him clambering skilfully up the wall, pulling some tools and the hook out of his belt before attaching them. Anxiety had wracked me as he did it. I was almost certain that at any moment, he'd slip and fall to his death.

But he hadn't. Before long, he was on the other side, smiling victoriously at me and urging me to follow his path across the gap.

He had assured me that, even if I were to fall, I would be fine. The hook would hold my weight and he'd pull me back up. I wasn't so sure though and I didn't want to stay in that world for long enough to find out.

"How does this table look?" the waiter asked me, gesturing towards a small booth table far away from the rest of the people in the restaurant.

"It's great," I said. "Thank you."

My mom said nothing as she slid into one side of the booth and I shot the waiter a smile as I sat on the other side. I could see into the kitchen from where I was sitting. The huge pizza oven at the back had pizzas cooking in it, chefs waiting nearby to pull them out as soon as they were baked to perfection.

"There are your menus. Can I get you some drinks or do you need a minute?" the waiter asked.

I picked up the menu that he'd placed on the table before me, my eyes already going to the pizza section as my stomach growled hungrily. I don't know why I even looked at the menu when I knew I was just going to get the same thing I always did but I still checked.

"I'll just have a sparkling water," my mom said.

"Can I just get a coke, please?" I asked, smiling at the waiter.

"Of course. I'll bring those right over."

I looked down at the menu again, my eyes unfocusing slightly as the urge to disappear back to Crete gripped me. I fought it though. I could feel what was happening and I didn't want to be there.

The rocks dug into my fingers and my arms shook with effort. My legs strained too. I had barely started climbing but I really hadn't thought it would be that hard. I just wasn't used to it. It had been so long since I'd climbed last and that was making me want to do it more.

Not because I was enjoying it, I just knew I needed to get better. I needed to be able to manage it next time because what if it wasn't just a fairly small chasm we needed to climb over? What if I needed to actually climb something properly? I wouldn't be able to do it.

"What are you feeling?" my mom asked, surprising me.

She never asked what I wanted normally.

"Um… I think just a cheese pizza," I said.

She nodded, her eyes scanning the menu.

"That does look good. Are you not having a starter?"

I looked at her in shock. Normally she told me I was eating too much, not suggesting we have more food. But I guessed that being in Scotland was rubbing off on her. It was probably making her want to rebel.

I glanced at the starters, my eyes taking in the options quickly.

"Oh, maybe the bruschetta," I said.

It sounded delicious. There was even a drizzle of pesto on it.

My mom hesitated before saying, "That does sound lovely."

Something told me she was biting back the urge to say something cruel. It didn't really matter to me though, I knew that I wanted to eat the bruschetta, no matter what.

"Are you going to have a starter?" I asked.

I saw my mom purse her lips before carefully saying,

"Yes, I think I will."

There was a moment of awkward silence between us before I made myself speak again.

"What are you going to have?"

"I think I'm going to have the scallops to start and then the pesto pasta," she replied, without looking up at me over the menu.

"Mm, sounds good."

I looked back at the menu awkwardly, starting to reach out for the comforting dizziness to escape the awkwardness that stretched between us, but the waiter returned, sparing me from having to experience any more of the rock climbing.

I was so close anyway. I was almost on the other side.

"There we go," he said, placing our drinks in front of us. "And have you decided on what you would like to eat? Or do you need another couple of minutes?"

I glanced at my mom who said, "I think we're ready. I'll have the scallops to start and then the pesto pasta."

She looked over her menu at me expectantly.

"Oh, can I have the bruschetta and a four pizza, please? And some garlic mayonnaise?" I asked.

"Great. Any other sauces or sides?" the waiter asked.

"No, thank you," my mom said, answering for me.

"Wonderful."

The waiter finished scribbling down our order before taking the menus and walking away from the table.

Once more, the silence grew between us. I smiled awkwardly at my mum, not sure what to say or if there was anything I could do to start a conversation.

"So," my mum said slowly, clearly searching for something to say too. "How are you finding school?"

"Oh, yeah. It's alright."

"What is your favourite subject at the moment?" she asked.

It surprised me. I didn't really expect her to say anything more.

"I'm not sure, really. Maybe philosophy? I'm really enjoying that."

My mother nodded, her smile only slightly forced.

"So... you want to become a Philosopher?" she asked, a hint of mocking in her voice.

"No," I said immediately, fighting back the urge to point out that I didn't think it was really a job anymore anyway. "I'm not sure what I want to do."

"No? Does your school not have a career advisor?" she asked.

"No, not really. I mean, there's a person who comes once a year and tells us what she thinks we should do."

Not that she was any good or actually listened to what we wanted.

"Oh? And what did she say you should do?"

"It varies every year, but she's said I should look into journalism, law or medicine," I answered flatly. "I'm pretty sure that she gives that advice to everyone though."

I saw my mom's eyes light up and I knew she had ignored the second part of what I had just said.

"Law or medicine, huh? Do you think you have the grades to study either of those?" she asked, her voice strangely excited.

I knew what she was thinking. She was hoping that I would go into medicine, study something that was better than any of my cousins and that would finally make my grandparents proud of me and, by extension, her. It wouldn't happen though. I didn't care about the subjects and I was pretty sure I wasn't smart enough to do either.

"I'm not sure. I'm not really interested in law or medicine though," I told her.

"That doesn't matter! You don't need to actually care about them. They're good jobs, you'd be able to actually make something of your life," she said.

I scrunched up my face in disagreement. I wanted a job that I did care about. Well, at least something that made me happy. Maybe before it wouldn't have mattered too much to me. I would have been content to just do anything, work mindlessly at whatever job I fell into or study whatever seemed achievable at university, but not now. Somehow, seeing Mitch enjoying his life made that feel less acceptable. I knew that he was just in my head probably, but still he made me want to actually do something I enjoyed with my life.

"Yeah," I said reluctantly, "but there might be something else I enjoy more or that I'm better at."

My mother looked at me like I had said something ridiculous.

"Does that matter? Why do you need to enjoy work?" she demanded, her tone quiet so that no one would overhear how she was talking to me. "Do you really think I enjoyed all of my jobs? When I practically ran that media company, do you think I had a good time? Or when I managed over one hundred people, do you think that was fun for me?"

I almost wanted to say yes. She brought those jobs up all of the time. Depending on what point she was trying to prove, she either found the jobs so easy and had a wonderful time or she had to put in extra hours, worked overtime and was never at home. Either way, she painted herself in such a positive light that I doubted the stories completely.

I settled for grunting noncommittally.

"Exactly! It's better to work a job that you don't really enjoy, but that means you can support yourself to have the lifestyle that you want!" she said. "And, if you are a lawyer or a doctor, you should be able to find yourself a nice wealthy man to settle down with!"

I fought the urge to roll my eyes at her. She brought that up a lot. Half of her advice to me was about how to find a nice wealthy man to marry and have children with. I was never sure quite what to make of it. I mean, most people had considered what their dream wedding would be like and how their futures would look, but I didn't think about it that much.

I didn't like to. I wasn't sure why but the idea of the future just filled me with such...dread. Talking to anyone about it made me anxious. I didn't want a future, especially not one like my mom was talking about. I didn't want to think about finding a person to marry and spend the rest of my life with, working in a job for the next however many years and popping out a dozen children, like she wanted me to.

None of that appealed to me. Well, some of it did, I guess I didn't mind the idea of marrying some guy, as long as it was someone who I actually liked and wanted to spend time with. That didn't sound like it could happen though. I'd never even had a boyfriend, how could I be thinking about a husband? It was impossible to find someone who liked me and wanted to even date me.

My foot finally touched the ground on the other side of the canyon but I couldn't let go of the rock just yet, even though Mitch had grabbed my arm and was pulling me further onto solid ground. My fingers stung from how hard I had been gripping the stone and my legs were shaking. I glanced back at the wall, marvelling at the fact that I had actually managed to climb it.

Not really climb, of course it was just a fantasy and I wasn't even there, but I had managed it. I didn't think I would be capable of it.

"Good job, kid!" Mitch cried, clapping my shoulder. "Ready to move on to the next bit or do you need a minute?"

I sucked in a deep breath, feeling some of the adrenaline drain from me now that I was firmly on the other side. I wanted to say that I didn't need a break, that I was ready to keep going and see what challenge or trap awaited us next, but my hands were trembling. My legs were too. I was genuinely worried that I might fall over.

"Is it alright if I take a bit of a break?" I asked sheepishly.

"That's fine, kid. I want to take some photos of this wall anyway, just in case the Sterlings do find us and blow it to smithereens," he said with a grin.

My stomach clenched at his words. Suddenly, it felt so stupid to even consider stopping, even if it was only for a few minutes.

"Are you sure?" I asked, glancing back at the other side of the cave, checking to make sure they weren't sneaking up on us somehow.

The light barely reached that side but I was pretty sure there was no one there. I couldn't see any movement at least.

"Of course. Take a seat, I'll get it all set up for the photos and then we'll keep going," he said in a reassuring tone.

I smiled at him and started to sink down before being ripped back into reality.

"The bruschetta," a waitress said, looking between my mom and me.

A thick cut of bread was on the plate in her hand, decorated with multicoloured tomatoes and sprinkled with pesto and balsamic vinegar. My mouth immediately started to water and I had to swallow before I could speak.

"Here, please."

"Great, and yours must be the scallops?" the waitress asked, looking at my mother.

I glanced at the dish she was holding. I didn't eat fish, but it did look pretty good.

Large scallops rested in a cream sauce, flecked with black specks of pepper, with a thick wedge of bread on the side of the plate.

"Yes," my mother said with a perfunctory smile.

"Great. Can I get you anything else?" the waitress asked, looking between us.

"No, thank you."

I stared down at the plate in front of me, suddenly so glad that my mom had suggested that we get starters. I'd only had the bruschetta a handful of times, but it was always so delicious.

I picked up a half of the slice, tomatoes tumbling to the plate below and the juices already running down my fingers, and took a huge bite. I had to suppress the urge to sigh happily. It was just so good. It was somehow sweet yet perfectly savoury, the tomatoes so flavourful with a hint of saltiness and the pesto was incredible.

I quickly took another bite, savouring the delicious dish before me. The juices had started to soak into the bread but it was like a sponge, taking on more and more flavour.

I wished there was a place back home that did a bruschetta that good, but there just wasn't. There was a chain restaurant in the next city over that served it, but it was always just a little… lacklustre. Nothing like the mouth-watering version they made at Tony's.

I finished the rest of the bruschetta quickly, not even leaving some on my plate so as not to seem greedy, and scooped up some of the tomatoes that had fallen off the bread as I'd been eating.

My mom was so absorbed by her own dish that she barely even sent me a disapproving look. Even so, she almost finished all of hers, leaving behind just a small chunk of bread and half a scallop.

I leant back, a satisfied smile coming to my lips as I tumbled towards the dizziness.

"So, how are things going with Duncan?" my mom asked, pulling me back.

"What do you mean?" I asked, the words coming out a little too sharp.

"Well, aren't you two dating? You used to spend so much time going on bike rides together."

Her tone clearly insinuated that there was more going on than that, but there wasn't. Under the table, my hands clenched into fists but I wasn't sure why.

"No. We're just friends, that's all we've ever been," I said in as even a tone as possible.

It was true.

"Mmm," my mom said, clearly not believing me. "Are you still just… friends then?"

"Yeah."

She took a sip of her drink, scrutinising me over the rim of the glass.

"I've not seen him around in a little while."

I didn't need to answer her, but I felt strangely defensive.

"I still see him sometimes."

I bit back the urge to say that we still texted a fair bit too. That would make her suspicious that there was something more going on between us when there really wasn't. We were just friends, we always had been, and we probably always would be. He'd never want to be with someone like me, he had too many better options.

Not that I even liked him like that. He was just a friend. Like, he was attractive, of course. He had a nice smile and he was on the rugby team, so he had a good body. I'd seen him topless enough times to know that, but I only ever saw him as a friend.

I felt my phone buzz in my pocket but I fought the urge to reach for it, trying to keep my facial expression as neutral as possible as my mother examined me doubtfully. I knew that it might have been Duncan and, for once, I didn't want it to be. If it were him and I were to read the text and smile, my mom would demand to see the message.

I really didn't want that. I hadn't cleared his messages in a while so the one with the picture of the bottle of vodka would be there and she'd see it. I could already hear the rant she would give me now and it wasn't worth it. It was always the same rant. She started by telling me how stupid drinking was and how drinking so early would ruin my brain and mean that I'd never achieve anything in my life, so I'd be mediocre forever.

It was one of her favourite rants and every single time, I had to fight the urge to point out that she'd told me stories about her drinking from the age of thirteen so... surely she had ruined her brain too.

That wouldn't be worth it. It would feel so satisfying for a moment but not for any longer.

"All done here?" a waiter asked as he paused by our table.

I opened my mouth to reply just as a deafening explosion sounded in my fantasy.

CHAPTER THIRTY-SEVEN

I looked around in fear as dust rained from the ceiling, my eyes finding the path we'd come through, certain that Sterling's people were about to burst out, guns blaring, and kill us both.

Mitch's hand found my arm and he started to pull me towards the archway in the centre of the mural.

"Follow me and keep moving," he said, glancing back over his shoulder.

I started to look back but he began pulling me forwards even harder.

"Is that them?" I asked stupidly, bringing my free hand up to wipe the dust from my eyes. "Did they find us?"

Mitch started to speak before being interrupted by another, smaller explosion.

"Yes," he said quietly, once the noise had died down again, "and they didn't spot the bomb I primed either."

His tone was grim. He clearly wasn't happy with that

even though it would probably slow them down. I hoped it would, I really didn't want to meet them. The idea of them alone scared me, I didn't want to know what they were actually like.

"What do we do?" I asked, my voice rising with panic.

"Keep moving. Hopefully, they'll get lost down here and we'll be able to reach the vault without them getting to us first," Mitch said, slowing down as we reached a fork in the path. "Left. We'll go left."

"Why left?" I asked as he continued to pull me onwards.

"It should bring us further under the island. They'd keep it in the centre, most protected," he told me. "And if not… we'll circle around."

I nodded and glanced back at the path we hadn't taken. It looked the same as the one we rushed down but I still worried. It made sense but it seemed like too big of a risk. If we were wrong, I didn't want to have to go back. How far would this path go? Would the Sterlings get to the fork before we found out if we were going the right way?

"Ah, stop a second," Mitch said.

I stopped immediately as he leaned forwards.

"The margarita pizza?" a waitress asked.

I blinked and looked around, my heart still racing.

"Oh, here, please," I replied, my tone a little breathless.

It sounded like I had been running, but luckily

neither my mom nor the waitress noticed.

"Would you like any parmesan?"

"No, thank you," I said, already slipping back into the fantasy.

"Okay, you need to follow my steps perfectly," Mitch told me.

"Why?" I asked quickly.

Mitch looked down at the floor before looking at me again.

"Some of the stones ahead of us are traps. There are bombs underneath but luckily, the ones we should step on have been worn enough that it should be simple. Do you see?" he asked, leaning to one side so that I could look at the floor past him.

At first, I wasn't sure what he was talking about but then I saw it. Before us, the passageway floor was covered in small square slabs, some of them worn whilst some were still completely flat and untouched.

"Are you sure it's not a trick?" I asked worriedly.

He considered my words for a moment, his head cocking to one side.

"That was a concern that I had," he said with a slight nod, "but I don't think it is. It would be a lot of effort to do that and if you look at the slabs that have been well used, it's not even. Do you see what I mean?"

I looked away from him, squinting at the nearest stone.

I think I understood what he meant. There was a

dent in the middle of it but it wasn't a perfect circle or even properly central.

"I've seen enough traps and enough badly concealed traps. Either they're very good at making this look perfect, which I don't think they are based on the last few things, or it should be an easy journey. Now, follow me," he said, starting to step onto the first stone.

My body tensed as I watched him, certain for a moment that I was about to witness his death but nothing happened. He simply continued along the thin passageway, stepping carefully.

"Do you know where to stand?" Mitch said, prompting me out of my paralysis.

"Oh, yeah. Sorry, I forgot I was meant to be following you," I replied with an awkward smile.

"Don't worry, kid. It happens!"

He continued to watch me as I slowly moved forwards, preparing to start my precarious journey across the booby-trapped corridor.

"Are you enjoying your pizza?" my mom's voice said, cutting through my fantasy.

I was whisked back to reality so abruptly that I almost choked on my mouthful. I swallowed the pizza down, my eyes watering slightly as dizziness threatened to overwhelm me once more.

Nausea wanted to rise within me and the restaurant swam in my vision as I reached shakily for my drink.

"Sorry," I said, finally managing to gain control of

my dizziness. "Yeah, it's really good."

My mom's eyes narrowed suspiciously at me, but she just nodded and continued to eat her pesto linguine.

I chewed in silence for a moment, not wanting to return to Spinalonga so soon. I was probably still trying to transverse the trapped corridor and I didn't want to go back to that. What if I got really dizzy and stumbled, blowing us both up?

No, I had to stay in reality for a little longer.

I didn't mind too much though. The pizza was incredible and the garlic mayonnaise was just how I remembered it. It was so creamy and tangy and garlicky, better than I'd ever found anywhere else. I already knew that it was going to make my breath stink but I didn't care.

My phone buzzed in my pocket again and I fought the urge to react in any way. I really wanted to check it. Intrigue was eating at me even though I knew it was probably just Phoebe. She was probably just hiding in the bathroom to text me about her latest difficulties in France.

I felt so bad for her but it was also kind of funny. I think she was having a good time, which made me feel better about finding it entertaining. She loved the food and she said she was getting on really well with her cousins so that helped, I think.

"How's your food?" I asked, suddenly realising that I hadn't asked my mom about hers.

"It's lovely, thank you. The pesto isn't as salty as it was last time," she said, her nose scrunching delicately.

I almost rolled my eyes at her.

She had complained so much last time we had come to Tony's that the pesto had been unbearably salty, however she had still finished almost all of her pasta, so it couldn't have been that bad. She'd even told the waitress that it had been delicious, so I think she just wanted something to complain about, which she did a lot.

"I'm glad," I said politely.

I felt myself reach out for the fantasy subconsciously, dipping gently back into that world for just long enough to get a glimpse of where I was.

My leg was stretched out, my foot was poised over a stone on the other side of the corridor, but I was too short. I'd have to jump slightly to reach it. Dizziness started to crowd my mind and I withdrew quickly, not wanting for it to hit just as I jumped.

It was too dangerous. I couldn't risk it.

"I'm just going to run to the bathroom," I decided, placing the crust of the pizza slice I had just finished on the plate in front of me.

I'd eaten most of the pizza, more than I normally would, without really realising. My mom had noticed though. I saw her glance at my plate as I slid out of the booth, her lips pursing slightly.

I ignored it though, slipping down the corridor that ran next to the kitchen. I waited until I'd locked the door to the cubicle behind me before pulling out my phone.

It wasn't a message from Phoebe, like I'd expected, it was from Duncan. My eyebrows drew together even as my lips lifted into a smile.

Hey, are you about? read the first text.

Sorry, I know you're in Scotland. Are you around to talk?

I bit my lip before texting back, *Yeah, I'm out for dinner with my mom, but I'm here. Is everything okay?*

I used the toilet whilst waiting for him to reply. Anxiety churned within me as I waited though. I knew that it was probably nothing, he was just bored or drunk or something, but still, I wasn't sure what he was going to say.

I saw him start to type before stopping a few times as I opened the cubicle door and washed my hands.

Yeah, it's all fine. I'm just at a house party and wish you were here. I always have the best time with you.

I paused, glancing towards the door before looking back at my phone and reading the message again.

He was so sweet, but I suspected it was just because he was drunk. I mean, he was sweet when he was sober too, but it wasn't like this. I wasn't sure how to reply. I kind of did wish I was there though, instead of sitting in Tony's with my mom, but I wasn't sure how to tell him. I didn't want to say something cringy that he might misinterpret.

My fingers hovered over the screen as my brain

worked furiously to try and find something I could say to him.

I do too, I typed before hitting send quickly, before I could change my mind.

It didn't feel like enough. I wanted to say more.

Who's throwing the party? I added.

He started typing immediately.

Ella. I'm hiding in the garden because she won't stop trying to get me to play drinking games with her, he'd written.

I snorted softly at that mental picture.

Why don't you want to? I typed before pausing and chewing my lip as I deliberated whether or not to add something else. *She's clearly into you.*

I grimaced as soon as I pressed send, immediately regretting it. It felt so awkward, so uncomfortable. Duncan and I didn't talk about things like that, it always made things weird between us.

I started to type an apology and change the subject, but he was already typing.

Yeah, I know but I've told her a bunch of times that I'm not into her. What else can I do?

I smiled softly and considered what to write. I kind of wanted to know why he wasn't into her. I mean, she was pretty and popular.

I think just keep telling her? Surely she'll get bored and move on soon? I sent instead.

I hope so.

The door swung open and I looked up in fear for a

moment, half expecting to see my mom walking through the door, but it was just some random woman.

I should go back to my mom, I typed.

That's fair, Duncan replied quickly. *I should probably go find another hiding place anyway, I've been out here too long. Text me later?*

I paused before typing back, *Sure*.

Slipping my phone into my pocket once more, I left the bathroom and returned to the table. I tried hard not to look guilty even though I did feel a little bad for spending so long in the bathroom texting Duncan. My mom had even finished her pasta whilst I'd been gone.

"You certainly took your time," she remarked as I slipped into the booth again.

"Yeah, sorry. There was a queue," I lied, the words coming easily.

"Well, I'm not surprised. The bathroom here is too small. I don't understand why they'd only have two cubicles," she said snootily.

"Are you finished with your plates?" a waitress asked, stopping by our table.

"Yes, that was delicious," my mother replied, her tone overly positive again.

"Oh, fantastic. Can I interest either of you in the dessert menu?" she asked.

I saw my mum hesitate before glancing at me.

"What do you think?"

I was taken aback. She didn't normally ask for my opinion on stuff like that, she usually just decided that we didn't want dessert because it wasn't healthy.

"Umm… I'd like to see the menu?" I said unsurely.

I mean, there was no harm in just looking. I didn't have to actually have a dessert. I knew that, if I did, she'd probably comment on it. But I was still tempted.

Also, I didn't care as much as I maybe should have. If she did start talking about it or saying that I'd need to go swimming again tomorrow or something like that, I could just disappear back to Crete.

Once I'd thought about Crete again, I couldn't help but disappear there.

We were in a different place from where we had been last time. We must have crossed the corridor without incident because now, I was padding rapidly down a different corridor.

It was much wider than the last one though, more cavernous. There were even sconces for lanterns embedded in the walls. Most of them held the rotten remains of wooden torches, but that told me we must be close to the treasure.

I sucked in a deep breath, almost too distracted by examining the space around me to notice the dizziness that gripped me. Not quite though, I still did stumble slightly.

"You alright, kid?" Mitch asked, glancing over his shoulder at me.

"Yeah, sorry. Must have caught my foot on a rock or something," I lied.

He glanced at the ground, where there were no stones, before looking up at me.

"I think we're almost there, should be just around this... ah."

He broke off and slowed to a stop.

I did the same, glancing between Mitch and the archway at the end of the corridor that he was staring at.

"What?" I asked before glancing back over my shoulder at the passageway behind us.

There had been no more noise. The Sterlings must have been following us, but I couldn't hear them. Mitch seemed too relaxed too. He was rushing, but he didn't seem panicked or anything.

"That's going to be it," he said.

"How do you know?"

"Just a feeling. There are going to be some traps though, I know it. Wait here."

I waited, watching as he moved forwards slowly, examining the wall and floor as he did.

He seemed to see something interesting because he crouched down. I had to fight the urge to edge towards him or ask him what he was looking at. I didn't want to distract him if it was something dangerous, but I assumed it would be.

"There we go. The desserts are on the back page and the specials are on the board," the waitress said with a smile.

I hesitated, half tempted to ignore her and stay in

Crete, but it felt so rude.

"Thank you," I replied with a smile as my mom took a menu too.

My eyes scanned the desserts before darting towards the specials board. The chocolate brownie sounded good, but so did the cannelloni. I wasn't sure which one I wanted, but I didn't even really think about it, I just blinked back to Crete.

"Ah, there it is. Somehow this gas trap is still primed. How about that, huh?" Mitch said lightly. "The last one was a mess, but this one is still intact."

I opened my mouth to reply, but my mom spoke at that exact minute.

"Well, I don't want anything," she said pointedly to me.

Frustration rushed through me, both at her tone and because I was being pulled back from Crete, making my tone snappier than I meant.

"I'm going to have the cannelloni," I decided.

Confusion washed over my mother's face and I wasn't sure if it was because she just expected me to go along with what she wanted and not have dessert or if it was because of my tone. Guilt churned in my stomach. I didn't mean to snap at her, I just really wanted to know what Mitch was going to do about the gas trap and I really wanted to be there when we saw the treasure.

"Are you sure?" she asked, trying to sound concerned even though her tone was cold. "I know you swam for a while today, but you still ate most of your pizza. I understand you're on your holidays, but that's not an excuse for gluttony."

"I know. I'm still going to have it though," I replied, refusing to react at all.

She seemed surprised, which made victory roar within me even though it was such a small win. I think she knew that I wasn't going to back down though because she glanced down at the menu again before speaking.

"Well, I might have to join you in that case," she said with a tight smile.

"That sounds good."

I felt my hands moving in the fantasy as Mitch handed me something and I started to lift it towards my face.

"Did you decide on a dessert?" the waitress asked as she returned.

"Yes, I'm going to have the cannelloni, please," I said quickly, just in case my mom had planned to say that we didn't want dessert.

It wouldn't surprise me, she'd done that before.

"Great, one cannelloni with cookie dough cream. And, what can I get for you?" she said, looking at my mom.

My mom made a show of looking at the menu, deliberating whether or not she truly did want dessert before sighing.

"I'll have the lemon sorbet," she said finally.

"Great. I'll bring that over soon," the waitress replied.

I handed her my menu and disappeared back to Crete.

For a moment, I was confused by the thing on my face. It took me far too long to realise that I was now wearing a gas mask again. It covered my mouth and eyes, wrapping tightly around my head, making my breath sound far too loud to my own ears.

"Got it?" Mitch said, looking at me expectantly.

I stared at him with wide eyes as I frantically tried to search my memory and work out what he had said but I came back blank.

"Can you repeat that?" I asked, worried that he might refuse or tell me off.

"Of course. Follow what I do and if there is any gas, try and just breathe normally. I assume that it'll be fine and that the gas will be gone by now but if I tell you to do anything, just do it, okay?" he said.

I nodded quickly, my eyes darting past him towards the corridor.

"It'll be okay," he promised.

I nodded again, fear starting to edge into me again, but Mitch simply turned and started down the passage-way carefully.

I tried my best to follow his journey exactly but I felt clumsy. Whilst Mitch's steps were sure, mine were sheepish. I felt like a baby deer, unused to walking. It was embarrassing. We were just walking down a corridor, not anything more strenuous or difficult, but I still felt like I was doing something wrong.

Maybe it was because I was horrifically aware that, at any moment, I could make the wrong step and probably poisonous gas would be sprayed at us. I knew that we were wearing gas masks, but I still worried it would kill us both.

"There you go," the waitress said, shattering my concentration and pulling me back to reality.

I blinked a few times to chase away the dizziness as I stared at the cannelloni that had been placed before me. It looked spectacular. The stack of three golden biscuits were baked to perfection with chocolate chip studded cream at each end. They were cold to the touch and so absolutely delicious that I wasn't even tempted to return to the fantasy where I continued to edge nervously down the corridor.

It wasn't until I had finished all three, ignoring the looks from my mother, that I returned to Spinalonga.

My timing was perfect somehow. Just as I blinked back into the daydream, we reached the end of the corridor. I watched as Mitch checked the archway and the entrance of the room beyond before he turned back towards me.

Most of his face was concealed by the gas mask but I saw wild excitement dancing in his eyes.

"I was right."

CHAPTER THIRTY-EIGHT

I stepped forwards excitedly, wanting to see what Mitch had been right about, but he held up a hand to stop me.

"Wait right there for a minute. I'll quickly check for traps and then you can come in."

I nodded at him, fighting back my impatience as he darted into the room and began searching it quickly.

My skin prickled as I waited. It felt like someone was watching me. I didn't think they were though; it was probably just paranoia. It didn't help that I knew that, somewhere behind me, the Sterlings were making their way through the caves.

I wasn't sure how far behind us they were though. I didn't even know how big the cave system was. I'd flitted in and out of the fantasy too much. I wasn't even sure how long we'd been underground.

Was it still even nighttime? Or was it creeping towards the daytime?

I had no way to tell. I didn't have my phone with me and my watch had run out of batteries whilst we'd been on the boat. It could have been any time.

There was no light down there either. Just the bouncing beam of the touch attached to Mitch's shoulder as he searched the room and turned back to me.

"Alright, I think we're good! Are you ready to discover some treasure?" Mitch called out to me.

I grinned and stepped forwards just as a voice broke through my fantasy.

"Are you finished?" my mom asked.

Irritation flared in me and I refused to return. I couldn't leave Spinalonga just as I was about to find what we'd been searching for.

"Yes," I said in both worlds.

Mitch walked towards me, finishing out another torch from his pocket, as my mother looked around the restaurant for our waitress.

It was weird being in both worlds at once. I was seeing everything that happened in Spinalonga, but also in my world but it looked more distant. It was kind of like I was watching it on a tv screen. I could feel my body move, but I wasn't exactly attached to it. I had no real control over it.

"Ah, could we get the receipt?" my mom called, holding up her hand to get a passing waiter's attention.

He paused, despite being laden down with plates, and said, "Sure, I'll bring that right over."

"Okay, do you want to know what we're looking for?" Mitch asked.

I blinked, pulling myself into that world with some difficulty.

A wave of dizziness hit me but it felt a little detached. It wasn't as severe as it normally was, maybe because I hadn't truly left the world.

"Yes!"

Mitch hesitated, his eyes flitting over my shoulder to scan the corridor outside.

"Start looking through the boxes and the shelves for any scrolls, books or statutes or anything like that. If you do find a scroll or really old book, don't touch it. It'll be really fragile, just call me over and I'll sort it. Sorry, kid," he said with a grimace. "I have a lot of experience with old books."

"That makes sense," I replied.

It did, honestly. I didn't want to be the person who picked up a really old scroll or book and destroyed it. Plus, I was pretty sure that I'd heard somewhere that people have oils on their skin that could ruin old books. I was happy not running that risk.

I swept the torch that Mitch had given me back and forth, my eyes widening as I took in the huge room. There were endless shelves, taller than I was, and made of dark wood. Most of them had crumbled over time, meaning that the artefacts and items that had originally lined them lay in piles.

But that wasn't it. There were also giant wooden crates that sat at the end of some of the rows. They looked like they had been left there in a hurry. Like someone had just dropped the boxes and disappeared.

Confusion hit me suddenly. How would they have gotten the giant boxes through all of the traps? The one closest to me was short but wider than I was. It would have been impossible to carry. There must have been another path, another way in.

"Do you want to start on that side and I'll start on this one, then we can take it one row at a time?" Mitch asked. "One sec, I should put a motion detector and a quick trap down so we have some warning when the assholes show up."

My skin prickled at his words and anxiety churned in my stomach. I watched him dig around in his backpack for a moment longer before rushing towards the side he'd mentioned.

My heart was beating too quickly. I knew that soon, Sterlings people would arrive and then we'd need to either fight or run. I wasn't sure which Mitch would do or even which I wanted him to do. He would want to find what he'd been searching for but... would that be worth risking death?

I reached the far end of the shelf closest to the door and shone my torch at the pile of stuff that had fallen, unsure where to start. I glanced back at Mitch who was placing a small device facing the doorway before looking back at the stuff.

I needed to start sorting through it but, as I moved my torch to get a better look at it, I became horrifically aware of how many spiders lived in the wreckage. It looked like there were hundreds. Well, maybe not hundreds but so many. Too many.

A shudder slipped down my back. I didn't want to touch any of it. But I wanted to help Mitch. I wanted to find what he was looking for before they got to us.

Mitch raced down the row towards me before slowing slightly and chuckling.

"Too many spiders?" he asked, his tone understanding.

I nodded hesitantly, not wanting him to be angry at me. I knew we were in a rush but I could already feel the bugs crawling over my skin and that made me feel horrible.

"Do you want a pair of gloves? They go halfway up your forearms. Well... maybe more for you," he offered, glancing down at my arms.

"Umm... if that's okay?"

"Of course, kid!"

"Are you coming?" my mom demanded.

I started to stand automatically, never really returning to reality fully, and began to follow her from the restaurant, my movements entirely automatic. I was still in Spinalonga, but I could feel myself moving in Tony's.

"Alright, they might be a little big, but they should

stop some of the spiders and creepy crawlies from getting on you. Actually…" He glanced at his shelf for a moment, watching the spiders crawling over the gold statue before nodding to himself. "I'm going to wear some too. It shouldn't be too bad, but I've heard these jumping spiders can bite."

I froze and glanced at the web-coated stuff around us.

The idea of spiders that not only jumped but also bit was so horrible it almost pulled me out of the fantasy. Part of me longed to return to Scotland where I was walking towards the car and half paying attention to Spinalonga, returning only when we had found whatever we were looking for. I couldn't do that though and the desire was little more than a passing whim.

I wanted to do this with Mitch. It was what I had been waiting for. I would not chicken out at the last moment because of some spiders. I needed to be better than that.

I slipped back into the fantasy fully, just as I reached out to pick up the first whole item from the broken shelves. The spiderwebs stretched and snapped as I lifted the delicate white and blue porcelain bowl. Delicate flowers were painted into the low yet wide rim of the bowl and in the centre was a bird. It was unlike any other I'd ever seen before with long thin legs and a ridiculously elaborate tail.

"Ah, that is beautiful," Mitch sighed from behind me.

I turned towards him, still holding the bowl.

He was holding a plate, clearly from the same set as the wreckage in front of me. The design was much busier though. Instead of flowers just around the edge, they spread over the entire plate. As overly elaborate as it was, it was still absolutely stunning.

They almost made the plates that my grandparents had look bad. I mean, their ones were obviously expensive and elaborate too but these were just… stunning.

"I hate that we'll need to leave these here, but they're just too fragile to bring. Sterling's assholes won't see the value of them. I've tried to teach him before that it doesn't need to be expensive to be worth acquiring but no, apparently he's still never learnt. Put that down over here, hopefully, they'll miss it," he said, placing the plate down to one side carefully before glancing out the archway. "We need to keep moving."

I nodded, putting the bowl down before turning back to the shelf. I dug through the rest of the shelf finding nothing more than broken crockery before moving to the next one. Mitch worked quickly behind me, pausing every few minutes to stare out the archway, but still managing to get to the end of the row before I did.

There were countless things, treasures, gold bars even, but nothing similar to books or scrolls. Even the statues I found weren't right.

The noise from the corridor was getting louder too. They weren't approaching just yet, but the distant bangs and explosions were definitely getting closer.

"Next one," Mitch instructed when I finally reached the end.

I nodded, following him around to the next row of shelves. We raced towards the far end of it, pausing only to listen intently.

Those shelves were different. I wasn't sure why, but they were more intact. The items on them were placed further apart which might have helped too. I left the shelf at the far end for Mitch to search through, he was faster than me so it made more sense, and started picking over the items.

There were no plates on that shelf, it was mostly carvings and busts. I was just about to turn towards Mitch and ask him if they were the items he was looking for when I heard him let out a soft laugh, full of disbelief.

I glanced towards the end of the row, terrified that Sterling's people had found us, but there was no one there. I looked back at Mitch, catching the look of pure wonder on his face as he stepped back, staring at the top of the shelf along the back wall.

He shook his head slightly, as if to clear it, before saying, "We've found it, kid. We got it!"

Excitement washed through me and I hurried to his side, staring up at the top shelf. I couldn't really see anything on it, I was too short, but I could tell by Mitch's expression that we'd found something great.

"I knew we'd find it but... damn," Mitch breathed.

I rose up on my tiptoes and craned my head to try and see what he was looking at but I couldn't see anything but the tops of some statues. Excitement and impatience washed through me, tinged with embarrassment. I hated not being able to understand immediately.

"What did we find?" I asked finally.

"Okay," Mitch said, pointing up at the top of the shelf with his torch. "What do you see there?"

I followed the direction of the light, my eyebrows drawing together as I stared.

"Some statues?"

"No, no. Behind the statues. Look at the wall behind the shelf."

I continued to stare blankly.

It just looked like normal stone and I wasn't sure what it was that he wanted me to see. It was exactly the same as every other part of the wall around us.

Wait. No, it wasn't. It was a slight difference, but there was definitely something there. The wall was… darker. It was just a little bit more weathered than the rest of the stone. A portion of the wall, an archway, was a different style. And there was something else. Carved into the rock were letters. Words, maybe? They definitely weren't English, though.

"Can you read it?" I asked, my words coming out hushed.

Out of the corner of my eye, I saw Mitch grin.

"Kind of. I mean, my ancient language knowledge

could do with some more work, but I'm going to take an educated guess based on what I can read and assume it says 'the cure of the soul'. Basically, it means we've found what we're looking for. We just need to get to it."

"What is it? What does it mean? How are we going to get there?" I asked, my questions coming out rushed due to my excitement.

Mitch chuckled softly and began taking items off the shelf in front of us and placing them gently on the floor out of the way.

"Start removing all this stuff, we don't need it. That particular quote was carved into the wall in the reading room of the Library of Alexandria. How much do you know about the library?" he asked, glancing at me.

I wracked my mind but I couldn't think of anything. I recognised the name, I thought, but I didn't know anything else.

I shook my head at Mitch, almost expecting him to judge me, but he just smiled softly and continued talking.

"The Library of Alexandria is one of the largest libraries of the ancient world and the scholars who lived and worked there were from all over the world. It was founded back in two hundred and fifty BC and it was part of a larger group of institutions known as the Mouseion dedicated to the Muses, the goddesses of the Arts. I mean, that's a whole other lesson though. Some people argue that there are three Muses, some say there are nine, it's a whole thing. We'll get into it another time," he assured me.

I nodded, staring at him as I picked up a surprisingly heavy vase and moved it out the way.

I kind of did want to know about the Muses. I didn't know anything about them, except that they were in that Disney movie, but I couldn't remember how many of them there were. I was sure it wasn't nine.

"The person who hired me has been hunting pretty much her whole life for proof that the library wasn't destroyed," Mitch continued. "I mean, of course, it was. People argue that it wasn't actually burnt down by Julius Caesar, but it absolutely was. I've found enough evidence to prove that, I'd say. That doesn't matter though. Do you want to know why?"

He glanced over his shoulder at me and I nodded immediately.

A crash echoed through the room and I froze. Mitch cocked his head before glancing at his smartwatch. Somehow it still had battery even though mine had died.

"Okay, we've still got some time," he muttered, almost to himself. "So, it was burnt down in forty-eight BC by Julius Caesar when he set fire to his own ships to limit Achilles' ability to communicate by sea because the fire spread to the docks. The library was pretty close to the docks because they had a fantastic policy of confiscating all books that came into the ports. They'd make copies and then keep the originals, sending the copied version back to the owners which I think is just incredible. Such a smart thing to do. Oh, be careful with that one!"

Mitch's warning was too late though. The wooden mount of the bust I'd just picked up crumbled, slipping away from the bottom of the statue and crashing onto my foot.

Brief pain shot through me but it wasn't too bad.

"Are you alright?" he asked quickly, taking the statue from me and placing it on the floor, his eyes searching my face.

"Yeah, I'm fine. Sorry, I didn't think that would break," I said sheepishly, worry burning into me.

I'd broken it. It was probably hundreds of years old and I just broke it. Tears burned behind my eyes.

"That's fine, ignore it. Are you okay? Did that hurt? Can you move your foot?" he asked, his hand cupping my elbow to help support me.

"Yeah, it's okay," I said, wiggling my foot and barely feeling any pain. "Let's keep going."

I knew that we couldn't afford to hesitate, we needed to hurry up. Sterling's people were too close.

Mitch continued to examine me for a moment before nodding and turning back towards the shelf again.

"Okay, where was I? Oh yeah, the library burnt down. So, it was a tragedy, the library was a great place but some scholars had already started fleeing because of the geopolitical situation at the time and, interest-ingly, the books appear to already have been removed. The information is a little spotty because of how long ago it was but from what I've learnt, there was an organisation that started at the library. Their core goal was to protect and further knowledge so as soon as there was the hint of scholars and information being purged in one hundred and forty-five BC, they started illegally removing scrolls."

I looked at him in fascination.

"A secret organisation?" I asked.

"Yeah. And I'm sorry I didn't mention them earlier, kid. I've known pretty much since the beginning that we've been chasing them, but I didn't want to tell you, just in case. They're the ones who funded the expedition to Spinalonga. I hid some of the paper from the key, but it said they were transporting some stolen goods that I assume will be behind this shelf. Sorry," he said, seeming genuinely apologetic.

"It's fine," I replied quickly.

I just wanted to learn more about the group and his apology made me uncomfortable. I wasn't used to people saying sorry when they did something or hid something from me, especially not an adult. I mean, my dad apologised for the way my mom acted quite a lot, but she never did.

"From what I can tell, the organisation still exists today. They have their fingers in a lot of pies, mostly research and development, but also education and some other more questionable ventures. They've swept in during a lot of disasters and near misses, always staying in the shadows until necessary. It's been very hard to learn about them even though they're everywhere. They've become a lot more competent than they were back in the time of the library too, that's for sure," he said with a slight shake of his head.

My mind spun and I almost wanted to leave the fantasy and start researching the group myself, even though I wasn't sure where to start. Would they even exist in the real world? If they did, I wanted to join them.

Spending my life protecting and furthering knowledge… didn't sound bad. Actually, more than that, it sounded like a good way to live. I'd actually be contributing to the world, making things better.

"Okay, back to the library," Mitch said, before pausing and listening again. "Nah, I'm hearing things. So, most of the books had already been transferred to the library in the Serapeum of Alexandria by the time it was burnt down. The Serapeum is a temple to the Graeco-Egyptian deity, Serapis, I'll explain that one later too if you don't know about them?"

I shook my head, the weight of all of the things I didn't know feeling a little overwhelming but I couldn't dwell on it long. Mitch had already started explaining again.

"The books stayed at the Serapeum for a little while

but were moved at some point before the temple was destroyed back in three hundred and ninety-one by either a Christian or Roman mob, depending on which report you want to believe. At that point, the group stopped being comfortable staying in Alexandria. They'd mostly been based in the city since their inception but it wasn't safe anymore. Man, I do wish we could go to the Serapeum though, that place is stunning," Mitch said, his tone wistful.

"Oh, really?" I asked.

My mind raced, immediately imagining a grand temple made of marble with Egyptian, Greek and Roman Gods carved into the walls. Stained glass was everywhere, illuminating the inside so beautifully and bathing it in colour.

"Oh yeah. I mean, obviously it's in ruins now, there's only a single pillar standing but the catacombs are great. There's not much to see there unless you want to blow a hole in some of the walls but some great items have been found there! It's pretty much all in museums now though. Well..." he hesitated and sent me a cheeky smile. "It was."

My mouth dropped open.

"It was?" I asked.

"Well, I had a contract to fulfil and the fake was great. I could hardly tell the difference, the museum won't for years! That reminds me, kid. If I'm ever going to break into a museum, I'm leaving you in a hotel somewhere and making sure you have enough money to last a few weeks until I can break out of jail again. Of all of the places I get arrested breaking into, the museums are somehow always the worst. I just don't know what it is. It's like I have some mental block or something with them," he muttered. "Alright, give me a hand removing this shelf."

CHAPTER THIRTY-NINE

I opened my eyes wearily, the sun blinding me as it snuck into the room around the blinds that never quite closed all the way. Confusion washed over me and, for a moment, I didn't know where I was. The room I was in was familiar but at the same time, it wasn't. The half-naked pictures of men and women on the walls were all the same as they'd always been, but they filled me with unease.

Something felt very wrong.

Panic gripped me as I realised that I didn't remember getting home or even going to bed last night. I'd been in Crete with Mitch the whole time.

I sucked in a breath. I'd fallen asleep and left Mitch alone! The Sterlings were approaching quickly and I'd just left him. Of course, he'd be okay, he always was, but it was so irresponsible of me. Anything could have happened there and I wouldn't even know.

I squeezed my eyes shut again, already reaching out

for the familiar dizziness, before hesitating. What if we were running away from the Sterlings and I did something to distract Mitch and he were shot? What if I stumbled because I was dizzy?

No, I needed to go anyway, I couldn't stay away.

"Okay, easy, easy," Mitch muttered to himself.

I stumbled backwards just a little as dizziness shot through me so strongly it hurt. My hand shot out to grab a barely intact shelf, my torch light weaving lazily across the room as I swayed uncontrollably.

But Mitch hadn't noticed. He was standing halfway inside the shelf that we'd been emptying whenever I'd fallen asleep before, the crowbar back in his hands and the tip wedged into the back corner of the shelf.

I blinked hard, my gaze floating in and out of focus for a moment before finally returning to normal as I stared at Mitch. Everything looked almost exactly as it had the night before, to my relief. We must have finished cleaning out the shelf because all of the items were neatly piled along the row, but apart from that, I wasn't sure how much time had passed.

There was something on the floor between Mitch and me too. A weird unrolled tarp or container of some kind. Probably in case we found some scrolls, I realised slowly, sleepiness making me dumb.

A bang came from behind us and my head whipped around. I almost expected to see the people in black tactical gear creeping towards us but the noise had come from further away. They weren't there for now.

"Okay, you ready, kid? This is stiffer than I thought so if anything falls, cover your head and try to dodge it, okay?" Mitch called softly.

"Yeah," I answered quickly.

"If this breaks and ruins anything on the other side, I swear to god, I will be so sad," he muttered before I saw him push all of his weight onto the crowbar.

At first, it looked like nothing was happening. There was no change or any sign that what Mitch was doing was working but then a loud crack split the room. He didn't even hesitate, he just continued levering the door further open.

Before long, he abandoned the crowbar, throwing it to the floor and squeezing himself into the gap. Bracing himself in the space, he slowly managed to get the fake wall all the way open.

I edged forwards, trying desperately to see into the gap behind the shelf, despite Mitch having told me to stay back, but I couldn't see anything around him. Instead, I settled for staring at his back, trying to work out if he had found what he wanted. He wasn't moving much as he slowly seemed to survey the space. My heart pounded in my ears as I waited and fear started to creep into me. What if there was nothing there? What if the space had been raided years ago and this was all for nothing?

A loud knock startled me and I looked around fearfully.

"Are you still asleep?" my mother asked.

I pulled myself out of the fantasy, my hands gripping my duvet as nausea washed over me.

"No, I'm awake," I said, blinking hard.

"Good, because it's almost ten. I understand that you're on holiday, but that doesn't give you the excuse to sleep the day away," she chided.

"I know," I replied, trying not to completely lose sight of what was happening in Crete.

There was a pause and I saw Mitch start to step back before my mom spoke again, distracting me.

"Are you not going to get up now?" she demanded.

"Yeah," I said, looking away from her and staring around the room, frantically looking for an excuse to be by myself for a bit and not be distracted by anyone.

My gaze fell on my swimming costume, still hanging on the radiator, but I knew that wasn't good enough. Someone could walk into the pool at any moment and start talking to me. Plus, I was still a little worried about drowning whilst in a fantasy.

If I were to drown whilst in Crete with Mitch, would I just die in real life and stay there? I wasn't quite sure what happened after death but if that were to happen, I wouldn't be too upset about it.

No, I couldn't do that. But I could go out for a run. The grounds around the house were lovely. I could go for a run through the forest and no one would bother me.

"Actually, I was going to go for a run before lunch," I said brightly, sitting up and smiling.

My mom looked a little taken aback by my sudden happiness. Suspicious crossed her face.

"Without having breakfast?" she questioned.

"Yup, I'm not really hungry today. I probably just ate too much yesterday," I lied, hoping that my stomach wouldn't choose that exact moment to grumble.

Luckily, it didn't.

"Alright," my mom said, still eyeing me suspiciously. "Have a good run and don't go too far out of the grounds."

"I won't," I lied again.

She nodded, watching me for a moment longer before leaving my room.

I hurriedly got up, already slipping back to Crete as I grabbed my running clothes.

"Is it there?" I was asking as I returned.

"Oh yeah," Mitch said with a huge grin, turning back towards me.

Another crash came from outside and the grin slipped from his face. His eyes darted towards the door before he checked his watch.

"Alright, kid," he started softly. "I'm going to start loading some things into my bag and making sure they're waterproofed. We're going to be leaving through the other passageway. It's not the nicest way to go and I didn't want to use it but I think it's the only way. Turn your torch off, I need you to keep an eye on the door and take this. It's semi-automatic so just point and shoot until you run out of bullets."

He took a gun out of the holster on his leg and held it out to me, handle first.

I took it with shaking hands, handing back my torch so that I could hold the gun properly.

"You want me to... shoot them? The Sterlings?" I asked.

It suddenly felt too real. I knew this was coming, I knew it was inevitable, but it was still terrifying.

What if I hit someone and killed them? It was just a fantasy, of course, but it would change how I thought about myself. I would become someone who could kill.

"No!" Mitch answered quickly. "You don't need to aim at them. Just point roughly in their direction and pull the trigger. It doesn't matter if you hit them or not. The chances of you actually getting a good shot on them are very low."

Somehow, his words did not reassure me.

I nodded anyway. I needed to do it. I couldn't just let the Sterlings attack us.

"Should I... Should I go to the end of the row?" I asked, glancing around.

"No, there's no need. Just find a part of the shelves where the back has crumbled away and you can see through to the door," he instructed.

I nodded and started to walk away from him, my eyes

scanning the shelves around us. I didn't need to go far, however. In many places, the wooden shelves had crumbled to nothingness.

I stopped, squinting through the gap and making sure I could see through to the door before lifting the gun slightly. It felt weirdly heavy in my hands.

"You got a good position, kid?" Mitch asked as he moved carefully back towards the tarp on the floor, an old crumbling paper in his gloved hands.

I hadn't even noticed him put the gloves on but the gloves were a pristine white plastic.

"Yeah," I said, snapping my gaze away from it to glance at the door again.

Still nothing.

"Okay, good. I'll try and be as quick as I can here and then we'll head to the port entrance," he said, bending down slowly and laying the scroll between two layers of thick plastic gently. "I'm going to warn you now though, kid. Lauren said that way is real bad."

"What do you mean?" I asked anxiously, unable to look away from the door.

"It used to be a port, back in the day, so it's open to the elements, but there was a rockslide at some point since then. I'm not sure if it was intentional or not, but she said it's almost entirely blocked the way. Lauren's cleared it out best she can and left the scuba gear in the opening but... apparently, the smell is... significant."

My nose crinkled up and I felt fresh air hit me in

the face. It took me a moment to realise that I'd left the house in real life and began walking toward the back of the gardens where the forest started.

"How bad is it?" I asked Mitch's retreating form as he raced back into the secret room.

"I mean… have you ever smelt a beached whale? You know, once the rot has really set in?" he asked as he returned with another disintegrating paper.

I wasn't sure how old the parchment was or if it was actually from the Library of Alexandria or just a more modern recreation but it looked really old.

"No," I answered.

"Well then, today should be a fun experience for you. There's no whale carcass there but… apparently, from the smell of it, you'd think there was."

My stomach clenched slightly in anticipation of the smell. I wasn't sure what to expect but I knew it would be bad.

"Alright, a couple more things and then we should be good to go. As much as it's going to pain me walking away from this place and leaving some of this behind, I've got the photos. Plus, Sterling won't keep all of this. It'll show up in auctions in a few years," Mitch said, starting to walk out of the room before pausing, having spotted something. "Oh, this though. I'm not leaving you behind, beautiful."

I looked away from the door, trying to work out what object he was crooning at, but it looked just like any other scroll. I wasn't sure what was so special about it, but I wanted to know.

Mitch had started to bend down, the scrolls clutching in his hands, but he paused. His gaze snapped to his watch.

I froze, my eyes returning to the door. We were out of time. It was too late, the Sterlings were approaching.

We needed more time though. Mitch hadn't finished loading the stuff into his bag and the waterproof wrap was still open.

I glanced back at him uncertainly. His stance hadn't changed but he'd placed the scrolls on the floor and had reached for his thigh. Slowly, he pulled another gun out and placed it on the floor next to him.

"Once they're in range, the electric trap I put down should buy us a little time. If you see them come through the door, start shooting," he breathed.

Anxiety and fear threatened to overwhelm me, making my hands shake and my knees weak, but I nodded.

I had to do this.

I brought the gun up to point through the hole, my chest tight. Part of me was excited though. I had wanted action and adventure, I'd wanted to feel like a character from one of my books and now, I basically was one. We had discovered proof of a secret organisation that protected knowledge and stole things from the lost Library of Alexandria, we had found scrolls maybe from the library. Everything had been building up to this point and now that I was there, I was terrified.

Then I heard them.

Footsteps in the corridor outside. Many of them, people running towards us. Their steps echoed. I ripped my eyes away from the door, needing to check on Mitch. He was carefully layering the papers on top of the plastic, making sure that nothing was overlapping before laying another sheet down.

I swallowed and looked back at the door.

The footsteps were getting louder. They'd be at the door soon. Why hadn't Mitch's trap worked? He said that it would buy us some time, so why hadn't it gone off? Was it broken? Or had he set it up wrong?

"Halt!" a voice shouted from outside, but they were too late.

A fizzing noise ripped through the air and I felt the hair on my arms stand on end as a bright light erupted from a small box in front of the door. I squeezed my eyes shut as lights burst in front of them, so bright and disconcerting that I was forced back to reality.

I stumbled, dizziness making the barely trodden path unsteady under my feet, before pushing myself to return to Crete. I stepped away from the shelves, my vision still hazy as shouts tore through the air.

"Get ready to run, kid," Mitch said, his voice almost blocked out by the noise. "I'm almost done."

I couldn't look away from the door though, I knew they were close.

The shouts slowly died down and I heard someone's voice speaking over the noise.

"Scan for more traps," she called. "That was too modern, it was placed by him!"

There was a moment of silence, occasionally broken by soft snuffling coming from the doorway, before I heard movement from Mitch.

This time, I did look away from the door.

Mitch had lifted another small box out of his bag, similar looking to the electric trap he'd placed near the door, and was loading everything else in. He slowly closed the zip before glancing up at me.

I looked away from him quickly, knowing that I needed to be staring at the door. I needed to be ready for when the Sterlings appeared.

There was a soft rustling noise again, moving closer to me this time.

"Alright, kid. What's going to happen now is we're going to make a run for it. Move slowly towards the end of the row, I'll go in front of you, and keep an eye on the door. They might find the other trap, but it's only a little one so I'm not sure. Either way, I'll set it off when we're in position. Once we get to the end, I'll prime this one and set it off to fill this place with smoke and then we run. How does that sound?" he breathed so softly I barely heard him.

I nodded, not trusting myself to be able to speak quietly enough.

"Okay, start moving. When we make a break for it, I want you to go first. My backpack is lined with kevlar and some other stuff so it should keep me fairly protected," he said.

I nodded again, wanting to disagree but not being able to.

He started to slip past me, his steps soft. I followed him, trying to peer through the broken shelves as much as possible whilst also trying to keep an eye on the floor and make sure I didn't kick any of the many rocks and broken pieces of wood there.

After what felt like an eternity, we stopped. Mitch slowly started to duck down, placing the trap out into the path just as the first person came through the door. I started to lift my gun but Mitch shook his head at me.

I stopped, holding the gun awkwardly as the guy who'd walked into the room looked around. Mitch still didn't move though. He seemed to be waiting for something.

Slowly, he lifted his arm, his other hand joining it and resting on his smartwatch. I looked away, glancing back at the man who was standing in the doorway, searching for bombs. How had he not seen the explosive on the floor or the one Mitch had put out next to our row? It felt so obvious to me.

"I think it's safe," the guy called.

That must have been what Mitch was waiting for because suddenly, smoke shot out from the small box, hidden behind a rock in the corner of the doorway. Thick white clouds burst to life from several of the rows. I hadn't even seen Mitch place the smoke bombs down, but he must have done.

Mitch didn't move as the room quickly filled with smoke and shouts again. He waited until the smoke was thick before his hand closed on my arm and he started dragging me towards the back of the room.

"I heard footsteps," someone behind us shouted, their tone victorious.

But Mitch was already pushing me to go fast.

"Keep going," he said, his voice barely audible over the noise. "I'm going to drop some smoke grenades."

His grip on my arm disappeared and I did my best to keep running straight towards the archway at the back of the room. It was hard. Even though the smoke was thinner towards the back of the room where we were, it still was so thick that I was basically running blind.

A heavy thunk followed by a hissing noise came from behind me before a hand closed on my arm again, pulling me slightly to the left.

"Almost there, kid," Mitch said. "We'll stop just out of the room so I can check the path for traps."

I scrambled to keep up with him whilst also listening to the noise behind us.

They seemed to be searching through the room for us still, seemingly not realising where we were or even that we were running away. I was glad. It felt like at any moment, someone would realise and they'd start to chase us.

I hoped that wouldn't happen though.

"This way," Mitch muttered, pulling my arm just in time as I crashed into the edge of the doorway.

I hadn't even seen it until just a millisecond before and if Mitch hadn't pulled me, I would have run face first into it, rather than just hit it with my arm.

"Stop here, are you okay?" he asked, glancing at me for just a moment.

Pain shot through my arm and I knew that it would be bruised if it had happened in real life, but I was okay. I tightened my grip on the gun, glancing back over my shoulder at the smoke-filled room. "I'm fine," I said quickly.

"Okay, good. Wait here whilst I check this and if they start shooting, shoot back. You don't need to aim, just fire. I just want you to scare them, that's all. The more scattered the better," he muttered, already crouching down and examining the floor of the cave.

I turned away from him, staring blindly back into the smoke filled room. My heart pounded and my hands felt slick as I squeezed the gun harder, bringing my finger to rest on the trigger.

I didn't want to shoot the gun, despite a hint of morbid curiosity. I didn't want to hit someone or kill them. I just wanted to be able to escape with Mitch and get to wherever we were going after this so that we could examine all of the things that he'd taken.

But I had to. I wanted to live out something like the adventure books I read and there was never an easy escape in those. They always had daring getaways, filled with gunfire and excitement. I thought that was what I wanted but now that I was actually in there, I just wanted to get away.

I could have just left. I could have blinked back to reality where I was running through the forest and just come back when we were somewhere safe but I couldn't leave Mitch.

"There!" a voice cried from somewhere too close to us.

Gunfire erupted from the room behind us, the noise much louder than I expected. My ears rang and I lifted the gun, pointing it towards where I thought the room was. My finger tightened on the trigger and bullets exploded from the gun, shaking my arms and making me almost stumble.

CHAPTER FORTY

After what felt like too long, Mitch's hand clasped my shoulder, gently pulling me away. I turned, lowering the gun shakily, and let Mitch drag me down the corridor. I ran numbly, barely paying attention to the clunks and bangs coming from Mitch as he alternated dropping grenades and shooting at the people following us.

He must have let off another smoke grenade, because it was getting harder to see in the passageway we were in. I wasn't even sure how he was navigating, but he was managing just fine. He barely even stopped or paused.

I'd shot a gun. I might have killed someone and I didn't know. I would never know. There was no way to find out and, although I knew it wasn't real, it still shook me.

Another smattering of gunfire came from Mitch and I forced myself to focus on what was happening despite the fear that was still coursing through me. I couldn't think about the fact that I'd potentially killed someone, I needed to pay attention and keep running. Mitch could get shot if I didn't and I couldn't let that happen.

"Left!" Mitch ordered under his breath and I rushed to follow his direction.

My heart was pounding in my chest, a stitch burning in my side, but I pushed myself to keep moving. We turned down another corridor, footsteps chasing us, and I kept expecting Mitch to stop us to check for traps, but he didn't.

It felt like we were weaving down endless corridors, a maze under the island, but I was suddenly hit with a smell. It was so horrifically strong, so nauseating.

The rancid scent of rotting fish assaulted me, causing bile to immediately rise in my throat. I swallowed it down, trying so hard to keep running, but the stench was worse than anything I had ever smelt before. I slapped a hand to my nose, trying to block it out, but it somehow still found a way in.

It was almost like I could taste it.

"Almost there!" Mitch insisted but I could barely see.

The smell was making my eyes water and blinding me. It drew all of my attention away from everything else that was happening. I couldn't focus on anything other than the festering stink.

I gagged again just as Mitch's hand shot out and pulled me to a stop. He dropped my arm and I blinked quickly, looking around. The smell was still horrific, but I knew that I needed to keep an eye on the corridor behind us.

Wiping the tears from my eyes, I blinked quickly, trying to clear my vision as I turned but immediately I saw the black-clothed Sterlings emerge around the corner far behind us. A shout went up just as Mitch stood and grabbed my arm again.

"Keep going!"

I started moving as fast as I could, my feet pounding against the stone floor, and I could feel myself running faster in real life too. Branches whipped against my arms as I ran too close to them down the thin, barely used paths, but I didn't care. I just had to keep moving.

The smell was getting worse the closer we got to wherever we were going. I should have expected it but I didn't. It was horrific and burnt into my nostrils, showing no signs of subsiding.

We turned one final corner and slowed.

The corridor ahead of us was blocked. The roof had collapsed in, stones and boulders scattered over the floor. There was no way forwards.

"Climb," Mitch ordered, pressing a torch into my hands again.

I looked at him, concern shooting through me. I couldn't see a way through and it seemed too risky to try. The stones were unsteady and the Sterlings were fast approaching.

But we couldn't just stand there. I trusted Mitch,

he'd been right every time before, so I quickly started picking my way over the stones, slipping on them, and trying my best not to fall. It was hard to balance on such uneven ground with the gun still clutched in one hand and the torch in the other. I was so worried that I'd fall and accidentally shoot Mitch even though I kept my finger far from the trigger.

A stone tipped under my foot and my ankle rolled. I started to fall but I dropped the gun, my hand finding the rough wall instead. The wall scratched my palm as my fingers scrabbled to find a grip. It was just enough to stop me from falling fully and I quickly jumped forwards onto a more sturdy-looking rock, ignoring the pain in my ankle and the stinging in my hand.

"You alright?" Mitch asked from just behind me.

I glanced back at him for just a moment, seeing his huddled form as he ducked to stop himself from hitting the ceiling, before looking back in front of me.

"Fine," I lied.

I was mostly fine. The pain was receding, leaving just a faint throbbing in my hand, but it didn't matter. I had just seen the way out. There was a gap in the rocks ahead and I was pretty sure we'd be able to slip through.

"Okay. Leave the gun there," Mitch said, "Just keep moving."

I nodded, my gaze fixed on the hole ahead of us.

I had to get there before the Sterlings rounded the corner. We were too out in the open, too vulnerable.

If they started shooting at us, they wouldn't be able to miss.

It felt like the footsteps were too close to us. They echoed in the tunnel, making it hard for me to actually work out where they were.

I climbed up the slope of fallen rocks towards the hole, the stones slipping under my feet and making me feel unsteady, until finally, I reached it. The hole was small, barely big enough for me to fit through and so high up that I had to just dive through it and hope for the best.

I was already hauling myself through it when I realised how stupid that was. My hands grabbed at the loose stones on the other side, trying to catch myself. There was too much of a drop though, the slope too steep, and I fell hard.

I hit the ground, the breath knocked out of me, and blinked in the sudden brightness. Confusion hit me at the same time as pain and I stared around the forest.

Pain shot through my hands and I was lying face down on the forest floor. I lifted my hands, tears springing to my eyes as I stared at the blood slowly oozing from them. It was surprise more than pain that was making me cry, but it did still hurt.

Rolling over, I wiped my hands together, trying to get rid of some of the attached twigs and leaves before pushing myself up. Even as I cried, I knew I had to return to Crete. I had to get back there.

"Are you alright, kid?" Mitch asked as he climbed much more skilfully through the hole, managing to land on his feet somehow.

Embarrassment washed through me as I climbed up from the slimy ground.

"Yeah, I'm fine," I said, breathing deeply and trying to stop myself from crying.

Mitch's face was concerned and he shone the torch over me.

"Are you sure? Your hands are bleeding!"

He took one of my hands in his, examining my scraped palms. He was gentle despite the urgency of the situation. Footsteps were racing towards us still.

It felt weird. Having someone care for me like that set me on edge and somehow made it harder for me to stop crying. It wasn't what I was used to. If I got injured in real life, I just dealt with it. My mom wouldn't care unless it was really bad and not even then sometimes.

"It's fine," I said, taking my hand back and wiping my eyes with the back of my hands.

Mitch glanced back through the hole before nodding.

"Okay, I'm sorry we can't stop and sort them out now, but we will as soon as we get to the plane. Here, get this on and put the respirator in," he said, hefting an oxygen pack off the ground and holding it out to me.

I turned, putting my arms into the straps he was holding, and tried not to stumble as he slowly lowered the weight onto me before passing me a weighted belt.

I turned back towards him, watching as he checked the dials and handed me the goggles. I wiped my nose with the back of my hand before putting them on and slotted the respirator into my mouth, biting down on the rubber.

Mitch dropped a pair of flippers onto the floor in front of me and I slipped my feet into them before looking up at him uncertainly. He'd already strapped his backpack to his chest and was pulling the oxygen tank into place.

"Alright, kid. Put this around your wrist," he said, holding out a strap to me.

It looked a bit like the kind of thing a kid would have to wear so that they didn't run away from their parents.

I looked down at it in confusion before sliding it onto my wrist and doing the Velcro up.

"You're going to go first so you'll need your torch back. Here," he picked it up off the ground and handed it to me before picking up a spear gun, "and this will stop you from getting too lost. Lauren's attached a guide rope down there too which should help. Okay, let me just trigger this."

I watched silently, tears still slowly leaking from my eyes and the plastic torch feeling skippering in my hands, as he typed something on a small device that was attached to his oxygen pack.

"That should do it. Go on, the rope has enough slack and I've got a few more tricks up my sleeves here," he said.

I nodded hesitantly as he started to pull another grenade off his belt and turned towards the hole in the ground.

Once I had goggles and a respiratory in, I couldn't smell it but looking at the green slime-covered rocks and dark hole in the floor was terrifying. I couldn't see much under the water, just murky water. I didn't want to go near it, but I knew I had to.

I started towards it, feeling the rope between me and Mitch trailing between us, and stared down into the hole. Even shining my light into it didn't help.

Gunfire roared behind us, slamming into the rocks that separated us from the Sterlings and I turned back.

Mitch threw himself to the side, shielding himself behind the bigger and more protective rocks before looking at me and calling, "Go, kid!"

I nodded, panic overriding my reluctance to get into the water, and I started to climb down the slope. It was uneven, worn away from the tide lapping at it for years and I was quickly in up to my waist.

I glanced back for just a moment, seeing Mitch throw multiple grenades through the hole before he whirled around and started rushing towards me.

"Go!" he called again.

I dove forwards, flinging myself into the water and paddling forwards as the water got too deep to stand. Just before my head dipped under the surface, I heard a thud followed by a skidding noise.

Fear pounded through me in time with my heartbeat as I swan deeper into the dark cavern. What if Mitch had been shot and I'd heard him fall? Then, I'd just left him. Sterling's people would find him and kill him if he wasn't already dead. And what would happen to me? I wouldn't be able to get to the plane or whatever we were going to without him. Not that I'd even want to. I didn't want to stay in this fantasy without Mitch.

So, I had to believe that he was still alive. That the noise I'd heard wasn't him falling, it was just him… kicking some rocks as he ran towards the water. That made more sense, right? There were a bunch of loose stones on the ground and it was so unsteady, of course he would have stumbled. That's what had happened, it had to be.

Not really. But I needed to believe it. Plus, there was that wall of rocks between Mitch and the Sterlings so it was unlikely that a bullet would have even been able to get through. Although, maybe one had. They'd been shooting at it a lot. What if they'd somehow managed to wear some away and a bullet had gotten through?

I couldn't help it. I couldn't keep swimming and not look back. One hand shot out to grasp the guide rope and I turned as much as I could in the narrow tunnel, contorting my body and searching for Mitch. My torch light quickly found him right behind me and, with a sign of relief, I turned back and continued swimming.

It was easier, once I knew that Mitch was alive, but

not by much. The tunnel was dark and the light from the torch only reached so far. I kept expecting to run into a wall or a dead end or for some horrific creature to suddenly appear and attack me.

That thought almost made me pause. I was bleeding. My hands were still bleeding. I could feel it every time I touched the rope, the slight sting of my cut palms.

What if there were sharks in Crete?

I was bleeding and everyone knew that sharks could smell blood from like a mile away. What if they attacked? Mitch had a harpoon gun but that wouldn't do much, surely. We wouldn't be able to fight them all off.

Or what about other creatures? Sharks probably weren't the only animal that could eat a person in the sea. What if there were other ones there?

Part of me was tempted to leave the fantasy, disappear back to Scotland and quickly google if there were sharks in Crete, but I couldn't. I was too terrified that I'd return in the midst of a shark attack or something. I couldn't leave. I wouldn't let myself.

I was somehow both relieved and more scared when I burst out of the seaweed-encrusted cave entrance and emerged into the sea. I looked around, frantically swinging my torch from side to side in an attempt to try and spot any of the dangerous fish or animals that could be swimming towards us.

I couldn't really see anything. It was still too dark and the torchlight just stretched out into the empty water. I could only vaguely see the light of the surface far above us. What time even was it? A hand touched my leg and I whipped around as quickly as I could, my heart racing.

Mitch was floating behind me, both hands held up reassuringly. Relief washed through me and I waved at him awkwardly. He returned the wave before pointing forwards. I nodded at him before turning and swimming in the direction that he pointed.

He swam next to me, checking behind us frequently for the Sterlings. They couldn't follow us though. There had only been two oxygen tanks down there, one for Mitch and one for me. They wouldn't have been able to make it through the collapsed cave and out the other side without one.

But then, there had to be more of them about. They wouldn't have only sent one team, they were better than that, I assumed.

Just as that realisation hit me, I saw movement. My head whipped to the side as quickly as I could underwater and I squinted at the distant vague movement. I could see things or maybe people floating in the water near what I assumed was a boat. I closed the distance between me and Mitch and tapped his arm, pointing as subtly as I could at the people.

He glanced at them before looking back at me and shaking his head. Confusion washed through me, but I didn't know how to communicate that to Mitch. We were underwater, I couldn't exactly just ask him and the basic scuba diving training we'd done didn't cover anything more than simple communication.

I lifted my arms in an exaggerated shrug, hoping to convey my confusion.

He glanced at the two people who were sinking slowly lower before looking back at me. He pointed at them before raising one hand in an 'okay' gesture, holding it for a moment before pointing back in the direction we'd been swimming in and then tapping his watch.

He was clearly trying to say that the people weren't Sterling's and that we needed to hurry up and get to wherever we were going, but I was still confused. I repeated the gesture back to him before starting to swim again.

I kept an eye on the two people as we swam, trying not to be too obvious about it, just in case, but I wasn't sure what was happening. They just seemed to be swimming slowly lower, holding hands. After a minute, they stopped and faced each other. They seemed to be communicating and soon, one of them lifted a hand to their bikini bottoms and began slowly lowering them.

My eyes widened and snapped forwards as the other person began to remove their swimming trunks.

Mitch had said that there were swingers about, but... I hadn't expected them to actually get in the water.

But then there was movement even closer to us. A woman, already naked apart from a scuba tank, was pulling her partner deeper under the water. They were so close to us and the light from the boat above lit up the water making it very clear what she and her lover were doing.

I fought to look away, embarrassment coursing through me. I couldn't believe that some people were doing that, so close to us. They didn't even seem to notice that we were there, or maybe they just didn't care.

I kept my eyes pointing straight ahead as my heart pounded. There were so many people in the water with their partners and we were just swimming through it. It was overwhelming and kind of scary. Surely it was too dangerous. The Sterlings would be following us or they could be watching us right then.

But... how would they see us with so many other people underwater too? Not everyone was entwined with their partner, some were just swimming like we were.

It was genius. With so many people in the water, the Sterlings wouldn't be able to distinguish us from the others. And surely they wouldn't risk just shooting people at random, right?

I wasn't sure, but the thought made me swim even faster.

A huge shadow and the hull of a ship appeared in the distance and I glanced at Mitch. He didn't change our direction at all. That must be our target.

I continued swimming forwards, keeping my eyes fixed on the boat and not looking at the many naked people in the water around us. My face felt hot, even underwater, and every time I breathed, the bubbles sounded so loud.

My stomach hurt. I was so self-conscious and conscious of everything that was happening around us that my stomach physically hurt, but luckily we reached the boat before long.

Mitch tapped my arm as we approached the shiny ladder that hung into the water and pointed to himself, then the ladder. I was pretty sure he was trying to tell me he would go up first so I nodded to him before hastily doing another okay symbol with my hands.

He returned it before taking hold of the ladder and starting to climb.

I hesitated, watching him climb before shooting a furtive glance towards the nearest couple who were flailing together. I looked away quickly, staring up at the ladder and realising that Mitch had reached the top. I quickly started climbing, my face flushing even darker. I really didn't want Mitch to think I was snooping or watching the couples underwater.

Emerging from the water was surprisingly hard. The tank on my back threatened to drag me down into the depths but Mitch's hand found mine and he hauled me up out of the water with a soft grunt.

"You alright, kid?" he asked softly.

"Yeah," I said, staring past him at the huge yacht we were now on.

"Andrew!" a voice called.

Mitch straightened, turning in the direction of the man.

"James," he replied in a deep, smooth voice. "It's been a while."

CHAPTER FORTY-ONE

Mitch buttoned his wet vest quickly as the man closed the distance between them.

"It really has, how have you been?" James asked. "Take that gear off so I can see you properly!"

The dark-haired man finally reached Mitch and kissed him on the cheek before embracing him tightly.

"I've been well, how about you? I can see your business is still booming!" Mitch said as he undid his scuba gear and placed it into a box full of other gear before moving his bag back onto his back.

I spat my respirator out, taking a deep breath of fresh air, and pulled my goggles off. The air tasted weird after using the oxygen tank for what felt like a long time. It was too salty.

"Ah, have you been keeping track of me? Well, I wouldn't mind if you have been! I'm fantastic. Time has been kind to you, Andrew!" James said, pulling back finally. "You've aged like a fine wine, I don't know how you do it."

"Ah," Mitch said. "You've aged well yourself! You don't look a day older than the last time I saw you."

James laughed, the noise rich and melodic.

"Well, with the amount I've spent on botox and surgery since then, I would hope not! What a thrill it was to get your call, even if it was just for use of my boat, but you know I can never say no to a good party! Despite your insistence that I keep it behind closed doors until after you've left..." James said, trailing off with a pout.

Mitch laughed lightheartedly.

"I know, it was a disappointment for me too, but I need to try and do right by the kid."

James' face lit up and he finally looked away from Mitch for long enough to glance at me.

"This must be her. I didn't know you had a daughter," he said, scrutinising me.

I felt my face flush under his gaze. I didn't know who that man was or why Mitch had given him a fake name, but I saw the way his hand lingered somewhat possessively on Mitch's arm.

Mitch chuckled easily.

"Me either! Imagine my surprise when I got a call from an ex thirteen years later and then Faith came to live with me," he said, smiling back at me. "Do you need a hand with your gear?"

I nodded at him, trying to look a little uncertain, and

undid the clips, turning around so that Mitch could lift it from my back and put it in the box too. I kicked my flippers off and put them in the box too, watching the man. I wanted to look like I was really Faith, a kid who was dumped on a father she didn't know after however many years. He'd said thirteen though. How old did he think I was? Or, was it just an act?

I couldn't actually remember if I had ever told him how old I was. Surely I had? It probably came up at some point, but I just couldn't remember.

Or maybe he was doing it on purpose. I mean, he had lied about both of our names, maybe he was lying about my age too so that we were even less traceable.

"You know, I do see it! She looks just like you," James said with a smile at Mitch before looking back at me. "It's lovely to meet you, Faith."

"It's nice to meet you too," I replied with an awkward grin.

"I like to think we look pretty similar too," Mitch told the man. "Did my transport get here alright?"

"Yes, yes. You know that Hannah would never disappoint you!" James said, gesturing with his head further into the boat.

They turned and started towards the stairs leading up to the rest of the boat and, for the first time, I got the chance to look around at the boat we were on.

My mouth fell open.

I could tell from underneath the ship that it was big,

but I hadn't expected it to be that huge. It was the largest and fanciest-looking ship I had ever seen in my life. It made the one that Mitch and I had been on the night before look tiny.

I stared at the small platform that James had been waiting for us on, taking in the comfortable-looking chair and half-empty glass of champagne resting on the table next to it, before following them up the stairs.

"Now, now, Alistair," James chided from in front of me, blocking the view of whoever he was telling off. "Remember what I said about keeping communal spaces appropriate and clean until I make the announcement. There's a child on board this ship now, we need to protect her innocence!"

My face flushed as James stepped aside, revealing the tanned man who was reclining on the sofa. One arm was wrapped around a woman, the other frozen in the act of unbuttoning her shirt.

He looked at me before sighing heavily, his hand falling away from her as his head dropped back against the sofa.

"Come now, James!" he complained in a thick accent. "She's barely a child!"

James' eyes narrowed.

"I would appreciate you not questioning me whilst you are on this boat," he said coldly.

Alistair's head snapped up and I saw his throat bob as he swallowed.

"Of course! I was merely saying that the girl looks older, not questioning you. I would never," he insisted.

James' smiled at him, seemingly enjoying the grovelling.

"Good. See to it that you don't. Now, Andrew, your helicopter awaits," he said, warmth returning to his smile, and gestured further into the boat.

Mitch nodded to him and we began following him along a corridor, past the bar where a black-suited waiter stood. I smiled at him politely, before sending a furtive glance out the large glass window that lined the corridor. I could see multiple ships around the area, most of them well lit which made them seem fairly innocent.

Well, not innocent, I knew what was happening on the boats, but it seemed unlikely that the Sterlings would have such a bright boat too. Unless they were trying to blend in.

They could be on any one of those boats.

A loud moan sounded from one of the rooms as we walked passed, almost drowned out by a rhythmic banging and I felt my eyes widen. My face felt hot and I found myself glancing at Mitch and James, trying to see if they could hear it too. They must have been able to, it was so loud, but they didn't react in any way.

"You know," I heard James say, "you really must join us next time. It was so fun last time you attended one of my little parties."

Mitch grinned at him.

"Ah, it was, but I'm a father now. It makes it harder for me to attend," he lied.

"We have a children's boat!" James said. "Really, you must stay. Even just for an hour or two."

"I wish I could," Mitch told him. "But unfortunately, we need to get out of here."

James sighed loudly.

"I assume that means I will be having company soon?"

"Most likely. They shouldn't bother you for too long though," Mitch said. "And I owe you one."

James looked over his shoulder at Mitch, his expression flirtatious.

"You owe me at least three or four at this point," he said. "Maybe even five or six."

Mitch chuckled.

"Four," Mitch countered.

"I'll accept that." He stopped just in front of a door and turned back towards us. "Hannah's just through here, but unfortunately, I shall leave you here. I have matters to attend to and I assume Alistair did not take heed of my warning."

He glared down the corridor over my head.

"Ah, go easy on the poor man," Mitch said to him, resting a hand on his arm. "He looks like he's new to this whole thing."

"He is, but that's not an excuse to ignore a rule,"

James said before sighing heavily. "Alright, just for you I will make an exception. But that means you owe me five."

Mitch laughed.

"Fine. Five it is. I'll call you soon."

"I'll be waiting. It was nice meeting you, Faith. Make sure you look after your dad. He's not nearly as young as he thinks he is," James told me before winking at Mitch.

"Hey now! I am exactly as young as I think I am!" Mitch argued. "Thanks again, James."

"Don't mention it. Now, I shall go find someone to mop up this floor before someone slips. Have a safe journey."

He embraced Mitch once more before smiling at me and walking past us.

I looked down at the floor, spotting the trail of water that we had caused before glancing back at Mitch.

"Ready to go, kid?" he asked.

I nodded.

He pushed the door open, the noise and wind hitting me immediately. A helicopter waited on the huge deck at the front of the ship. I squinted, the wind making it hard to see, but Mitch wrapped a hand around my arm, leading me towards the aircraft.

I could barely see, my eyes were mostly shut, but I managed to make out some steps. I climbed aboard, falling into the nearest seat as Mitch shut the door behind us and sat opposite me. He grinned widely and pointed at a headset which hung on the wall next to me.

I slipped the headphones on and pulled the microphone down as Mitch did the same. The noise was immediately muffled and the silence that followed was a little disconcerting.

"Hello, Lauren, can you hear me?" Mitch said, his lips moving a little faster than his words were coming.

"I can indeed. You're right on time. Ready for lift-off?" the familiar voice asked.

I craned my head, looking through the gap in the seats and spotting her bright red hair sitting in the cockpit.

"Damn right, let's get out of here. Are you ready, kid?" he asked, looking at me as he slung his bag off his back and opened it quickly.

He grinned at the items inside, clearly happy that they were undamaged before looking back up at me.

I gave him a thumbs up before realising I could probably speak.

"Oh, yeah! Sorry," I said quickly.

"Not a problem! Take us away, Lauren. Once we're in the air properly, I'll have a look at your hands, kid. How are they feeling?" Mitch asked.

"What happened to your hands?" Lauren asked quickly, sounding worried as the helicopter lifted into the air.

I looked down at them, staring at raw, red skin. They looked worse than they had before. The water had washed away all of the blood leaving deep gouge marks on my palms, but at least most of the stones had been washed out of them. The skin around them was red and strangely puckered from being underwater.

I wasn't sure what to say to Lauren though. It felt so embarrassing to explain that I'd fallen climbing through the hole. It made me feel so stupid and inexperienced.

"She took a bit of a tumble," Mitch explained for me. "But luckily it wasn't as bad as the one you took back in Majorca. I'm not a squeamish person, but half your chin was hanging off!"

I looked up in horror, the mental picture running through my head.

"I told you I'm clumsy!" Lauren shot at Mitch. "Plus, it was nothing that sixteen stitches and some light surgery couldn't fix. Are you okay, Grace?"

I swallowed, feeling the weird and uncomfortable feeling that I'd felt when Mitch had worried about me before returning. It sat heavily in my stomach, making me feel a little nauseous.

"Yeah, I'm fine," I answered, looking out the window at the sunrise.

I could feel Mitch's eyes on me, but I didn't want to look at him. I was too ashamed.

"Where's the first aid kit? Still under the seat?" Mitch asked, leaning forwards and groping blindly under his seat.

"Nah, I got it here," Lauren said, leaning over and

grabbing the red bag from the passenger seat and holding it out behind her.

Mitch stretched to take the kit from her with a wince.

"Are you okay?" I asked quickly, suddenly remembering the noise I'd heard just before I'd gone underwater.

"Ah, I'm fine, kid," he said, not looking up from the
first aid kit that he was unzipping.

I watched him, concern washing through me. He
looked fine. I couldn't see any injuries, but it was hard
to tell. His clothes were still wet and the vest he was
wearing was such a dark colour that I wouldn't have been
able to see any blood stains on it.

He slipped a pair of rubber gloves on before leaning
forwards towards me.

"Can I see your hands?" he asked, the words coming
through my headset after a slight delay. "I worry about
them getting infected because the water in that cave was
probably not the most sterile."

I shuddered lightly at that. I had to agree with him.
The thought of that horrific-smelling murky water
being anywhere near my cuts made me anxious. Most
of it would have been washed away during the rest of the
swim, but I was still worried.

I edged forwards in my seat and held out my hands
to him.

He examined them carefully for a moment, gently
touching the skin around the cuts and watching my

face to see my reaction.

"Does that hurt?" he asked.

"Mmm, kind of," I said. "I think it's just a normal cut though, not anything bad."

He nodded distractedly, looking back at my hands.

"Okay, I'll remove the rest of the gravel now and disinfect them. I'll wrap them just to keep them clean for now, but I'll do it properly when we get to the plane. I want to give them a chance to breathe and for the scabs to form properly."

"Okay," I replied, not sure what else to say.

"This might hurt a little but I'll be as gentle as I can," he promised.

I nodded, not moving my hands as he began to carefully remove the stones.

Even so, it hurt. I sunk my teeth into my lower lip, biting down hard to distract myself. It stung, sometimes becoming a sharper pain, before settling down into a soft throbbing. They started bleeding again too, wherever Mitch had removed the stones. I was almost a little glad that it hurt, which felt strange. I could feel exhaustion hovering just out of reach and I knew that whenever it did hit me, I would crash hard.

Eventually, Mitch leaned back and brushed the final stone off my hand and onto the floor between us.

"You have someone who will disinfect in here, right?" Mitch asked Lauren over the comms.

"Yeah, of course. It's hired through a company that

has surprisingly good cleaning policies which… now that I think about it, is pretty concerning," she replied.

Mitch laughed.

"Well, I'm glad, but let's just not look into that any further until we are far away from this island," he said.

"Agreed."

He grinned up at me.

"It's probably not as dark as it sounds, right?" he asked. "Alright, I'm going to disinfect them now. This is going to sting."

I nodded, watching as Mitch tipped some disinfectant solution onto a cotton pad before gently swiping it across my palm.

Pain spiked in my hands again making me bite harder on my lip but it faded quickly.

"How are they feeling?" Mitch asked, finally finishing disinfecting my hands and looking up at me again.

"Alright," I said uncomfortably.

They hurt, obviously, but it was fine. It wasn't too bad.

He smiled at me, the skin around his eye crinkling.

"Okay, let me just wrap them up and I'll be done," he said.

I nodded, watching as he tucked the slightly pink cotton pads into a clear plastic bag with the rest of the rubbish before pulling out two large plasters.

"These will be pretty loose," he told me, "but the scabs won't stick to them."

I nodded.

Mitch carefully unwrapped one of the plasters, gently pressing it over my palm and making sure it was stuck down around the edges before doing the same with the other hand.

"How do they feel now?" Mitch asked. "Are they still stinging?"

I shook my head.

"They're not too bad."

Mitch gave me a look that told me he knew I was lying.

"Okay," he said after a moment. "Lauren, how far out are we?"

"Mm, not too far. Should only be five to seven minutes," she replied. "I'll let Oscar know to start getting everything switched on and ready to go. I've already bribed everyone I need to, so we should be able to get in the air again pretty much straight away."

Mitch slumped back against his seat, one hand resting gently on his stomach.

"Oh, good. I should pay you more."

There was a pause before Lauren spoke again.

"Ah, my rates are high enough already. I wouldn't charge you more."

"At least let me pay full price then," he shot back.

"Never."

Mitch sighed loudly before grinning at me.

"She does this every time," he said. "But every time I

try to send her more money, she either shuts down the bank account or moves out of the country."

Lauren's laugh echoed in my ear.

"I do what I have to. You know that Oscar and I already have more than we need. You're paying too much for us as is and we owe you everything. I refuse to charge you a cent or penny more."

Mitch shook his head and started to open his mouth but Lauren started talking again.

"Did you find what you were looking for?" she asked.

Mitch's hand patting his bag, seemingly subconsciously.

"Oh yeah. I got a good few scrolls, some artwork and a bust or two. Obviously, none of the scrolls are originals from the library, but there's enough of an age range there to prove that the organisation is still at work. Or at least they were at the beginning of the last century when the items were stashed there, I assume."

"Oh, really? You didn't find anything more recent than that?" Lauren asked.

"Nah. I'm not sure if they assumed it was a safe hiding place or if they forgot about the stuff. I reckon it was intentional though. There was too much there for it not to be, but I know for damn sure that they're going to be pissed. What do you reckon the fallout of this will be? How long do you think we'll have to hide?" he asked.

Lauren deliberated for a moment.

"I really don't know. You said they're still pretty

powerful, right? Do you think they had access to any of the cameras on the island? I assume they did, right? Oh, one second, got to speak to Air Traffic," she said.

I watched through the gap in between the seats as she lifted a hand to her headset, speaking quickly before touching it again.

"Yeah, I reckon they do. I mean, it would be foolish if they didn't," Mitch said. "They have to be better than that, I'll be so disappointed if they aren't."

Lauren laughed.

"You'll be disappointed if they don't have pictures of your face?" she asked.

"I mean... a little! They're a huge, international organisation, funded by some of the richest people in the world. They need to be good."

"You know, Mitch," Lauren started. "Sometimes, I worry about you. Are the Sterlings not enough of a challenge that you want to piss off whatever this lot are called too?"

"I don't specifically want to piss them off!" he insisted. "I'm just saying that if I have pissed them off already doing this work for Georgia, I want to see what they can do. It's morbid curiosity more than anything else."

Lauren laughed.

"Damn right it is. You reckon she's going to want you to keep searching after you've found this or will this be the end?"

Mitch let his head fall back against the headrest, his eyes shutting softly.

"I reckon there will be another job. This is what, the sixth? She wasn't content with the research I found for her nor the World Chronicles I stole from the Pushkin Museum. Even when I got her the gold plates from the Serapeum, it wasn't enough. I think this is enough concrete evidence of the organisation to mean that nothing will ever be enough again. She won't be happy until she joins them or dies trying," Mitch explained.

"What, you reckon they'll kill her?" Lauren asked.

"Mmm, I don't think they will. Her interest is innocent enough. She's just a collector, you know? Plus, with her fortune and funding, it would be a waste. I think they'll recruit her. Especially after this."

"What does that mean for us? Surely they won't be comfortable hiring such scummy lowlifes," she teased.

"Wow, lowlifes? Hardly. I'd say we're at least middlelifes," Mitch joked. "I'm not sure. I'm going to assume we're not the first people who have stolen from the organisation and probably not the most skilled either. I think they'll either recruit us too or Georgia will be our liaison and we'll never officially know they've hired us. It'll be pretty obvious though, I think."

"You reckon?"

"Oh yeah, she'll start either asking for really specific things like specific items or she'll have more to give us. Rather than just saying 'get me proof' or 'find them', I think she'll tell us to hunt down an item that was stolen by a specific person or organisation."

"Huh, makes sense. That could be pretty fun though. More money, right?" Lauren asked as the airport came into view.

"Probably. I feel like they'll be less okay with me keeping artefacts for myself though."

CHAPTER FORTY-TWO

Oscar waited outside the plane, a gun in his hands, his eyes scanning the skies, as we landed. Relief crossed his face as we stumbled out of the helicopter, but he quickly returned to looking around, waiting for any sign of trouble.

Lauren raced across the tarmac ahead of us, her hand finding Oscars briefly before she threw herself up the stairs and into the cockpit. I reached the steps first, pounding up them and sinking into the chair I'd sat in what felt like weeks ago. It had only been a few days, maybe a week, but it felt longer. So much had happened in that time and I felt like I'd changed a lot too.

My limbs trembled, my muscles sore, as adrenaline drained out of me. We'd done it. We had gotten back to the plane, we must be safe. Lauren had said that she hadn't seen anyone following us and Mitch had agreed, even if he had said he'd feel better once we were in the air.

A loud slamming noise came from behind me as

Oscar shut the plane door and Mitch fell into the seat in front of the table, dropping his bag onto it and barely missing the first aid kit that waited there.

"Can you wait until we're in the air before we sort you out?" Oscar asked Mitch, shouting over the noise of the plane as it idled towards the runway.

"I'm fine," Mitch said, wincing as he shuffled to do up his seatbelt.

Oscar sent him a disapproving look before sinking into the seat opposite me and buckling up.

"What about you, kid? Any injuries or bullet wounds?" he asked, his eyes scanning me.

I glanced down at my hands, unsure whether to mention them. They didn't feel like a proper injury, just something dumb that I'd done. I could feel them in real life too. They stung but I didn't want to think about it too much, it would pull me out of the fantasy.

"No, I'm fine," I called back over the noise.

"What happened to them?"

Oscar nodded towards my hands.

"I fell," was all I could think to say, my cheeks flushing again.

"Ah, we've all been there," he replied with a grin.

"Haven't we just," Mitch added with a cheeky grin. "But this is nowhere near as bad as the injury you got in... where was it? McNab's island?"

"Oh, come on, man," Oscar groaned, dropping his head back against his headrest as the plane lifted from the runway. "Don't bring that up again!"

I smiled slightly, looking between them.

"What happened?" I asked.

I knew it was silly, but it did make me feel better to know that others had injured themselves whilst with Mitch too. It made me feel less stupid, like it was something that happened to everyone.

"Nothing, it was nothing!" Oscar objected.

"Nothing?" Mitch chuckled. "I would hardly call it nothing."

Oscar groaned loudly.

"Alright, fine. I'll let you tell it if you let me deal with that," he said, gesturing towards Mitch. "Looks like you should have done something with it before now anyway."

"Hey! I put pressure on it," Mitch argued.

"Is that all?"

Mitch shrugged.

"I didn't want to scare the kid," he said.

Oscar glanced towards me, but I couldn't react in any way. I was frozen in my seat as fear raced through me. What had happened to him? How bad was it?

"I get it, but that's stupid. You need to sort it out. How bad is it?" he asked.

"Not bad," Mitch replied. "Didn't hit anything important, I'm more worried about it getting infected."

Oscar's eyebrows drew together.

"Get that shirt off now. Let's have a look at it."

Mitch glanced at me before sighing and rolling his eyes.

"Alright, alright," he said, undoing his seatbelt and opening his vest.

"Do you need a hand with your shirt?" Oscar asked.

"Man, Lauren's right through there. Have some self-restraint," Mitch teased.

Oscar glared at him.

"I'm not hitting on you, asshole, I'm trying to make sure you don't die. God, I forgot how annoying you are when you're injured."

"Hey, now! I'm annoying all the time, not just when I'm injured."

Mitch slowly lifted his shirt over his head and my eyes immediately found the surprisingly small oozing hole. It looked deep.

"Well, you're right about that, but you definitely are more annoying when you're injured. Bullet hole?" Oscar asked, his eyes on the wound.

"Yup. No exit wound so I'm pretty sure it's still in there. It probably came through the stone so it won't have been going too fast," Mitch reasoned, probing the edges of the wound carefully.

I swallowed, unable to look away from the bullet hole.

Mitch leant back, looking down at his wound before reaching towards the first aid kit.

"You aren't dealing with that yourself," Oscar said

sharply. "I don't trust you to fix bullet holes on your-self anymore. Last time you didn't stitch it properly and almost passed out from blood loss. Turn towards me."

Mitch held his hands up in defeat and pulled a leaver under his chair, swinging it around to face Oscar.

"You say that like it's a bad thing. I know you've been eyeing up some of my crap for years. You sure you're not hoping that I finally croak and you can have my stuff in the will?" Mitch asked, eyeing him with a smile.

My heart clenched at the mention of Mitch dying, even if it had been playful. He couldn't die. I couldn't have him die.

"I'm still in the will?" Oscar asked. "I thought you took me out."

"Nah, you're still on there. Somewhere towards the bottom but... still on there." Mitch grinned before his expression sobered. "I don't mind doing this myself."

"Oh, shut it. You know this is part of my job," Oscar said, reaching for a nearby headset that I hadn't even noticed before and speaking into it. "Darling, I need to fish a bullet out of Mitch, nothing too bad though. Am I safe to do it now?"

There was a pause and I watched as Mitch grabbed some gauze, wiping away some of the blood.

I couldn't hear Lauren's reply over the noise of the plane, but Oscar nodded.

"Ah, perfect. Thanks, love." He took the headset off and looked at Mitch again. "Lean back, old man. Let me have a look at that."

Mitch did as instructed, leaning back and lowering the gauze so that Oscar could examine it.

"Thanks, man. I forget how bossy you get when you're fixing me up," he said with a warm smile before glancing at me. "At least tell the story of what happened on McNab's whilst you sort me out to distract Grace."

Oscar groaned again before glancing at me, and I became aware that I'd just been staring at them for the last however long. I felt like I couldn't move or look away though. I could barely even blink. I felt dizzy and nauseous.

Mitch had been shot.

Was it my fault?

"Ah, no need to look so worried, Grace," Oscar told me as he picked up a pair of gloves and started to put them on. "I've picked more bullets out of this grumpy old man than I can count."

"Which isn't saying much because he dropped out of school at fourteen," Mitch added.

"How did I drop out? I finished all my exams and graduated. School was holding me back, there was no point being there," Oscar said distractedly, dropping to his knees in front of Mitch and beginning to put white sheets on his lap and the table.

"Eh, same thing. Go on. Do you want me to start the story? You know how much it cheers me up."

Oscar glared up at him.

"Yeah because it makes you look like a hero and I look like a dumbass," he shot back.

I didn't get how they were acting so normal. They were just chatting, bickering as if Mitch didn't have a bullet wound. I knew that he'd been shot before, he was covered in scars, but I didn't understand how it wasn't more of a big deal. He had been shot, he could die. He could be dying at that very moment but instead, he and Oscar were just sitting about joking.

It felt wrong, it all felt so wrong.

"You don't look like a dumbass," Mitch said. "You were one."

"I know. Alright, fine," Oscar sighed as he pulled out a syringe and a glass vial. "I guess it's the least I can do to distract you whilst I root around in your body looking for this damn bullet. But if I get so distracted that I hit you in the kidney..."

He shot Mitch a threatening look but Mitch just snorted.

"Please! It's nowhere near my kidney. If you manage to hit that, you'd have to be actively aiming for it."

"Whoops," Oscar muttered darkly, sinking the needle into Mitch's abdomen around the bullet wound.

I watched as he slipped the cap back onto the needle and placed it on the table before leaning forwards. His body blocked my view of Mitch's wound and although I was glad, it also made my anxiety rise.

I wanted him to move. I wanted to be able to see

exactly what he was doing. I needed to be prepared. If anything went wrong or if he needed my help or something, I'd be lost. Even if I could see what was happening, I would still be lost though. I just needed to.

I needed Mitch to be okay, I didn't know what I'd do if he were to die. It had been my fault. I wasn't sure how but it was. I'd hesitated, taken too long. I was the reason Mitch had been shot.

"Alright," Oscar started reluctantly. "Ready to hear the story of how Mitch saved my ass and taught me a valuable lesson about stupidity?"

He glanced back at me as he reached for a pair of long tweezers.

I nodded numbly, my body feeling strange. It felt like I wasn't attached to it. Like I was watching it on tv or something. I couldn't feel my body. It wasn't like when I first started fantasising. I knew I was there, but I just couldn't feel it. I could barely move, I felt like I was staring, my eyes needing to see more.

"Okay, in my defence, I was young and dumb as dirt. I thought I was smarter than that, but clearly, that is not true. But, just know that I truly thought it would be okay," Oscar insisted.

Mitch snorted.

"Enough excuses, get to the story," he prompted, clearly enjoying himself. "Kid, do you know where McNab's is?"

He looked up at me.

It took me a minute before I realised he was talking to me and shook my head.

"Alright, start by telling Grace about that. I mean, how is she meant to know how dumb you were if she doesn't know the background? Although," he paused and grinned down at Oscar, "I think she'd know that hitching a ride with Sterling's people and telling them exactly where to find me is a dumb as hell move."

Mitch burst into laughter, his hands twitching towards his stomach.

"Be careful, old man. No movement or laughter whilst I'm doing this. I'm not telling the story if you can't keep it together," Oscar warned.

Mitch's hands returned to the armrests, smearing blood on them.

"Alright, I'll try my best."

"Good," Oscar said, leaning back and dropping a squished hunk of metal onto the sheet on the table. "Do you want me to start with the night we first met or by explaining what the deal is with McNabs?"

Mitch cocked his head, thinking about it.

"Eh, the night we met is irrelevant. You can go straight to McNabs if you want?" he suggested.

"Irrelevant?" Oscar repeated, feigning offence. "Wow. I mean, I thought that night was pretty fun and important, but apparently not."

Mitch snorted softly.

"Just tell the damn story."

"Alright, alright. So, this asshole climbed out of my hotel window at four in the morning after hinting that he was going to go rob an abandoned military base and gold mine and I think it's worth pointing out that my room was on the sixth floor which, honestly, is pretty impressive. Then, he had the sheer audacity to act surprised when I showed up at the military base the next day," Oscar said.

Mitch laughed, earning a sharp look from Oscar.

"Sorry, sorry. No laughing, got it," Mitch told him. "It was a test and you know it. I expected you to get to the island, I just didn't expect you to rock up with the Sterlings!"

"How did you expect me to get there then? Swim?"

"I don't know, I thought you'd steal a boat or something! You spent the whole night boasting about how you could hot wire anything! What was I supposed to think?"

"So your mind immediately jumps to crime rather than just hitching a ride with a nice group who were heading there anyway?" Oscar asked. "You need to get out of the field, mate. It's corrupting you."

Mitch chuckled at Oscar's long-suffering tone.

"It's been corrupting me since long before you were born. Keep going."

"Alright. You know the drill, this is going to hurt," Oscar warned him.

I scanned Mitch's face carefully, watching the slight

twitch of his eyebrows as Oscar did something to the wound, his body blocking it.

Part of me wanted to stand so that I could get a better view of it, even though the mental picture of what was happening was making me nauseous. It still felt too distant though. It was like my body was feeling sick, but it didn't really impact me in any way. Almost like I wasn't connected to my body.

"I'm going to go out on a limb," Oscar said as he dropped a blood-soaked cloth onto the table, "and assume that you've never heard of McNab's island?"

He glanced at me and I shook my head, unable to speak.

"Ah, not many people have. I mean, I hadn't before I met Mitch. It was dumb luck that I was even in Canada at the time."

"It wasn't," Mitch muttered under his breath.

Oscar glanced up at him but Mitch just smiled innocently, causing him to sigh and continue as if he hadn't been interrupted.

"So, the island is just off Halifax Harbour in Nova Scotia. It's been there forever, and it has a pretty interesting history actually. It's been used for leisure and by the military fairly extensively, but right now, it's mostly a historic site. They run tours and stuff of it for kids now, right?" he asked, glancing up at Mitch for clarification.

"Yeah. I mean, a few people live there, but hardly

any," he replied with a slight wince.

"Right! I'll save you the long history lesson but basically, way back in the late 1800s, some people who lived there reported that they saw some people, probably American pirates, heading towards one of the coves with some form of treasure or something. They searched the area the next morning, but didn't find anything particularly suspicious."

"Mmmm, they kind of did though," Mitch interrupted.

"I was getting to that!" Oscar chided.

"Slowly! Are you really saying that a big hole with a cherry tree planted over it isn't weird? They even mark the spot with stones."

"Well, now you've ruined it! Yes, they found a hole, a cherry tree, and some markings, but they didn't find any treasure."

"Because they were looking in the wrong place!" Mitch added animatedly.

Oscar leant back and looked up at Mitch.

"Do you want to tell the story?" he asked.

"No, you're doing a good job. You can keep going," Mitch replied, trying to suppress his grin.

"Oh, I can? Thank you so much for allowing me to tell the story you forced me to tell," Oscar shot at him sarcastically. "So, as Mitch so rudely spoiled for you, they weren't looking in the right place. Neither were the people who searched there about fifty years later."

There was a pause as Oscar dropped another wad of blood-covered gauze onto the table before grabbing a large white bandage and microporous tape from the first aid kit.

I watched as he carefully unwrapped it and placed it over the wound.

"Hold this, but don't get your grubby hands on it," Oscar ordered.

"I can do one or the other," Mitch replied.

Oscar glanced at his hands for a moment before looking back at mine.

"Both horrible options," he muttered under his breath. "Put this glove on."

Oscar held a glove out to Mitch so that he could slip it on easily before readjusting the bandage again.

"I got it," Mitch said. "Tell the kid what we found."

He grinned up at me, but I couldn't bring myself to smile back at him.

"Well, it turns out the cherry tree was marking the entrance to an abandoned gold mine that the French set up when they occupied the island years before," Oscar said as he picked at the tape, trying to find the start of it.

"And, remind me how you got to the island?" Mitch asked innocently.

Oscar paused to glare at Mitch.

"I knew this asshole was testing me and honestly the mystery was too tempting. I overheard a tour group saying they were going to the island, so asked if I could hitch a ride too."

"Just a nice friendly tour group all dressed in black with visible weapons," Mitch teased.

"They were perfectly friendly to me!" Oscar objected. "We just chatted a bit and I said nothing about you. Then they dropped me on the island and we went our separate ways."

"Mmm, you sure about that? Nothing at all?" Mitch asked, a smile playing about his lips. "Are you sure you didn't tell them just enough to know exactly who you were meeting?"

"I mean… I might have briefly mentioned that I was meeting a friend on the island, but that was it! I didn't say anything that could have given it away, I don't think. I reckon they already knew you were going," Oscar said before sitting back and examining his handiwork critically. "How does that feel? It should keep you from bleeding out before we can get you to a hospital."

"I don't need a hospital. 'Tis just a scratch."

Oscar stood with a groan and stretched his legs.

"We're taking you to a hospital, even if I have to sedate you and drag you there against your will," he threatened, his tone surprisingly lighthearted.

"You've done it before, you'll do it again, I guess," Mitch said with a slight shrug. "Finish the story, I'll tidy up."

Mitch started to turn towards the table but Oscar stopped him.

"Nah, I got it. You relax," he insisted before looking at me over his shoulder. "To cut the long story short, those assholes followed me to where Mitch was hunkered down in a mining shaft, held me hostage, and tried to murder us both. Mitch took them all out, saved me, got us both off the island, and then I met the love of my life."

Mitch's mouth fell open in outrage.

"Hey! No fair, you missed out so much! What about the heroic way I pushed you out of the way of gunfire, sacrificing myself? Or how I carried you back to the seaplane despite having a gaping bullet wound in my arm?" he argued.

Oscar sent me a smirk as he loaded the used medical equipment into a trash bag.

"Oh yeah, he did all that stuff."

Mitch sighed and dropped his head back against the seat.

"Damn, I can't believe how long ago that was," he said after a while.

"I know, it's wild. I can't believe how much my life has changed since then," Oscar said, a smile on his lips as he tied the bag shut and slung it behind his chair. "I wouldn't change it for the world though."

"Me either," Mitch replied, smiling fondly at Oscar.

There was a pause as they both reminisced for a moment before Oscar began rolling up the first aid kit.

"So, what's the plan now? Hospital first, then

what?" Oscar asked.

"Mmm… we should probably lie low for a little while. I think we pissed off the Sterlings pretty spectacularly, so I'll give them some time to stop wanting to kill me quite so much, then we'll anger them again," Mitch smirked.

"That's a good idea. I mean, I'm pretty fond of you and I'd rather you don't die any time soon."

"Ah, you're just in it for my money," Mitch teased.

"No, I love you and your money. It doesn't need to be one or the other."

Mitch laughed at him, a hand going to his stomach.

"You and Lauren got enough saved up to see you in beer and food for the next six months or so until I need your service again?" he asked gently.

"Yeah, man. You know we're good."

"I know, I know, just gotta make sure."

"Appreciate it. Which house are you going to go to?" Oscar asked.

Mitch scrunched his face up.

"I'm not sure really."

"It had better be somewhere where you've actually registered with a doctor. You're going to need antibiotics and follow-up appointments. And, no exercise or strenuous activity until it's fully healed, so it had better not be that place where you have to climb about a hundred steps to get up there," Oscar warned him.

"You're not out of the danger zone yet and you're not

as young as you once were, old man."

Mitch's face fell and my heart clenched.

"Well, it's not going to be that place now, I guess," he said, feigning disappointment before looking at me. "Ready for me to have a look at your hands now, kid?"

I looked down at my hands without speaking, staring at the white bandages which were speckled with blood where it had soaked through.

"Oh, shit," Oscar said before I could answer. "I completely forgot. I shouldn't have packed everything up!"

"Don't worry about it. I don't think unzipping it will count as strenuous activity. Go on, trade places, you two."

I reached for my belt, my hands trembling. It took me a few tries to actually be able to undo it.

I stood and edged around Oscar, dropping into his chair.

"Hands," Mitch asked, undoing the kit and leaning forwards slightly.

I lifted my hands, laying them face on the table.

They were shaking. My fingers were trembling so hard that they looked like they were twitching. I couldn't make them stop.

"You alright?" Mitch asked me softly.

"Yeah," I forced out, feeling embarrassed by how unsteady my voice was. "I don't know why they're shaking."

I let out a laugh that felt flat and looked away from Mitch's sympathetic face.

I stared at the last empty seat, trying to force away the tears that were burning behind my eyes.

"It makes sense," Mitch said gently. "You're new to this and it's scary. In the last twenty-four hours, you've been shot at, almost stabbed, almost blown up, and you've seen all that happen to me too. It's a lot to process."

A hot lump of emotion sat in my throat, making it hard to breathe. My chest felt tight too. Even when I managed to suck in air around the lump, it didn't feel like enough.

"I promise, Grace. It's normal to feel overwhelmed," Mitch said, starting to gently peel the plasters off my hands.

"How do I make them stop?" I asked, hating how weak they made me feel.

"Give it time. Just let yourself feel overwhelmed and scared, it gets easier with time. It might help to go run your hands under cold water for a little bit too?" he suggested.

I nodded before stopping.

"Is that okay? I mean, it won't make them worse?" I asked stupidly.

I wasn't even sure why I asked it. Surely washing them with water wouldn't make them infected or anything.

"No, they'll be okay. Just be gentle when you dry

them, and make sure to just dab, not rub."

I nodded and pushed myself out of my seat. I started to pass him before stopping.

I shouldn't have asked. I knew that. I didn't want to hear him lie to me.

It would have eaten me alive even if I hadn't though.

"Was it my fault you got shot?" I asked softly. "Is it because I took too long?"

"No!" Mitch cried immediately, but I knew it was a lie.

If I had been quicker, if I had just gotten in the water when he told me to, he wouldn't have been shot. He might still die.

I couldn't stay there. I couldn't stay in my fantasy any longer. I could feel the tears coming and I didn't want to cry in front of him. I slipped into the real world, my hands stinging and dripping blood onto the forest floor, and stopped running. Tears escaped my eyes and my breath came in gasps.

I couldn't take it. He'd been shot because of me.

My knees gave way and I fell onto my knees, barely able to breathe, sobs threatening to choke me.

But I hadn't left Mitch's world. Not fully. Part of me was still in the bathroom, glaring at myself in the mirror and the back of my hand pressed against my mouth to muffle my blubbering.

"How did she do out there?" I heard Oscar ask through the door.

I pressed my ear against it, needing to hear Mitch's response.

"She did good."

Another lie.

ABOUT THE AUTHOR

Alexa Lee was born and educated in the United Kingdom, where she continues to live. Her over-active imagination and experience working in mental health inspired her to begin writing in 2021.

Follow us:

riverfolkbooks.com

Facebook /riverfolkp

Twitter /riverfolkp

Instagram /riverfolkp

If you want to discuss our books with other readers and maybe even the author, join our discord server using the link on our website.